LONDON PREP
BOOK 3

those three
little words.
jilliandodd

LONDON PREP

BOOK 3

JILLIAN DODD

FRIDAY, OCTOBER 4TH
Don't sleep with him tonight.
11:45PM

"I …" I stutter, feeling caught in Noah's hand.

Caught in his words.

Don't sleep with him tonight. Promise me?

I can smell Noah all around me. His musk is so thick that I can barely breathe.

"You can't ask that of me," I finally say, tears pooling in my eyes. One escapes, rolling down my cheek and searing a line into my skin.

I wish I were crying because I was angry. Because I was mad at him.

But I'm crying because … I feel heartbroken.

At my words.

At the expression that forms on Noah's face as he nods his head, understanding.

Because he looks like he might cry too.

It looks like with one statement, I've shattered him.

And my stomach feels like it might bounce up and out of my throat or fall through me.

Noah doesn't say anything else. He just holds on to my hand, nodding his head, his eyes staying closed.

He looks perfect.

Lying in bed, drunk and broken, he still looks perfect.

"Get some rest," I whisper, wanting to soothe him. Wanting his expression to relax. I drop his hand, and my lip starts quivering. My heart feels as if it were being ripped out of my chest.

I rush out the door, wanting to scream at the sensation. Or cry. I'm not sure if I'm hurt or scared or actually injured, but I can't even distinguish what I'm feeling.

But then anger rises in me. I want to slap Noah for asking that of me. I want to go back in and yell at him and tell him that I can do *whatever* I want.

And that I *will.*

He doesn't have a say in what I do.

In who I'm with.

Tears burst from my eyes, and I rush into the nearest bathroom, falling onto the floor in a heap.

How did everything get so messed up?

Where did I go wrong?

I cry, knowing I did this to myself.

I cry because I have real feelings for both Harry and Noah.

And tonight, I let Noah get into my head. I let him get to me.

I put myself into this situation.

My whole body shakes as Noah's words echo in my ears.

Don't sleep with him tonight.

Promise me.

I let out a sob, thinking about his expression. About how helpless he looked. Because even if Noah wants me, he will never have me.

I could never just be *his.*

No matter how *he* feels, Harry cares about me too.

And despite my connection with Noah, I care about Harry. Which is what makes this so hard.

So confusing.

If Harry knew what Noah had just said to me and saw how I'd reacted, he would never speak to me again. He wouldn't be able to look at me.

I didn't promise Noah. But I didn't tell him off either.

I just stood there, feeling myself break apart. With Noah, it's like I'm stuck in limbo, in this space where I can either be nothing or everything. In which Noah wants all of me for a moment. For even a second.

He wants everything I have to offer.

Please.

Don't sleep with Harry.

We have a connection.

Promise me?

But then, as usual, the moment is gone.

And he's asleep.

And he's back to being my friend.

Or hating me.

Or wanting me to be with Harry.

And that isn't fair to me.

That isn't what I want.

What—or who—I want is Harry.

The boy who is waiting for me.

The boy who is sweet and gentle.

The boy who isn't willing to give me up.

The boy who cherishes me, who says I'm his angel.

I sit on the bathroom floor and cry, getting it all out.

I let myself mourn what could have been with Noah. Because I know that it—*we*—will never be anything.

Despite my feelings for him, I don't want that.

This whole time, we've been lying to ourselves. At least, *I've* been lying to myself. I like Noah. I care about him deeply. And there has been more than one moment when I've wanted

him.

But nothing has ever happened.

I've never let it.

And neither has he.

We've been dancing around one another like magnets for so long that, at some point, we're bound to give in and come together—or break apart.

And tonight … tonight, I think we broke.

I don't know what this means for our friendship.

Or if we can even have one after this.

Maybe we shouldn't.

What I need to do is pull myself together.

I need to pick myself up and go back to Harry.

Because despite being dragged through emotional torture, love doesn't have to feel that way.

Relationships should be beautiful.

They don't have to be earth shattering to be important.

And tonight can still be special for Harry and me regardless of if we have sex.

Tonight isn't ruined because Noah is constantly conflicted.

Because he's always stuck, trapped by his emotions.

But I'm not.

My life can continue on regardless of what we are.

Regardless of how he feels.

And I want it to continue with Harry.

I'm not going to let Noah's words or his inaction ruin what Harry and I have built.

I let out a groan, wiping at my face. My insides are twisted up so tightly that I'm stuck between feeling furious and relieved.

Because Noah never seemed to care what was going on in my relationship with Harry.

But now, once I'm happy, that's when he decides to speak up?

When Harry and I have finally found our footing and are starting to get serious, that's when Noah decides to tell me he wants me?

After he told me that he retracted his offer?

Noah says we have chemistry.

That he wants me.

That he cares.

But he asked me not to sleep with someone else even though he knows that he will never sleep—or be—with me.

And it's bullshit.

The thought pisses me off even more.

I get up off the floor, pushing my shoulders back.

I'm not going to spend another second crying over Noah or his words. Because Noah's a wreck.

He's beautiful and alluring. Timeless. But he will take me down with him, and together we will sink.

I turn on the faucet, bringing a handful of water up to my face. I wash off my makeup, clearing away the streaks of mascara running down my cheeks.

Once my makeup is gone, I press my hands down over my hair, making sure it's still in place. I look at myself in the mirror, taking in my reflection. My eyes are red, but my skin is clean. I look like a blank canvas. Like I've washed away my makeup, my tears, my disappointment.

And I needed to. But now, it's time to turn things around.

To have fun. To go back to Harry.

To show myself that I'm not weighed down by Noah's words.

That he can't get to me.

Special, special, special.
12:10 AM

I WALK OUT of the bathroom, feeling like a different person. I don't feel like someone who just had their chest cracked open. Like someone who was lying on the floor, crying. I feel like someone who has made a decision.

I feel like someone who knows exactly what they want.

I feel powerful. Like nothing can stop me.

I quicken my steps until I'm back in the billiards room, my whole body searching for Harry. I scan the room, easily finding him. He's relaxing on a sofa, a glass hanging lazily in his hand. I take in his wide grin, watching as he sits, talking to Mohammad and Olivia.

I move toward him, past Naomi and George, who are in the middle of a game of pool. She's leaning over the table, aiming her shot.

Harry must not notice me because he looks surprised as I sit down on the couch next to him.

"Hey," he starts.

But before he can continue, I kiss him, pressing my lips against his, forcing his mouth open, slipping my tongue in. I place my palm against his jaw as he kisses me back, feeling like I can finally breathe again.

I break our lips, pulling back to find Harry looking at me happily. I turn my attention to Mohammad and Olivia, who are both gawking. Mohammad's eyes are the size of saucers, and Olivia's mouth is about to come unhinged from hanging open so far.

She forces her mouth shut and narrows her eyes at me.

"Noah all right?" Harry asks, breaking the silence.

His blue eyes are on me, and I instantly feel bad for being such a disaster upstairs.

Because I know *this* is what I want.

"He's fine." I nod, the reply falling easily out of my mouth. "But now that he's been put to bed, I'm ready to have some fun."

"Anything particular in mind?" Harry asks, cocking his head to the side.

His eyes are sparkling at me, and I bite my lip, taking in his strong jaw and wide smile.

"Shots," I declare, glancing over to Mohammad and Olivia.

Because I am very ready for a drink.

The entire drama that just unfolded with Noah had a sobering effect, and at the moment, I can't think of anything better than feeling happily buzzed. I don't want to think about Noah or what he said. And now that he's finally upstairs and asleep, it means I can let loose. I know that he won't be silently judging me from a corner or longingly looking at me like our lives are some Shakespearean tragedy.

No.

I want to have fun with my friends and flirt with Harry.

I want to be happy.

And dammit, I'm going to be.

"Fuck it, let's do some shots," Harry says, standing up from the couch.

I take in Mohammad's expression, watching the wheels turning behind his eyes.

"What are you thinking?" I ask, trying to figure out what he's so focused on.

"We can't just do shots," Mohammad finally says.

"Don't tell me you're already done for the night." I pout.

Because Mohammad is probably the most fun out of

everyone here, and if he's having a good time, I know everyone else will too.

"Hell no, Miss America," he says, swatting his hand at me like I just insulted him. "I'm thinking one better. *Body* shots."

He wiggles his eyebrows at me, and I grin, not even thinking before I answer, "I'm so down."

Harry looks at me, stunned, but before he can say anything, I pull Olivia up off the couch.

"We're doing body shots," I call out, capturing everyone's attention.

"That sounds disgusting," Olivia says at my side as I drag her over to the pool table.

"It sounds *fun*," I correct, not taking her attitude.

Because if I'm going to have fun, then she needs to have fun too.

I turn my gaze to George and Naomi, realizing that this is going to interrupt their game.

"Do you mind if we clear off the table?" I ask.

"For body shots?" George laughs, already pushing the balls into the pockets. "Not. At. All."

I walk over to the liquor cabinet, Mohammad at my side.

"We need limes," he says, shifting around the bottles until he finds some tequila. "And salt. Lots of salt."

Before I have a chance to say anything, he's out of the room. I pour myself a shot of tequila, deciding that I might as well do one now, just to take the edge off.

I down the shot, letting it burn.

"Already started?" Harry says at my side.

I can feel his breath on my cheek, and it warms me more than the tequila.

"Don't worry. I promise I'll stay standing long enough to do a shot off of you." I look up at Harry through my lashes, wishing that it were just the two of us alone in this room. I pour myself another shot, deciding one more won't hurt.

"Someone's getting a little heavy-handed," Harry says, stopping the shot glass at my lips.

"For you then?" I ask, holding it up for him.

He glances between my lips and the glass, leaning in closer. His blue eyes are on me as he takes the glass from my hand and throws the shot back.

I smile at him as Mohammad rushes back into the room.

"All right, we've got everything we need," he says, setting down a plate of lime wedges and a saltshaker next to the tequila.

"How are we supposed to do body shots when we're all in dresses?" Naomi asks, now at my side.

I look between us, realizing she's right.

"That's a fair question," Olivia adds, crossing her arms.

And I can tell from her tone that she isn't too happy about me kissing Harry so openly.

"The boys will have to just make do with licking salt off of us," I reply, shrugging.

Because even though body shots sound fun, I'm not about to hike up my dress to let them suck tequila out of my belly button. If anything, the fact that we're all wearing dresses sort of saves us from getting sticky.

"That's not as fun." Mohammad pouts, pouring tequila into a shot glass.

"Cheer up. We can still take the shots off of your stomachs." I smile and raise one eyebrow at him.

"I think that's fair," Harry cuts in, his eyes on me.

I flush, wishing Mohammad would just let us skip the whole *body shot* part and move straight to the *drinking tequila* part.

"All right, who wants to go first?" I ask.

I glance between Olivia and Naomi, but neither of them

looks convinced. George has a huge smile on his face while Thomas seems more hesitant. Katherine and Collin look excited but stay quiet.

"Fine, I'll go." I push my shoulders back and decide that if I want this to happen, I need to take the initiative. "And I'm calling upon Naomi to be my body."

I grin at her.

She tilts her head at me, a smile forming on her lips.

"I accept." She giggles, bouncing up and down like she's proud to be the first one chosen.

And I think just about everyone in the room watches her boobs bounce, more distracted by her chest than her excitement.

Naomi moves to the edge of the pool table, her hands preparing to brace her weight. But before she can jump up, George's hands wrap around her. He picks her up and then sets her down in one fell swoop.

"There you go." He smiles at her, nodding his head in approval.

She beams back at him.

I roll my eyes and move past him.

"All right, lie down," I instruct.

Naomi scoots her butt further onto the table, splaying herself across the dark green fabric. Her dress tumbles out around her, and she really does look beautiful.

"Here," Mohammad says, handing me a lime.

"Would you mind holding the shot glass?" I ask.

I contemplate letting George do it, but I think he might be too distracted to stay focused on the simple task. His eyes have glazed over, and he's looking at Naomi laid out on the table like he's never seen anything so perfect.

And I can't blame him.

"No problem," Mohammad agrees, handing Naomi the

salt.

"Where do you want it?" she asks, leaning up with the saltshaker.

"Wrist." I lick her wrist and pour some salt onto it. I hand her the lime, instructing her to lie back down and put it into her mouth.

"Tequila?" Mohammad asks, holding out the shot glass.

My eyes slip down Naomi as I try to decide where I could set the glass.

"Cleavage, obviously." I grin at him, poking one of Naomi's boobs.

"Hey ..." she says, but with the lime in her mouth, it comes out muffled, and she starts laughing instead, her chest shaking.

Mohammad tries to place the shot glass down on her, but it won't stay still.

"No laughing," I say, willing my voice to be firm.

But I just end up laughing along with her. And I'm not the only one. Everyone else seems to be chuckling, watching Mohammad struggle to set down the glass.

"If you don't stay still, the tequila's going to end up on you," Olivia warns, looking amused.

Naomi nods, finally collecting herself.

"Ready?" Mohammad asks, his fingers still resting on the shot glass.

I nod, grabbing Naomi's wrist and licking the salt off of it. When I set her wrist back down, Mohammad lets go of the shot glass. My lips wrap around the edge of it, and I throw my head back, downing the shot. The taste is strong in my mouth, and I move to take the lime from Naomi's lips, sucking the juice out.

Harry lets out a whistle.

"That was exciting," Naomi says brightly, sitting up.

"Thanks for being my first body." I grin at her and then bite my lip, looking toward Harry.

I take in his brilliant blue eyes and wide smile.

"You're next," I say, cocking my eyebrow at him. I hold his gaze as he takes a step closer to me.

"We're supposed to rotate," Mohammad disagrees.

But Harry doesn't say no.

"I didn't realize there were rules," I counter, trying to prove my point.

"Of course there are rules. Besides, it's my turn," Mohammad says at my side.

I glance over at him and roll my eyes.

He can wait.

"I'll be quick," I promise, gripping Harry's sweater.

I push him against the pool table, his eyes on me the entire time. It's like everyone else in the room disappears, just leaving the two of us. I vaguely see Mohammad and Olivia from the corner of my eye, watching as Mohammad pours tequila in a shot glass for Naomi to take off of George. Or for George to take off of Naomi. I'm not really sure because I can't focus on anything, except Harry.

His gaze is on me as he strips off his sweater and white T-shirt, pulling them both off together, painfully slow.

My heart is pounding when his shirts finally fall onto the table next to him.

I take in his long, lean torso, watching as his abs become even more defined as he leans back until, finally, he's flat on the pool table. He tilts his head to the side, his blue eyes focused on me the entire time.

And I don't feel like we're playing a game anymore.

This isn't just fun.

This is … *sexy*.

After how intimate things got on the balcony, I shouldn't

be surprised.

But that's what is confusing.

I want Harry. I *really* want him. But I expected him to rip off his shirt, laughing the entire time. I expected it to be fun. Crazy.

I thought he and Mohammad would joke together, fighting over who got to pour tequila on who and drinking straight from the bottle.

But not right now.

Right now, his eyes are glued to mine, and it's like I'm seeing his bare chest for the first time.

I shake my head, realizing that we aren't alone and that I need to pull it together.

"Hold it still."

I hear Naomi laugh next to me.

She's struggling to get her mouth around the shot glass because Mohammad keeps moving it. She finally throws it back before her mouth comes down onto George's, retrieving the lime. She makes a sour face after, but her cheeks are flushed, and she can't stop looking at George or his megawatt grin.

"Ready?" Mohammad asks Harry, turning his attention to us.

"Of course." Harry nods, but his eyes stay glued on mine.

Mohammad chuckles, his body shaking with laughter as he pours a shot straight into Harry's belly button.

"Hey …" I scold, wanting the shot glass. But some of the tequila drips down across Harry's flat stomach, and my eyes are easily distracted by the droplet.

"This is more exciting," Mohammad replies, already looking a little too entertained.

I lick Harry's stomach, grab the salt and pour it on his skin, trying to stay focused on the task.

"Hurry up," Mohammad insists, his eyes glued to Harry's belly button.

I think he's worried about the tequila spilling out.

I just roll my eyes. There's always more tequila.

"Lime?" Harry asks, reminding me of the last thing I need.

Salt. Tequila. Lime. Harry.

I nod, placing it into his mouth.

I lean in, taking in his scent. Cigarettes and alcohol. I lick the salt off of his skin, doing my best to go achingly slow. I want to tease him.

George lets out a whistle, and I hear Naomi giggle next to me.

Then, I move my mouth down to his stomach and start sucking. Harry's stomach bounces as he laughs, and I can't help but laugh too.

Because it's not at all as sexy as I was hoping it would be.

I just end up making a terrible slurping noise, struggling to get the tiny amount of tequila out of his belly button.

Finally, I'm up to his lips, grabbing the lime from his mouth.

I suck the juice, my lips pursing at the taste.

"Whoa," I breathe out, letting the salt and tequila and lime hit me all at once.

"That was the funniest feeling," Harry admits, his nose wrinkling as he sits up.

"You should have put the salt on his stomach," Katherine jokes.

"Care to show her how it's done?" Collin questions.

And before I know it, Collin is stripping his shirt off, and Katherine is taking extra care in licking his stomach. George, Naomi, and Thomas are watching her, chuckling to themselves.

Collin must catch it because he points to Thomas, saying, "You're next."

"I think the belly button was a fail," I say to Mohammad, setting down the lime.

"I disagree. It was hilarious," he replies, shaking his head.

Mohammad pours another shot of tequila. Katherine decides instead to balance the glass on Collin's stomach, wrapping her lips around it to down her shot. Suddenly, her mouth is on Collin's, taking the lime from him. He sits up, grinning.

Harry's still sitting at the edge of the pool table, watching, but he moves to get up.

"Whoa. You're not going anywhere," I say, stopping him. "Lie back down."

I press my palm against his chest, feeling more relaxed.

Harry grins at me and complies.

"Olivia, you're up," I say, my eyes shifting over to her.

She has her arms crossed in front of her chest, looking a little too detached and sober.

"You're serious?" she asks, her eyes growing wide.

I roll my eyes at both of them. "Mohammad, she'll have a double. She can handle it."

Mohammad smirks at me, pouring a double of tequila before handing Olivia the salt. She looks at it in her hand, glancing between the salt, me, and Harry.

"Mallory," Harry says, leaning up on his elbows.

I push him back down.

"Why not? It's not like she hasn't licked you before. Relax. It's just a shot."

I look at Harry, wanting him to know that I'm fine with this. I'm not sure if it's the shots or all of the shirtless boys or the late hour. Maybe it's the flush on Naomi's face and the sparkle in Mohammad's eyes, but I want Olivia to have that too. She looks rigid, and I just want her to let loose.

We all deserve to have a good time.

"Fuck it then," Harry lightly banters back, not too upset that I just invited his ex to take a shot off of him. "Well, come on, Olivia. Let's crack on."

I nod for her to scoot closer, and for a minute, I wonder if I made a huge mistake.

But she breaks a smile, and I know that she's not reading that much into it.

"Fine," she says, like she's not the least bit interested. But she moves to the edge of the pool table and pours a line of salt onto Harry's stomach. Mohammad places the shot next to the salt. I put a lime in his mouth and smile at him.

I want him to know that this is okay.

To have fun.

His eyes stay on mine, but a second later, Naomi is hooting as Olivia licks the salt, throwing back the double.

And I have to admit, I'm impressed.

She grabs the lime from Harry's lips without issue, and a second later, he's sitting back up.

"That was hot," Mohammad says next to me.

"What was?" I ask, smiling at him.

"The way she threw back that double. A true woman." He nods, looking convinced.

I pat him on the shoulder.

"Mohammad, I think you're next." Olivia laughs after apparently overhearing him.

"Hey, whoever wants to put their mouth on me is welcome to," he says, shooting Olivia a wink.

Olivia rolls her eyes, but she doesn't look disinterested.

Harry gets off the table, goes over to Mohammad's phone, and turns the music back up.

"I want another," I say, walking up to him. I bite my lip,

taking in his shirtless chest.

"Is that right?" Harry looks down at me, tapping me on the nose with his finger.

I don't answer him. I kiss him instead. His breath is warm, and I let my tongue slip against his lips.

"Mmhmm," Harry says, sounding caught off guard. But I can tell he likes it.

I bring my hands to his chest, pressing my fingers into his skin.

"Mallory," Harry says, breaking our lips apart, his hand coming down onto my waist.

But I want him. I really want him.

I lace my hand through his, pulling him out of the billiards room. I lead him down the hallway, trying to find somewhere private, where we can be alone. I skip the sitting room that I took Noah to, going into an empty bathroom.

"Where are you taking me?" Harry laughs, amused as I shut us in the bathroom.

"I want privacy." I grin at him and push him up against the door.

"Yeah?" he asks, tilting his head at me.

His expression is light, but I can see the want in his eyes.

"Yeah," I repeat before kissing him again. I press my body flat against his, wanting to be as close to him as possible.

I fumble with my dress, trying to figure out how to get out of it.

I need to be free of it.

I can feel Harry smile against my lips, and I start to wonder if he thinks this is funny. But a second later, his hand is cupping my cheek, and he's kissing down my neck.

I bring him back to my lips, letting my tongue slip into his mouth. Harry's kisses are warm and reassuring.

Which is all I need.

I move my fingers across his chest and down to his belt. I quickly get it undone, sliding it from around his waist and tossing it onto the floor.

"Someone's serious tonight," Harry says, looking down at me.

I nod at him, not responding. A second later, I have his pants unbuttoned and am trying to pull them down his legs while still kissing him.

"Mallory," Harry whispers again, biting his lip when I finally get them off.

"No more talking," I argue, dropping onto my knees.

I kiss down his stomach, liking the way he tastes like salt and tequila. I sit back on my heels, wanting more of him. I want to show him how much I want him. I let my fingers dance across the edge of his boxers and then glance up at him, connecting our gaze. All I can see is his flat stomach, hard jaw, and glowing eyes looking down at me.

"Fuck," he breathes out.

I get my hands wrapped around his boxers, ready to pull them down when Harry lifts me up from the floor.

"Harry," I whine, "I want you." I look at him, pouting, not sure why he stopped me.

"Not here," he says, shaking his head.

His face softens, but his blue eyes are still glowing, and I can tell I've got him worked up.

"Here," I disagree, turning him.

I push him down, so he's sitting on the toilet, and I straddle him. My dress slips up my legs, and Harry's palms instantly move to my exposed skin.

"I know you want me. I want you too. Now the only thing separating us is this measly fabric."

I look down to his boxers, getting a glimpse of my own underwear.

Just two little pieces of fabric that need to disappear.

"What's going on?" Harry asks, pinching my chin.

I swat his hand away, not wanting him to treat me like a child.

"Nothing," I push out. I stare at him, wondering if he's going to change his mind. If he's going to let his hand slip further up my thigh and back into my underwear.

But he doesn't.

I get up, fixing my dress. Because if he doesn't want to do anything, then we won't.

But I'm not going to be happy about it.

"Come here," Harry says, taking my hand.

He pulls me back down onto his lap, kissing me gently. I give in to his lips for a minute but then lean away.

"I want you," I insist, sticking out my bottom lip.

"I want you too," he agrees. "But not like this. It should be special for you."

I roll my eyes. "*Special, special, special.* I'm in a *new dress.* I have on *lingerie.*"

"You're not playing fair," Harry groans, his eyes slipping back down my legs.

"You weren't playing fair when you stripped naked in front of me earlier tonight. This is your punishment." I grin at him.

I stand up from his lap again, taking in his darkened eyes.

"You can even have a peek." I lift up my dress and turn around in a circle in front of him.

He bites his lip, shaking his head.

"Very, very unfair." Harry runs his hand up my thigh, grabbing my ass.

"Is it working?"

"It's definitely working," he says, his eyes on my legs. "But we still aren't shagging in the loo."

"Fine," I huff.

Harry pulls his pants back up and rebuttons them. A second later, my cheek is back in his palm, and he's kissing me.

"I'm trying to be a gentleman," he finally says.

"I appreciate that," I admit, still trying to figure out how to coerce him into going straight up to his room.

But a second later, Harry is pulling me out of the bathroom and back into the billiards room. I barely have time to make sure my dress is in place before Mohammad is at my side.

"Holy shit," he starts, speaking a mile a minute, "I got to grab a lime wedge out of Olivia's mouth, and I swear, she looked at me the entire time I was leaning over her!"

Harry rolls his eyes.

"I'll make us a drink," he comments to me before walking toward the liquor cabinet.

"Really?" I ask Mohammad once it's just the two of us.

"Oh yeah," he agrees, his brows dipping in. "She's playing hard to get for sure. But I know she's interested."

"Well, that's good." And I wonder if maybe that's what I should do instead with Harry. Play hard to get.

I glance over at him, and he smiles warmly at me. And I instantly know that the answer to that is no.

Because Harry and I don't play games.

I take in his shirtless body. How his muscles snake around him, making him look lean and extended. Everything about him is tight and beautiful. And it's funny because I'm not sure how someone with such a long, trim body can have such a hard, square jaw.

But Harry does.

"Obviously," Mohammad replies, interrupting my thoughts.

I fan myself, disconnecting my gaze from Harry's body. "I might need that condom after all," I whisper.

Because I can more than imagine slipping it onto Harry, finally being able to feel every piece of his skin against mine.

"Miss America," Mohammad says, turning to me with a grin. He tilts his head, searching my face.

"I know," I admit, my eyes going wide. "But I can't help it. He's standing over there, shirtless. It's torture."

"Where did you two sneak off to anyway?" Mohammad asks, leaning closer.

"Well, after the tequila and striptease, I had to get him alone," I spill out, wanting to talk to Mohammad. My forehead creases as I think about Harry not giving in to me in the bathroom. "But he didn't want to do anything but kiss."

Mohammad throws his arm over my shoulders. "Don't read into it. I'm sure he just wants to chill before having that kind of fun."

But I'm not convinced.

"You're telling me that if Olivia pulled you into the bathroom and tried to take off your pants, you'd stop her?"

"Fuck no, I wouldn't stop her," he says, shaking his head. "I think you need another shot."

"Can I do one off you?" I ask excitedly, deciding to ignore his comment.

"Hell yes, you can." He leads me over to the pool table and removes his shirt, dramatically tossing it onto the ground.

I half-expect him to start dancing for us.

"Oh Lord," I comment, rolling my eyes.

Mohammad's pearly whites are out, and I think it's the first time I've ever seen him shirtless.

And I'm not surprised to find that he has rounded shoulders and a thin, tight waist.

"Uh-oh," Naomi says, bounding up to me. "Decided to

go for another round?"

I take in her pink lips and rosy cheeks. George comes up behind her, wrapping his arms around her. I search his face, finding his lips to be tinted the same color as Naomi's.

Hmm.

"Well, someone demanded I have another shot," I say, glancing down at Mohammad.

Olivia walks over to us, looking like she's lost in a world of her own. She has an easy smile on her face, her eyes drifting across Mohammad's shirtless torso.

"Where'd your friends go?" I ask George, not seeing Thomas, Katherine, or Collin anywhere.

"They headed out," he replies. But he's quickly distracted by Naomi's neck, kissing up to her cheek.

She lets out a giggle, and Olivia looks like she might burst out laughing, watching them. I'm not sure if she's repulsed or happy for Naomi, but her expression makes me laugh.

I turn to Harry, raising an eyebrow at him. "Care to do the honors?"

"Going again, are we?" Harry asks, pushing off the liquor cabinet.

He fills up a shot glass while I grab a lime, handing it to Mohammad.

"We are," I reply.

"She's been putting them back tonight," Mohammad says enthusiastically, taking the salt. "Where do you want it?"

"How about your hand?" I comment, keeping my eyes on Harry.

He brings the shot glass to the table, turning his attention to Mohammad.

"How about not?" Mohammad replies, wetting down a piece of his stomach, adding salt.

I narrow my eyes at him, but he just chuckles.

"Let's keep it in the shot glass this time. I don't really feel like sucking tequila out of Mohammad's belly button. No offense."

Besides the fact that it's slightly gross, I have no idea who else's mouth has been on him. And I would rather not think about it.

"None taken," he replies. "But so you know, every shower I have, I clean my belly button as well. No bits left unscrubbed."

I laugh, thinking about Mohammad in the bathroom. I can imagine him fussing over everything—from making sure he gets every part squeaky clean to leaving the conditioner in long enough for it to have its softening effect.

"Always good to know," I reply, popping the lime into Mohammad's mouth. I lick the salt off the side of his stomach and then wrap my mouth around the shot glass, throwing it back.

The taste is stronger than I remember, and I blink a few times, moving to Mohammad's mouth to get the lime and kill the taste.

But all of a sudden, Mohammad starts talking, causing the lime to fall, and I end up with my lips directly on his.

I stay on his mouth for only a second, momentarily shocked, before ripping my face away.

My eyes grow into saucers, my mouth falling open.

"Mohammad!" I start, but he looks equally as stunned.

His expression is a mixture of shocked and distraught, like he just saw his sister naked on accident or something.

"You kissed me," he says, sitting up.

"I didn't mean to kiss you," I argue back. "You dropped the lime!"

Harry buckles over in laughter.

Olivia and Naomi are both laughing now, too, mostly

23

from watching Harry, who is practically crying.

"You put it in backward," Mohammad states, raising his hands in front of him.

I roll my eyes at him.

He glances over to Harry, a grin pulling at his lips, and I know he's already come up with a way to twist what just happened.

"If you wanted to kiss me, you could have just asked, you know," Mohammad says, practically beaming now.

I shake my head, not letting this feed his ego.

"You should have seen Mohammad's face," Harry says, finally catching his breath. His cheeks are tinted red, his chest still heaving. "His eyes were open the entire time. He looked like he was snogging his gran."

"Always appreciate the compliment," I say under my breath.

Harry wraps his arm around me, pulling me against his side.

We move toward the couches. Apparently, me kissing Mohammad took it out of everyone, and we all sit down with a collective sigh.

I drop onto the couch effortlessly, curling up next to Harry. Mohammad and Olivia sit down on another sofa together, and he drapes his arm around her. She looks tired, and she leans into him. Naomi and George are already kissing.

"This is nice." I smile, feeling my eyes form into little slits. I lean my head back, falling against Harry's strong arm.

I'm not tired, but Harry is warm and it's dark and I just want to absorb everything.

To sit here happily with him.

The alcohol settles into me, and it makes me feel really relaxed.

I lazily run my hand over Harry's arm, my eyes slipping

up his skin. And suddenly, I can't stay seated next to him.

I press my mouth onto his, sliding onto his lap.

I can't help it.

Harry kisses me back, his hand coming up into my hair, running down my back.

But then he pulls away.

"I think we need to get you up to bed," Harry comments, those blue eyes giving nothing away.

Yes, let's go to bed!

I wiggle my eyebrows at him, and I'm trying so hard not to burst out into a full grin. "Finally."

Harry chuckles at me. "Someone looks like they plan on misbehaving," he whispers, his arm wrapping around my waist.

He pulls me up off the couch, and I lean into him, letting him steady me.

My head feels foggy, but I let the fog stay. Because as long as I have Harry, it doesn't matter if my head is foggy. Or that my arms and legs seem to be heavier than before, like they're filled with sand.

"You're so helpful," I sigh, putting my head against his shoulder.

"It's not a problem," Harry says, holding me firmly.

"Good night," I call out, waving at everyone still in the room. Which I guess is just Olivia, Naomi, George, and Mohammad.

Hmm. I'm not sure where the others went. *Did George say they left?* I can't remember.

But I give them a wave, too, just in case I can't see them. Maybe they will be able to sense it.

"I'm getting this one up to bed," Harry says when Mohammad stands up, walking toward us.

"Good night, Miss America." Mohammad smiles at me.

And I instantly want to fall into that smile.

I pick my head up off Harry's shoulder, my hands aching to be around Mohammad. I hug him tightly.

"Steady on," Harry comments, his hand on my arm.

"Good night," I say, squeezing Mohammad.

I let go of him, letting Harry lead me out of the room.

"Let's get some water first," he says, taking my hand and leading me into the kitchen.

Next thing I know, he has me seated up on the counter and is digging through the fridge.

A second later, he has a water bottle in my hand, making me hold it up to my lips.

"I can do it," I whine, letting the cold water fill my mouth.

"I know you can," Harry says, moving between my thighs.

He watches the bottle at my lips, and my eyes easily move across his strong jaw. I set the water down, my fingers aching to be on Harry's cheeks instead. My hands fall down his neck and onto his shoulders, my thumb rubbing across his collarbone.

Harry lets out a groan, his eyelashes fluttering closed. I watch his blond lashes, pretending that they aren't inches away from me but tickling my cheeks instead.

"Mallory," Harry whispers, gazing directly at me.

I look between his eyes and his lips, wanting him to make a move.

Wanting his lips to be the ones to press hard into mine.

I want to taste how much he wants me.

Because Harry's the master of nonchalant. It's like the first day we met. He kissed me right away. He put his hand down my shirt on the double-decker, a silly grin on his face. He's always doing what he wants but in a way that makes you not sure if he's just trying to get away with it or if that's actually what he desires.

My hands leave his collarbone, my finger coming up to his lips. I trace their outline over and over, my finger moving up before dipping down at the center, just to go up again. His lips are long and beautiful.

I flick my gaze up to Harry's just as he takes my wrist in his hand, pulling it away from his lips.

A second later, his mouth is crashing against mine, his tongue pushing my lips apart. I open my mouth, feeling my skin tingle. He drops my wrist, his arms sliding around me.

He moves me toward the edge of the counter as I wrap my legs around his waist.

All I can feel are his hips pressing into mine, and I moan into his mouth at the sensation.

"I want you naked. Now," I whisper, biting his lip.

"Here?" Harry asks, practically panting.

"What's a kitchen good for, if not this?" I ask, letting my hands slip up into his hair.

"Food." He chuckles against my mouth.

"I could be your dessert," I push, my lips trailing down across his jaw.

"You're relentless tonight."

"I thought you were the one who wanted me naked and covered in chocolate. Or did you have a different idea when you came up with *date night delight*?"

"You have a good point." He shakes his head, and then suddenly, his hand is moving under my dress, his fingers slipping into my underwear.

I gasp at the sensation as his lips press into the skin at the nape of my neck.

I lean my head back, letting the feeling overcome me.

Because *this* is what I've been wanting.

I want sexy, *I'm going to stand here and do exactly what I want to you, right here in the kitchen* Harry.

And he's finally giving me that.

I squeeze my legs around him tighter, his mouth finding mine. I trail my fingers down over his chest, my nails scraping against his soft skin.

"Let's go to bed," Harry whispers, pulling me down off the counter.

I wasn't expecting it, and I stumble a bit.

I laugh at myself, feeling lighter than normal.

Everything is moving around me, like the world's axis is off or something.

I nod at him.

Harry slowly walks with me to his bedroom, and I feel immense relief when he finally shuts the door behind us.

"Here, have some more water," he insists, handing me the bottle from the kitchen.

I take a few gulps before setting it down on the bedside table.

Harry's bedside table.

I smile to myself because it's finally just us. No more excuses. No more *eat this* or *have some water* or *not here.*

No.

No more excuses.

I move my hand over my shoulder, trying to grab the zipper at the back of my dress to pull it down. Because if I could just get this dress off, I know that I could easily win Harry over with my lingerie.

"Here," Harry says from behind me.

He unzips my dress, but when I turn around, he's moved. He's over at his dresser.

"Let me get you something to sleep in," he comments, fumbling through one of his drawers as I slip out of my dress.

He turns back to me, holding a T-shirt, finding me standing in nothing but my lingerie.

His eyes scan across my exposed body, his gaze lingering on my chest.

I smile at him. "Do you like it?" I try to pop out my hip, wanting to make myself look curvier.

Harry smiles back at me, tilting his head. He's looking at me almost like I'm a child.

"You're stunning, Mallory," he says, extending out the top.

I look down at it, furrowing my brow.

I'm not sure why he looks so amused or why he's holding out his shirt to me, but I don't want it.

I take the shirt from his hand and then drop it onto the floor.

Harry cocks his head, his tongue coming out and licking his bottom lip.

I take a step back, unhooking my bra.

"I don't want your clothes," I start, letting my bra fall to the floor. "In fact, I don't want to wear anything."

I watch Harry suck in a breath as I pull down my underwear, kicking them off from around my feet.

"What do you want?" Harry asks, swallowing hard. His eyes scan up and down my body, his mouth slightly ajar.

"I want to be naked in your bed," I state, looking directly at him. I hold his gaze for a minute and then turn around and walk over to his bed. I crawl onto it and then prop myself up onto my elbows. "And I want you on top of me."

I watch Harry blink a few times. He brings his hand up to his cheek, running it down across his face. He lets out a shaky breath, like he's trying to slow down his heart rate.

I start to wonder if he might just stay standing like that forever, but a second later, he's striding toward me.

I spread my legs apart, so ready for him.

He climbs on top of me, his weight settling into my body as his mouth finds mine. His hips rest between my legs, and I run my hand down his back, my nails scraping across his skin.

Harry kisses me wildly, like he's finally giving in.

Good.

His hand moves between us, finding my chest. He teases my skin, his palm gliding across my ribs and down over my hips. My fingers slip around his waist, and I try to grab his butt, but all I feel is fabric. Then I try to push off his pants, wanting to feel every piece of him against me.

"I want you," I mumble against his lips, finally just shoving my hand down into his boxers.

Harry kisses across my jaw, and I can hear his breathing catch in my ear.

"I know," he whispers back, his voice shaky. He presses up off my chest, supporting his weight with his elbow.

I search his eyes, trying to figure out why he's pulling back.

"How about, tonight, you just let me kiss you?" he asks, his blue eyes on me.

"Kiss me …" I mumble, frustrated.

I need to feel him.

I want more than just kissing.

Harry smirks at me, looking amused again. I'm about to tell him off when he drops his mouth down onto mine, softly biting my lip.

A second later, he's trailing his mouth down over my neck and across my chest. His mouth is warm and wet, and he pulls at my skin, sucking on one spot before his tongue moves to another. He kisses every inch of my stomach, his teeth teasing me.

He scoots further down the bed, letting his hands slip up and down my thighs as he bites my hip. I suck in a gasp, the sensation surprising me.

I hear Harry let out a groan as he picks up my legs, resting them over his shoulders.

I tense up, my body not sure what to expect.

"Just lay your head back and relax. Or you can watch," he says, his eyes on me.

But then his mouth dips between my legs, and my head instantly falls back.

I let out a moan, the feeling better than anything I could have ever imagined.

Because this is *definitely* not what I thought when he said *let me kiss you*.

SATURDAY, OCTOBER 5TH
What happened last night?
9:30AM

I WAKE UP with a headache. A *pounding* headache.

Ughhh.

I sit up in bed, trying to orient myself. I glance around, taking in Harry's room. I bring my hands up to my eyes and rub them, willing them to open more.

But everything hurts.

The light coming in through the window is too bright. The sound of the fan, too loud.

What happened last night?

But suddenly, everything comes flooding back to me. Well, at least pieces of it.

Kissing Harry on the balcony.

Noah's words.

Crying in the bathroom.

I squeeze my eyes shut and slip back under the covers, wanting to crawl into a hole. But I kind of already am in one.

A fluffy one.

A fluffy one that smells like a boy—that smells like Harry.

I glance down, realizing that I'm in one of Harry's shirts.

I don't remember putting on his shirt.

I peek out from under the covers, looking around. *Because where is Harry?* I glance over to the bedside table, finding a note that reads:

In the kitchen.
Come down when you wake up.
X

There's also a fresh bottle of water and an ibuprofen. I take the tablet into my mouth, trying not to cough when the cold water hits my dry throat. I want to lie in bed all day, never venturing downstairs, but I know that I need to.

Not only because Harry told me that's where he would be, but also because if my memory's right, Naomi might still be here.

And Mohammad.

And Noah …

I let out another grumble, not wanting to face any this. But I know that I have to.

I decide to just get up and get it over with. I throw the covers off and move to stand up. But the small amount of motion sends a shooting pain through my head, and I grab on to it, wanting to cry.

I move slowly to the bathroom, almost tripping over clothes.

A pair of pants.

My bra.

My dress.

Oh my God.

My eyes go wide as I take in the state of Harry's room. Our clothes are littered all across his floor. I pick them up, hoping that at least if I put them into a pile, it won't seem as bad.

Well, at least, it won't *look* as bad.

I finally make it to the bathroom, getting toothpaste into my mouth and rinsing off my face. By the time I'm back in

Harry's room and I find a pair of pajama bottoms to throw on, I'm not feeling any more awake.

Or any less hungover.

I slip out of Harry's room and can easily hear noise coming into the hallway. I hear a pot banging in the kitchen, and my stomach does a little flip.

I'm not sure if it's a *you cannot eat a thing right now* flip or if it's a *I can eat everything in my path right now* flip, but I guess I'll find out soon enough.

I'm halfway down the hallway when I hear a door creak open.

I stop, watching Olivia come out from a bedroom.

And my first instinct is to hide.

I go around a corner, not ready to face her this morning. Well, not really ready to face anyone. But I peek back around the corner, curious.

Olivia sort of looks like she woke up with all of her makeup still on. She looks ... perfect. Her hair is a little messy, but it's got volume to it.

I instinctively bring my hand up to my hair, patting it down.

She walks in the opposite direction of the kitchen, so I decide it's probably safe to reenter the hallway. I'm walking past the room she came out of when I run straight into a naked chest.

A naked chest belonging to Mohammad.

Holy shit.

My mouth is gaping open.

Because he came out of the same room.

The same room.

And he's shirtless.

Like, *shirtless!*

My eyes go wide in shock. Mohammad steadies me and

then throws me a quick wink.

I'm so stunned that I can't even say anything.

I just stare at him.

He squeezes my shoulder before slipping past me and into a bathroom. I try to push words out of my mouth, but I can't. I end up forcing my jaw closed, deciding I need to get to the kitchen, where it's safe.

I move through Harry's ginormous house, trying to convince myself that *that* just actually happened.

Because Olivia came out of the same bedroom as Mohammad.

Mohammad!

Did they just fall asleep together? Maybe she asked him to bring her something?

Or maybe something did happen …

By the time I get to the kitchen, I'm too freaked out to continue thinking about it.

I'll just have to wait and let Mohammad explain.

I walk into the room, finding Harry at the stove. He's stirring the contents of a skillet, and Noah is seated on a barstool at the island, watching him.

Noah is hunched over, and all I can see is his curved back and messy hair.

I slide onto the stool next to him, letting out a groan.

Harry must hear it because he turns around, looking at me brightly.

"Well, good morning," he says, sounding way too chipper. His blond hair is brushed, and he has on a long-sleeved shirt and thick sweatpants.

I glance between him and Noah, not even sure how to form words yet. I'm confused, my head is pounding, and I'm still slightly frightened about seeing Olivia and Mohammad together.

"Coffee …" I finally get out, creasing my forehead.

"Someone's grumpy," Noah mutters next to me.

Someone's grumpy, I internally mock.

Are those really his first words to me this morning? After everything last night? After he was the *grumpiest* of them all?

I would roll my eyes at him, but I'm not sure I have the energy.

"Someone's *sleepy,*" Harry sweetly corrects, coming to my side. He softly kisses my forehead, his hand running down over my hair. He smells fresh and clean but with a hint of food and coffee. "You have the cutest morning hair."

I look up, taking in Harry's easy expression and crisp blue eyes.

I barely glanced at myself in the mirror this morning, but I know he's being kind. If anything, my hair looks like that of a wild woman. I mindlessly touch it, feeling it sticking up in the back. I try to give him a smile anyway, but for some reason, my lips pulling across my cheeks adds pressure to my face, and my head starts to hurt again.

"Ugh," I mumble, laying my head down into my arms on the counter.

"Look at you two. Who would have thought that I'd be the only one *not* hungover?" Harry chuckles, easily moving about the kitchen.

I peek up at him, taking in the contents spread across the counter. He already has a French press filled with coffee and a box of eggs and a package of frozen potato cakes out.

"You're hungover?" Noah asks, finally looking over at me.

And it's the first time I've actually seen his eyes since last night. I search his face, taking in his pale complexion. He looks tired and worn down, but he doesn't look half as bad as I expected. Not that I expected him to look bad. I just expected him to look more … hungover.

"Fuck, I forgot you went to bed. You should have seen her last night." Harry laughs. He pours me a cup of coffee, setting it down on the counter.

I give him a thankful smile and take a sip.

The liquid warms my throat, and instant relief hits me.

"What?" Noah asks, confused.

"Harry," I push, not wanting him to go there. Because, for one, it's not funny. And two, I don't really want Noah knowing everything I did last night.

I don't even want to know what I did last night.

"She came downstairs after putting your drunken ass to bed and started pounding the liquor," Harry continues, obviously excited to share the story. He's looking at me like he's somehow proud of me, but a second later, his back is to us, and he's fussing over the stove.

"Really?" Noah asks, his eyes fully on me now.

I hold his gaze, taking a sip of coffee.

Because at least if my mouth is full, I don't have to answer him.

"Oh, she went wild," Mohammad confirms, walking into the kitchen.

"I did not," I argue, dipping in my brows.

Because I'm too hungover to get scolded by Noah or made fun of by Mohammad. I want to have my coffee, eat some food, and fall back asleep, wrapped up in Harry's warm arms.

"You did," Harry confirms, examining the package of frozen potato cakes. He rips open the box, dumping them out and onto a baking sheet before Mohammad moves him aside.

A second later, Harry's leaning against the counter, watching as Mohammad throws away whatever was in Harry's skillet on the stove. Mohammad cracks a few eggs, mixing in salt and pepper, and then he turns on the oven and puts the potatoes in.

Harry continues, addressing Noah, "She started doing body shots. She sucked tequila out of my belly button."

"She took a shot from between Naomi's boobs." Mohammad smiles. His eyes slip up to the corners, and it looks like he's reflecting on a fond memory.

"She even snogged Mohammad," Harry adds, shooting me a wink.

I flush, the memories flooding back. Noah's mouth is hanging open, his eyes still on Harry.

"You kissed Mohammad?" Noah asks, turning to me. His voice is rough, and his eyes are filled with disbelief.

"She did," Mohammad confirms, not letting me answer. "I'm not sure it was intentional though. I mean, she was sort of going for the lime in my mouth, but then I dropped it, and she just kept going—"

"It was fucking brilliant," Harry cuts in with a sharp laugh.

"I *might* have grazed his lips," I admit, closing my eyes with my words.

Because I do not want to be recalling all of this right now.

"See, Noah," Mohammad says, walking around the island and wrapping his arm around Noah's shoulders. "That's what happens when you get plastered too early and pass out. You miss all the good shit."

"Apparently," Noah mumbles, not seeming at all amused by our conversation.

"Speaking of *fun*, where's Olivia?" I ask, cocking my head at Mohammad. Because I would give anything for this conversation to not be about me anymore.

And I think if anyone needs to explain themselves, it's him.

And I'm curious what he's going to say.

LONDON PREP: BOOK 3

Mohammad drops his arm from around Noah, moving back to the eggs. He's practically beaming.

"She went to find Naomi and George," he answers, dumping scrambled eggs onto a plate. He slides it toward me and Noah before adding more eggs to the skillet, checking on the potatoes in the oven.

"How do you know that?" Noah asks, grabbing a few forks from a nearby drawer.

"That's a great question." Mohammad grins, waggling his eyebrows. He turns the skillet on low, coming to sit down next to me. He steals a sip of my coffee and takes a bite of the eggs.

"It *is* a good question," Harry repeats, like he's trying to figure out what Mohammad's answer is going to be.

I look at him, wondering if he's going to be happy or upset at whatever did or didn't happen between them.

"Well?" I push, but a second later, Olivia comes into the kitchen, causing Harry to roll his eyes, evidently not ready for the interruption.

"Morning," Olivia says.

"Morning," I reply back because no one else has.

"A lively bunch," she comments, walking straight to the coffee.

She pours herself a cup before looking at the scrambled eggs with distaste. She moves easily through the kitchen, and I watch her, captivated. She grabs milk out of the fridge, adding it to her coffee before pulling open a cabinet to reveal a loaf of bread and then putting a few pieces into the toaster.

"Where's Naomi?" Mohammad asks next to me when she finally settles, leaning her elbows down onto the island as she waits.

"Getting ready. I found her asleep in one of the bedrooms," she replies.

"No George?" Harry asks, surprised.

Olivia shakes her head. "Not in her room anyway."

"Got some action and then snuck off?" Mohammad asks, confused.

"Sounds like George," Olivia offers.

"He seemed into her last night though," I disagree, thinking about the way he looked at her.

Olivia shrugs, taking a sip of her coffee.

Well, okay then.

She's either just not chatty or she doesn't know the answer, but I can't decide which. Or maybe it's a slow morning for her too.

Mohammad gets back up, tending to his eggs. He grabs the potatoes out of the oven, tossing them onto a plate.

"Let's all sit at the table," Mohammad instructs, turning off the stove, his second batch of eggs ready. He's already zooming out of the kitchen, a plate in each hand.

"He's too awake this morning," I mumble, taking another sip of my coffee.

"Not feeling so good?" Olivia asks, peering over at me.

"Not the best," I admit.

There's no point in lying.

She nods understandingly. "Yeah, those shots weren't the *best* idea."

"No," I agree, but a second later, Mohammad is at my side, ushering me up and to the table.

I walk slowly, carrying my coffee cup with me like it's the most precious thing in the world. Noah shifts next to me, and I glance over at him.

His expression is a mixture of tired and confused, but he stays silent.

Olivia sits down across from me, bringing in a pile of toast, already sliding jam onto one of the pieces when Naomi walks into the room.

And she's radiant.

"Good morning," she sighs, practically falling into her chair. She has her hair up in a scrunchy, and she has on a pair of pink pajamas.

"Morning," I reply, taking in her shiny eyes and rosy cheeks.

Olivia hands her a piece of toast, and she takes it, absent-mindedly biting into it.

"You're glowing," I comment and instantly feel a little bad for saying it out loud.

"You are," Olivia agrees, peering over at her, looking amused.

Harry takes a seat next to me, pouring more coffee into my cup.

"Thanks." I smile at him.

I want to hold his gaze forever, but Naomi continues.

"Last night was fun," she evades, her soft eyes shifting from the table down to the toast in her hand.

"Spill," Olivia instructs. Apparently, this morning, she's not about playing games or being subtle because her words are direct and clear.

Everyone at the table looks at Naomi, interested. I think we all want to know what happened.

For a minute, I consider shutting down Olivia's question, but Naomi can hold her own. If she doesn't want to answer, she won't.

Naomi rolls her eyes. "Don't get any ideas. I made George sleep on the couch."

"Really?" Mohammad asks with surprise.

Naomi nods her head, grinning at us. "We kissed. He walked me into my room and said good night. Of course, he wanted to *just* sleep in the bed with me, but I told him no."

"Good for you," Olivia replies with admiration.

I glance between Harry and Mohammad, who both look confused. My eyes slip over to Noah, who is digging into his eggs, barely paying attention.

"I don't get it. I thought you liked him?" Harry finally asks, biting into a potato cake.

"I do like him," Naomi answers.

"Then why kick him out of your room?" Mohammad asks, shoveling in a mouthful of food.

I let out a chuckle, realizing that guys and girls really do think differently.

"She likes him. She doesn't want to just hook up," Olivia answers, rolling her eyes.

"It is possible to sleep in the same bed and not shag," Mohammad replies quickly, arching an eyebrow directly at Olivia.

She narrows her eyes and shoots him a glare before looking back to Naomi.

"It sends the wrong message. And it's too much temptation. Besides, I think it drove him crazy. When he woke up this morning, he came in to say good-bye. Kissed me and told me he wanted to go out this weekend."

"You got him to commit to a date," Harry says, seemingly impressed.

"I did." Naomi beams.

"Well done," Olivia approves.

"Last night was fun," Naomi gushes, taking another bite of her toast. "I mean, I'm a little tired this morning; don't get me wrong. But it was nice, all of us hanging out. It felt like old times."

"Definitely," Mohammad agrees, still shoveling food into his mouth.

I glance up, thinking about what she said.

Old times.

Olivia's eyes are on Harry. Mohammad and Naomi are so focused on eating that I'm the only one who is paying attention to the way that she looks at him.

My stomach twists when I place the emotions in her eyes.

Longing.

Sadness.

I swallow hard, looking back down at my plate. I know I should eat something, but my head is pounding, and now, my stomach feels all knotted up.

But a second later, Harry's hand is resting on my leg. My body relaxes at his touch, and I decide to try a few bites of egg.

I chew slowly and then swallow.

"I'm not sure my stomach's ready for food." I bring my gaze up to meet Harry's, who has stopped to watch me eat.

"I'm not sure everyone here feels the same." Harry laughs, looking between Mohammad and Noah, who are both inhaling their food.

Normally, I like the smell of eggs, but this morning, they make my stomach churn.

I push my plate away, trying to keep from looking repulsed.

"You're feeling a little sick this morning?" Naomi asks, sympathetically looking at me.

"A bit."

She slides some butter on a piece of toast and then says, "Here, have some." She leans across the table, handing it to me. "It's easy on your stomach, but it will help fill you up."

I bite into the toast, feeling relief when I swallow it and don't instantly feel sick.

"Thanks." I flush, embarrassed.

"How are you feeling, Noah?" Mohammad asks, his eyes flicking up from his plate.

"Shit, mate," he replies, setting down his fork.

"We're a fucking mess this morning, aren't we?" Harry chuckles, admiring everyone at the table.

I sigh, feeling a little less embarrassed. Because at least I'm not the only one who drank too much.

"We are," I agree.

"At least we're a mess together," Naomi encourages, her rounded eyes slipping from Olivia and moving around the table to Noah, Mohammad, me, and finally Harry.

I smile at her optimism, finishing off the piece of toast she gave me. The warm butter and bread have settled my stomach, and mixed with the coffee, it makes me feel a little more awake.

"So, what are everyone's plans today?" I ask.

"I've got to head back to the house soon. Get changed for my match," Noah replies first.

"Right." I nod, thankful that at least he's talking to me. "You're playing … Highgate, right?"

"That's going to be an intense match," Mohammad says enthusiastically, his pearly whites coming out.

"You'll come then?" Noah asks, his eyes lifting to Mohammad.

"For sure." Mohammad nods.

"Do you think you'll win?" Naomi asks.

Noah shrugs. "They're a great team. And I'm not feeling the best this morning, but hopefully."

"Bollocks. You'll rally," Harry cuts in.

"You think?" Noah asks, looking doubtful.

"Well, you'd better fucking rally. I'm only coming if you promise to kick some Highgate ass," Harry banters back.

Noah grins at him. "I'll do my best."

"That's the problem with drinking on a Friday night," Mohammad says.

"What do you mean?" Olivia asks, her eyes flicking toward him.

"Friday night should be the warm-up for Noah. Then, Saturday, after football, he can go on a bender. He needs to be strategic."

"Fair point," Olivia agrees.

Noah rolls his eyes.

"You're only saying that because you want Kensington to win," I cut in.

"I'm only saying that because I care about Noah's reputation. Which, in turn, affects my reputation. And right now, he's looking hungover," Mohammad points out.

"I'll be fine," Noah replies.

"We might have to come up with a different solution to winning this match," Mohammad disagrees.

"Like what?" Harry asks, sitting up straighter with interest.

"Like ... a distraction," Mohammad says.

And I can see the wheels turning in his head.

"A distraction?" I ask.

Mohammad's eyes widen, his whole face brightening. "You two should come," Mohammad says, looking between Olivia and Naomi. "Dress up sexy and start waving at the Highgate players. They'll be so distracted that they'll forget how to kick a football."

Olivia's brows dip in, and she looks unamused. Naomi flushes, like Mohammad's idea was some sort of compliment.

"That's devious," Harry says energetically, nodding his head.

"It won't work," Noah disagrees.

"No, Mohammad's right. It could work," Olivia replies, apparently reassessing her previous unamused stance.

"Brilliant fucking idea, Mohammad," Harry agrees.

"Aren't you forgetting something?" I ask, wondering if I'm the only one who's thought of the alternative effect.

Because they all look too pleased with themselves.

Well, everyone, except for Noah, who looks like he can't believe this conversation is happening.

"Forgetting what?" Mohammad asks.

"Well … if Naomi and Olivia are so distracting that they make Highgate forget how to play football, it is assumable that they might also distract Kensington's team."

I look between everyone, taking note of their reaction.

Olivia and Naomi sway their heads back and forth. Harry just looks confused, like he can't decide if he agrees or disagrees.

"Shit," Mohammad mumbles. "You have a point."

I just shrug, moving my attention back to my coffee. Because as much as I want to have the energy to banter back and forth with Mohammad on distracting the players or winning the match through a secret operation, I don't.

"Well, I'm sure the team will appreciate the support either way," Noah says, getting up from the table.

"Need to get back?" Harry asks.

"Yeah. I need to shower and change. Maybe sneak in a nap," Noah replies.

"I should probably get back too," I agree.

I'm sure that Helen will suggest that I go to Noah's match, and just like Noah, I think I'm going to need a shower and a nap before I'm ready for that. Part of me wants to text her and tell her that I'm going to hang out with Naomi today and then really stay here with Harry. But Harry's going to want to watch Noah play, and I already know that I'm not going to get the quiet morning in bed with him that I hoped for.

"Aww," Naomi says, pushing out her bottom lip.

I smile at her as Noah picks up his plate, moving to the kitchen. "What are you up to today?"

"I have a dress fitting actually." Naomi beams.

"Ooh, for what?"

"It's for a launch party. One of our family friends is opening up an art gallery in Mayfair."

"That's amazing. There are always cool art exhibits popping up at galleries in New York. I think it's one of the best perks about living in a city."

Naomi nods. "I'm not always the biggest fan of doing things with my parents, but I think it will be fun. I love getting dressed up, and being there to support them will be nice."

I nod at her, deciding I'd better get up too. Mohammad rises with me, grabbing a handful of plates. When we get to the kitchen, Noah's already putting his plate into the dishwasher.

"I'm going to grab my stuff and then head out," he says, barely looking at me.

"All right. Give me, like, twenty? I want to help clean up before we go."

Noah nods, but a second later, he's out of the kitchen. Harry, Naomi, and Olivia all move into the kitchen, setting plates down onto the counter.

"Help me with the dishes?" I ask Mohammad, wanting to talk to him.

Alone.

And I'm hoping if we offer to do the dishes, then everyone else will disperse.

"No, I've got it," Harry interrupts, grabbing the plate out of my hand.

I shake my head at him. "I'm not going to leave you with a messy house. I want to help pick up."

47

"Why don't Olivia and I work on the kitchen?" Naomi offers.

I flare my eyes at Mohammad, hoping he'll see that I want to talk to him.

"Mallory and I can get the billiards room," Mohammad agrees, raising his eyebrows at me.

"I think I'll pop out for a quick fag then," Harry comments, setting down the plate he took from my hand onto the counter.

"Always *so* helpful," Olivia says under her breath.

Naomi dips her chin down, pretending she didn't hear her comment.

Harry waves her off.

"I'll give you two a sec," Harry says into my ear, looking between me and Mohammad.

I smile at him, grateful that he could see that I need a minute alone with my friend. I squeeze his hand before leaving the kitchen with Mohammad.

"PLEASE TELL ME you two shagged," Mohammad says the second we're alone in the hallway. "Because at least, if someone else got some action, I wouldn't feel so sorry for myself and my lack of getting any."

Mohammad lets out a huff as I snap my head in his direction.

"But I saw you two this morning. You came out of the same room. You were *shirtless*."

Mohammad glances around like someone might overhear us. And the second we're in the billiards room, he shuts the door.

"We snogged. Which I have to say was a fucking feat in and of itself. But that's all we did."

I tilt my head, sort of agreeing with him. Because Olivia

does seem like a tough nut to crack.

"It's more than I expected," I admit.

"True," Mohammad agrees. "When you and Harry went to bed, I thought I might be done for at that point. I mean, I knew Olivia chatting me up was just to annoy Harry. Or make him jealous. But anyway, you two left, and she still sat close to me."

"Then, what happened?" I ask, trying to piece everything together.

"Then, she told Naomi and George that we were going to bed and pulled me up off the couch. I kind of thought she'd pull me into a bedroom for effect and then kick me out. Or make me sleep on the floor."

"But she didn't?" I ask, a little confused by Olivia's motives.

Mohammad shakes his head. "She acted normal. Used the loo. Rinsed her mouth. That sort of thing. I kind of just sat there, unsure of what was going to happen."

"That had to have been awkward," I say, taking in Mohammad's embarrassed expression.

"A little." He flushes.

"But?"

"But then she came out of the bathroom, and suddenly, she was kissing me and pushing me onto the bed. She kept my hands strictly at her waist, but I wasn't going to try anything."

"No way," I gasp, my eyes turning into saucers.

Because Olivia came on to Mohammad?

"I know," Mohammad agrees, looking almost as confused. "But I wasn't about to question it. I mean, I woke up next to Olivia Winters. It was like a dream."

I shake my head, trying to clear my mind because nothing is making sense.

"Well, I'm happy for you." I give Mohammad my best

smile. I want him to know that he can always talk to me. And that despite his choices in women and tactics, I support him.

I just want him to be happy.

Mohammad grins at me, giving my shoulder a push. He moves to the liquor cabinet, grabbing a trash bag. He holds it open as we move through the room, collecting the leftover food boxes and empty alcohol bottles.

My stomach twists as I remember the variety of alcohols I consumed last night.

The bottle of wine that Olivia had gone and gotten.

The wine that I finished when Noah started acting weird.

How he had that glass up to his lips as he glared at me.

I push the thought out of my mind.

"I appreciate that," Mohammad continues. "I mean, Olivia is a challenge. But the fact is, I got to kiss her. It was kind of like kissing a witch. Or a goddess. You never believe it will actually happen, but when the chance comes up, you take it. Mostly because it sure as hell will never happen again. And you're curious what it will be like."

"I'm not sure Olivia would appreciate you comparing her to a witch." I laugh.

Mohammad grins at me.

"Well, I have to know," I say, urging him on, "what was it like?"

"What was what like?"

"Kissing a goddess."

Mohammad tilts his head back, like he's looking up at the sun with squinted eyes. "It was magical. She has these lips that, man, they just suck you in."

"Uh oh. It sounds like someone's a little smitten."

"No smitten-ness here," Mohammad assures. "Anyway, what about you? Did you use my *gift* last night?"

Mohammad waggles his eyebrows at me as I shift away

from the couch, moving to the pool table to grab an empty bottle. I throw it into the trash bag Mohammad's holding open.

"Unfortunately, no," I reply, thinking about the *gift* of condoms that Mohammad is referring to.

"Why not?"

"What do you mean? You saw the state that I was in last night. I was beyond tipsy."

"Yeah, I was a bit surprised. Something in you shifted. You really were having a good time."

"Too good of a time," I correct.

I glance over at Mohammad, wanting to tell him everything. All of the things that Noah said to me. How I cried in his arms. How I felt so helpless. But I can't bring myself to do it. To even repeat what Noah said. I don't want to dwell on his words for one more minute. I can't give them—or him—any more power.

"Something in me did shift."

"Talk to me," Mohammad says, tying off the trash bag before pulling me down onto the couch.

"I … I was overwhelmed last night. And I sort of tried to declare that I wasn't overwhelmed by letting loose and having fun," I say, trying to make sense of it.

"Declare to who?"

"To myself."

Mohammad looks at me, his lip twitching. "The sex stuff freaks you out, doesn't it?"

I watch his eyes soften as he waits for my answer.

I let out a heavy sigh, falling back into the couch. "The sex stuff is confusing."

"I never meant to push you," Mohammad says, his forehead creasing.

I shake my head at him. "You didn't. I mean, to be honest, last Wednesday, nothing made me worry about the stuff that Harry and I were doing. And yet, we did it. I think, for me, when sex finally happens, it's going to just have to happen. No hype. No planning."

"I respect that." Mohammad nods. "I was just taking the piss, you know that, right?"

"I knew it was all in good fun." I pull him into a hug.

"So, neither of us got any action, huh?" Mohammad chuckles at my ear.

"I mean … I got a little action," I admit with a flush.

Thinking about last night with Harry, I definitely remember parts of it. And I clearly remember Harry kissing across my stomach and down between my legs.

"From the looks of it, it was some good action." Mohammad grins.

I can't help but grin back at him. "It was … hot."

"You really like Harry, don't you?"

"I really, *really* like Harry."

I pull Mohammad up off the couch, almost losing my balance in the process. My head still aches, but the medicine and food and coffee seem to have helped take it from a sharp pain to a dull throb.

"I feel like shit," I huff, fluffing the pillows on the couch.

"I don't know why we're even cleaning. Harry has maids," Mohammad says as he puts the rest of the liquor into the cabinet.

"I've never seen any." I laugh.

"They're here at his beck and call. They're supposed to be around the house all the time, but I think Harry ends up sending them away more often than not."

"Doesn't that sort of defeat the purpose?"

"Essentially." Mohammad chuckles. "But I think it's more of an *if no one's around, there's no one to tell* sort of thing."

"So, the secrets stay secrets."

"Harry used to not care. We would drink and hang out, and the next morning, the maids would draw him a bath or make him breakfast. I remember, one time, a woman came into my room and opened the curtains and started to clean around me. I was freaked as shit."

"I can imagine." I laugh. "I'm not sure what I would do in that situation."

"I didn't know what to do either. Harry had never mentioned it before then, and let's just say, I sleep naked."

"No," I reply, my eyes growing wide.

"Mmhmm. So, I was stranded in bed until after she left, just sitting there, shitting myself."

"Oh my God." I burst out laughing, imagining Mohammad stranded in bed in one of the many plush bedrooms in Harry's house.

"I was freaked. I thought word would get back to his parents and that they would call my mum. I was terrified."

"Did they?" I ask.

Mohammad shakes his head.

"I think Harry's parents are more concerned about keeping that stuff to themselves. It's all about discretion, so there's always someone there to clean it up. Whatever happens behind closed doors is fine as long as it stays that way."

"Do you think they would rather Harry party at home than go out?"

Mohammad nods. "I mean, someone restocks the liquor cabinet."

"You're kidding ..." I search Mohammad's face, hoping to find a hint of amusement or sarcasm. But I don't find either.

Mohammad shakes his head.

"Anyway, I came downstairs that morning to find Harry

in his boxers in the kitchen. He asked me what I wanted the cook to make me for breakfast, who was right there, at the stove. It was the strangest thing."

"Sounds like it," I agree.

"But Noah and I got used to Harry's lifestyle pretty fast. We grew up together, but as we grew, I guess there were always things that surprised me. Like the constant maids. Or Harry's ability to just dismiss them without his parents' input. The restocking of the liquor cabinet. His parents' constant absence after his mum went to work." Mohammad shrugs, scanning the room. "Well, I think we're finished."

"I think we are," I agree. I open up the door, knowing that I need to get dressed and get going with Noah, but Mohammad stops me.

"You said something *did* shift last night," Mohammad says, his eyes on me.

I freeze, feeling like I've been caught. And I know that I need to talk to someone about this. About the way I acted. How I threw myself at Harry. What Noah said.

"Is that what led to the whole tipsy thing?" he asks, looking concerned.

"Tipsy?" Harry says, coming into the room, catching me off guard.

My eyes flash at Mohammad as Harry places a kiss on my cheek. Mohammad must understand that I can't talk about this yet—or right now—because he drops my arm.

"You were relentless last night," Harry says.

"Oh God." I close my eyes, feeling embarrassed.

"Well, that's my cue," Mohammad cuts in, scrunching up his nose like he's grossed out. "I'm going to go shower."

He picks up the trash bag, taking it with him.

The second he's out the door, Harry continues, "Mallory, you literally had my pants around my ankles and dropped down onto your knees in the loo," he says, his blue eyes holding mine.

"Oh …" I stutter, not sure what to say. Because I don't know what Harry is thinking.

And suddenly, I feel embarrassed and hungover and slightly dizzy.

"It was fucking hot. Until I realized you were a few too many drinks in."

"I vaguely remember."

Harry grabs on to my hand, moving me back to the couches that I just fluffed up. He pulls me down onto his lap.

"Well, do you remember stripping naked in front of me?" He peers up at me, his eyes sparkling.

I gasp, blinking hard. I bite my lip, scolding myself.

Because how could I have done that?

I remember being with Harry in bed. I found my clothes all over the floor this morning, but I definitely don't remember stripping naked in front of him last night.

Harry nods, tightening his hands around my waist. "I turned to get you a shirt for bed, and a second later, your knickers were off."

"Harry," I mumble.

But he continues, "I eventually got you into one of my shirts—by the end of the night at least."

I open up one of my eyes, peeking down at him. He's grinning up at me.

"I know. I mean, I woke up in your shirt. And I do remember *most* of last night …" I say, thinking about my legs draped over his shoulders.

"You were a demoness or something. I swear, I've never seen you so determined."

"I threw myself at you."

"A bit." Harry chuckles.

I bring my hands up to his cheeks, cupping them. "I'm so sorry."

I search his face, hoping that he can see my embarrassment. And that I am sorry. I shouldn't have gotten so drunk. I shouldn't have thrown myself at him. And I shouldn't have tried so hard to make him give in to me. It was like I was possessed or something.

I wanted to sleep with him. I wanted to so badly.

"Don't be. I enjoyed last night," Harry says, bringing his hands up onto mine.

"Yeah?"

"Mmhmm. It was fun seeing you so ... *ready*." He grins again.

"It's embarrassing ..."

"Did you at least have a little fun?"

Harry's face shifts from amused to concerned, and I wonder if he thinks I'm more embarrassed about last night than anything else.

"Of course I did. I'm just embarrassed about the way I acted. Hearing you say out loud exactly what I did ... it's nerve-racking. I'm not usually like that, and ... I don't know ... I don't feel good about pushing you. And I don't feel good about having been drunk."

"Mallory ..." Harry stutters.

"I remember a lot of things. Being on the balcony. Being in the kitchen. A few things are blurry, like the underwear. The bathroom ... but I remember how I felt. And you always, without a doubt, make me feel amazing."

"Someone's smitten," Harry says fondly, trying to conceal another smile.

"Someone is," I agree, smiling back at him.

I drop my lips down onto his, kissing him. He kisses me for a minute before breaking our lips apart.

"I meant what I said about sex though. When it happens, I know you want it to be special. You deserve more than a quick shag in the loo and a hungover memory of it."

"But yours wasn't romantic," I state.

"Yours can be though. And it should be. I've been thinking about that a lot lately."

"Really?"

"Surprisingly." Harry chuckles.

I laugh at his honesty.

"And what have you thought about?" I ask.

Harry brings his eyes up to mine. "Things feel natural between us. And if—*when*—that happens, I want you to feel good. I want to make you feel comfortable."

"You always make me feel that way."

"Well, I should hope so." Harry's whole face lights up. "If not, I'd be a shit boyfriend, now wouldn't I?"

"You could never be."

Harry moves his hands to my waist, his fingers pressing into my ribs. His gaze slips from my hair to my cheeks before moving to my lips and then down to my chest.

"I like this."

"You like what?" I smile.

"I like you in my shirt. I like waking up next to you. I like having you here with me."

Butterflies form in my stomach, and I press my lips back against his, letting his tongue slide into my mouth. His breath is warm, and it makes me feel like I'm being held in a hug.

A warm, delicious hug.

And everything feels better.

My headache goes away. My insecurities about last night disappear. Everything falls away when Harry kisses me.

"Mallory." I hear my name come from the doorway and instantly feel my stomach drop.

"Yeah?" I say, breaking my lips off Harry's, turning to find Noah.

"We—*well, I*—need to head home." His voice almost cracks, but his expression remains fixed and cold.

"Okay." I nod, pulling myself up and off of Harry. "I'll go change."

I rush past Noah, practically running to Harry's room and throwing on my clothes.

Noah looked pissed. And I really don't feel like keeping him waiting.

By the time I get to the front door, Naomi and Olivia are there, and Naomi hugs me and says good-bye.

"I'll see you at the match," Harry says, pulling me into his arms.

"Okay," I reply, flushed. Because Noah is staring at me blankly and is not so patiently waiting.

I step out the door, following Noah, but then turn back to Harry.

"Wait, where's Mohammad? He'll be there too, right?"

"He'll be there," Harry says with a nod.

A second later, Noah and I get into a cab, and we're headed back to the Williams' house.

I open my mouth to say something but immediately close it.

I don't know what to say.

I feel like I'm in trouble. But I'm also hurt.

And at the same time, I'm upset with him.

I feel like I could both scream and cry, so instead, I keep quiet.

I stare out the window, watching it start to sprinkle. It's a cloudy, gray day. I recognize the route we drive, taking comfort in the familiarity.

"Will you play in the rain?" I ask, finally deciding to break the silence.

"We will," Noah confirms, not adding anything else.

I glance over at him, but he keeps his head straight forward.

He doesn't crack and glance over to me.

He doesn't twitch or smile or even look like he's fighting to.

I shift my eyes back to the window, wishing I had something better to say.

Wishing I could come up with anything.

But I can't.

Even when we get to the house, both Noah and I take off our wet shoes in silence.

Noah is lying.
11:30AM

"THERE YOU TWO are," Helen says, suddenly standing in front of us.

I take a step back, her close proximity and voice level taking a minute for me to adjust to.

"Hey, Mum," Noah says, kissing Helen on the cheek.

"Hi." I smile at her, dropping my bag.

"I thought you were going to be back well before now," she says, glancing to the clock. "You'll still need food then before your match?"

Helen looks like she's about to short circuit, glancing between Noah and me and the clock at a constant interval.

"Don't worry about it. Mohammad made a huge breakfast for us this morning. Even invited the girls round," Noah says nonchalantly.

"Oh?" Helen asks, tilting her head.

I bite my lip, trying not to freak out.

Because I feel like she's going to put two and two together, and then *she's* going to freak out and lose it on us.

Well, me specifically. Because I'm the one who lied about where I was sleeping.

"I didn't know Mohammad could cook," Helen comments, ushering us into the house.

"He actually made a great breakfast," I admit, thinking about the eggs, potatoes, and toast.

Even though he didn't actually make the toast I ate, he did scramble the eggs. And everyone seemed to enjoy them.

"He only cooked because Olivia flirted with him yesterday at school, and he's trying to get with her. He messaged her this morning, inviting the girls to Harry's," Noah explains.

My eyes move to Noah as my mouth falls ajar.

Because Noah is lying.

Like, *lying!*

And he's sort of good at it.

He lets out a huff about Mohammad as he sits down on the couch.

Helen's back is to me, and I'm thankful that she's looking at Noah and not me because it takes a good few seconds for me to get my bearings. I close my mouth, shake my head, and walk into the living room. I take a seat on the sofa that's opposite Noah.

"Oh, Mohammad," Helen replies.

"It's a useless effort. Olivia was just trying to make Harry jealous by talking to him," Noah informs.

Helen glances to me, looking almost appalled.

I just shrug at her. "Noah's right. It was a pretty weird morning."

"Well, that's enough about that. Your father ran out to

grab those bagels from the shop, and he should be back anytime now. I'm going to start preparing the food for tonight." Helen turns to me, looking almost proud.

"The fondue?" I ask, remembering Noah's suggestion that we celebrate.

I look over to him, trying to find some common ground, but he won't even look at me.

Helen nods.

"Mum, I think you should stay here and get the food ready for tonight," Noah says, grabbing both my and Helen's attention. "Harry and Mohammad are coming to the match, and I'm sure we would all love something warm when we get back."

"Are you sure?" Helen asks. She sounds conflicted as she sits down on the couch next to him.

"Yeah. I would rather have a warm meal after playing in the rain than you at my match."

"All right, sweetie," she says, apparently agreeing. "Well, that gives us a bit more time then."

Helen visibly relaxes into the couch.

I'm not sure if what Noah said is true or if he just wanted to give his mom an out from watching his match in the rain, but either way, she seems to appreciate it.

"The same for you, Mallory. You don't have to come watch me in the rain," Noah says, finally connecting his eyes with mine.

"I don't mind," I reply, giving him a flat, straight smile. I want to cross my arms over my chest and glare at him for being so rude, but I don't.

And it doesn't matter anyway because I'm not going for him.

I'm going because Harry and Mohammad will be there.

And because I want to get out of the house.

It would be fun to have a day where Helen and I just hung out but not today. I'm too tired to be any good at lying, and I think if I lay around in bed all day, she would know something was up. This will force me to get out of the house.

"Well, that's supportive of you, Mallory." Helen beams.

I grin at her and shrug my shoulders. "I don't mind. Besides, it sounds like it's going to be an intense match. Plus, with the rain, maybe I'll see some players fall into the mud or something exciting like that."

"It's going to be cold, so make sure to bundle up. Why don't I go find you a raincoat? Did you bring a thick enough jumper? Oh, never mind. I'll go pull out a few things for you," Helen fusses.

She waves her hand at me, getting up off the couch.

"Mum, Mallory already has a raincoat," Noah interjects, sounding annoyed.

"Of course she does," Helen says, shaking her head. "I'll grab you a jumper anyway, just in case."

"Thanks." I smile at her.

Even though I have a million sweaters, I appreciate the sentiment. And it's kind of nice, having Helen fuss over me. She's the sort of mom that you complain about having but secretly love.

Helen shuffles upstairs, leaving Noah and me alone in the living room.

"You don't have to come to my match," Noah breathes out. His face is still hard, and he keeps his eyes on the floor.

"Oh, so we're talking now?" I ask, raising my eyebrow at him.

"I thought you said your hair didn't do well in the rain," Noah replies, not answering my question.

"I'm coming," I state, ignoring his rude comment.

"Whatever."

Noah rises from the couch slowly and dramatically, shaking his head in apparent disappointment at my decision.

But before he can be the one to walk off, I fly up off the couch. I grab my bag from the door and try not to stomp up the stairs. Because I'll be damned if he's going to be the one to walk away, all pissy.

I toss my bag onto the floor the second I get into my room, frustrated. But then my annoyance dissipates, and I fall onto my bed, exhausted.

Ugh.

I close my eyes, feeling so many emotions.

I can't help but feel dreamy about Harry. Or embarrassed about last night. I'm upset with Noah and grateful for Mohammad. The thought of seeing Harry at Noah's match gives me butterflies, and then the fact that Noah doesn't even want me at his match ... well, that just hurts.

I inhale a long breath, finally letting it out as my mind calms. I roll onto my side, pulling my comforter on top of me.

A KNOCK ON my door wakes me.

"Mallory?"

I blink a few times, realizing that I fell asleep. I look over to my door, watching as Helen walks into my room. Her dark, curly hair is pulled back at the nape of her neck, and she has a sweater in her hand. She sits down at the foot of my bed as I sit up.

"I brought you a jumper."

"Thanks," I say, wiping my hand across my eyes.

"You were tired." Helen smiles, patting my leg.

"I was." I nod, trying to wake myself up. "I love sleepovers, but they're kind of exhausting."

"They are," Helen agrees. "It's good you got in a nap."

"Wait ... Noah's match," I say, trying to throw the comforter off of me. Because even though part of me is annoyed with him, I wouldn't want to miss such an important game.

"Relax. That's why I came and got you. Gene got back a bit ago with bagels. Noah's getting ready to leave."

"Thanks," I sigh, letting my body lean back against the headboard.

"Noah said you were asleep and that he didn't want to wake you. But I could tell you were excited about going," she says, her eyes on me.

"I actually really enjoy watching Noah play," I admit.

Helen smiles at me. "He is fun to watch. Noah's going to leave soon to be there for warm-ups. If you want, you can go with him now or leave a little later with Gene, closer to the match."

"I should probably go over with him now," I reply. Because I think it would be good if we had some time alone to talk.

Helen nods, rising from my bed. "Make sure to cheer a little extra for me."

"Don't worry; I definitely will." I smile at her, getting up too.

"And don't forget to wear your wellies. It's been raining off and on all day."

Her eyes shift up to the corners, and I can see that she's running through a mental checklist in her mind.

I smile, watching her.

She catches my gaze and replies, "I know Noah teases me about fussing over these things, but it's what mums do. We fuss."

"I like that you fuss. And I appreciate the jumper."

"Well, I know that Noah appreciates you being there to support him, as do I. These are the events that you don't have to participate in, but you do. And it means a lot to our family that you're there."

I nod to Helen, understanding her completely. "I wouldn't have it any other way. I'm really grateful to be here with your family."

Helen smiles at me before walking out of my room. After she does, I quickly change, making sure to grab a hat and put on an extra layer of socks. There's nothing worse than being wet and cold, and I would rather be bundled up than look adorable. I decide to not do my makeup or mess with my hair because, well, I'm going to be outside and in the rain.

And because I know that if I don't hurry downstairs, Noah will leave without me.

I take the steps two at a time, grateful to find Noah still in the kitchen, finishing off a bagel. I glance around, looking for Gene.

"Where's your dad?" I ask.

Noah shrugs, keeping his gaze down on his food.

All right then.

Noah has on workout pants and a thick sweatshirt, and I easily spot his bag lying beside the kitchen table.

"Are you ready?" I ask. Because Noah's silence is deafening, and I feel like the second I sit down, he's just going to get up.

"So, you're coming then?" Noah asks, finally looking at me.

"Yes, I'm coming," I reply, narrowing my eyes at him.

I watch as he sucks in his cheeks, his leg bouncing. His antsy-ness makes me uncomfortable, and I shift back and forth on my feet, not sure what to do.

Noah lets out a loud, audible sigh. His chest pushes out once before concaving in, and he nods at me. He purses his lips, looking between me and the table. I look with him, trying to figure out what he's thinking.

Maybe he's considering throwing the bagels at me?

It's what I would do anyway.

But what I don't really understand is why he's being so dramatic.

If anyone should be upset, it should be me.

I roll my eyes, deciding to break this weird Noah versus me versus the bagels standoff, so I reach out to grab one.

"No," Noah says, his hand stopping mine.

I flick my eyes up to his, wondering if he's really about to tell me that I can't have a bagel.

He keeps his hand atop mine for a brief moment but then drops it.

"I set yours aside," he says, grabbing a bagel and holding it out in front of me.

And it's my favorite.

Strawberry and honey.

I look from the bagel in Noah's hand up to his eyes. They're already brighter, and his cheeks have a hint of color back to them. His hair is brushed. And it seems like his hangover from this morning has all but disappeared.

"Thanks," I finally say, wondering if I should take the bagel from him.

I decide not to.

I'll let him give it to me.

When *he's* ready.

Because if I know anything about Noah, it's that he scares easily, and I wouldn't want to rush toward him—or *my* bagel—like the bulldozer I am and freak him out.

Because *everything* is about Noah.

I try not to grumble to myself.

"Can you walk and eat?" Noah asks, glancing at the clock.

"Yep," I reply.

I grab the bagel straight out of his hand, throwing caution

to the wind. I move to the front door and push my hair over my shoulders. I grab my raincoat off the hook, put it on, and then slip into my waterproof boots.

When I get my coat zipped up, I feel like a puffy marshmallow.

Or like Paddington Bear.

My raincoat isn't as bright as his, but we both have the *boots and raincoat* thing going for us.

Noah shifts at my side, pulling up the hood of his sweatshirt before putting on his own jacket and sliding his feet into his wellies. I assume his cleats are likely in the bag resting on his shoulder.

I grab my hat, deciding that I would rather add another layer than have cold ears.

I pull it on, but a second later, Noah's hands are on it.

"What?" I ask, looking up to him.

"The logo isn't centered," he replies, adjusting it into place.

I scrunch up my face, irritated that he's treating me like a baby.

"I can do it," I say, fixing my hat. I bring my hands up to it, making sure it's in place.

"Well, apparently not because it was crooked," Noah mutters.

I pull up my hood and open the front door. I want to scream into the fresh air, but I don't. The rain is trickling down in a steady dribble, and it's surprisingly soothing.

The second I hear Noah close the front door, I start walking.

Noah walks alongside me, and I can feel his eyes burning into my skin. I continue walking, willing myself to look straight ahead and not over at him. Which is surprisingly difficult because I can feel him glaring at me, and every few seconds, I hear a huff come out of his annoying mouth.

"What?" I practically yell, stopping on the sidewalk.

The rain has faltered off, but it's still cold, gray, and gloomy. And the weather, mixed with Noah's attitude, makes me feel nothing but angry.

"Come on," Noah says a few steps in front of me. He stops walking but won't look up at me.

He keeps his eyes glued to the sidewalk. His face is set, but I watch his jaw twitch.

"No."

"Fine," Noah says, starting to walk away from me.

I watch his body move, and I instantly let out a heavy sigh. Because maybe Noah just needs time. Maybe he's not upset. Maybe he's hurt.

And maybe I'm being childish.

I catch up to Noah, feeling guilty for my outburst.

"You know what I find interesting?" Noah says, still walking.

He quickens his pace, and I do my best to speed up and stay with him.

"What?" I ask.

Part of me wanted to stay silent.

To make him suffer.

But another part of me thinks that maybe if we talk like normal again, things will go back to being normal between us. To the way they were before last night happened.

"The fact that you needed liquor to go through with things last night." Noah snorts.

My eyes go wide at his statement, and I feel like the wind has been knocked out of me.

I stop walking, trying to catch my breath.

Because how could Noah say that?

But a second later, all I feel is anger, my blood boiling in every part of me. Noah hasn't stopped walking, but he's turned, looking over his shoulder at me. I see a flash of concern on his face, but then it hardens again.

"You're an ass," I seethe, pushing past him.

"Tell me, why am I an ass? It's true, isn't it?" Noah says at my side, apparently ready to talk.

"We didn't fuck," I practically yell. "In case you cared to know what actually happened."

I glare at him, wishing I could actually hurt him with my eyes.

"Wow, such a beautiful idea put so eloquently," he fires back.

"We need to talk about last night, Noah." I grab on to his arm, forcing him to stop.

"I was drunk. Don't read too much into it."

I search his face, trying to figure out if he actually believes that.

"Don't read too much into it?" I repeat.

I feel like this isn't even my body.

This isn't my life.

I don't even recognize how Noah and I got to this place. How I could be standing here, having this conversation with him.

I shake my head.

"Noah, last night, you told me you wanted me. You might as well have told me you … loved me."

I feel all the anger leave my body as the memories from last night come flooding back.

The way that Noah's hand felt on my skin.

How upset he looked in bed.

How heavy his body was leaning into mine for support.

Noah sucks in his cheeks, his eyes practically glowing. "And you reacted by getting pissed and trying to shag my mate."

My stomach feels like it's falling through me at his words, and I try to breathe through the sensation.

I can't keep reacting to what he says.

I need to stay focused.

"Why did you ask me not to sleep with him?"

"It doesn't matter," Noah says, shaking his head.

He closes his eyes before turning away from me. He starts walking, and I can see his head still shaking back and forth.

And it really, really upsets me.

"Noah Williams!" I shout.

A couple across the street stop walking, looking over at me, but I don't care. I need to get his attention. Because I feel like all we keep doing is walking and stopping, pushing out a few harsh words and then remaining rudely silent.

And it needs to end.

Noah's head snaps around at my voice, and I know that I finally have his attention.

I stride toward him until he's forced to look at me.

Hear me.

"You always want to talk when *you* want to talk. Well, guess what. *I* want to talk. And you're avoiding it. You're avoiding me and this conversation. And you can't. I won't let you. So, start talking."

I stare at Noah, hoping that my firmness will make his crack.

Noah pushes his shoulders back, standing almost rigid in front of me.

"What do you want to know?" he says, his eyes flaring.

"I want to know why you said those things to me."

"I was drunk," he replies.

"That isn't an answer."

Noah shakes his head again, his mouth falling open like

it's being weighed down.

His jaw twitches.

"I … I was having a moment of weakness that should be disregarded. My decision about things hasn't changed."

"Your decision?" I gape at him. "You would have been fine if I had kissed you last night. I could have ended things with Harry, and you would have let me. A moment of weakness?"

"You and I both know you wouldn't do that."

"Right. I wouldn't do that because I care about Harry. And because even though you don't want me with anyone else, you don't want me either. And that isn't fair, Noah. You can't ask that of someone."

"We can't have this conversation," Noah says, turning his gaze away from mine.

"*Exactly*, Noah. Regardless of the fact that you and I haven't done anything, you've said things to me, held me in ways you shouldn't have. And I've allowed it. All of it. And it's wrong of us. We can't do that to Harry."

"Then, why are you forcing me to talk?" he says, taking a step closer to me.

"Because … you owe me an explanation," I say, my stomach swaying.

Despite being upset with Noah, I have to know what he's thinking. What he's feeling. *Where do we go from here? What does this—all of this—mean?*

"An explanation?"

"For your actions. Your words. You keep saying that you were drunk and that you couldn't stand seeing us together. Me and Harry. But I don't understand why you push me toward him. Why you say you don't care about me in that way when you do. Why do you keep lying to me? Just be honest."

"Be honest?" Noah repeats, pursing his lips. His eyes darken, and he crosses his arms like he won't budge, but I know that he's going to answer me.

Because despite his hard expression, I can see right through him.

"Fine, I'll be honest," he continues, his eyes stilling. "Honestly, the thought of you and Harry in bed together had me going fucking mental, and I snapped."

"Because you don't want me with him."

"Because it's different. You and Harry together aren't the worst couple. I've seen better. But he cares about you. And I know you care about him. Fine, be together. Date. Kiss. But sex … it's not something to be taken so lightly. And the fact that you just threw yourself at him with little regard …" he says.

"You don't have the right to judge my decisions, Noah."

And how does he even know that I threw myself at Harry?

Is that what Harry said I did?

Would Harry have talked to Noah about me like that?

"You asked me for an explanation," Noah states clearly. "Well, here it is. You shouldn't just *sleep* with Harry."

"Why not?" I growl.

"Because," Noah says, his eyes looking like they might burst into flames. But then his hardened face cracks, and his eyes slip down to my lips.

"Because you want me to sleep with *you*," I almost gasp.

"Stop," Noah says, shrugging me off.

"Because you want my first time—this huge, important event—to be with *you*."

"You sound ridiculous."

"And you don't have a different answer," I argue.

"Yesterday morning, you were in bed in tears. You were scared about getting your heart broken. Well, it's going to break. And I don't think adding in sex will do you any good; it will only cause you more hurt. So, there's your answer. I don't want to see you—or Harry—more hurt than you're already going to be when you leave."

Noah glares at me and then walks ahead.

I stay frozen in my spot, feeling like some piece of me just cracked.

Does he really believe that?

Does he think I'm going to hurt Harry?

And that I'm going to leave here, brokenhearted, just like Anna said I would?

I glance up, watching Noah walk up the sidewalk. I follow behind him, feeling like a puppy who was just scolded yet is still following their owner. Not that Noah's my owner. Or that he physically hurt me.

But his words hurt.

And they hurt because they're true.

Everything in his statement was true. And he knew that it was the one thing I was scared about.

Getting attached. Getting hurt. Getting my heart broken.

When we get to the field, the rain starts up again, and part of me just wants to run away. To run off this field and never come back. This is how I could leave Noah. I could book a flight and go home. I could have my stuff sent to me. I would tell my parents that I couldn't handle being away from them.

I could lie.

I wouldn't have to say good-bye to anyone.

Helen.

Gene.

Mohammad.

Harry.

I could just leave.

I know I would hurt them. But at least they could be mad at me. They could be angry that I just left. They could put all their energy into hating me and moving on from me. In a few weeks or months, the guys would talk about me at lunch— that girl from New York who just walked out on them.

Who needs her anyway?

Not them.

The thought is comforting. Because at least if they hated me, they wouldn't be hurt. They wouldn't feel brokenhearted. Maybe it would be for the best. I can deal with my own pain. I can handle the weight of knowing what I did was to hurt them just a little less.

I think I could live with that.

I look out onto the field, watching as Noah throws his rain jacket and duffel onto the ground by the sidelines. He stomps onto the field, letting the water splash onto his legs as he strides toward his team. I watch the water darken his hair, his face looking fixed and determined as he listens to his coach speak. My eyes scan to the spot where Olivia and I sat, handing out water my first week here.

It wasn't rainy then, and I remember seeing Harry come to the field. I was so nervous to see him standing on the sidelines. I remember watching with amazement as Noah played, trying to stay focused on something other than my feelings.

Everything about this place holds memories, nostalgia.

Which barely makes sense because I've only been here a few times. I've watched Noah practice here twice and play here once. But it already holds so many memories.

I grab at my stomach, feeling like all the air is gone from within me again.

Maybe I *should* just leave.

Just walk away.

I scan the field, watching as the team starts practicing. There are only a few people on the sidelines. And all I can hear is a whistle, the rain trickling down, and feet pressing into wet, muddy grass.

Tears form in my eyes. But then I catch Noah's gaze. He's out on the field, in his position, but he's looking at me. His plump lips are pulled into a straight line, but his brows are dipped in.

I expect to see anger in his eyes.

For his face to harden the second he sees me looking back at him.

But he doesn't.

His eyes are filled with … pain.

He looks as upset as I feel.

A tear slips down my cheek when Noah looks away from me, turning his attention to another player.

I wipe the tear away, forcing it off of my face. I need to pull it together.

Noah said everything that there was to say. He told me how he felt. He was honest.

I'd thought that would make me feel better.

I'd thought that his honesty would bring me clarity.

But all I feel now is more confused. I was a fool to think that talking through things, opening up that box, would do me—us—any good. Because the truth is, all it did was inflict more pain.

More people start to show up, and I search the thin crowd, hoping to find a familiar face. Every part of me aches to see Harry's eyes. To find Gene. To have someone to tell me it's going to be okay.

More tears well up in my eyes when I finally spot him.

Mohammad.

He has on a windbreaker, his hood pulled up, but I easily

register his face. When his eyes find me, he smiles.

He smiles at me. That bright, pearly, megawatt-status smile.

And with that one smile every wall I was about to build up, every cell in my body that was ready to run away, stops. Everything stops.

I rush toward him, running into his arms.

"Whoa," Mohammad says, steadying us.

His arms slip around me, and he hugs me back. He starts to pull away, but I don't let him.

"Just hold me." I feel like I might start crying again, but I beg myself not to.

"Okay," he replies softly.

My arms tighten around his neck, and Mohammad's hands stay firmly on my back. He doesn't try to move again.

I look over his shoulder, out onto the field. Noah's watching us. He looks confused, but I close my eyes. I rest my head by Mohammad's, doing everything I can to calm myself down.

"What's going on?" Mohammad asks, pulling back to look at me.

His forehead creases when his eyes land on mine, his pearly smile gone.

"Things with Noah aren't good," I admit, my lips pulling to the side. I'm not sure what to tell Mohammad. Mostly because I don't know how I'm feeling or what to say.

Mohammad tilts his head. "Did you have a fight?"

I nod. "It was terrible, Mohammad. He told me that I was going to leave here with a broken heart."

Mohammad's eyes soften. "Come on," he says, rubbing his hands up and down my arms. "Don't let him get to you. He's always been a real tosser when he's hungover."

"You're probably right." I chew on my lip, wanting to

believe his answer.

Noah's just grumpy.

Angry.

He'll blow off some steam on the field and apologize.

My hands start to shake at my sides. Mohammad looks down, noticing.

"Miss America," he says, pulling me back into a hug, "I promise, it will be all right. I always know what I'm talking about, don't I?"

I let out a small laugh against his chest.

"You do," I agree.

"See. You don't have anything to worry about then. Mohammad will always be here to help."

"And always in third person." I chuckle, actually feeling better.

"What's really going on?"

"I wish I could talk about it, but I can't yet. I don't know what to say, and even if I did, I'm not sure it would do any good."

"Then, don't talk about it," he says, glancing between me and the field.

"What?" I look up at him, surprised.

He waves his hand at me. "Not everything has to be talked about and worked through. Sometimes, you just need to get a hug and move on. Let it go. You know?"

I blink a few times, wondering if he's right.

Can I just let this go?

We had a fight. It was just a fight. It isn't the end of the world, even if it feels like it.

"I think you're right," I finally agree.

Mohammad smiles at me. "Of course I'm right."

I shake my head, smiling back.

"Where's Harry?" I ask, wondering where he is.

"I don't know. I came from my house."

"How was everything once Noah and I left? I didn't get to say good-bye to you," I say, thinking about how Naomi and Olivia left the same time that Noah and I did.

"It was calm. We just ate and watched television."

"Sounds relaxing." I smile. "I napped."

"Probably for the best. You were a zombie this morning."

I roll my eyes, shoving Mohammad. "I still can't believe I saw you shirtless this morning. *And* with Olivia. I swear, I had an out-of-body experience because of it."

Mohammad beams. "Please. You've been lucky, Miss America. Most of the girls at school would *kill* to see me shirtless. Plus, you stole a kiss. That makes you even more of a threat."

"Because the girls at school all want you," I say, following along.

"Obviously." Mohammad nods.

"Well, let's hope they don't *actually* see me as a threat. It's not like I need any more girls at Kensington to hate me," I reply, my eyes flaring.

"They don't *hate* you," he corrects. "They're just madly jealous. But that's the price you pay when you're friends with us."

I glance over at Mohammad, taking in his serious expression. He looks over to me, convinced that he's right.

"Is it?" I laugh.

"Well, *friends* might be too narrow a term for you."

"What do you mean?"

"I mean, *friend* doesn't even begin to cover the walking chaos that you are. That's what makes you intriguing—and maybe threatening. You're best friends with me—clearly," he says, pointing to himself. "And I only have cracking friends. You also happen to be Harry's girlfriend, which, up until you got here, was a spot strictly reserved for Olivia. You're also close to Noah, who, despite being an ass this morning, is usually likable."

"You make it sound like I hit the trifecta," I say, shaking my head.

Because Mohammad's description of himself, Harry, and Noah, it all has to do with their outer appearance. What the school thinks of them, what they're known for. It's all about what other people think.

But I don't see them like that.

I just see … *them*.

Playing video games, studying together, supporting one another, having embarrassing conversations, watching pizza grease drip down Mohammad's chin …

"You did," Mohammad confirms. "Though, I have to say, we got lucky too. And I'm sort of impressed with myself. From day one, I knew that you had my boys all tangled up."

"Well, you don't have to worry about that now," I huff, looking out to the field. To Noah. "There's nothing tangled between us anymore. Any friendship that we had is probably over. So, that means, no tangles. No confusion. It means, we're … nothing."

"Could you be any more dramatic? You'll make up with Noah. You always do."

I tilt my head, weighing his opinion against mine when Gene walks up to us.

"Terrible weather," he mutters. He has on a navy rain jacket and is holding up an open umbrella.

"It is," I agree, letting my mind focus on the chill in the air. "But at least it's just sprinkling."

"Better than a downpour," Gene agrees, pushing his glasses up.

"I see everyone's arrived."

I turn instantly, recognizing Harry's voice. He's walking toward us, and within an instant, he is pulling Gene and Mohammad into hugs.

"Hey," he says, leaning in to kiss me on the cheek.

"Hey," I reply, feeling a mixture of emotions.

I feel relief at seeing him. But I also feel a massive amount of guilt for everything that was said between Noah and me. But at the same time, a flash of annoyance shoots through me because of what Noah said earlier.

And because Harry was the only one who could have told him.

"All right?" he asks, catching my eye.

Harry has on dark jeans and a creamy brown sweater that sits under a deep chocolate brown raincoat. He looks almost too dressed up to be on the edge of a wet soccer field. I glance down at myself, taking in my bundled-up appearance, feeling a tinge self-conscious.

"Fine," I reply, trying to figure out what to do.

Gene looks at me, his brows dipping in. I glance over to Mohammad, hoping to find a friendly face, but he's looking between Harry and me with concern.

It's probably because I can already feel myself getting more frustrated as Harry stands next to me, and I think they can see it written all over my face.

"Actually, no," I correct, turning to face Harry. "Can we talk?"

My arms want to cross over my chest, but I don't let them.

"Sure," Harry replies, but it almost sounds more like a question than an answer.

I shift away from Mohammad and Gene, walking a few paces to give us a little distance and privacy.

"What's up?" Harry asks. His forehead is creased, and he

seems confused.

"Did you tell Noah about last night?" I come right out and ask the question.

"Tell him what?" Harry's eyes stay on me with the question.

I shake my head, frustrated, because he should already know what I'm asking.

"About *us*. About last night. About … me." I narrow my eyes at him, hoping he gets the point.

Harry sucks in a long, slow breath. But then a smile cracks on his face, his eyes brightening. "I told Noah that you were a bit … *determined* last night."

He's still smiling at me, and I can't help but groan.

"Harry …"

"What?" he says, taking a step closer. He places his hands on my arms, holding me firmly. "I was flattered."

"I'm mortified."

"It's just Noah," Harry says lightly. "He doesn't care."

"Did you tell him that I … threw myself at you?" I stutter over the words, feeling slightly sick at them.

"No, Mallory—" Harry says.

But I hold up my hand, stopping him.

Because I'm about done with these boys.

Both of them.

"What's wrong? You tell Mohammad everything. And now, suddenly, it's not all right if I talk to Noah?"

Harry looks upset, and I can't blame him.

"I tell Mohammad …" I start but then let out a growl. Because he's right, and I hate that he's right. "I tell Mohammad things, and he keeps it to himself."

"Really?" Harry cocks his head to the side, looking amused.

"Fine. Maybe he doesn't always keep things to himself.

But for the most part, he does. And even if he doesn't, he doesn't judge me, Harry."

"What are you upset about?"

"I'm upset that you told Noah something so private."

"Noah doesn't care," Harry says, his eyes flashing.

"He does care," I correct, trying to make Harry understand. "And I care."

"What?" Harry asks.

I close my mouth, silently scolding myself.

I should have just kept my mouth shut.

"I told you the other day that Noah cares about his virginity. And I got a not-so-subtle lecture today on being a respectable woman and not throwing myself—and my virginity—away in one drunken night." The words tumble out of my mouth in frustration.

I connect my gaze to Harry's, wondering what his reaction is going to be. Maybe he'll be mad. Or upset. What he should probably be is concerned with *why* Noah cares about my virginity so much.

I expect a million different reactions, but Harry just laughs.

Not a mocking laugh. A warm, full-belly laugh. He tosses his head back, his whole face brightening as he stands in front of me, laughing.

Laughing.

"That sounds like Noah," he finally says, his blue eyes coming back to mine. He pulls me against his chest, running his hand down across my back.

I instantly pull away from him. Because he can't be serious.

"Harry, I'm not joking."

"Guys," Mohammad says, interrupting us. He's looking at me with disbelief.

How long has he been standing there?

"What?"

"The match is starting," Mohammad says, looking out to the field.

I rip my eyes away from him, watching as the players get set up.

"Come on. Let's go back over to Gene," Harry comments, moving next to Mohammad.

"No." I cross my arms over my chest, standing firm.

But a second later, Mohammad is ushering me back over, Harry still chuckling to himself.

I look at Harry the same way that Mohammad was just looking at me—with actual disbelief. I open my mouth to fight with him, but then I close it.

Now is not the time or the place.

And part of me knows Harry is right. He didn't tell Noah, knowing that Noah would get upset and then get upset with me.

He was talking to Noah as a friend.

At least, he made it sound like he was.

I glance over at him, feeling a little guilty for being so rude. Because Harry was sweet to me. He's been nothing but sweet, and the first chance I get, I attack him.

"I'm sorry," I whisper as the match starts. I look at him briefly, too chicken to hold his gaze.

Harry's eyes flick over to mine, his lips pulling to the side.

"I'm sorry that what Noah said upset you," he replies, leaning closer to me until his arm bumps against mine.

"I was already embarrassed about last night," I whisper, knowing that I need to be quiet. Gene is at my other side, and I don't want him to overhear. "And then, when Noah said … anyway, I just thought you had told him, and I was freaking out already."

"I promise I didn't give him any juicy details," Harry says, turning to me. "But I had to talk to someone about last night, get some relief. You *were* a demoness," Harry whispers the last words in my ear before bringing his mouth to mine. He kisses me hesitantly. It's like he's not sure if I'm willing to accept his apology, his words.

I bring my hand up onto his cheek, kissing him back.

Because he's right. I can't fault him for talking to Noah. Noah's reaction was my fault, not Harry's.

I quickly bite his lip, bringing it between my teeth before pulling back. Harry smiles down at me as he pinches my chin.

He wraps his arm around my waist and looks out to the field.

I look out, too, watching as Highgate gets the ball. They send it flying down the field and rolling out of bounds.

One of Kensington's players goes out to throw it back in when Noah looks over at us.

I'm not sure why I expected him to look happy. Maybe because every time he sees Harry, he becomes a *happier, better* Noah. But when he looks at us, he doesn't smile. He barely moves his chin up, throwing Harry a nod.

I keep my lips in a straight line. I don't give him a wave or a smile.

I don't give him a single ounce of encouragement.

Noah grabs my gaze, holding it only for a second, but it's enough time to tell that he's moved beyond being sad or grumpy.

Now, he's angry.

And that is a look I know well.

Noah turns his attention back to the field, and a second later, he has the ball. I flinch as someone falls to the ground, tripping another player. The rain picks up, and I pull up my hood. Mohammad opens his umbrella. I glance over to Harry, watching as his blond hair darkens from the water.

The match is intense, and all of the players are wet and covered with mud and grass. It seems like everyone has fallen at least once, and the coaches are constantly screaming out directions.

The air surrounding the field feels heavy with electricity.

You would think it would be hot to see a bunch of guys wet and filled with testosterone, playing with this much intensity.

But this feels almost more serious.

Noah's eyes look like coals, and his body is moving so quickly that it seems impossible to keep our eyes on the ball.

Mohammad walks around Gene, giving me his umbrella to stand under. He hands it over like he can't be bothered with it anymore, his eyes glued to the field.

"Fuck, our boy is in fine shape today," Harry says, his eyes on Noah.

Noah easily moves past his opponent, dribbling the ball down to the goal.

"He's killing it," Mohammad agrees, looking like he's ready to shout out with applause.

A second later, Kensington scores.

I watch Noah, wishing that this wasn't about something more.

That this wasn't about us.

But he doesn't even look happy about the goal.

"He's angry," I state. Because they should know the truth.

Noah is dominating because he's pissed.

He's hurt.

And he's taking all that energy—that energy and emotion stored away for me—and he's showing it now.

"What?" Harry asks, looking over at me.

Mohammad looks over, too, even though I already told

him.

"I told you, we got into a fight."

Harry rolls his eyes. "You always fight. I swear, it's like you're siblings or some shit."

"That's because Noah's infuriating," I state, wishing that what Harry said were true.

Wishing that we fought like we were siblings.

Things would be easier if it were like that.

But they aren't.

The match continues. I listen to Gene cheer, throwing his hands out in front of him in excited fists. I smile, watching him, seeing how, every once in a while, he jumps with excitement.

And then there's Harry next to me, holding my hand now. Every so often, he glances over at me, smiling, when he's not cheering Noah on.

And then there's Noah, practically strutting across the field. He's taken ahold of everyone's attention, his hardened jaw never faltering.

But then the match is over, and they've won.

Mohammad and Gene are clapping, and everyone along the sidelines is cheering.

Even Highgate fans.

Because despite Kensington winning, it was an intense match for everyone. It was a close game.

"Bloody hell," Harry screams, extending out his hands as Noah runs over to us.

Noah's beaming, a wide smile set on his face. He's sweaty and dirty, but he looks relieved.

"What a match," Gene boasts, his face lit up.

"You destroyed it out there," Mohammad agrees, looking just as happy.

Their mood is contagious, and despite not wanting to

crack a smile, I do.

"Thanks," Noah replies, wrapping his arms around Harry in a hug.

When Noah pulls back, he glances down to me, and then his eyes quickly shift to Gene's.

"Great match." Gene smiles at him, his cheeks tinting pink.

"I cannot believe what you did out there. You decimated them. Dominated. You were a fucking champion," Harry goes on, getting louder with each word.

I scrunch up my nose, watching as he marks the occasion with his speech.

"The glory that Kensington is going to get," Mohammad agrees. "This definitely just upped our status."

"Your status?" I ask.

"Anyone who was here, watching Noah, was left practically panting along with him. I mean, every girl in school is going to want him after this. Which means every girl is going to want to be friends with me to get to him. It's brilliant," Mohammad boasts.

"Oh, boys, that's enough now," Gene interrupts, shaking his head.

"He is right, Mr. Williams. I think everyone is going to want Noah after today. I mean, I even find myself attracted to the man." Harry grins.

"Well, don't let me get in your way then," Gene banters, taking a step back.

Noah glances over to Gene, still grinning.

I expect them to hug, but instead, Noah gets a soft pat on the back from Gene. And the angry Noah that was on the field is completely gone.

Now, he's standing here, almost blushing at their compliments, a wide smile on his face.

I narrow my eyes at him, not convinced.

Because this Noah cannot be trusted.

He could turn at any second.

"I'd ask if you were going to stop in at the pub before coming back to the house, but I'm not sure you'd be let in, in your state," Gene comments.

I glance across Noah, taking in his wet and muddied body. He's standing between Gene and me, and I can smell the grass and sweat mixed into his skin.

"I think I need a shower first," Noah replies.

"I think so too," I decide to finally add.

Noah's eyes land on mine, and I instantly regret speaking. I feel like with one look, all of my insides do a flip. He holds my eyes, tilting his head. But a second later, he's looking back at his dad.

"It doesn't matter anyway. Mum's making fondue to-night, so we'll just head straight back."

Gene nods, apparently just now remembering about the fondue. "Right, well, I'm off. I'll see you two at home. And maybe you boys," Gene says, looking to Mohammad and Harry with a smile.

Harry nods, his eyes on Gene.

"See you," Noah calls out as his dad walks off, giving a small wave.

"You'll come over?" Noah asks, looking between Mohammad and Harry.

"For fondue?" Harry says, already nodding his head. "Absolutely."

"I can't," Mohammad replies. "My aunt wanted me back after your match to help get ready for my parents' return tomorrow."

Mohammad drops his eyes, looking down to his feet, like he's both sad and disappointed by the news himself.

"Get ready?" Harry asks, sounding confused.

"Yeah. She's ordered them a cake. Wants to put up streamers and make a sign. She's making us go greet them at Heathrow tomorrow." Mohammad rolls his eyes, but I think it might be for show.

"Awww. I'm sure your parents and sisters will love that," I encourage, thinking about how excited his family will be to see him.

He just shrugs, waving his hand in the air like he couldn't care less.

"I don't know about Mohammad greeting them at the airport, but his sisters will love the streamers," Noah says, a smirk on his face.

Harry lets out a loud laugh, looking with bright eyes between Noah and Mohammad.

Mohammad shakes his head but doesn't look upset, and he cracks a smile.

"Well, fuck, what are you doing later? I mean, we need to celebrate. Noah destroyed it out there," Harry says.

"Uh, no. I don't think I could manage another bender," Noah says, shaking his head.

His brows drop in, like the thought of drinking grosses him out. And honestly, I'm right there with him.

"We have to celebrate," Harry says.

"We *are* celebrating. Just with chocolate fondue instead of alcohol," Noah replies.

"I can't believe I'm missing fondue. Do you think your mum will save me some?" Mohammad asks, his shoulders falling.

"I'm sure she would," I answer, wanting Mohammad to feel included.

"Chocolate fondue? I am so down. What's the occasion?" Harry asks.

"Helen probably knew what the score of the match would be," Mohammad answers, looking frightened. "I'm telling you … women."

I let out a laugh, watching as Noah rolls his eyes.

"It's actually for Mallory."

My name on his lips draws my attention, and when I look up to him, his eyes are on me.

"Oh?" Harry asks.

I break my eyes from Noah, turning to Harry. "To celebrate my grade in Latin. The test I did good on," I clarify.

"Well, any excuse for chocolate." Harry grins at me, wrapping his arm around my shoulders.

Noah chuckles, glancing over to his duffel. "I'll grab my stuff, and then we should go. I think it's going to start pouring again."

Harry nods. I glance up to the sky, taking in the darkening clouds above us.

"Brilliant job, mate," Mohammad says, patting Noah on the shoulder before pulling me into a hug.

"I'll make sure to have a little extra chocolate tonight for you." I smile.

"It's a nice sentiment, but I think that might make it even worse."

He hugs me back, nods to Harry, and then is off. Noah runs across the field to grab his duffel.

I take Harry's hand into mine. "I'm glad you're coming for fondue."

"Of course you are. It's what you were begging me for last night, right? Me, you, and chocolate." He beams.

I shake my head, a smile forming on my lips.

"I think it might be a little different tonight. Add in clothes, Gene, Helen, Noah, and nothing sexual."

Harry waves his hand at me, his blue eyes connecting to

mine. "I'm just happy to spend time with you."

I raise my eyebrow at him, not convinced.

Harry lets out a light chuckle. "All right, fine. Maybe it's just an excuse to watch you lick chocolate off your finger. But a man can dream, can't he?"

"And we get to the real motive." I grin.

Noah walks back up to us, his duffel over his shoulder. "Ready?"

"Ready," I agree.

As we walk off the field, a few people nod and smile at Noah saying, "Great match."

I want to tell them to shut up. That they shouldn't be feeding his pride. But I keep my mouth shut.

Because he did do a great job.

And because he looks ... almost peaceful. And I'm not going to push my luck.

If Noah wants to be happy now, then fine, let him be happy.

The walk back to the house is in a sort of comfortable silence. The rain darkens the sidewalk, and a chill runs through me. Noah glances over at me, noticing, before looking away. I wrap my arm through Harry's, and he tucks me against his side.

"I can't wait to be out of this rain," I finally say, breaking the silence.

"I'm still fucking impressed," Harry comments. "After how much you drank last night, the fact that you could even make it out to the field was a feat."

Noah lets out a chuckle. "It was a good thing I missed the rest of the fun then. I felt like absolute shit this morning. But after having a rest and a bagel, I felt better."

Noah's shoulders shrug easily, annoying me.

Because he's acting so nonchalant. Like the fact that he

put me through emotional hell last night doesn't mean anything to him.

He was just a little drunk.

Went to bed early.

No biggie.

And to make it even worse, Harry is eating it up. His eyes are sparkling at Noah, a huge grin on his face. I let out a snort.

Because I am *not* going to take part in the Noah Williams Fan Club that's happening right now.

"All right?" Harry asks, glancing over at me.

"Fine," I mutter, deciding I just need to stay quiet.

We're almost to the house, and then we will have other people as buffers. I can focus on Harry while Gene and Helen praise Noah.

The thought makes my throat tighten.

Stay here forever.
4PM

WHEN WE GET back to the house, Harry's the first one inside. He's already pulling off his shoes as I stand in the doorway, Noah still behind me on the front porch.

"Look at the three of you," Helen says, eyeing us from the kitchen.

She rushes to our sides, helping me pull off my wet raincoat. It reminds me of the first time I met her, when she picked me up from the airport. I remember her shuffling toward me through the crowd with a sense of urgency and determination. I was a little freaked out when she finally made it to a flustered stop. But quickly, her nerves put my own at ease, and then we were off, driving back to their house.

And that's when I think I clicked with her. Listening to her talk about Gene, Noah, and Mia. Admiring her speeding skills.

"It's frightful out there." Harry nods, hanging up his jacket.

"I knew it would be," Helen replies, her face flashing with concern. Her eyes widen when she looks down across Noah's body, her gaze lingering on his muddied legs. "You cannot come into the house like that."

"Mum," Noah huffs, stepping into the house and closing the front door.

I shift on the rug, trying to make sure I stay on it while also making enough room for him.

"You will do no such thing. I just spent the morning cleaning," Helen replies, her hands coming down to rest on her hips.

And with that one motion, I know she won't give in.

Noah glances around, looking like he's confused about what to do. He lets out another long sigh as I start to pull off my shoes.

"You will strip off those clothes immediately."

"Here?" Noah asks.

"I'll go find you a towel," Harry offers. A second later, he's gone, walking toward the laundry room.

"I'll take off my shoes and be careful, I promise," Noah says, trying to convince his mom.

Helen raises one eyebrow at him, her hands still at her hips.

"Fine," Noah finally concedes.

He must realize that she isn't going to budge because he takes off his shoes and drops his bag onto the floor. Helen stands firmly between him and the house. It's like she's protecting it from Noah. And it's sort of satisfying.

"Well, I think I'm going to change into something dry," I cut in, breaking their staredown. I smile to Helen, hoping she'll let me pass.

I glance down at myself.

"I don't see any mud. Is it all right if I go change?" I decide to ask before making a move.

"That's fine, dear." Helen smiles back at me. "Just make sure to put your damp clothes in the laundry room."

"I will," I reply, slipping past her as Harry walks back to them with a towel in hand.

I give him a quick smile but then take the stairs two at a time. Because I'm definitely not going to be anywhere near Noah while he strips down into his underwear. I rush into my room, closing the door behind me with relief.

I want to fall down onto the bed and go to sleep, but I don't. Because Harry is here. Because my clothes are damp, and when I finally get into bed, I want it to be warm and dry. I roll my eyes to myself, getting out of my clothes. I pull on a fresh pair of jeans and a cozy sweatshirt. I sit down at my desk, bracing myself for my reflection.

I look at the mirror with horror. My hair is frizzy, and the whole front section is wet while the back is dry.

Wonderful.

I brush through it once, deciding the only option is to pull it into a bun. It feels good to run a comb through it and get it off my face. I add some ChapStick to my lips and a spritz of perfume, feeling better.

I hear the stairs creak, and I focus on the sound as the footsteps move down the hallway. I let out a breath, knowing that means that the coast is clear. Noah's stripped-down body is safely locked away in his room or the bathroom, and I can go back downstairs in peace.

I open up my bedroom door, peeking my head out to the

left, looking at Noah's shut door. The bathroom door is also closed, and I feel myself relax a little.

I quickly rush out of my room, keeping my eyes on his door.

But suddenly, I'm slamming straight into a body.

I groan at the impact, putting my hands out to steady myself. My fingers press into a bare stomach, and it's like all the blood drains from my body in a single moment.

"Shit." Noah's voice is all around me, and I let out another groan, this time from frustration.

I do everything I can to avoid his eyes. When I look down, I instantly regret it. Because all I can see are his naked chest and stomach. I move my eyes further down, trying to find something other than his creamy skin. But then I get a glimpse of his bare legs and boxers and feel my stomach flutter.

"Watch it," I say, realizing that I need to look up at him. I need to keep my eyes off his skin, and glaring at him is the best option at this point.

"You ran into me," Noah replies, insulted. He puts his hands on my shoulders, moving me to the side of the hallway.

Out of his way.

And he walks right past me.

I turn, watching him as my mouth falls open. His legs are covered in mud, but his back and shoulders are clean. A second later, he's slamming the bathroom door shut.

I shake my head, trying to get his shirtless, rude body out of my mind.

WHEN I'M BACK downstairs, I find Harry sitting on the couch. He's leaning back into the sofa, looking relaxed.

"I feel so much better," I say, curling up onto the couch with him. I try to keep my mind on my clean, dry clothes and the sweet boy sitting next to me.

"Don't get too comfortable," Helen says, popping her head out of the kitchen. "Dinner's almost ready."

"What are you making?" I ask.

I take a minute to absorb the scent wafting through the house. It's onion and garlic but mixed with something sweeter.

"I decided on a nice pumpkin soup to warm you up from the rain. Noah loves pumpkin, and Gene will eat just about anything if it's accompanied by fresh, buttered bread."

"Uh, that sounds amazing, Mrs. Williams," Harry says at my side, his eyes practically rolling back in his head at the thought.

Helen's cheeks tint pink. "I thought so too," she agrees before disappearing back into the kitchen.

"It's kind of funny that Gene will eat anything if it's accompanied by bread. It reminds me of Mohammad and his constant need to stick his chips into my soup." I smile.

"Mohammad can't help himself." Harry smiles back, his blue eyes capturing mine.

I feel myself get lost in them. My heart rate slows down, and I ease into the couch, lacing my fingers through his. I can't help it when my gaze slips down to his lips.

"You want to kiss me, don't you?" he says quietly, wrapping his arm around my shoulders.

I nod my head. Because there's always this conflict surrounding me.

And it's constant.

And exhausting.

But the second it's just Harry and me, I relax. I can take a breath. I can just be me.

I can be happy.

"Well, if the lady wants a kiss," Harry says, his hand

coming to my cheek.

He pulls my mouth toward his but doesn't press his lips into mine. He keeps me suspended, our noses dancing together. My cheeks flush with his face so close to mine.

He runs his thumb across my jaw, causing my heart to start pounding.

I lick my lips, wanting this kiss.

And Harry gives it to me. He drops his mouth onto mine. I sit up straighter, feeling my back arch. His lips are firm and warm. I practically fall into them.

Into the feeling.

He has his arm still wrapped around me, his other hand on my face. I bring my hand to his forearm, grasping on to him.

I want his lips to stay here forever.

"I love kissing you," Harry says against my mouth. Then, his lips move, sprinkling kisses all across my cheek. He turns my head, starting on the other cheek.

I let out a stream of giggles, feeling like a little flower getting showered with sunlight.

"I like kissing you too," I admit, feeling a flush on my cheeks.

"Dinner," Helen calls out. Her loud voice grabs my attention, and she must have wanted Noah and Gene to be able to hear her upstairs.

Harry and I get up off the couch and make our way into the kitchen.

"Wow. It smells great, Mum," Noah says, joining us. He has on shorts and a long-sleeved shirt, his hair wet from his shower. He places a kiss on Helen's cheek before sitting down.

"Oh," Helen says with surprise. "Thank you, dear."

"Can I help with anything?" I offer.

"No, no. Gene," Helen calls out again, moving the large

pot from the stove to the table.

Harry slides down into the chair next to mine as Noah grabs the bread out of the oven, sets it on a plate, and brings it to the table.

"For heaven's sake. Gene!" Helen moves out of the kitchen, looking up the staircase. "I swear, that man," she mutters, going upstairs.

"Where's your dad?" I ask Noah, a laugh escaping my lips. Noah just shrugs at me.

Harry looks from Noah to me, concerned. I know he's finally noticed Noah's shortness, and he wants an explanation, but all I can give him is a shrug of my own.

"I found him," Helen says, walking with Gene back into the kitchen. She has her hand wrapped around his forearm, like she won't let him out of her sight again.

"Sorry, guys. That was your gran," Gene says to Noah as he takes a seat at the table.

"Oh? How is she doing?" Harry asks.

I glance over at him with surprise, but he's looking to Gene with interest.

"She's doing well. I have a slight suspicion that she wants to come for a visit soon. Couldn't get her off the phone," Gene replies.

"Would you like that?" I ask as Helen pours us each a bowl full of soup.

"It can be a challenge, having family visit. The different routines. But I know she wants to see Mia and hear about her trip," Gene replies, bringing his first spoonful of soup to his lips.

I do the same, blowing on the warm liquid.

"Well, I suppose we'll have to have her out then," Helen says matter-of-factly. "Now, Noah, tell me about your match."

"It went good," Noah replies, biting into a piece of bread.

"It went brilliantly. Noah dominated," Harry interjects, slurping a spoonful of soup.

Gene lets out a small, concealed chuckle, watching him, and I can't help but smile.

"I knew you would do great." Helen beams.

"Thanks, Mum."

Noah and I don't talk at all through dinner. He laughs at Harry's jokes, maintains conversation with his dad, and always blushes at his mom's compliments.

But with me?

Nothing.

And honestly, it's crappy.

Because this whole night was his idea. Coming back after his match, having fondue.

As Harry and Gene clear the table and put the leftovers in the fridge, Helen brings a tray full of dipping options over. Apples, strawberries, biscuits, and marshmallows are stacked high.

I look at the tray, feeling slightly defeated.

The idea of having to sit here, being forced to celebrate with someone who won't even look in my direction makes the soup in my stomach churn.

"I'll be right back. Need to use the loo," Noah says, getting up from the table.

No one pays attention to his statement.

I look between Helen, the fondue pot on the counter, and Noah, who is leaving the kitchen.

And I can't deal with things being like this.

"I'll be right back," I say as Gene and Harry sit back down at the table.

I push out of my seat, making my way out of the kitchen.

"What was that about?" I can hear Helen's voice from the kitchen.

"They were in a fight or something earlier," Harry replies as I'm walking upstairs.

"Noah," I say, catching him just as he's walking into the bathroom. I follow him in, closing the door.

"What?"

"We're celebrating my grade tonight," I state, looking at him.

"Yeah?"

"So, we are celebrating. Not … fighting. This whole night, the fondue, it was your idea."

I look at him, feeling defeated. Something about the silence at dinner got to me. The way he diverted his eyes from mine.

He nods, his lips pulling to the side. "Okay."

"Okay?" I ask.

"We're fine," he confirms, his face softening. "I'm … sorry that I yelled at you."

"I'm sorry that I pushed you."

"I don't want to talk about last night anymore." Noah blinks a few times, like he's trying to clear something from his eyes.

"Neither do I," I agree.

"Okay."

"So, we're okay?" I ask awkwardly.

"We're always okay," Noah sighs. But then he nods his head toward the door.

"What?"

"Want to give me some privacy, or do you want to watch me use the loo?" he says, raising his eyebrows at me.

His lips hold out a smirk, and I let out a relaxed laugh.

"All right, all right," I reply, getting his point, "I'll leave."

"You can stay," he banters back. "I mean, it's not like you haven't seen most of me naked anyway."

"What …"

"Don't you remember? I thought you were going to murder me when you were banging on the bathroom door your first week here. And then you followed me into my room, and I stripped off my towel. You were so angry … until I did that."

"Noah!" I want to smack him for bringing that up. Because he was such a little crap to me.

But suddenly, he's ruffling my hair, rolling his eyes. "But then you just got … flushed."

My eyes form into saucers as I think about that day. How I do *clearly* remember seeing Noah's butt.

"I actually need to use the loo now," Noah says, ushering me out of the bathroom. He moves me into the hallway, closing the door between us.

I shake my head, deciding it's best not to ask questions. Because I think we've made up.

Or at least, we've agreed not to fight.

I walk back down to the kitchen, seeing that Helen's moved the fondue pot to the table. The whole kitchen smells like warm chocolate now.

"You get it sorted?" Harry asks as I sit back down.

I nod apologetically to all of them.

"You're not a *sweep it under the rug* kind of girl." Harry smiles.

"I'm not." I flush.

"I think that's something admirable about Americans. They like to address things right away," Helen admits.

"I prefer the rug," Gene says wittingly, smiling down at his empty plate.

"I'd like to think I prefer the rug too. Normally, I hate confrontation. But it's almost worse when you know you just need to get it out of the way."

"I think there's a distinction," Helen offers. "Sometimes, it's best not to latch on to every small thing. It can become overwhelming. But if there's an issue that must be addressed, it's better to get those things sorted."

Gene nods in agreement. Harry glances over at me, a smile on his lips.

"Well, your son likes to compare me to a bulldozer." I laugh as Noah sits back down at the table.

"A true compliment." Gene chuckles, shaking his head.

"My thoughts exactly." I grin.

"Noah's always had a way with words," Harry says, laughing now too.

I watch his eyes close as he laughs. I think he can completely see Noah saying that, but at the same time, he's almost in disbelief that Noah *actually* would.

"Oh, Noah," Helen scolds, looking across the table at him.

"It wasn't an insult," Noah defends, rolling his eyes. "It was an … observation."

"How thoughtful of you to observe," I tease.

"Well, I'm not sure about a bulldozer, but I like your personality," Harry interrupts, his mouth falling open slightly. "You know exactly what you want, and you always make it crystal clear." He gets a boyish grin on his face, his hand coming down onto my leg.

"Aww," Helen coos, causing Gene to actually break into a smile.

My cheeks tint pink because of the way Harry is looking at me. Because, well, he has a sparkle in his eye that goes beyond fondness.

He's teasing me about last night.

About how I apparently was extremely direct with what I wanted.

"A bulldozer charges forward without any regard. It's frightening, but it's powerful. That's what I meant … in case you were wondering," Noah mumbles.

"I'm not sure that makes it any better, mate." Harry chuckles, his eyes slipping to Noah. "But the real question is, what would you compare me to?"

"Oh, do tell, Noah," Helen encourages. "And dig in, everyone. Congratulations again, Mallory."

"Thank you." I smile at her.

Noah shakes his head, keeping his lips sealed.

"I'd like to think of myself as a dashing gentleman or a Roman god of some sort. I could be like Napoleon, leading the world ahead," Harry continues, grabbing a chocolate biscuit and dunking it straight into the fondue.

"Those are very bold comparisons," I offer, trying to decide between the apple and strawberry.

"They have to be. I have a big personality." Harry grins, his eyes lingering as I bring the strawberry I dipped in chocolate to my mouth.

"That you do," Gene agrees.

"See, I would say you're like a wise sage, Gene. Or a brilliant alchemist. You give great advice. You're cracking at finance and predictions. Always overly knowledgeable but also willing to share what you know," Harry says.

"Well, I'm not so sure I would agree that I am a sage. But I suppose, with age, we all do get wiser."

"See, you can't help but even reply wisely," Harry banters back.

"That's our Gene. Brilliant, isn't he?" Helen beams.

I glance over to Noah, wondering what his take is on all of this. But his eyes are down at the table. They're shifting, and I can tell he's thinking hard about something.

"Noah?" I ask, grabbing his attention.

He looks up at me before moving his eyes to Harry.

"I was just thinking about what Harry would be. I think if I had to compare him to anything, it would be to … light."

"All right, you'll have to explain that one," Gene replies, seeming confused.

And I'm right there with him.

Light?

"You're bright and reflective. You love attention. You can become any color. You move quickly. You attract people to you. Spending time in the light makes everyone feel good."

"Those are some deep sentiments," I reply.

"Well, I think I rather like that. Light. I'm like light. Such a compliment." Harry beams, licking the chocolate straight off of another biscuit.

"What's the downside to light?" I question.

Because I was a bulldozer.

Strong but forceful.

And I feel like Noah's not finished talking.

"There's only one real question I can come up with when thinking about light. What does it see?" Noah asks.

"Light cannot see," Helen says, dipping her brows in.

"Darkness?" I answer, understanding what he's saying.

"That's tragic," Harry says, pulling his chin back, sitting up straighter.

"Well, no one knows," Noah says. "You could be surrounded with so much of your own light that it's blinding, which could be good. But on the other hand, maybe light only ever sees darkness. Or maybe it's up to the light what it sees."

"Light wouldn't have a choice. It would just experience, wouldn't it?" Gene adds.

"What do you mean?" I ask.

He sounds so certain, but I'm not following. I reach for an apple and dunk it into the warm chocolate.

"It's human nature to ascribe something as good or bad. We make connotations. Light is good. Dark is bad. What Noah is saying is, projecting that light is good, and darkness is bad. But the truth of reality is that it is experienced and ascribed meaning through the human lens."

"This is getting a bit philosophical." Harry chuckles, breaking another biscuit in two. "What does that mean, the *human lens* thing?"

I glance over at him, taking in his curious, cautious eyes.

"It means that nature does not *see* good or bad. Nature— or light—does not assign a meaning to an experience. So, the light in this example might see light or darkness. The point is that it doesn't matter because that is its experience. Humans, on the other hand, experience something and then put a meaning or value to it. We argue that if we only see darkness, that must say something about us. It leads to the assumption that we are a dark person. Maybe we have a bad temperament. Bad thoughts that lead us to view the darkness."

"So, nature just ... experiences," I say, trying to sum up his point.

"Exactly," Gene confirms.

"A little deep for dessert, dear," Helen comments, trying to lighten the mood.

"Well, it's all just hypothetical anyway. I mean, Harry isn't light, and Mallory isn't an actual bulldozer," Noah comments, finally partaking in dessert. He drops a piece of apple into the fondue before bringing it to his mouth.

"I don't know ... she might be." Harry grins, causing all of the seriousness in the air to dissipate.

I grab another strawberry, dunking it into the chocolate so it's well coated. I bring it to my lips, trying to figure out how to bite into it.

"I might need a bib." I chuckle, having to put the whole

strawberry into my mouth. I try to break it with my teeth, but juice seems to be seeping out of it.

"You're a disaster," Harry teases, wiping at my chin as I tilt my head back, trying to keep the juice in my mouth.

"Apparently, I am today."

"That's all right. This is a messy treat. It should be fully enjoyed," Gene adds, taking a sip of his wine.

Harry shoots me a wink after getting the chocolate off of my face, and I grin back at him. I glance over, watching Helen pick at a biscuit. Noah dips his finger straight into the chocolate. I raise my eyebrow at him, a little surprised. Because if Helen had seen that, she would have lost it.

Noah brings his finger into his mouth, sucking the chocolate right off of it.

I don't let my eyes linger, quickly flicking my gaze away.

"Well, I am stuffed," Helen declares, pushing away from the table.

"It was wonderful, dear," Gene replies.

"It was," I agree, feeling a little stuffed myself. "I could definitely keep eating, but I know I shouldn't."

"We'll leave it out for a bit. Maybe have some tea to settle our stomachs." Helen practically sighs.

My face falls flat at the suggestion of tea.

"This is delicious," Noah agrees, nodding his head.

He's dipping his finger straight into the pot again, and this time, Helen catches him. She swats his hand away, causing Gene and Noah to both let out laughs. I glance over to Harry, who has officially moved beyond the carrier of the fruit and biscuits.

"Whatcha doing there?" I ask, looking at his plate.

He has a huge pile of fruit that all of the chocolate has been sucked off of.

"That chocolate sauce is bomb," Harry says, his eyes

rolling back.

"But apparently, the fruit wasn't," I tease.

"Fruit's … fruit," Harry replies.

"Harry, you up to playing chess?" Noah asks, his eyes coming to meet Harry's.

"Why not?" he agrees, leaning back in his seat, running his hand through his hair.

"Come on then," Helen says, the first to get up. "Let's get on our comfies and make a night of it. Harry, you're not in a rush, are you?"

"Not at all," he replies.

"I'll put on the kettle then," Gene says, getting up.

I decide to help Helen with the dishes, watching as Harry and Noah set up the chessboard in the living room. They're sitting on the floor in front of the coffee table.

"Well, even if they're not changing, I am," Helen confides.

"I'll change with you."

"That's lovely of you," she says warmly. "There's something about a rainy evening. You've got your family—well, almost all your family—under one roof. Your comfies are on, and you're tucked under a blanket. It's a mother's dream."

"I'm with you there. I think I could easily fall asleep on your couch." I laugh.

"You wouldn't be the only one. I bet Gene won't last five minutes in his chair before snoring."

I grin at her, thinking about Gene.

WHEN WE FINISH the dishes, I run upstairs and throw on pajamas, not really caring that they're not my cute ones. They are soft and cozy and perfect for tonight. By the time I get downstairs, Noah and Harry are well into their game.

"Who's winning?"

"Depends on who you ask," Noah replies.

"Which means Harry has the advantage." Gene chuckles.

I glance up at him, watching from his chair. He's started a fire, and Helen's coming from the kitchen, carrying a mug and wineglass into the living room.

"Tea anyone?" she asks, setting down Gene's wine beside him.

He glances up at her through his thick glasses, his cheeks tinting pink.

"I'm okay," I reply, snuggling up under a blanket.

"I'll have some," Harry replies. Noah doesn't even answer. He's too focused on the board. "Three sugars, please and thank you."

"I know how you take your tea." Helen almost giggles, hurrying back to the kitchen.

"That fire feels nice," I say, holding out my hands toward it.

I settle into the couch, thinking about what Helen said. Everything she needs, aside from Mia, is in this room. And it's strange, but I can relate to her. Even though I don't have my parents here, I have the Williams. Harry. And the fact that I even thought about leaving all of this because I was upset, scared … it makes me a little ashamed of myself.

"We should go out for tea tomorrow," Helen says, pulling me out of my thoughts, "while the boys are off at the pub. I thought you might enjoy that. I've booked us a table, but of course, it's up to you. It's no problem if I cancel …" Helen goes on, sitting down next to me.

"I would love that." I grab her hand, giving it a small squeeze.

"Good. It's a date then," she replies, scrunching up her nose. She grabs the remote, turning on the TV and flipping through the channels.

She lands on one of those holiday home shows, her face brightening.

"Shit!" Noah shouts, looking completely caught off guard.

"Noah," Helen scolds, turning to glare at him.

I keep my lips in a tight line, trying to keep from laughing.

"This isn't possible," Noah groans, intensely looking at the board.

"What?" I ask, not able to help myself.

"How in the hell did you beat me? You actually did it," Noah says, stunned.

I glance over to Harry, taking in his relaxed demeanor and glowing face.

"I know you, mate. It isn't about knowing how to win. It's about knowing how to beat your opponent."

"We have to play again," Noah says, staring at the board.

Gene sits up, glancing at the match. "Well done, Harry," he congratulates.

"Cheers," Harry replies.

I watch Noah reset the board. As they start another game, my phone goes off.

I grab it off of the coffee table, reading a new message.

"It's Naomi. She's invited me out for brunch tomorrow," I say, reading the text aloud.

"That's lovely, dear," Helen replies, glancing over to me. But just as quickly, her eyes are back on the TV.

"Well, it seems everyone wants some of you tomorrow." Harry chuckles, looking at me. "What would you say if I threw my name into the hat as well?"

I connect my gaze with his, feeling butterflies in my stomach. "What do you have in mind?"

"Dinner, of course," he banters back.

"Of course," I repeat. "Well, it sounds fun. But I would

need to check with Helen and Gene first."

"It is a school night," Helen says, glancing between the two of us, not seeming convinced.

"Oh, Helen," Gene interrupts, bringing his wine to his lips. His glasses slip down his nose, and he pushes them back up into place.

Noah looks up at his mom now, too, and I turn toward her, wondering if she'll cave.

"I suppose, as long as you're back and tucked into bed by ten, that should be all right."

"That shouldn't be a problem." Harry grins.

"It *won't* be a problem," Helen corrects, eyeing him. But I can tell it's all for show because she looks too pleased with herself to actually be concerned that we will break her rules.

Though I guess, with Harry and me, it's kind of hard to know.

Harry and Noah finish their second match, Harry winning again.

Noah gets upset, throwing his king onto the living room floor. Helen looks like she might lose it on him while Gene is trying not to laugh out loud.

"Well, I think that's good enough for one night," Harry says, getting up.

"I'm not sure I could take losing again," Noah agrees, standing too.

"You're off?" Helen asks.

"Yeah. I should get home. Get some rest for that date tomorrow night."

Helen shakes her head at him but then pulls him into a hug.

"I'll walk you out," I say, grabbing his hand. But a second later, I have to drop it as he puts on his jacket and boots. I decide to slip on shoes too, hearing the rain still falling outside.

"That was fun," I say when we're out front and alone.

"I'm not sure anything will compare to last night," Harry disagrees, putting his hands on my shoulders.

"Not even the chocolate?" I offer.

"It was delicious. But I loved last night."

"It's embarrassing."

"I loved the parts before too, you know?"

"Yeah?" I ask, looking up to him. My face flushes, even as the cold night air settles into me.

"Yeah. I loved dancing with you. Sitting on the balcony. Kissing in the kitchen."

"That *was* kind of fun," I agree, biting my lip. "And a little more than kissing was going on."

Harry nods. "Plus, you were in my bed again. Even Helen's fondue can't beat that!"

I shake my head, slightly in disbelief. Because here Harry is, being sweet and funny. Spending the day hanging out with me and the Williams. He could have blown it off or just gone home after the match.

But he didn't.

He's here, asking me out for tomorrow.

Standing out in the cold, talking with me.

I pull him down to my lips, letting my hands wrap around his neck. I open my mouth, feeling my heart in my throat.

Because time and time again, Harry shows me how he feels about me. That he's committed to me.

"I'll see you tomorrow," he says, breaking our lips apart.

I grab his hand as he turns away, stopping him. I hold on to him, looking him over. The way his jacket fits perfectly to his body. His sparkling eyes and happy expression.

"You're going to be home alone tonight. Are you going to

be okay?"

"I told you, you don't have to worry about me," Harry replies, his lips pulling to the side.

"I will anyway," I say, wanting him to understand.

"How could I not be okay? I know that I've got an angel looking out for me," he says, bringing my hand up to his lips. He places a quick kiss on my fingers, and then he's off, walking down the street in the rain.

I stand there for a minute, watching him walk, trying to figure everything out.

WHEN I LIE down in bed, yesterday runs through my mind like a movie reel.

Crying with Noah before school that morning. Being so excited to be with Harry. Feeling so nervous.

I was, in a word, a disaster.

But then I wasn't.

I felt good about things, about Harry. Until Noah opened his mouth. Until his finger came down onto my lips. Until he held my hand and asked me not to sleep with Harry.

And then I had to go and get drunk.

It wasn't my proudest moment, and thinking about it makes my stomach flutter.

Because I shouldn't have done it.

I shouldn't have just attacked Harry.

It would have been one thing to drink to have fun, to forget.

Maybe Noah was right.

Did I drink to try and loosen myself up to do something with Harry?

I ponder it, but I think the answer is no.

I drank because I wanted to have fun. Because I wanted to prove something to myself. Not to anyone else. And being with Harry is easy and fun. And I don't regret anything. The only thing I regret from last night is letting Noah get to me.

Letting him upset me.

I roll onto my side, trying to get comfortable. I hear footsteps in the hallway and see a shadow outside my door. It stays there, not moving. I hold my breath, wondering what the shadow will do. But a second later, I hear the floor give, and the shadow is gone.

I let out the breath I was holding in.

Noah told me today that he didn't want me to sleep with Harry because I was going to get hurt.

Because I was going to hurt Harry.

And maybe that is true.

Maybe if I do, it will hurt us more.

But the truth is, he was lying to me. And maybe he's lying to himself too.

He doesn't want me to be with Harry because he wants me to be with *him*.

The thought of sleeping with Noah crosses my mind. What it would be like. It's hard to imagine. Not because of the fact that we haven't done anything, but because it's hard to imagine how it would feel. I think about the way his hands feel when they hold mine. How my cheek warms against his chest. How soft his lips are. How much his smell overpowers me. Each of those things alone is overwhelming.

And the idea of them all coming together, around me, against me, with me … I can't even imagine it.

I *shouldn't* be imagining it.

I grumble into my pillow, wishing I could just fall asleep, feeling in love with Harry. Feeling only blissful about hanging out with him tonight.

But I can't.

And maybe that's my problem. Maybe I'm trying to deny

my feelings instead of just accepting them and moving on.

Who knows?

One thing is for sure though: I definitely have no clue what I'm doing.

SUNDAY, OCTOBER 6TH
Give this a chance.
8:30AM

I STRETCH OUT my arms, glancing over to the window as I wake up.

The curtains are pulled closed, but a sliver of light finds its way into my room. I allow myself to stay in bed, enjoying just sprawling out.

Because Sundays are nothing if not the day of rest.

And I plan to do nothing this morning, except brunch.

And then tea …

And then my date with Harry.

I really do have a full day. But those things all sort of count as resting—or at least, they're relaxing.

Well, maybe they don't count.

But I am excited to hang out with Naomi. And it will be nice to have some time alone with Helen.

And then my date with Harry. I smile to myself, thinking about spending the night alone with him. Well, a few hours of it anyway. The thought crosses my mind that he said his mom is out of town.

Maybe we'll just hang out at his place?

Get some alone time.

The idea sends butterflies through my stomach. I grin at my ceiling before pulling the covers up and over my head, burying myself under my blankets. I close my eyes and picture being with Harry. About the way he looked Friday night. How he stripped down naked right in front of me. The past few days have been … hard. And I'm excited to be spending the evening with Harry. I think I've realized though that I'm not ready for sex.

At least, not yet.

Because when I lose my virginity, I don't want any doubt.

And Noah has placed so much doubt and confusion in my head that I don't know which way is up.

But I feel like, for the first time in days, I can see things clearly.

I throw off my covers, standing up to twist back and forth, giving my body a small stretch. I feel amazing, and I skip over to the desk, plopping down into my chair.

And then I look at myself in the mirror and almost scream.

Because I look a little scary.

My hair has turned into some type of freaky bird's nest, my straight, dark strands sticking out in places that they definitely shouldn't be. My entire left cheek is red, likely from sleeping like a rock all night. I shake my head.

Today is unquestionably a shower day.

I decide to shower before going downstairs for coffee— that way, my hair can dry as I enjoy a slow morning.

I glance over to the clock, noticing it's only eight thirty.

Not exactly sleeping in, but it's better than waking up to an alarm for school.

I smile to myself as I shower, deciding that if I want my life to be simpler, I need to make it that way.

And today is going to be simple.

Coffee, homework, brunch, tea, and Harry.

I make myself take extra time in the shower, letting the

hot water seep into my skin. There's something cleansing about it.

The warm water.

The repetitive droplets.

There are no distractions.

No input.

But then you turn the water off, and it's like you fall back into the physical world. You have to dry off, put on lotion, get dressed, brush your teeth, and walk out that door, which kept everything silent and perfect and your way.

But I guess that's life. And it's not just you and your thoughts.

It can be like that.

But it wouldn't be very special.

Because you wouldn't have the people you love around you.

The people who break the silence.

I pull open the bathroom door, quickly running across the hallway to go back to my room to get changed. I throw on a clean pair of pajamas and then head down to the kitchen.

I have a plan. I'll sit at the table, quietly drinking my coffee. I'll lay out my homework, making sure to get it all done and show Helen, so that way, she's even more confident in her decision of letting me go on my date.

But when I get to the kitchen, that's not what I find.

"Oh crikey, I've burned the toast," Gene says, running his hand through his hair. He has on a button down with a blue sweater over the top, his collar sticking out.

"Well, that's how these things tend to go, don't they?" Helen says, flustered.

I stand in the doorway, watching her dash around. She pours herself a cup of coffee, practically swallowing it in one gulp.

Noah's in the kitchen, his chestnut hair a disaster. I watch as he stands up from the table and unplugs the toaster. He forks the burnt piece of toast out before plugging it back in, adding fresh slices.

"Morning," I say with hesitation, stepping into the kitchen.

"Morning, lovely," Helen says, sweeping past me to a cupboard. She pulls out a to-go coffee cup, filling it up.

"Morning," Noah says, turning to me.

My gaze flicks to him before moving back to Helen. She has papers spread out across the kitchen table and is definitely overdressed for a Sunday. She has on a matching two-piece suit, her dark, curly hair styled to the side.

I want to ask her why she's in such a hurry, but I dare not to.

Her heel is tapping impatiently on the kitchen floor, so I decide to just sit down and stay out of the way.

"Noah, can you please jam and butter the toast and fold it into a sandwich? I'm going to have to take it to go," Helen asks, shifting past me. She collects her papers off the table and then points between her folder, her coffee cup, and her car keys.

"Are you heading out?" I ask, my eyes on the keys.

She nods at me before glancing to watch Noah pop the bread out of the toaster. "I have a potential client who came into the city unexpectedly. They rang to see if they could get a meeting with me, and, well, here we are."

I'm not sure whether to congratulate her on the potential client or feel sorry for her for the last-minute meeting on a Sunday.

"That's … probably hard, having such short notice."

"Exactly as I said," Gene agrees, moving next to Helen.

He rubs her tense shoulders, and Helen visibly relaxes.

"Here you go," Noah cuts in, handing his mom the toast to go.

"All right, I'm off," Helen replies, taking the toast from Noah with a smile.

She moves to get her purse and folder but then looks between her already-filled hand to the coffee mug on the counter, and I think she might explode.

"I've got it, dear," Gene says, picking up the coffee and folder.

She gives him an apologetic smile before grabbing her purse and moving to the back door that leads out to the garage.

"Oh, Mallory," she says, quickly turning around, her brown eyes fluttering. "I don't expect the meeting to go past lunch, but just in case it does, I will text you with the name and address of the hotel where our tea is scheduled, and we can meet there."

"Great," I reply, giving her an enthusiastic smile. "I can't wait."

She nods, looking like she has something more to say but doesn't. Gene follows her into the garage along with Noah. I get up, peeking my head out the door. I watch as Helen gets situated into her car, rechecking she has everything.

"I'm off. Now, be good, you three. I want to come back to my house intact," she says, her eyes narrowing at us. But then she cracks a smile and is waving as she pulls out into the driveway.

"Well, that was quite chaotic," Gene says, shaking his head.

"She *was* a little flustered," I admit. Because I can't imagine how worked up she was before I got downstairs.

"She was more than flustered. She went mental. I can't believe she didn't wake you up sooner," Noah says, walking back into the kitchen.

"Really?" I laugh.

"Mmhmm," Noah says. "Dad can confirm it."

"Helen enjoys excitement, but I think on her own terms," Gene replies.

"Her terms." Noah laughs out. "She all about lost it. She was running up and down the hallway like a madwoman. I'm pretty sure I saw her in two different suits before she decided on the one she has on."

"Three," Gene corrects with a fond smile.

I shift to the counter, pouring myself a cup of coffee before sitting back down at the table. Gene stays standing, his arms resting on the back of a chair. Noah puts two more pieces of bread into the toaster.

"Aww," I sympathize, feeling bad for Helen. "I hate feeling unprepared too."

"She'll be able to handle it," Gene replies. "And I suppose that means we have the house free to ourselves today."

"Any big plans?" I raise my eyebrows, noticing his eyes brighten.

"I'll read the paper this morning, and then I have a book I would like to finish before the pub this afternoon. What about you two?"

"Homework this morning for me," I reply, taking a sip of my coffee. "And then brunch with Naomi at eleven."

Gene nods before looking at Noah.

"I'm just going to hang around. Maybe play some games, do some homework."

"Homework first preferably," Gene says before patting Noah on the shoulder. "If you need me, I'll be in my chair."

I watch Gene leave the kitchen, looking almost suspiciously happy. Noah sets the toast on the table.

"Want anything on yours?" he asks, glancing at me. "Your

usual?"

I nod.

A minute later, he's sitting down at the table, handing me the honey, almond butter, and a banana.

"Why is your dad so happy?" I ask while assembling my toast.

Noah looks between me and the living room, like he's making sure we're alone. "Mum usually makes Dad spend Sunday mornings helping her around the house with little projects. Like I said before, about *the man being the man*," Noah says the last words as he puffs out his lips and chest, apparently trying to show me that he means manliness.

A giggle escapes my mouth at his bad imitation.

"So, he got out of housework. Makes sense."

"Mmhmm," Noah replies, a smile pulling at his lips.

I bite into my toast, letting my eyes roll back at the flavors. There's something comforting about having things that you love. It's like, no matter where you are or how out of whack you feel, you can always depend on those things to remind you that no matter what changes, you're still you.

No matter where I go, I'm always going to love almond butter and bananas on toast.

And I'm always going to love coffee.

And not be a morning girl.

I smile at the internal list I'm creating.

"You're chuffed," Noah comments, pulling me out of my thoughts.

"I am," I say back, sipping my coffee. "Hey, I was wondering. What do your parents do? I can't believe I haven't asked until now, but … seeing your mom rush off to work made me realize I don't know."

"Dad's an actuary," Noah says, taking a bite of his own toast.

"What does an actuary *actually* do?" A laugh escapes, and I watch as Noah's cheek pulls his lips into a one-sided smile. "Did you get my play on words?"

"I did," Noah says, letting out a deep belly laugh. I'm not sure if he's laughing at me or laughing because my joke was *amazing*, but I don't really care. "Anyway, he analyzes the consequences of a risk."

"Analyzes a risk? What do you mean?"

"Basically, he analyzes the possible financial consequences of a risk for a company. He looks at events and tries to determine their risk through math and theory."

"That sounds extremely technical," I say, impressed.

"It is. But he loves it. He deals directly with a board, helping them make decisions on the right direction to take the company in," Noah replies.

"And what about your mom?" I ask, taking another sip of my coffee.

Noah finishes his toast, spilling a little jam on his finger. I watch him suck it off before he answers, "She's an HR consultant."

"Human resources. Now, that sounds even harder than your dad's job." I laugh.

"What?" Noah chuckles, tilting his head.

"I can't imagine what it would be like to have to make sure a whole bunch of people were appeased and working together. The thought freaks me out. I'm not sure I'm a people person," I admit.

"Of course you are. Isn't that kind of the whole job of a realtor? Getting to know a person's wants and needs and finding them the right place?"

I roll my eyes. "Yeah, *one* person. Or a family. Not a whole company. And once you get them what they want, you move on to the next one. The focus is on the property, not really the people."

"I don't know. I don't think you give yourself enough credit," Noah argues.

"So, what exactly does an HR consultant do?" I ask, moving the subject back to Helen.

"She consults with companies to help figure out succession plans—who the future leaders will be. She also helps with the corporate culture as well, making companies a better place to work."

"Wow. That's a pretty big role."

Noah nods. "She basically goes into a company and helps them solve problems."

"That's really cool," I say, finishing off my toast.

"I don't know about cool, but I guess it suits her," Noah replies, taking his plate to the sink.

"I can see it suiting her. It's probably why she's such a good mom. You have to be able to see what people say versus think. You have to be able to identify talent and leadership skills and then somehow organize it into a company that works. It's probably a lot like running a household. Making everyone work together."

"I like that." Noah smiles. "So, what are you doing this morning then?"

"Homework, I guess."

"Sunday mornings are supposed to be spent resting, not doing homework."

"Are you encouraging me to slack off?" I ask, getting up from the table. I rinse off my plate before looking back at Noah.

"I'm encouraging you to make sure you rest. But it sounds like you've got a full day." Noah drops my gaze, moving his attention to his hand at his side. He's fidgeting with the hem of his shirt, and his antsy-ness makes me a little uncomfortable.

"I did rest. All of last night. I ate chocolate, sat by the fireplace, and went to bed early. It was a good night."

"It … was," Noah replies, his eyes flicking back up to me. "Well, I'll be in my room."

And a second later, he's out of the kitchen.

I WORK ON my homework throughout the morning, deciding to go sit in the living room for Gene's company. I scribble out my answers to my statistics homework, knowing that they're probably all wrong. Then, I read through my chapter in Latin after deciding to *actually* do the reading for Monday.

Noah stays up in his room, probably playing video games just to avoid me.

But I don't care.

Because I can't tiptoe around the house, and I won't.

Things weren't awkward at breakfast, but they didn't feel normal either. I guess I just need to stop caring so much about him and how he's feeling and doing. What he's thinking.

I need to start thinking about me.

About what I want.

I give myself enough time to get ready, putting on eye shadow and mascara to make my eyes pop, finishing it off with a subtle lipstick. Since it's brunch with Naomi, I decide to go girlie for the day. I pull on jeans and calf high black booties that have a short block heel. I pair them with a black and burgundy tweed jacket, which has gold buttons dotting the front.

After looking myself over in the mirror, I add a headband to make myself appear a little younger. I glance from my shoes up to my hair, knowing that this will be cute and appropriate for both brunch and tea. I'm not sure how long brunch is, but I want to be ready to meet Helen for tea right after. And if there's extra time, maybe I'll spend it shopping.

Have some time to myself.

I decide to throw a book into my purse just in case I stop for a coffee. It was one of my favorite things to do in New York City. There's something about getting bundled up, going out to shop, and then stopping to warm up inside with a coffee and a good book. Especially somewhere by a window, where you can people watch. I think I usually spent most of my time watching people instead of reading, but it always gave me something relaxing to do either way.

I wave to Gene as I head out of the house, but he barely looks up at me from his book. He looks as content as Noah said he would be, and it puts a smile on my face. I pull out my phone, opening up the message from Naomi.

The place she suggested is only a twenty-minute walk, and I gave myself enough time to get there without taking the tube.

It's fun to walk and people watch. Letting the cool, crisp air reset you.

I push my hands down over my jacket.

I remember the day that I got it in New York like it was yesterday. It's one of the better memories that I share with my mom. It was actually a day like this, chilly but not too cold, spent walking through the park. We stopped to see the birds and then had a long drawn out lunch. It was right after my thirteenth birthday, and my mom wanted to do something special.

As a little girl, I always would sneak into her closet, trying on her tweed jackets. Not the most normal thing for a little girl, but I loved how her jackets made me feel. I saw all the ladies wear them and always thought they looked so mature and put together.

I used to want that.

I dreamed about that.

Feeling like I was someone who was heard and respected.

So, Mom took me into a shop and said that since I was becoming a woman—I was a teen now after all—it was time I got a jacket of my own. She made me buy it two sizes up—thankfully—but I wore it everywhere until, one day, I finally grew into it.

I liked that experience with my mom.

It was like she somehow knew that I put a dream—a dream of growing up—into an item. And she understood that in a way I hadn't expected from her. It surprised me.

And now, here I am, walking down a sidewalk in London on my own. I'm almost seventeen—a young woman most would say.

And I've adjusted.

I've taken someplace unfamiliar and made it into a home.

And I think that's special.

It's really special.

WHEN I GET to the restaurant where I'm meeting Naomi, I practically fall over on the sidewalk, looking into the display window. There are rows and rows and rows of desserts. There are mini chocolate cakes and full-sized layer cakes covered in edible flowers. There are towers of eclairs and meringue cookies. Everything is bright and dusted in colored powder or flowers. My eyes are the size of saucers when I walk into the restaurant, but I try to pull it together—at least for the sake of the hostess.

"Hi," I stutter, my eyes drifting back to the desserts. "I'm meeting a friend …"

But then I see Naomi at a table in the corner and give the hostess a sympathetic smile.

"I see her actually," I clarify.

But I now see that she isn't alone.

She's with Olivia.

Uhhh.

Part of me wants to turn around and just walk out the door, but the other part of me knows I can't do that.

I need to give this a chance.

I move through the restaurant until I get to their table. Olivia glances up at me, her mouth fixed in a flat line.

"Hi." Naomi grins, rising up from her chair, pulling me into a firm embrace.

"Hey," I reply, my gaze still on Olivia's indifferent expression.

She doesn't get up from the table, and when Naomi pulls away, I decide to take a seat.

"I'm not sure why we're having brunch together," are the first words out of Olivia's mouth as I sit down.

Apparently, she's decided to get straight to the point.

"Naomi," I say, feeling defeated.

Because why did she ask us both here?

She had to have known that it wouldn't go well. And I was really looking forward to this.

"Enough," Naomi says sternly. She holds out her hands in front of her, her palms stopping both Olivia and me from talking. "We are having brunch because everyone loves brunch. We got through a party together, and I need to gush."

I take in her excited expression and know I need to give in.

I know she's just trying to help, but I'm not convinced it's going to work.

"The party where Mallory was all over Harry?" Olivia asks, staring directly at Naomi.

Olivia has her shoulders pulled back, one eyebrow raised at her friend, and I definitely know this isn't going to go well.

"You were all over Mohammad," I argue, capturing Olivia's attention.

"And I was all over George!" Naomi cuts in.

Olivia drops my gaze, looking back over at Naomi, confused.

"My point is, I like George," Naomi clarifies. "But, Olivia, you've flirted with him before. You also snogged Mohammad even though I'd told you that I thought he was fit."

Naomi's matching Olivia's expression now, her features set pointedly on her delicate face. I raise my eyebrows, impressed.

"You're not serious," Olivia says, her voice pouring out like honey. She glances away from Naomi in annoyance.

"You and Mohammad *actually* kissed," I stutter, realizing the full truth of it now that I'm in front of her.

Because she didn't deny it. And even though Mohammad told me that they did, it's just so hard to picture.

And I really want to know her motive.

Olivia glances over at me, her brows dipping in as she narrows her eyes.

"I'm serious about this. Mallory met Harry before she ever met you. Now, if we had been friends first, maybe we could have explained to her your history, and things might have been handled differently," Naomi suggests.

"I don't know about that …"

"We're on the same side!" Naomi says, flashing her eyes at me.

"What side is that?" Olivia says through gritted teeth.

"The girl side, obviously," Naomi replies, rolling her eyes.

"I think taking sides is a bad way to look at this," I say.

I don't want Naomi to choose sides between Olivia and me. And I definitely don't want her thinking that if I had known Olivia first, I would have let that get in the way of me being with Harry. Because I get the whole *girl code* thing, but that certainly wasn't my mindset when I got here. And I'm going to be with whoever I want to be with.

Whoever I like.

"All right, you two," Naomi says sternly, "having girlfriends is important. We need to be kind to one another. We need to be friends. And that starts by talking. Maybe if we hang out and open up, we can have those soft sides for one another. We're all women here. We need to support each other."

I can't help but smile a little at Naomi's sentiment.

"I can't really argue with that," Olivia comments, her shoulders dropping.

"Mallory?" Naomi asks, glancing to me.

I think about my options. I don't want to just agree with her to avoid an issue.

I want to be honest.

"You're right. Olivia and I met in a … weird way. It wasn't my most shining moment. And things just went downhill from there."

"I agree." Naomi nods. "Now, the only question is, do we have topics we want to rule out, or are we committing to this openly?"

I look to Olivia, my hands fidgeting in my lap. Her lips are pulled flat, and she looks sort of frustrated. Like she's internally arguing with herself.

"Olivia?" Naomi asks, letting her answer first.

"It depends on the day," she says, fluttering her eyelashes. "It … it depends on the day and when it comes up. If I have an issue, I'll tell you. So, for now, let's just talk about whatever."

My stomach falls as I watch her. I can see that this is hard for her. That she's struggling with it. But in her way, I know she's trying.

Maybe she's not trying for me, but it doesn't matter.

She's trying.

And I need to try too.

"Okay," I agree, nodding at her. "I'm not going to pretend like I'll be okay with you talking about wanting Harry back. I think that would make me uncomfortable. But, yeah, I think us talking openly about our feelings might be a good idea."

"How about we stick to the feelings and leave the H-word out of it?" Naomi offers, glancing across the table at me.

"We can try," Olivia replies as a waitress comes over to our table.

"Hiya. How are we doing over here? Can I get you something to drink?" the waitress asks.

"I'll have the peppermint tea, please," Olivia says, starting us off.

"And I'll have a matcha latte," Naomi says with a smile.

"I'll have a cappuccino," I answer.

The waitress leaves our table to go put our drink order in. I decide to look over the menu, seeing the different breakfast and lunch options. There are things like avocado toast, smoothie bowls, healthy pancakes, and extravagant egg dishes listed. There are rows and rows of specialty coffees and infused tea concoctions, not to mention the half-page list of desserts.

"This place has amazing food," Naomi gushes, her eyes brightening. "I would recommend the pancakes. They're super healthy, but they have this delicious coconut fluff on top of them. The eggs are good, too, and of course, the desserts."

"I was practically drooling at the front window." I chuckle, looking back over at the meticulously displayed treats.

"Olivia and I always splurge on brunch here. My favorite

is the chocolate cake," Naomi confides.

"It's sensational," Olivia agrees. "Something about the chocolate and peppermint tea together is …"

"Magic," Naomi finishes.

"Maybe we could share a dessert," I reply, wanting to make an effort. "I don't know if I could get something all for myself though. Helen's taking me for afternoon tea, and I'm sure I'll get my fair share of sweets then too."

"Oh, I love afternoon tea," Naomi coos, pushing her hands together in front of her chest.

"The cakes are delicious, but it can drag a bit." Olivia looks unimpressed.

"No," Naomi cuts in, swatting her hand at Olivia. "I love getting dressed up and going with my mum and gran. We can sit there, eating and chatting, for hours."

"It sounds like my personal nightmare," Olivia says dryly. But I see her lip pull up at the corner, and I know she's teasing Naomi.

"I'm excited for it. Mostly to spend time with Helen. She's been really good to me while I've been here." I smile, thinking about the affection that Helen has shown me.

She's been like a mom to me these past few weeks.

"I wish I could have met her more properly," Naomi says, referencing our sleepover.

"You know, Naomi mentioned your sleepover," Olivia says, pushing her blonde hair over her shoulder.

I glance across at her, taking in her creamy sweater and expertly done makeup. She has on gold jewelry that highlights how perfectly put together she looks.

"I never thought I'd hear the end of shirtless Noah."

"Well, I had to tell someone about it! Mallory was oblivious to his body, and I needed someone to gush to about how fit he is."

"You were gushing about Noah?"

Her words pique my interest, but I try to ask the question with indifference because I can feel Olivia's eyes on me.

"Of course I was. And then I started imagining what it would be like to be on a foreign exchange, sleeping one room over from a lush boy. Maybe next year, I'll beg my parents to send me off. Let me go to Australia. I'm sure the boys have to be rugged there. I could find myself a surfer," she says excitedly.

"And what about George?" Olivia questions, tilting her head.

"Oh, George …" Naomi pouts, putting her chin into her palm as our waitress comes back.

"Here we are," she says, setting our drinks on the table. "Are you ready to order, or do you need a few more minutes?"

We order our food before picking the conversation back up.

"Speaking of George and the party"—Naomi smiles mischievously—"can we please get back to talking about you and Mohammad?"

"There's nothing to talk about," Olivia responds sharply, looking at Naomi like she's betrayed her.

"I'm not judging you, Olivia," I interrupt.

"You don't have a right to judge me," Olivia replies.

I'm not sure if she's trying to assess my intentions or prove her point, but she sounds conflicted.

"What's said at this table stays at this table," Naomi says sternly. "It will not be used in any manner to break friendships or relationships. That was my point before."

"We kissed," Olivia states blankly, relaxing into her chair.

"And?" Naomi pushes.

"And it was fun," Olivia says, glancing over at me. She shrugs, like she's as surprised as we are. "I've known Mohammad forever. He used to be scrawnier. A bit of a loudmouth, always grabbing everyone's attention in class—and not in a good way. But he's changed."

"There's definitely something sexier about him now," Naomi agrees, her cheeks tinting pink.

I glance over to Olivia, wondering if she notices.

She does.

"So, he was a good kisser then?" Naomi continues.

And it sort of sounds like she's digging for information. I'm not sure if it's for herself or just to keep the conversation about kissing going.

Olivia hesitantly looks over at me.

I nod at her, wanting to be encouraging. I don't want her to feel like she has to filter what she says.

"Not bad actually. It was fun. Obviously, it was a decision made after a few drinks. But it's not like I did anything I regret."

"That's fair," I reply, sort of liking that. I like that she's owning up to it. And not trying to lie her way out of it or twist her actions into something they weren't.

"Do you think it could be something more?" Naomi asks.

I snap my head in her direction, my eyes going wide.

"Don't even go there." Olivia snorts.

"I'm just saying, even if you wanted—or want—H back," she says with a whisper, "that doesn't mean you can't have fun or date now."

Olivia rolls her eyes, letting out a huff. "We know that stands for Harry, Naomi."

"You're not allowed to say Harry!" Naomi squeaks.

"We were having a good time, and things happened. That was it."

"I'm glad you had fun. I had fun. I mean, at least up until my hangover the next morning," I say, trying to change the subject.

Olivia ignores my efforts.

"You do make a good point. I deserve some fun now. Maybe I need to think about this. I could date Mohammad"—Olivia smiles and looks at me—"or Noah."

My stomach instantly rolls.

But then she waves her hand in front of her, throwing aside her ideas. "I think I'd rather be single. Plus, if I were going to date someone, they'd have to be on Harry's level."

"Maybe I could see if George knows anyone?" Naomi offers.

"No. It would have to be someone new. I know all the guys at Westminster. Eaton. If I'm going to move on, it has to be with someone worthy."

"I agree. The best for my best friend." Naomi smiles, grabbing Olivia's hand, giving it a squeeze.

I'm thankful when the food finally arrives. I dig right in, having ordered a smoothie bowl and a square of carrot cake. I take a bite, letting the banana, blueberries, honey, and granola all mix in my mouth.

Then, I take a sip of my coffee to wash it all down.

"I'm a little offended no one has asked me about George," Naomi says, stabbing into her chocolate cake.

"Is there more to tell?" I ask.

"He asked me on a date," she says, reminding us.

"Shit," I mutter, feeling bad for having forgotten to ask how it went.

"He actually took you out?" Olivia questions.

"I know." Naomi nods. "I was surprised, too, when he messaged me. I thought for sure he'd just said it as a way to try to get into my knickers. But he took me out last night."

"I'm impressed." Olivia smiles in approval.

"That's the whole reason I asked you both here. Because I

wanted to tell you about how it went in person," Naomi explains.

"I thought you asked us here to force us to become friends," Olivia replies with a smirk.

"Well, that too." Naomi scrunches up her nose, giving us a grin.

Olivia and I listen as Naomi tells us about her date. George picked her up, and they had dinner in the West End before seeing a show. Supposedly, it was *amazing*. He held her hand in the theater, they kissed for what felt like hours after, and he begged to see her again this week. Her face is lit up the entire time she talks about him, and both Olivia and I listen, adding in words of encouragement when needed.

"I'm GLAD WE did this," Naomi says, hugging me when we get out front of the restaurant.

I glance down at my watch, taking in the time.

One o'clock.

"I am too," I reply, hugging her back.

When I first arrived and saw Olivia, I thought it would be a disaster. But once we got over the awkward beginning of brunch, it was actually fun. We ate delicious food, and Naomi insisted that I take more than a few bites of her chocolate cake.

"See you at school tomorrow, Mallory," Olivia says, giving me a nod.

"See you tomorrow," I reply with a closed mouth smile.

She doesn't try to hug me, and I'm grateful for it.

Naomi waves good-bye.

Helen texted me while I was at brunch, telling me to meet her at the One Aldwych at three. She went on about getting cash from Gene to take a taxi, but I messaged back, insisting I'd be fine. The One Aldwych is a pretty hotel right off the river and in the heart of the city. Or so Naomi and Olivia told me when I asked if they'd heard of it.

Instead of going back to the Williams' before tea, I decide to use the spare time to explore the city.

When I look up directions on my phone, I realize I'll have to take the tube to make the journey there.

I go into the Underground and study the map. The closest stop to the hotel is on the Piccadilly line at Covent Garden. It's only four stations away with no transfers. And since Covent Garden is supposed to have great food and shopping, I think I can definitely kill a couple hours, exploring there.

Have some time to myself.

Maybe do a little shopping.

Walk off this food.

I can't imagine eating another meal in two hours, let alone everything that is supposed to go along with tea. Sandwiches. Desserts.

And then there's the tea.

And from the sounds of it, it just keeps on coming and coming and coming.

Maybe I can find a way to sneak some instant coffee into it when Helen isn't looking.

But that would require instant coffee.

And insisting to Helen that it was in fact tea and not coffee.

I can already picture her face flashing with disapproval as I get onto the tube. It's less than a ten-minute ride, so I decide to stay standing. The sea of people flowing in and out is chaotic but peaceful in its own way. I pull my headphones out of my purse, letting myself get lost in some music.

Before I realize it, I'm already at my stop, the doors pushing open.

I squeeze past a pack of tourists, their thick white sneakers standing out in the sea of black. When I'm finally off the tube, I let the flood of people moving in the same direction as I am lead the way.

I figure they have to be going somewhere, and I follow them until I'm standing in front of a tall building, each level a different restaurant, with ivy and flowers climbing up the brick walls.

I spin around, taking in the open layout before me.

Bricks line the street in every direction, leading to a columned building, set on each side with green iron ceilings that close in the gaps between the central and surrounding buildings, forming a sort of complex.

When I get under the covering, I realize it looks like you're walking into a train station with restaurants and shops on each floor.

I glance in one of the shops, deciding to go inside.

It's a tea shop, of all places.

But there isn't just tea.

Scented candles are stacked along one wall with hot chocolate mixed in with spice packs and various painted plates and mugs displayed on shelves throughout the store. My eyes explore as I listen in on conversations about which flavor they like the best or which *two for ten pounds* deal they should get.

I feel my phone buzz in my bag, and I pull it out, seeing two texts on the screen.

Harry: *I'll be outside at 7. x*

Harry: *Wear something special.*

I reread his text a few times, butterflies forming in my stomach.

But what does he mean by special?

Special like special?

Like sex special?

Or are we talking just something dressy? A date night outfit?

I furrow my brow, confused. Because when he took me out for Italian, he didn't tell me to dress special. I did, and so did he, but he hadn't said to. Which makes me think that, tonight, I need to be extra dressed up. But then there are so many possibilities. Do I go with something more formal? Or maybe overly romantic? I huff, knowing that I need to stop overthinking it.

I read his text again, transcribing it to the basics in my head.

He'll get me at seven.

Dress nicely.

Okay.

That I can do.

I walk out of the tea shop, moving down the sidewalk and discovering a fun window display in a clothing store I recognize from their Kensington location. A place I've always wanted to go into but never had the time to stop.

My hands slip across the fabrics, moving from one beautiful piece to the next. I pick out a few dresses, deciding the only way to tell if I like them is to try them on.

I put on a long, flowing dress. It's a mixture of metallic earth tones with a deep V in the front that is matched in the back.

When I come out of the changing room to look myself over in the full-length mirror, the salesperson says, "That's stunning on you."

"It is." I examine myself, taking in the dress.

The fabric is luxurious, a floral gold lamé with shades of teal and rose. The neckline cuts so far down that it meets the dress's cinched waist. A gathered skirt flows delicately over my hips.

It's gorgeous.

I go back into the dressing room and slip into the other pieces I picked out. None of them have the same effect, so I decide not to purchase them. I'm not sure if this is the dress I'll wear tonight, but I know it's a dress that I'll wear at some point.

I usually don't pick out such delicate items. I typically choose clothing with hard lines and structured fits, but something about this dress is different. It's soft and beautiful and understated.

It's the perfect dress.

I just don't know for what yet.

I check out and then leave the shop, feeling excited.

I wander farther down the street, going in a few interesting stores I pass, looking at handbags and jewelry.

I'm searching for a coffee shop when I suddenly stop, taking in an iconic two-storied store.

Burberry.

Classic but modern pieces are showcased in the window displays, single lights illuminating the sparse mannequins. I smile to myself as I walk inside.

Because nothing says British like Burberry.

"Can I help you?" A woman saunters up to me, tilting her head to the side, a pleasant smile on her face.

"Yes. I'm looking for a dress." I smile back at her.

She nods in approval, turning to guide me farther into the shop. "Right this way."

WITH ANOTHER SHOPPING bag in hand, I leave the store and then stop in a small but busy café that's only a block away from the hotel. I order a coffee and find a table in the corner. I let my bags rest in the opposite chair as I pull out my phone since I still have a little time before tea.

I take a sip of my coffee and look over at my bags. It only took trying on two dresses to find *the* dress for tonight.

It's different from the first dress I bought.

Sexier.

It sits off the shoulders, cutting across my chest in a straight line. It has fitted long sleeves, and the skirt falls just below the knee. Even though it's longer than I might usually choose, it fits snugly at the waist and skims perfectly over my hips. The dress is a soft gray jersey knit on the top, moving into a tightly pleated gray and white patterned skirt. It gives the illusion of being two separate pieces.

It's classic and reserved, but at the same time, it's modern and sexy.

I look out the window and think about home. About New York. About how a day like today—filled with brunch, shopping, and coffee—would be exactly the sort of day I'd have with Anna.

It makes me miss her.

I pull up her name on my phone, deciding to call her.

I know that she owes me an apology, but she's never been good about being the one to make the first move.

She's stubborn like that.

But she's also sensitive.

And she won't call me to make her point.

That I hurt her too.

That I was a bad friend, and that with one phone call, I somehow ruined her idea of our perfect junior year.

Dreams are important to Anna, and she usually has big, elaborate, and overly dramatic ones. They're usually all in her head, but to her, they are well thought out. And despite there not being anything tangible to them, they're real for her.

And I have to support her.

Which means that I need to make things right.

I hit her name, listening to the phone ring.

"Anna," I say into the phone when she picks up.

"Hey," she replies, sounding caught off guard.

"Anna, I'm sorry," I spit out, knowing that I need to get the words out of my mouth. "I'm sorry I didn't call you sooner. I was a shitty friend. And I know that what you said, you meant well."

"Mallory—" Anna starts, but I interrupt her.

"No, let me finish," I continue. "You were right about everything. But you have to understand that it's been so different than I expected. I didn't plan any of this. And …" I stutter, feeling stuck in my words. All of my emotions come rushing back to me.

"It was inconsiderate of me to say those things. I was hurt and wanted to hurt you too," she admits.

"Are we okay?" I ask, desperate for this to just be over between us and for things to go back to normal.

"We're okay," she says.

I can hear her voice lighten, and relief floods through me.

"How are you doing?" I ask, knowing that when Anna's upset, she doesn't hide it.

She usually acts out in retaliation, but since I'm not there, I'm not sure how she handled our fight.

"Well, things have been amazing actually. I mean, apart from our fight. I hate to say it, but I … well, I burned our friendship photo."

"Anna!" I gasp.

I expected her to be upset but not *that* upset.

One summer a few years ago, Anna had made me spend a whole day on a quilt in the park with her. She knew I wasn't good at art, but I sat there and decorated a picture frame for her while she decorated one for me, and we put the same photo in each frame.

Anna thought that friendship bracelets and necklaces were *lame*. I knew she secretly loved the idea, but once, she asked me, "How are you supposed to match these to your outfits?"

It was always an ongoing struggle for her. Keychains hadn't even been considered, so she had decided on frames, saying that we would wake up each morning, seeing our best friend's face on our bedside table. I was a little freaked out at the idea because of how disgustingly sentimental it felt, but deep down, I loved it too.

I'd liked that I was as important to her as she was to me.

"Look, I was upset. You should have seen me. I was inconsolable," she defends, her voice rising.

"I can't believe you burned it. It took me forever to make that thing."

"Oh, I didn't burn the frame. Just the photo," she corrects.

I let out a sigh of relief. "You could have led with that."

I can almost hear her rolling her eyes through the phone.

"I thought our friendship was over, Mallory. And you were as good as dead, coming back to me, brokenhearted. Every vision I had of us dating best friends and setting the town on fire was torched with that photo."

I take a sip of my coffee, flaring my eyes with her overdramatic statement.

"But with a little perspective?"

"But with a little perspective, I realized that was childish."

"I love you, Anna."

"I love you too. So, how are you doing? Or should I even ask?"

"It's probably best not to ask," I reply quickly, shoving my hair behind my ear.

"Spill."

I can hear what sounds like Anna shifting on her bed, probably getting comfortable. Which is smart since she knows me and realizes we might be here for a while, talking my emotions around in circles.

"Actually, things are fine," I say, deciding to get a little perspective of my own. "I feel good today. I went shopping. I'm drinking a coffee. I'm glad we're talking."

"I'm glad too. But I still want you to spill."

I run my fingers across the rim of my coffee mug, weighing my words. "I have strong feelings for a lot of people here, and it was sort of getting me down. But I've decided that, instead of dwelling on it, to just be happy. To feel lucky. I guess that's it."

"You sound determined," Anna says, laughing softly.

"I am."

"It's a little freaky."

"Enough about me. Tell me about you."

"You've been missing a lot actually. I've been to Nori twice already, and it's absolutely delicious. It's my new favorite spot for sure, and I know you'll love it. The leaves are starting to change color, and everyone's bringing out their fall wardrobes."

"And what about Anthony?" I ask, knowing that she probably wants to talk about the guy that she's "dating" this year.

They aren't really a couple, and I'm not sure she even likes him that much, but once Anna sets her mind to something, she's off and gone.

And last I heard, her mind was set on Anthony.

"Ugh, I'm so over him," she says with indifference, like her former crush has now somehow become repulsive.

"Really?" I ask, surprised.

"I can't believe I haven't told you. Well, actually, I can,

seeing as it only happened yesterday. Anyway, I'm totally over Anthony. But that's only because I've moved on to someone new." She sighs into the phone, and I can hear it in her voice.

"You're in love," I tease.

She doesn't miss a beat. "His name is Jordan Marks. He's six foot one, blue-eyed, and absolutely gorgeous. We met at a party last night."

"Did you get his number, or what did you guys do?" I ask, trying to figure out if this love is just in her head or if there's some reality to it.

"We stole glances for a while. It was like something out of a movie. He has the darkest, most beautiful skin. He's a swimmer, I later found out. Anyway, he finally came over and introduced himself. I think he must have noticed that I was interested. But I was still down about our fight. He held up a bottle of champagne and asked if I wanted to talk."

"Aww, romantic," I say, letting her continue her story.

"We shared a few drinks and talked for hours, I swear. And he's the best kisser."

"Anna, that's awesome."

"I know. We've been texting all morning."

"I can't wait to meet him."

"I miss you, Mallory. I can't wait for you to be home next weekend."

"I miss you too, Anna. Call me this week. I want an update, all right?"

"Of course," she replies brightly before hanging up.

I check the time, throw my phone into my purse, down my coffee, and head out the door. It only takes me a minute to get to the hotel, and quickly enough, I'm standing in the lobby of the One Aldwych before being directed up to the restaurant, where tea is held. It's on the second level of the hotel, overlooking the lobby. Everything is bright and airy, the windows on the main level lighting the entire room up. I search around for Helen but don't find her.

"Can I help you?" a hostess asks.

"Yes. I'm actually supposed to be meeting someone. It should be under Williams."

"You're the first to arrive. I can take you to your table if you'd like," she offers.

I nod. "That would be great. Thanks."

I follow her to our table, letting her take my coat. Just as I'm sitting down, I see Helen rushing toward me.

"Oh, dear, I'm so, so sorry," she says, flushed when she gets to the table. "Traffic was horrid, and finding a place to park … and here you are, seated alone at a hotel."

"Don't worry about it. I literally just got here," I say, placing my hand on her wrist.

She glances down at it before bringing her gaze back up to mine, visibly relaxing.

"Well, in any case, we've both made it, so I suppose I should take a deep breath," she says with a chuckle.

"You should," I agree, withdrawing my hand. "How was your meeting?"

Helen picks up her menu, mindlessly flipping through it before setting it back down onto the table. I'm not sure she actually read anything, but it gave her hands something to do.

"They've agreed to hire me as a consultant." She shoots me a wink.

"Congratulations! I think you might need a glass of champagne instead of tea to celebrate." I raise my eyebrows, wondering if my suggestion will tempt her.

She pinches in her lips, her cheeks rising up as her mouth pulls into a conspiratorial smile.

"I won't tell if you don't," I urge, grinning.

"Well, I suppose one won't hurt."

The waiter comes over and takes our order. Helen orders a glass of champagne to be followed by a pot of rose tea. I order peppermint, remembering how Olivia said it goes well with chocolate.

A FEW MINUTES later, the waiter brings us our drinks. I watch Helen enjoy her first sip of champagne.

"Better?" I ask, but I already know the answer based on the content sigh she lets out.

"I have to say, I've never once had champagne accompany my afternoon tea. Though it's quite relaxing," she admits, taking another sip.

"It's good to celebrate accomplishments. Just like my chocolate fondue last night."

"You and Noah, always going on about celebrating."

"Is Noah big on celebrations normally?" I ask, taking a sip of the peppermint tea. I get it down, but it doesn't settle well. I always thought peppermint tea was supposed to soothe a stomach, but drinking it without food makes mine ache.

"He's always going on and on about celebrating. I swear, I don't know where that child gets it from. Mia would forget her own birthday if you let her, and Gene, sweet as he is, can't see an important date approaching if it hit him square in the forehead."

"I'm sure that makes anniversaries frustrating." I laugh.

Helen waves her hand in the air, taking another sip of her champagne. "I use to subtly remind him when we were younger. But now, I just kiss him on the cheek, whispering in his ear that yet another year has passed us by. With age, you tend to not care about those things as much."

"I thought you were always big about keeping the romance alive?"

Helen smiles at me. "True romance is very different from

romance on paper. Gene woos me in unexpected ways. It would be easy to wish that you had a partner who, say, drew you a bath every night or showed up home from work with a bouquet of roses on each anniversary. But that isn't a connection."

"So, do you think that we're taught to expect romance in just one way? Like the guy should pick you up, sweep you off your feet?" I say, quoting her previous words.

"Romance is ... romance. It's different for everyone. For you, it could mean having someone shower you with flowers or take you on fancy dates. But romance also means support. It means helping someone when they struggle. It can be anything from doing the dishes to a slow, unexpected kiss."

"I like that you talk to me about romance." I smile at her, feeling a little flushed. "I feel like I talk with my friends about it differently. I love them, and I want them to be happy. And I know love isn't the same for everyone. But sometimes, it seems so ... one dimensional. And I don't mean that about my friends ... maybe it's because of everything I've gone through here with Harry; I'm not sure."

"Something that you'll learn, Mallory, is that just because it doesn't seem maybe deep to you, it doesn't mean it isn't for someone else," Helen says.

"You're right," I admit. "Maybe I'm more judgmental than I thought."

Helen lets out a chuckle, her thick curls bouncing at her shoulders. I glance down to my tea, feeling embarrassed, as the waiter comes back to the table. He sets down a large three-tiered platter.

My eyes widen, taking in an entire row of mini sandwiches, the plates above it filled with mini desserts.

"This looks great," I say, licking my lips. My previously full stomach has now made room, and I scan the tower, trying to figure out what to test out first.

"It's always a treat," Helen agrees, picking up a sandwich. As she chews, she brings her attention back to me. "How are you doing, dear? You seemed exhausted yesterday. And you mentioned that you saw Olivia."

Helen looks across the table at me, and I shift under her gaze.

"I feel pretty good. I was tired yesterday, and things with Olivia were definitely strenuous, but Naomi invited her to brunch with us this morning," I confess as I bite into what looks like a blackberry tart.

"Naomi seems to be doing that quite often lately," Helen says, her brows dipping in. "Girls can be deceiving like that though."

"I know. I was completely caught off guard," I reply, taking another bite of the delicious treat. "I know she had good intentions. I just wish she had told me, so I could have been mentally prepared. But it went fine. We actually sort of came to an agreement about being friendly. Even friends maybe."

"Do you believe that can actually happen?" Helen asks before polishing off her champagne.

I take another bite of the tart as I think about her question.

"I guess I have two options. I can see her as an enemy, which means I won't like her and I won't go along with the *being friends* thing. Or I can try and get to know her. Honestly, we have a lot in common. Which is a little creepy. Well, maybe not a lot in common. But we both speak our minds. We're direct. I try not to think about it though because then I start dwelling on the fact that Harry obviously has a type, and then I start to freak myself out."

I flash my eyes at Helen, getting a chuckle in response.

She sets down her empty flute and rests her hand on my arm. "Oh, Mallory. I think you are just a breath of fresh air. I know you've had your troubles here, but I hope this exchange is doing you some good. I know you've certainly made an impact on our family."

"Really?" I ask, feeling butterflies in my stomach.

"Of course, dear. I've never seen Noah so happy. Despite his melodramatics, I know that he is fond of you. And Harry is quite clearly smitten. You've cracked into the hearts of my boys. Normally, I would be cautious of it, but I know that you have a good heart."

"I really appreciate that. I have been struggling a lot lately with the idea that I'm leaving in a week. I know that what I'm about to say will sound childish, but I don't want to go."

"It's a hard thing, isn't it? But all good things must come to an end. And think about all the new friendships you've made."

"But I know that things will change when I leave," I argue.

Because I want her to understand.

I need her to see how big of a deal this is to me.

"They will," Helen confirms, not easing my unsettledness. "But that's to be expected. Let me tell you something. I believe that we are put through tests in life. We are taken down a path filled with experiences. These experiences form us into who we are meant to be. They help teach us about ourselves. They show us the meaning of true friendship. These are lessons. These relationships you've built will require maintenance. But I promise that if you work at them, they can last."

I set down my fork, focusing all of my attention on Helen. "Do you think that Harry, Noah, and Mohammad will *want* to maintain them?"

Helen slides a scone onto her plate. "I think you've made friends for life here. I have no doubt about that."

I want to smile at her response, but I decide to keep my eyes down on my plate. I trust Helen, and if anyone knows them, it's her.

AFTER WE FINISH our tea, we find our way back to Helen's car and then make our way home.

And I still love the way that Helen drives.

She could put fear into just about anyone with her terrifying and impressive skills—how she effortlessly weaves in and out of traffic.

I smile, thinking about what my mom would think if she were riding with us. She'd probably have her eyes closed, saying something about how this was how she was going to die.

My mom's like that. Dramatic.

Sort of like Anna.

"Helen, I really appreciate you taking the time to take me out today."

"It was nice," she replies, glancing over to me. "Do you miss your mother, dearest?"

I nod. "A bit actually. Despite us being so different and her having her own set of quirks, I do. Sometimes, I think we're so different that we shouldn't get along. I mean, I know that sounds weird, but sometimes, it's hard for me to picture how she raised me."

Helen nods, keeping her eyes on the road. "Family is very important. You shouldn't ever negate the work that goes into parenting."

"I don't mean to. I guess what I mean to say is, you feel like my family too. Everyone here does. Not just my parents."

"You're a good girl, Mallory."

"I'm not so sure. I've managed to find myself in a fair amount of trouble here." I laugh, looking out the window.

Talking to Helen is easy. She always has sound advice, and even though she's opinionated, she's a good listener.

"Don't tell Noah this, but mistakes are how you learn," she replies. "As much as I want to just lead you children down the right paths, you have to walk them yourselves."

"Noah and Mia are really lucky."

"Aww, hush now." Her cheeks tint pink.

"You know, Noah told me about your job. It sounds really cool. I feel silly for never asking you about your work before. I'm not sure how you manage all of it." Because the realization hit me today that Helen not only works, but she's also a present mom and a wife.

"I'm traditional, but I also love what I do. Anytime the stress gets to me, I just think about what my life would be like without my job, and it humbles me. My children are also aging and will be off, living their own lives, soon enough. And my husband, well, he's not exactly too much to manage. Gene's what I like to call a low maintenance man. It's one of the things I love about him. The whole world can be in chaos around him, and he's happily asleep in his chair."

I laugh, thinking about Gene and his chair. Even this morning, he was so happy to sit there and just read.

"Does he help around the house? Stuff like that? Or is that your thing?" I ask, remembering my talk with Noah this morning.

"He's very organized. He always offers to cook, but I'd never allow it. I was raised and taught to take care of my husband. But Gene spoils me in different ways. He's always planning date nights out and making sure that I have what I need. He works very hard to provide for me and our children, and his job can be stressful at times, but he never brings it home. And the best gift that he gives me is being a good father to my children."

"Well, he definitely is that." I smile.

"He really is."

WHEN WE GET back to the house, it's empty, Noah and Gene are still at the pub. I go upstairs and start getting ready for my date with Harry. Even though it has been a busy day, it's been fun.

And I feel energized from all the excitement.

Or maybe it's just the never-ending coffees and sugary foods I've eaten today.

Either way, I'm buzzing.

I pull out my phone, checking my texts. I don't have any new ones, but Mohammad comes to my mind. His family arrives home today, and I'm sure he's excited.

Me: I want photos from today.

I set the phone down and am hanging up the dresses I bought when it vibrates with his response.

Mohammad: Photos?

Me: Of the decor. The arrival. I want to see your sisters.

I stare at the screen, waiting for the little typing bubbles to pop up but they don't. I decide to work on my hair while I wait. I brush through it, wanting to keep it slicked back and straight to go with the dress. I add some shine cream to the ends before stripping down and rubbing lotion on my arms and legs.

A text comes through, and it's an image of a modern sitting room. There are cutout paper flowers spread across a coffee table and streamers hanging from an oversized fireplace. There's a large cake in the middle of the table, already cut, with used plates surrounding it.

Me: *Mohammad! That's beautiful!*

It dawns on me that I've never been to Mohammad's house, and it's fun to see a glimpse of it. We always seem to hang out at school or at Harry's.

Mohammad: *It's overdone.*

Me: *I'm sure they loved it.*

Mohammad: *They didn't hate it.*

Me: *And your sisters?*

Mohammad: *One sec …*

A few minutes later, Mohammad sends me another photo. It's a selfie of him with three little girls, all grinning brightly at the camera. One of them is on his back, and the other two have their chins raised up toward the camera.

Me: *Oh my goshhh. They're so adorable!*

Mohammad: *Satan's spawn in the flesh.*

Me: *Mohammad!*

Mohammad: *I'm teasing, Miss America. Besides, even if they were, no one would believe me. Everyone says they're angels.*

Me: *And what do you say?*

Mohammad: *I missed them.*

Me: *I want to meet them this week. And your family. Think you can make that happen?*

Mohammad: *I'll make it happen.*

I don't reply, letting Mohammad have time with his family. But a second later, he's calling me.

"What's up?" I ask with surprise.

"I got sick of texting. Told my mum you wanted to meet the family, and she wants to have you round for dinner this week. Is that cool?"

"Yes! This is so exciting." I can't help but grin to myself. "I can't wait to meet your parents. Your sisters."

"Yeah …" Mohammad replies.

And his response is *definitely* lacking in enthusiasm.

"What?" I question.

"Well, she also told me that since the girls missed me so much, she wants me to take them out after school tomorrow."

"I'm sure they did miss you," I encourage, trying to cheer him up.

"Which means I'll be spending my Monday night at the Natural History Museum," he moans.

"Could I tag along? I've never been, and I've heard it's actually a great museum."

"Gladly!"

"Aww. Mohammad and his four women. Your sisters and, of course, me." I grin into the phone.

"Way to leave out my mum. Maybe I should bring that up at dinner," he banters back.

"I thought your mom scares you?" I laugh.

"She does. Which is why I don't have a choice in taking the devil's spawn out for hot cocoa and then to the museum."

"Three sweet little angels, drinking hot cocoa. Sounds like a nightmare," I tease.

"It is," Mohammad insists. "And you're a little off. It's more like three little girls pretending their loving, older brother is something to be climbed upon or dressed up. They will drink their cocoas, be wired from the sugar, and then proceed to run around the museum. And trust me, if you try to stop them, they will get this terribly cute, pouty face. Tears flood down their cheeks, like you've just ruined their whole lives. I can't tell you the amount of times that they've been terrors and then fake cried to get out of trouble."

"It sounds like you could use my help then," I reply as the front door downstairs opens and closes.

Gene and Noah must be home.

"See you tomorrow," Mohammad says into the phone.

"See you tomorrow," I repeat, hanging up.

I touch up my makeup, deciding to add a gray shadow to my eyelids. I glance between my reflection and the dress. It's neutral and understated, so I put on a creamy nude lipstick. I brush out my eyebrows, adding a little color to give them some thickness and shape. I'm applying perfume to my wrists when my door opens.

Noah's voice echoes in my room. "Mallory?"

"Yeah, come in."

Noah moves into my room, closing the door behind him.

And his presence hits me like a wall.

"Mum said you were up here," he states.

I take in his thick sweater, dark jeans, and uncomfortable expression. His jaw is loose, but his brows are dipped in, and his arms are crossed, covering his chest.

I wait for him to say something else, but he doesn't.

"You want to talk about things, don't you?" I suck in a thick, slow breath, trying to prepare myself for the conversation to come.

"I told you I was drunk. You don't need to worry about me slipping up again," he says, moving from the doorway to the edge of my bed. He sits down, watching me in the mirror as I put the cap on my perfume bottle.

My stomach tightens with his words, but I don't react to

them.

"Okay," I offer. Because I'm not going to do this with him. "Well, I was honest with Harry anyway. I told him that you were upset with me yesterday."

"Really?" Noah asks. He looks more curious than surprised as his eyebrows draw up.

"Yep," I say, shifting in my chair to face him. "I told him that the topic of my virginity—and my apparent need to *throw it away while drunk*—didn't bode too well with you."

Noah's lips crack into a smile. "What was his reaction?"

"He said that sounded like you. That you always care about that stuff."

"Well, he does know me," Noah replies.

"He told me that if that happened for us, him and me, he would want it to be special," I add.

Noah drops his gaze from mine, looking down at the comforter. "How did that make you feel?"

I roll my head, stretching out my neck with his question. "Do you want the long or short version?" I say, straightening back up in the chair.

"What do you think?"

"Right. Speak my mind. Well, it made me feel almost more nervous, honestly."

"Why?"

I let out a heavy sigh.

Another question.

I get up, pacing back and forth across my room. "Because … before, it was light and fun. I'm not saying that things weren't serious, but it felt like no matter what happened, Harry and I would be good. Then, you went all crazy on emotions and sex and love at school on Friday. And that made things confusing enough. Then, after the things you said … well, it didn't help. Anyway, I guess I just thought that I needed to lighten up. So, I tried. And I ended up getting a little carried away. Harry was a total gentleman. He didn't take advantage of the situation at any point even though I was basically asking him to."

"Harry's not that kind of guy," Noah replies.

"Then, after everything, Harry started talking to me about my first time, and now, I feel like it's this huge deal."

"Do you want to tell me what he said?" Noah asks, glancing back up to me.

I take in his warm brown eyes and know that I can talk to him. "He wants it to be special for me. He said that if or when anything happens, it should be romantic."

"He's right."

Noah's words take me by surprise.

I stop pacing. "I thought you would be upset."

"I told you, your body, your heart, your choice. Nothing is right or wrong, good or bad. You have to go with how you feel."

"But how do *you* feel?" I question, sitting down on the edge of the bed.

"The question is, how does what Harry said make you feel?" he corrects.

I divert my eyes, not wanting to answer him, but then I finally whisper, "It scares me, Noah."

"Why?"

"Because … everyone keeps telling me to have fun and not take life so seriously. Enjoy my time here. Relax. And it would be easy for me to, well, do that with Harry. I know you might not want to hear that, but it would be. I like him. He likes me. I think—I *know*—I would enjoy sex with him. But then just when I started to feel ready for it, he started adding in these emotions. This heaviness. That it needs to be special and right. What happened to *no fucks given* Harry? What happened to kissing a random girl at a pub? I mean, there wasn't romance in that, yet here we are."

"Mallory." Noah laughs, his chest bouncing. He shakes his head at me.

"What?" I huff.

"This has nothing to do with you wanting to see a different side of Harry. You're putting the blame on him to avoid your feelings."

I roll my eyes, annoyed with his assessment. "Fine, what is it about then?"

"Why don't you tell me?"

"I'm scared."

"About what?" Noah asks.

"I'm scared that things are getting too real. Too serious. And I feel like an ass for saying that."

"As relationships progress, it's normal to get scared. That's just a defense mechanism. Because at the end of the day, we all crave deep, meaningful connections."

I let my shoulders drop, knowing that he's right. "So, what do I do?"

"Just be mindful of your fears. You don't need to overcome them or run from them. Just watch them," he says.

"Watch them?"

What does that even mean?

"You just need a little balance. You can't have fun without seriousness. You can't have serious moments without fun ones too," he clarifies.

I scrunch up my nose, not liking his answer. "I feel like you and Harry are tricking me or something now."

"What do you mean?"

"Before, he was fun and light and easy. And you were this stubborn, grumpy butt. Now, things feel serious and intense with Harry, and you're so … *c'est la vie.*"

"You're not being tricked, Mal. But people can't just be one way. One thing. You know better than that."

"I guess I just make these boxes in my head to sort of organize things. Define people. And I had my boxes all figured out," I emphasize, wanting him to understand.

"But they aren't working," he states, raising his eyebrows at me.

"Nope."

"You have to be flexible." Noah smiles.

"I don't like being flexible," I say, standing up. I need to move. "I like being organized. See, I don't get it. I thought you would be mad that I told Harry. I'm surprised you just let me tell you that I told him and then let it slide."

"Why would I be upset?" he asks, cocking his head to the side.

"Well, it's sort of a revealing piece of information. I mean, it tells Harry that you care about me. The fact that you got upset shows you care."

Noah blinks a few times, dragging his eyes away from mine. "Harry already knows I care about you."

"Oh …"

"We're best friends. He knows me better than anyone. And I know him."

"I know you do."

"What are you thinking about now?" Noah asks, his lips pulling to the side.

"About?"

"About Harry. About love," he says.

My eyes go wide, and I let out a nervous laugh. "So many big questions tonight. Uh … honestly, I don't know. I guess I'm worried. I could let him in, Noah. I could really let him in. And I could fall for him. I already am." I shrug. "I care about him."

"I know you do." Noah nods, sucking in his cheeks.

"But I'm not sure if I should. You told me I would get hurt. That I would hurt him. I'm scared of that. Of moving too quickly. Too slowly. Sometimes, it feels like I'm scared of everything. Everyone always thinks I'm this strong, no-bullshit person."

"You sort of are." Noah grins.

"But I have doubts. I get scared."

"Do you feel like you have to pretend with other people?" Noah asks.

"People are always going to see what they want to. I don't care what people see. I guess I do care though about ... *who* sees me. If I really let someone in, it's a big deal."

"You're not alone in feeling that way, Mal. Everyone gets nervous about rejection."

"I guess you're right. Our actions can't be taken back. The things we do and say, they mean something. Your dad was right yesterday when he said everything had an effect. It has a cause, a reaction. It has meaning."

I watch Noah run his palm across his thigh, his hand shifting back and forth.

"Maybe you need to let go of that a little. It sounds like a lot of pressure."

"It sounds like the human reality," I disagree. "At least, it's my reality."

"You really do worry about a lot," he says, his lips pulling into a smile.

"Sometimes, I think you don't worry about anything," I offer.

"Do you really believe that?"

I roll my eyes. "Fine, tell me something you worry about. Enough about me." I sit back down on the bed, ready for this conversation to focus on Noah.

"I'm worried that this conversation hasn't helped you."

"It's helped me go in a circle," I tease.

"Has it?" Noah asks, his eyes squinting closed as he grins.

"No." I shake my head. "It has helped. You're easy to talk to—for the most part. And you're right. I build this stuff up in my head. I layer on so many fears and future meanings that I probably get lost in the simplicity of it."

"Look at you, boiling down a whole conversation into a sentence," Noah teases.

"Tell me something you actually worry about," I push.

"What fun would that be?" Noah says, his eyes meeting mine.

My mouth falls open. "Noah! You're telling me you get to ask me all these questions, making me go search through my heart and all these locked-up boxes to come up with an answer, and you won't even give me surface level here?" I ask pointedly.

"Annoying, isn't it?" Noah says, wiggling his eyebrows.

"You. Are. Infuriating," I say, picking up one of my pillows and smacking his arm with it.

He holds up his hands in defense, but I keep swatting him with the pillow. A second later, he takes the pillow out of my hand and tosses it off the bed.

"Hey," I scold, reaching for the pillow with a grin.

But Noah grabs my arm, pulling me away from it.

I try to wiggle toward it, but he holds both of my wrists in his hands, stopping me.

"I was having fun," I say, wanting him to let me go so I can keep hitting him with my pillow.

I try to pout but end up grinning at him. Because playing with Noah makes me forget about everything going on in my head.

"I could tell," Noah says, his face softening.

"I promise to be gentle," I tease.

"I have no doubt you'd be gentle," Noah replies in a sultry tone.

His voice captures my attention, and I connect my eyes to his. They're darker than before, but they have a sparkle of playfulness in them.

"But then again, you're always misbehaving."

"Am not," I argue, feeling breathless.

"No?" Noah asks, tilting his head to the side, not looking convinced.

"No. I'm always well behaved. You know that."

"Sure, out there you are," he says, nodding his head toward the door. "But in here, I'm not convinced."

"Is that a challenge?"

"No challenges." Noah smiles. "I just know you. You have very good manners."

"Thank you."

"You feel a lot though, Mal. And I think anyone you're with can see that. You're usually pretty good about staying in control. Obviously, not all the time. You do have your moments." He chuckles.

"I feel like I could say that about you though. Under your buttoned-up exterior, there's a lot of emotion. Passion even."

"Passion?" he asks.

"Yeah. It's obvious with things you care about. Or with your strongly felt opinions. You're usually very open to listening and not judging. You're a great listener. But I think there's also a huge vat of pent-up and held-back emotions and thoughts just waiting to explode."

"That doesn't sound pleasant," Noah says, his eyes flashing. "But you don't have to worry about that. I'm always in control."

"Mmhmm," I say, not convinced.

Because we both know he's not. And he especially wasn't on Friday night.

"If that passion were given," he says softly, "what do you think would be the result?"

"Well, that's a hard question. But in general, I think you shouldn't be so scared to show your passion. Because anytime you do, it's really beautiful. Like with football. Everyone watching can see how much you care. It's mesmerizing. Or like in art. I think your passion can inspire."

Noah scrunches up his nose. "Mesmerizing, huh?"

"Blinding," I emphasize, making myself sound even more dramatic.

"I'm glad we talked," Noah says, getting up.

"Me too." I smile. "Now, shoo. I need to finish getting ready for my date."

Mr. Brooks
7PM

WHEN THE DOORBELL rings, I check myself in the mirror, adjusting the dress at my shoulders. I turn to my side, running my hands down over the fabric before walking out of my bedroom and down to the front door, which Gene is in the process of opening.

"Hello, Harry," Gene says, his back to me.

"Hey …" Harry starts. But he quickly goes silent. His eyes drag their way up my legs and over my torso and chest, meeting my eyes.

Gene turns, following his gaze.

"Well, you look lovely this evening, Mallory." Gene smiles but then turns back to Harry, flustered. "I'm sorry,

Harry. I'm afraid I've just nicked your line."

Harry's lips pull into a smile. His eyes briefly flick over to Gene before returning to me again. "Don't worry, Mr. Williams. A girl can never be told she's beautiful too many times. Mallory, you look absolutely stunning."

My heart practically stops at his words.

Because Gene has finally shifted out from between us, and I take in all of Harry.

He has on a three-button suit that is perfectly tailored to fit his long, trim figure. Under the suit is a blue and gray striped spread-collared shirt that makes his blue eyes look even more brilliant.

Between his slicked back hair and strong jaw, I find myself conflicted on what part of him to admire first.

Which piece of his skin is more daunting.

I flush, knowing that I've been staring at him for a little too long.

And Harry knows it. His eyes have been locked with mine.

They're magnetic tonight, and even as I thank Gene, I can't seem to break his gaze.

Harry wraps his arm through mine when Helen's voice echoes in my ears. I turn back toward her, not sure what she even said.

I glance up to Harry, wondering if he knows, but he's just smiling back at me.

"Mallory?" Helen says.

"Yes?" I turn myself toward her, willing myself to focus on what she's saying.

"I said, I'd like a photo," she states like she already said it before.

And she probably did.

"Yeah, of course," I agree, looking up to Harry to make

sure he's okay with it.

But his focus is on Helen.

"Helen, they aren't off to formal," Gene objects.

"Hush," she says, her fingers messing with the screen on her phone.

"A photo would be great," Harry says.

He pulls me close against his side, and I can't help but stare at him as the flash goes off.

"One more," Helen instructs.

I turn toward her and smile because I know that's what she wants.

"All right, you two should be off," Gene says, moving between us and Helen.

"Bye," I mumble as Harry takes my hand, opening the front door again.

"Look at them, so lovely," I hear Helen say as I step outside.

And before I know it, a car door is being opened.

"Harry?" I question, glancing between him and the driver.

"I want to take you somewhere special," Harry replies, walking me to the car.

I slip into the seat, and then the door shuts, Harry moving around the car to the other side.

"This is too much," I insist as he slides in next to me.

Because I'm already feeling light headed. Harry looks beautiful.

Like unworldly beautiful.

He's put together in a way that I've never seen before.

And there's a different energy about him tonight.

He's quieter. *Sexier.*

Something is radiating off his skin that I haven't felt before. He's not bantering back and forth with me. Making silly expressions.

Making jokes.

"It isn't," he disagrees. "It's time you're taken for a proper night out. I want to show you how important you are to me. I want to let you in more, into my world."

I search Harry's eyes, trying to make sense of this.

"I thought we were going out for a simple Sunday night date," I reply as the car starts moving.

Harry shakes his head, taking my hand into his. "We ate at a modest Italian restaurant. We ate dessert at a diner. We rode on a tour bus. We've done simple. And it was fun. But I thought it was time for something different."

"Well, I like different." I smile, running my hand across his jacket. "And I especially like this suit."

Harry's lips pull into a smile. "I had a feeling you might," he says, dropping his lips down onto mine.

It's a soft kiss, and my fingers glide across his shoulders.

He brings his hand onto my cheek, and I want to deepen our kiss, opening my mouth to him.

Harry doesn't miss my invitation. He tilts his head, letting his tongue dance with mine, his fingers falling from my cheek to my exposed neck and shoulders.

I try to kiss him harder, but he keeps his mouth gentle on mine.

His fingers lightly graze across my skin, making each movement feel more intense.

Every piece of skin he touches, from the center of my throat to the tip of my collarbone, tingles with energy. Goose bumps rise on my arms, sending a shiver through me. And I know that Harry feels it. Because his fingers stop.

His hands slip up into my hair, and his lips get more frantic.

"I'm not sure we're going to make it out of the car," Harry whispers in my ear before trailing his mouth down across my neck. He sucks against my skin, causing it to flush.

"I think we should skip dinner altogether," I insist, biting my lip. Because I want to be out of this dress.

There's too much fabric between us, and my whole body knows it.

And it's revolting.

I can feel in the pit of my stomach what my body wants.

And that's for Harry's hand to trail up my legs.

For his hand to slip across my exposed ribs.

"I think you'd let me deflower you right here and now," he teases, his lips moving back up my jaw.

"It would make for a good story," I insist, closing my eyes as he tugs at my lip.

"I'm not sure how I'd feel about having a third party present," Harry counters, his eyes flicking up to mine.

I glance toward the front of the car, feeling a little guilty for being so hot and bothered with Harry's driver present.

I groan, letting my shoulders droop. "I can't help it. Your lips do something to me. And my body just reacts."

Harry chuckles, his blue eyes shining. "Do you think your body can behave itself long enough to make it through dinner?"

I roll my eyes, pressing my hand against his chest. "If it's forced to," I mumble, looking away from him.

But Harry brings his fingers to my chin, turning my face back to his and pressing his lips against mine.

I'M NOT SURE how long we've been in the car for or when it even stopped, but Harry breaks his lips apart from mine.

"I think it's time to get out of the car now," he whispers as the door opens.

A second later, I'm being helped out of the car, and Harry is back at my side, taking my hand in his. I pat my hair down with my free hand, knowing that it probably has been, at the least, mussed from Harry's hands constantly in it during the ride. My hand slips down onto my lips, tracing around them.

I feel like I've been lying out in the sun for too long.

Everything seems out of focus.

The colors off. Too bright.

I tilt my head back, looking up to take in the building that we were dropped in front of. Exposed brick encases oversized windows, and industrial metal reflects out from behind the glass walls that make up the front of the building.

"Wow," I gasp, appreciating the architecture of the place.

"It used to be an old hotel," Harry says, hearing the admiration in my voice.

"It's beautiful," I reply.

It's classic Chelsea architecture.

A doorman opens the door as Harry escorts me inside.

The restaurant gives off a warm glow, the deep red brick closing in the large interior. Three large light fixtures break up the dining room, the circular lights illuminating the space. There's a staircase that leads up to a loft, the rich wood looking like a remnant from the hotel that was too beautiful to get rid of.

I gawk at the space.

"I've seen a lot of beautiful restaurants, Harry, but this place is really something," I whisper, leaning into his arm.

"It's a great place," he responds, easily pulling me in the direction of the hostess.

But when we get to her, he doesn't stop. He continues walking past her. She glances at us, her narrow eyes moving to his lapel, and then she picks up the phone, tipping her chin in acknowledgment.

"Where are we going?" I ask.

I look around, wondering if maybe he reserved a special

table.

But wouldn't we still have to check in with the hostess to be seated?

I glance at his lapel, noticing a pin on it that I must have missed earlier.

"The restaurant isn't the only cool part," Harry says as we walk down a long hallway, up a set of stairs, and around a corner. "This place also happens to have one of the top wine bars in all of London. But those are just the parts of it that are open to the public."

"The public?" I ask as Harry stops us in front of a thick, engraved elevator and presses a button.

"Yes, you see, upstairs, hidden in plain sight, is one of the most exclusive clubs in London."

I furrow my brow at him as the elevator chimes, and the doors open.

"Welcome, Mr. Brooks," the elevator attendant says, startling me.

I glance over to Harry, not believing this is actually happening.

Mr. Brooks?

I stay silent as we ride in the elevator, wanting to talk in private without someone else a foot away from us.

Harry squeezes my hand as the elevator chimes again, the doors parting.

"Welcome to The Arrington."

I take in the wood-paneled room as we step off the elevator. There are numerous tables and chairs with fragrant floral arrangements on every available surface.

"The Arrington?" I ask, wishing Harry would just explain.

"The Arrington is a private club that my family belongs to. Come on. I'll give you a tour."

I want to respond to Harry, but there is so much to take

in that I don't have time to say anything. One moment, we're in what looks like an oversized sitting room, and the next, he's leading me into a cozy room, featuring leather couches and a long, formal bar.

"There are numerous rooms and endless corners of this place to explore. This is the private bar," Harry says, motioning around him.

"How many rooms are there?" I ask, glancing to a group of men seated on the couches, heavy crystal glasses resting in their hands.

Harry blows air out of his mouth, his eyebrows rising. "There are endless rooms. There's a billiards room, a smoking room, a space for dining, a game room. There are multiple floors, and each room is unique. The rooms can be used freely or rented out by the club members for private events."

"Do you come here often?"

"I like to when I can," he says, taking me into another room. "There are books and drinks and always interesting, high-profile people here. It's my oasis."

"I thought that was Marco's place?" I ask, thinking about his secret Italian hideaway.

"It is. But it's sort of a two-worlds thing. I'm just regular Harry there," he replies, his eyes on me.

"And here?"

"And here, I'm Mr. Brooks, the son of a shipping tycoon, set to inherit everything." Harry searches my face, his lips twitching at the corner. "I've made us special dinner plans, but we have time for a drink first."

Harry shows me two more rooms, one themed solely around an African safari.

There are heavy rattan chairs with deep cushions and paintings of game animals. There's a mixture of timeless and modern pieces, giving off a grand library feel as opposed to what you might think of when you imagine a *club*.

Before I realize it, we're back in the bar, and Harry's pulling me down onto a sofa. He unbuttons his suit jacket and the top button on his shirt, looking relaxed.

"You really feel at home here, don't you?"

Harry smiles at me as the bartender comes over to us.

"As you requested, Mr. Brooks," the man says with a formal nod. He sets down a champagne flute and a crystal glass filled with what smells like scotch.

Harry hands me the flute before taking his own glass, leaning back into the sofa.

"I do. Any member can bring guests here to entertain. My father usually graces this place when he's in town, sometimes before he even makes it home," Harry says, his jaw tightening. "But it's probably one of the best investments my family's made. Everyone who is anyone in society circles comes here. Plus … I don't know … I like it. It's sort of a second home."

I hold out my flute to him. "Thank you for bringing me here."

Harry smiles, clinking his glass against mine before taking a heavy sip of his drink.

"So, tell me, what do you like about it?" I ask, glancing around.

A couple quietly slips into the room, moving to sit at the bar. The woman has on high heels and a designer dress, the man with her wearing an exquisitely tailored suit.

I can smell expensive perfume wafting toward us as she shifts on the stool.

"I like that everyone here, in some way, is like me. Most of the families or individuals who belong are obviously well off. And you get the international club members who come when they're in town for business."

I take a sip of my champagne, trying to absorb Harry's

words. "But I thought you said this sort of stuff feels suffocating. Or is it different from being at your family's country house?"

Harry nods, understanding. "It's different. I know a lot of guys here. Though not to the same scale as me, a lot of them feel the pressure to go into the family business. There's a sense of loyalty and discretion that goes with my name. And I'm not the only one to experience that. I think, here … most people feel like that. They can relate."

"So, you have friends here?" I grin.

"I have a lot of acquaintances." Harry smiles back at me, taking another sip of his scotch.

"Have you brought Noah or Mohammad? Or is this another one of *your* places?"

"I've brought Noah. We played billiards and had a few drinks. It was chill, but I don't know." Harry shrugs.

"It has to be hard. Feeling like you live in two worlds," I say, noticing Harry's knee bounce.

He glances at me, pushing a piece of hair behind my ear and giving me a quick kiss.

But when he pulls back, I can tell he's thinking about what I said.

"It's a mixture of things, I suppose. Sometimes, I feel like a scared little schoolboy who gets told off by his professors. I can't … stand up to my dad. Yet, at the same time, there's this and my family and my expected duty to them."

"It's kind of strange." I laugh, bringing the champagne back to my lips. "The fact that we're in high school. That we deal with professors and mean girls and pass notes and can't kiss after class. But then, like you said, here we are, at a place like this. There is your family and their expectations. Do you ever feel like you just want to scream at your parents and force them to pick one?"

"Pick what?" Harry says, tilting his head at me.

"Adult or child," I clarify. "If they treat you like a child, at least then they have a right to check if you've done your homework or give you a curfew. But then they say you're becoming an adult and you need to act like one, and they want you to talk a certain way and expect you to fulfill these duties. So, which do they want? It's like, right now, either way with your parents, you lose."

"That's the way it is," Harry replies, looking around the room. "I'm a child of ... a bad man who happens to be successful. And my future depends on maintaining his legacy."

Harry downs the rest of his drink before watching as I take another sip. His eyes stay on my lips, even after I put my glass on the table, and I instantly wish we were alone.

"Come on," Harry says, extending his hand. "I want to show you my favorite room."

Harry leads us down a long hallway, slipping into a room with oversized windows and a high ceiling. "This is one of my favorite spots. The East Asian room."

I glance around, taking in the statues and artwork lining the walls. Red and black embroidered fabric covers a group of couches clustered together. There's a large mural hanging on one wall. Candles are lit on every table, giving the room a warm glow.

In the midst of everything, there's a dining table, set for two.

"Harry ..." I start.
He did this for us?
For me?

I look over at him with disbelief, but he just smiles, escorting me further into the room. He pulls out the chair for me, waiting for me to sit down.

"You planned all of this?" I stutter, suddenly feeling very

overwhelmed.

By the size of this room.

By the enormity of his gesture.

"Don't get too flustered. I just put in the request," Harry says, sitting down across from me.

There's a bottle of champagne chilling in an ice bucket next to the table, and I see Harry glance up at the doorway over my shoulder and nod at someone.

I turn around, seeing a waiter enter the room. He pours us two glasses of sparkling water before popping open the champagne and filling our flutes. I stay silent as he serves us.

"Harry, how are we allowed to be drinking here?" I question, leaning across the table as the waiter leaves.

"It's just how things are here." Harry shrugs. "Besides, I requested it. And after all, this is my family's contribution to the club."

"Wait, what is?" I ask.

"This room," Harry replies, gesturing around us.

"This room?" I question.

"Yes, my father had it curated for the club to enjoy. It's his personal collection, shipped straight from our home in Shanghai."

"That's …"

"Cool? Mad? Extravagant?" Harry says, attempting to finish my sentence. "It's all of the above. But I like it regardless. Despite my father being an ass, he's always had an eye for these sorts of things."

"Which explains your house," I reply, thinking about Harry's beautiful home. "Have you talked to your dad since … everything?"

"A bit. Here and there. Quite sporadically really," Harry says quickly. "Usually, he's upset over something, so I prefer that we don't talk."

"Nice of him to just check in," I state, shaking my head.

The thought of Harry's dad makes my blood boil. I glance around the room, wondering how someone who could see and curate so much beauty could be so cruel.

"Let's not talk about my dad," Harry says, spinning the ring on his pinkie finger around in a circle.

I nod, taking a sip of the champagne, trying to calm my insides when the waiter is back, setting down a plate in front of us. I look at the plate, confused, before bringing my eyes up to Harry.

"It's pizza?" I question, looking at the small, beautifully cut square.

"It's flatbread à la margherita actually," Harry replies with a straight face.

I narrow my eyes at him, waiting for him to crack.

"Fine"—he smiles—"it's pizza. But it's just an appetizer. We've got a whole night filled with delicious courses to come."

"Some things never change." I laugh, biting my lip. "Let me guess ... the second course will be something accompanied by homemade crisps?"

"I'm still a secondary schoolboy, Mallory. What did you expect? Caviar? A simple, gently cooked white asparagus atop a delicate quail egg, sprinkled with Parmesan? We aren't that fancy, are we?" he banters, his blue eyes sending butterflies into my stomach.

I raise my eyebrows. "Of course not." I grin.

The second course *is* actually fancier than the first. It's a lovely roasted squash soup, topped with chili oil and toasted pumpkin seeds.

"You know, it's kind of weird. I sort of feel at home here," I say, taking the first sip of my soup. "This reminds me of New York."

"What, private clubs?" Harry asks.

"No. I mean, I'm used to getting dressed up. Going out for nice dinners. All of today made me feel sort of nostalgic. Going for brunch, exploring the city. Shopping and having a coffee. I felt so much like myself. And now, here, tonight … you just … you make me really happy. You're always surprising me. I think I underestimate you sometimes."

Harry picks up his champagne, bringing it to his lips. "Maybe you do it so that way, if I fall short, you won't be disappointed," he offers.

"I think I forget sometimes that we have a lot in common. We're different, obviously, but we're kind of the same. We come from the same world. I know yours is a bit beyond mine. But we have families who are in the center of things. With business. Socially," I reply.

"Is it weird, staying at a warm home like Noah's?" Harry asks, catching me off guard.

"No." I shake my head. "I love it. I think I want that for myself, honestly. And that's not to say my home isn't warm. It's just …"

"Not like that," Harry finishes.

"No, it's not," I say, thinking about Noah's house. About Gene and Helen.

"I want that too, you know," he says, shifting in his seat.

"You have that with them, Harry."

He grins at me. "I guess I do. They *are* quite taken with me. Well, at least they haven't thrown me out yet."

"You know they never would."

"I'm not their son, Mallory."

"You're close enough."

Harry thinks about it for a moment. "I guess Noah and I are like brothers."

"But?" I ask, noticing his hesitation.

"But nothing. I guess I just ... I am close to them. But it's good to have distance too," he offers, pushing his soup away.

I set down my spoon, thinking about his words. "That distance is a defense mechanism, isn't it?"

His eyes flick up to mine. I can feel the intensity in his gaze, but his face remains soft, his jaw not setting.

"Maybe I push people away because I'm terrified."

"You're scared?" I ask, my conversation with Noah coming into my head.

"I'm scared all the time," Harry says, not flinching or looking away. "You seem surprised by that."

"I am a little surprised."

"I have the courage to admit it," Harry replies with ease. "It's easy to get hurt by the people who aren't supposed to hurt you. It's easy to get let down. So, if you don't care, what's it matter?"

My gaze flicks across Harry's relaxed face, my stomach twisting. Not because what he thinks is wrong, but because I've felt that way before. "I was sort of talking to Noah about that today."

"About what?"

"About you." I flush. "About how things are changing between us. I think that they're getting more serious. It makes me nervous. For the same reasons."

Harry's lips pull at the corners as his eyes soften. "I swear, Noah would make a fine shrink."

I can't help but laugh at his response. "He does have a way of helping you sort through things, doesn't he?"

"He does," Harry agrees. "Do you think things are getting more serious?"

My stomach rolls with his question. "I think they could be," I reply, trying to avoid the subject. Because admitting it would mean that we'd both have to finally recognize it. It would mean that I couldn't push the seriousness away anymore.

It's here, staring across the table at me.

"I'm not scared of you leaving, Mallory."

"Shouldn't you be?"

Harry shakes his head.

I blink a few times, looking down at my bowl of soup.

"I guess we can sort of see each other anytime we want. It's not like we can't visit. But how are we supposed to have a relationship, being apart?"

"I don't have the answers. But I do know that I like you," Harry says, extending his hand out across the table.

"I like you too." I take his hand, my fingers running across his palm.

"We have something, Mallory."

I glance up to Harry, finding his gaze on our hands. He's watching my fingers dance across his palm with a smile on his face.

"That sounds serious."

"You're meant to be in my life. I've never believed in ... anything really. But I believe in you."

"Harry," I push. Because his words are just going to make this harder.

We're going to fall.

And we're going to get hurt.

"No, I think you need to hear this." Harry pulls his hand away from mine. He gets up from his chair and moves around the table until he's hunched down next to me. He turns my chair to face him, taking both of my hands into his.

"This isn't necessary," I say, tensing up. I have so many emotions flowing through me.

"It is. Mallory, we have a cracking time together, and you've been there for me, as a friend. I do take notice of it. I know I laugh things off, but it's important to me. *You're* important to me."

I know he's right. I have been there for him. And even though he laughs most things off, I know that he appreciates it. And in so many ways, he's been there for me. Which is what makes this so hard.

He's looking up at me through his delicate blond lashes.

"Harry, why did you bring me here tonight?"

"To impress you," he replies smugly.

"That's not the truth." I smile down at him, tilting my head with question.

"No, it's not. I brought you here to see what you'd make of it. I wanted to let you in more. To show you everything that goes along with being a Brooks."

"Well, if being a Brooks gets you this delicious champagne, it can't be that bad," I tease with a wink.

I pick up my glass, taking a small sip. Harry's looking back at me with surprise. But then his eyes start to sparkle as his mouth sets into a pleased smile.

"Maybe you should give me a taste." His gaze falls down to my lips.

I bring my mouth to his, my hands instantly finding their way into his hair. Harry tilts his chin up, opening his mouth to me.

I kiss him, letting him taste my lips.

The champagne.

He breaks his lips from mine, rising back up and moving into his seat again.

I smile across the table at him, but my lips straighten as I switch my tone. "Do you think we're the same, you and me?"

"I think you have a lot more on your mind than just being a girlfriend or getting good marks," Harry replies and then takes another spoonful of soup from his bowl.

"Are you trying to say most girls are boring?" I question, wondering where he's going with this.

Harry shakes his head. "What I'm trying to say is that I've never met anyone like you, Mallory. Not to bring up my ex, but with Olivia, I knew she would love this place because of the status. She wanted a boyfriend; it was all she cared about. Looking good. Being seen out. Which, at the time, I didn't mind. But it never crossed my mind to take her to Marco's. It was too … personal. Too low key for her."

My stomach tightens at his comment.

"I think you underestimate Olivia," I reply, for some reason defending her. Because even though I don't know their history, I know that Olivia cares for Harry.

"I used to wonder what it would be like if I had a girl-friend who was a part of the club. Someone who didn't care about it the way that Olivia did. But then I figured that even if we fit together here, it would be weird with my mates. I never thought I'd meet someone who fit in both places. Bringing you here, I wasn't nervous. I knew we'd have fun. But we also have fun in class and on tour buses, at diners and at Marco's."

Harry's words pour out of his mouth like one long thought, and it takes me by surprise. How calmly he came to those conclusions. How he thinks that he has to choose one or the other. His gaze slips to the doorway as the waiter comes back in.

He picks up our soup, setting down a clean white plate with a beautifully arranged pile of food—a circular base of rice with drops of sauce scattered around it, vegetables layered across the top.

"I think I'd have fun with you just about anywhere," I reply when the waiter leaves us alone again.

"I know. The car ride here proved that." He grins, shooting me a wink.

"I didn't mean that kind of fun," I say, my mouth falling open.

I watch Harry across the table, digging into his meal.

"So, I know you always have things on your mind. Tell me what you think about."

"Will you tell me too then?"

"Always," Harry replies quickly, his eyes flicking up to me.

"Well … I do like the idea of living in a city. At least for a while once I graduate."

"To build your name." Harry nods, understanding.

"Mmhmm." I smile. "And I want to travel. But not to the annoying touristy places. Sorry, that sounded bad. What I meant is that I want to go to places and actually experience them."

"Like?" Harry prompts.

"Like I want to see reindeer. I want to cook outside in Peru. Did you know that they make these little ovens out of dirt, cook the potatoes in them, and eat them right there, on the side of the mountain?" I reply, thinking about everything I'd like to do. Everything I want to see.

"Really?" Harry says, cocking his head to the side with interest.

I nod, picturing myself there. Overlooking the endless hills. Eating something straight from the earth. It's one of the most foreign ideas to me, but that's what makes it sound so amazing.

"I want to get so lost that I can't remember who I am anymore."

"Just to go back to New York?" Harry asks.

"I need balance in my life, I guess. Lose yourself, find yourself. Sleep in the dirt, dine in the sky. That kind of thing."

"So, what you're saying is that you're going to drag me up a mountain to see alpacas, have us sleep in the grass with them, and then beg me to take you to a five-star hotel for a spa weekend afterward?" Harry chuckles, sitting up straighter in his chair.

"Exactly." I grin.

"I think I could get on board with that. Though I'm not sure about this hiking stuff. What if you left me at the base of the mountain, and I'd have a glass of champagne waiting for you when you came back down to the bottom?"

"How about you come up with me, and I'd let you sneak a flask?"

"Deal." Harry nods, taking a long drink of his champagne. He sets down his fork, and his eyes drift off as he thinks. "We could just graduate and go."

"Really?" I ask, trying to figure out if Harry's just being idealistic or if he's really offering it.

"I'm going to have to start working at some point. Maybe if I take the initiative of figuring out my future, I can pretend like what I'm actually doing is my choice."

"Fine, I'll play along. What would we do?" I ask curiously.

"Well, we would obviously take a gap year. We could travel. Spend time in New York for you," he replies seriously.

"I've been in New York enough." I laugh. Because if we're hypothetically taking a gap year, I want to visit new places.

"We could work our way around the world then."

"Backpack through Asia?"

"Five-star hotel through Asia." Harry chuckles.

He's almost glowing across the table, and it makes me smile.

"Right, continue."

"We could go to an island, just the two of us," he says, his eyes drawing up to mine. "Go sleep in an igloo."

"And find the reindeer," I say with excitement.

"I'm sure we could." Harry nods.

"But what about London? You love it here."

"I do. But traveling for a bit sounds freeing."

"Aren't you supposed to do a gap year with friends? New place, new girl. Come back … experienced?" I ask. Because I sort of thought that was the point.

"I feel like you should know better by now. Besides not always being the best boyfriend, I actually do like it," Harry says, his forehead creasing.

"You like what?"

"Having … I don't know … one person who's yours. For you," he says, clearing his throat.

I sit back in my chair, searching his face. He looks a little uncomfortable under my gaze, and it brings a grin to my lips.

"Are you a romantic, Harry Brooks?"

His nose squishes up as he smiles back at me, his brows rising. "I always thought not, but good God, look at me now. I've become total mush in the presence of an angel. What's happened to me?"

"Stop." I giggle, watching him become more expressive and sarcastic with every word.

"No, I think you're right. What *has* become of the once highly sought after party boy?" Harry teases.

"You've found someone." I smile.

"I've found someone incredibly special," Harry replies warmly.

He holds my gaze, and I feel that fear again chewing at my stomach, but I push it away.

"This actually makes me less freaked out," I admit, trying to relax.

"Hearing that I'm taken by you?"

"Hearing that you see us staying together. Being friends. Traveling together. It means a lot, Harry."

"Well, if we're traveling together, I don't want to just be your mate. Unless there are major benefits involved." He smirks.

"You always get what you want." I grin back.

"I do," Harry agrees.

I take a bite of my food, thinking about everything we've talked about. "So, the future is ours?" I ask, trying to pinpoint exactly what our conversation means.

"I think it could be. We could create something together, you know?"

Harry says it so casually, and it almost makes me think that he isn't serious. But I know that he is. And just like he said, he'll downplay anything to try not to make it a big deal.

To try to avoid being hurt.

"I like the idea," I offer with a smile. "But you know that I will have to go to a university."

"Are you only looking at universities in New York?" Harry questions.

"I mean, I've marked a few business schools there. Obviously, London has great ones too," I add.

"They do."

"Will you go to university?"

"Depends on how things go. Maybe I'll go straight into the business. Or maybe I'll have to attend first." Harry sounds unsure, and it doesn't seem like he really cares which way it goes. Which isn't surprising for someone who feels like they don't have control over their life.

"You don't have to do anything that you don't want to do. You know that, right?" I pull Harry's hand back into mine, lacing our fingers together.

"You know I do. If I don't attend university, my dad will

likely send me out to Shanghai to work under someone else in the company. Learn the trade. It wouldn't be the end of the world, I guess. Even though Dad's always in Shanghai, I actually like it. It's a cool city," Harry says, squeezing my hand.

"It really is." I nod.

"You've been?"

"I went once. It was magical. Everything is so modern. I love the way that they mix tradition with this super hip, progressive viewpoint."

"I know." Harry nods. "I like the culture. Maybe we should run away to Shanghai. Leave my parents and their mess in London and start over there."

"It's an idea," I agree, taking another sip of my champagne. "I didn't realize you liked traveling so much."

"At first, I didn't. I hated being dragged from one numbing event to another, but my parents were always adamant that I show my face every once in a while. But I started going out by myself, just walking. It's interesting, the places you end up. And despite hating my name, it's known. So, I always have people there to take me out and show me a good time if I want."

"Because of who you are?"

Harry nods. "It's expected. A nice courtesy extended out from other families."

"It sounds like it might be awkward," I comment, thinking about what it would be like to hang out with someone because our families had sort of arranged it.

"You'd think, but we've all done it. Plus, it makes traveling along with my parents a bit more entertaining. And it ensures that the circle goes round and round. My dad actually messaged me today about that," Harry says, clearing his throat again.

I furrow my brow. "He messaged you about what?"

"One of his client's sons is coming into town, and I'm expected to … show him a good time," he says hesitantly.

"When?" I ask, taken aback.

"Tonight."

"Tonight?" I cough, surprised at the suddenness.

"Yeah, I know. Not much of a warning," Harry says, not sounding at all excited.

"What exactly does a *good time* entail?"

"Do you really want to know?" Harry smirks.

"I don't know …" I stutter, my stomach knotting up.

"I'm joking," Harry cuts in, taking my hand. "No, it's just the usual. I'll bring him here. Take him out to a club. There's always a party. It's just a matter of what kind of a good time he wants to have."

"Won't that be weird?"

"This wasn't a suggestion from my father. It's my duty. My one use," he says, his lips pulling back in a flat line.

I open my mouth to say something, anything, but words don't come to me.

Harry must see that I'm struggling because he starts speaking again, "Sounds different when I actually say it out loud to someone." He shakes his head. "Anyway, he made it clear. His dad's important to our business, and my dad has booked him a suite at the Mandarin as a courtesy."

My eyes widen as I think about him going out tonight. "Do you have to go soon?" I ask, still feeling unsure.

"He's here, visiting a university and having dinner with alumni. I'm meeting him at the hotel for drinks at half past ten."

"Wow," is all I can manage to say.

"Yep," is Harry's response.

"Well, are you excited?" I ask, trying to brighten things.

Because I trust Harry, and it's obvious that he's not in the mood to party. This is something he's doing for his dad.

"He has a reputation."

"For?" I ask.

"Partying." Harry laughs.

"Like, drugs?"

Because if it were just drinking, I don't think Harry would have mentioned it.

"Yeah." He nods.

"Well, that's not exactly what I wanted to hear," I say solemnly. My heart starts racing in my chest at the thought of him going out tonight.

"Mallory, I don't dick with drugs."

"But he does," I state.

"He does."

"This isn't good," I say, my brows dipping in.

Because I don't like this.

I don't like this at all.

"I'll take him out, and it will be fine. Promise. Don't let the fancy hotel fool you. He isn't high class. Hopefully, we'll just get a drink at the hotel and end up at a pub. Or maybe he'll want to see the club and play some billiards," Harry replies, pushing his plate away.

"You're almost convincing," I say, knowing that he's just trying to calm my nerves. "But if he likes to party, he's going to want to go out."

"Worst case, we hit up a club. He'll chat up some girls, get plastered, and then I'll take him back to the hotel. He'll wake up hungover and then be on his jolly way. Dad will be off my back, and all will be right in the world," Harry replies, downing the rest of his drink.

The waiter is back, clearing out plates and pouring us fresh glasses of champagne.

Harry's face has hardened, his jaw tightly set.

"Harry, you have to let me back in. You put on this front about these things. It's okay to admit that it's wrong. That you're unhappy. That you ... hurt."

I search his eyes, wanting him to know that it's okay to be upset.

"I don't hurt with you, Mallory. I don't hurt with Noah, Mohammad, or the Williams. I'm not some tragedy. I just feel stuck sometimes."

I nod, knowing that I need to drop the subject for to-night.

"Come on," Harry says, abruptly getting up. For a mi-nute, I wonder if he's going to say we have to leave, but he extends his hand out to me. "Let's move to the sofa. Dessert is on its way."

I take Harry's hand and grab my champagne with the other and follow him to the couch. He easily falls down into it, pulling me against his side. Since he's getting comfortable, I decide to kick off my shoes, tucking my feet under me as I take a drink.

"Shanghai. Traveling. I like the idea of it," I say, my gaze moving across the decorated walls.

"Really?" Harry asks, his voice breaking.

I turn to take in his expression. He looks ... hopeful.

"Yeah, I do. I love spending time with you. And it sounds like an amazing adventure."

"I don't know," Harry starts, his lips pulling into a smile. "What happens if you get sick of me? Try to poison me with a scorpion bite in the desert? Abandon me at the Four Seasons spa? What will I do then?" Harry's tongue moves across his lip.

He's beaming.

"Well, scorpions freak me out, so you're safe there. And as

far as being abandoned at the spa, I can think of worse fates," I tease.

"You're serious?" Harry asks.

And I know he's not talking about the scorpions or spa.

He's talking about us, together, in the future.

I hold his gaze as the waiter comes back, putting a huge arrangement in front of us. I examine it, realizing that it's a bouquet of chocolate-covered strawberries. He lays out two napkins and sets down two delicate china plates onto the coffee table before nodding at us and leaving in silence. I look over to Harry, feeling him sit up straighter.

"I didn't bring you a bouquet of flowers tonight because I wanted to give you them as dessert."

My stomach tingles with his words, and I instantly press my lips against his. His hands find the small of my back, pulling me toward him.

I'm not sure if it's our conversation or the champagne or how sweet Harry is being, but an overwhelming sensation floods through my body. He opens his mouth to me as I sit on his lap. It's not the most appropriate thing I've ever done, but I don't care.

I hear the door close and break my face away, looking up.

"It's fine," Harry mumbles, pulling me back down to his lips.

I dig my nails into his shoulders as his hands move down my back to my butt. His fingers press into me, forming a warm pressure deep in my belly, and I moan at the sensation.

"That's not fair," Harry whispers in between kisses.

"It feels too good. I can't help it," I reply, kissing across his jaw.

His hands slide around my body, up my stomach, and to my chest. His fingers dance against my exposed skin before dipping below the fabric of my dress.

"Harry," I mumble, feeling light headed. But I glance to the door, afraid someone will walk in at any minute.

"Don't worry; we won't be interrupted," he insists as he slips me off of his lap. He pushes me flat on the sofa, parting my legs so he can lie between them, on top of me.

"This is so inappropriate," I try to insist. But for some reason, the words come out as a giggle as Harry kisses across my chest.

He sucks lightly against my neck before pulling back.

"It's not that bad," he says, shaking his head. "Here, have some dessert."

He leans up enough to grab a chocolate-covered strawberry, propping himself onto his elbow to feed it to me with his free hand. He lets it hover over my mouth, watching as I part my lips and bite into it. His eyes are all over me, looking between my hair and lips to the half-eaten strawberry in his fingers. I chew, letting the flavors take over my mouth.

"Are you going to share?" Harry says, dropping his mouth down onto mine.

He sucks on my lips, twisting his tongue with mine. All I can taste is Harry, chocolate, and the fresh strawberry. At some point, he must drop the rest of the strawberry onto the plate because both of his hands are on my body. He grabs my butt, grinding against me. I moan into his mouth, leaning up slightly.

"Harry," I insist, feeling flushed.

"I'm sorry. I can barely control myself when I'm around you."

"Are you sure no one's going to come in?" I ask, holding his blue eyes.

"I promise they won't. I gave instructions for dessert to be delivered and then for the waiter to be dismissed."

"What if a stranger walks in?" I ask, trying to think rationally.

Harry shakes his head. "There's a marking on the door. It's the one rule of the club. If the marking is up, you can't go in. The room is in use. Usually, it's meant for the purpose of keeping a meeting private, but …"

"So, you thought you were going to get lucky?" I ask, raising my eyebrows at him, trying to stay serious.

But it's too hard, and I crack a smile.

"I'm already lucky," he replies, dropping his lips back down on me.

He laces his hand through mine, pulling it above my head while his other wraps around my waist. I wiggle under him, pushing my body up toward his.

Harry must notice because he pushes back, sending a shiver through me.

"For someone who is always worried about getting caught, your body sure has other ideas," Harry groans out.

The gravelly sound of his voice goes straight to my head, and before I know it, I'm pulling his shirt out from his pants, so my hands can press against his bare skin. My dress slides up my thigh as Harry's hand explores my legs, his fingers tickling against my skin. I bite his lip, trying to keep myself under control.

"Does that feel good?" Harry smiles against my mouth.

"Mmhmm," is all I can manage to say because I'm so focused on his fingers and where they are headed.

They move painfully slow, inch by inch, working their way up and down my thighs.

"Harry," I beg, pushing my hips up against his.

Because he can't keep doing this to me. It's torture.

"Is this what you want?" he asks, his hand coming all the way up to between my legs.

His finger moves my underwear to the side before running freely across my skin.

I gasp at the feeling, my eyes fluttering open the same time that Harry's do. His mouth falls open as his fingers move between my legs.

I pull his shirt up, sliding my hand down his pants. When I finally feel him, it sends another shudder through my body.

"Fuck," he whispers, attacking my lips.

I can feel his whole body move with my hand, and the rhythm is overwhelming.

His fingers, his smell, the way we both taste like champagne and strawberries.

When I can't take it anymore, when the sensation becomes so overpowering, I let it go. And all I feel are rolling waves of pleasure moving through me. My chest is pounding, but at the same time, it feels like I'm not even within my body.

I see Harry suck in a breath above me.

He looks flushed.

I trace his lip with my finger, capturing his interest.

"You all right there?" I ask.

He nods, his lips pursing together as he pushes out a steady breath.

"Just trying to calm myself down," he says, his lashes fluttering.

"Well … I feel calm." I grin at him, scrunching up my nose. "Actually, I feel amazing."

His whole face brightens as his mouth forms a smile that matches my own.

"I'm sure you do." He chuckles, shaking his head.

"I'm spoiled." I laugh, knowing that this situation isn't exactly fair.

Because time and time again, Harry is forced to hold back. While I, on the other hand, don't have to.

"You're definitely spoiled," Harry confirms, dropping his lips back down onto mine for a quick kiss. "We have time for a few more strawberries, and then I need to get you back home."

"We wouldn't want to break curfew," I say sarcastically, still smiling up at him.

"No, we wouldn't," he says, pinching my chin before grabbing another strawberry and feeding it to me.

MONDAY, OCTOBER 7TH
Some secret Noah way.
6:30AM

THE SOUND OF a door closing wakes me.

I rub my eyes, trying to orient myself. There are footsteps coming from the hallway, and I listen as they move past my room and down the stairs. Then, I hear the front door shut quietly.

I roll away from my door, glancing over to my clock. It's six thirty, which means that the footsteps were Noah's.

He's left for his run.

And he didn't ask me to go with him.

I let out a sigh. Despite my optimism, I know things are going to be different between us now. Especially after my date with Harry last night.

Because he took it to a whole other level.

Not only did he let me in on his past, but he also seemed genuine in wanting a future that extended beyond school.

A future where we traveled and figured out life together.

One where we made our own plans.

And talking about that made me really happy.

I've been scared all along about leaving here and having things be different. I know that things will change; it's obvious that they will have to. But at least now, I know that Harry doesn't seem afraid of that change. He seems sure that we have a connection, that we will always be there for one another. And I find a lot of reassurance in that.

I smile, feeling like I couldn't have started off the week any better.

I decide to take advantage of Noah being gone and make use of the shower. I go into the bathroom and turn on the water, get in, lather up my body with soap, and let the whole room fill up with warm steam. I can't help it when my mind drifts back to last night.

It feels like a dream.

The champagne.

The dinner that Harry planned.

Requesting pizza as an appetizer in honor of our date at Marco's and a bouquet of chocolate-covered strawberries because we always talk about chocolate fantasies and date night delights.

I feel my breath catch in my throat, thinking about after, having Harry's body pressed on top of mine. He looked beautiful and acted different.

He was mature.

And definitely sexy.

I wanted him in the car ride to dinner and then again with dessert. I find myself always wanting him. But I also find myself constantly scared of giving him more. Part of me thinks it's because I'm afraid of hurting him. He's gone through so much, and he doesn't deserve yet another person letting him down. But I know that's just an excuse. I am the one who is scared of getting hurt.

I run my hands over my wet hair and across my shoulders, feeling the water pound into my skin. It reminds me of how my chest was pounding last night.

Of the way that Harry looked when he was breathing heavily over me.

Butterflies form in my stomach but quickly fly away when someone knocks on the door.

"Yes?" I squeak, feeling like my personal thoughts have just been infiltrated.

I cover my chest, not sure what to expect.

"You've been in there for ages. Care to let anyone else in the house shower?" Noah's voice echoes into the bathroom, and I turn off the water.

"*Shit*," I mutter, reaching for a towel and wrapping it around my body.

Have I been in here the entire time he was on his run?

That had to have been almost half an hour.

I immediately feel guilty.

"Sorry, sorry, sorry," I say, opening up the door, holding my towel in place. Because I could have kept Helen or Gene from getting ready for work. "Did your parents try to shower while I was in there? Can you even run the water in two showers? Will it work?" The words spill out of my mouth as I make eye contact with Noah.

A few beads of sweat run down his cheek, and my eyes slip down to his sweat stained T-shirt.

It looks like he pushed himself hard today.

"No, that's all right. You're fine," Noah says softly, seeming caught off guard. His brown eyes widen as he looks me over.

"What?" I flush. I shake my head, feeling insanely guilty for daydreaming in the shower for that long.

"Nothing," Noah replies, dipping his brows in. "I just didn't expect you to apologize."

I roll my eyes, being brought back to reality.

Because this is Noah I'm dealing with here.

I step back into the bathroom, reaching for my toothbrush and toothpaste.

"I lost track of time," I admit, pushing the door open wider so he can come in too.

"It's like a Turkish steam bath in here," he says, hesitantly stepping into the bathroom, swatting at the air.

I watch the steam seep out the bathroom door, the cold air sending a chill through me.

"Close the door. It's cold," I order. "I just have to brush my teeth, and then I'll be out of your way."

"Your skin's all pink," Noah comments as he closes the door, his eyes on my shoulders.

"I had the water pretty hot," I say, squinting my eyes, bracing for his reaction.

"Lovely, you used all the hot water then." Noah's mouth drops into a frown as he looks over my skin.

"Probably," I reply, shoving the toothbrush into my mouth. Because there's no way I'm talking myself out of this one.

"Well, luckily for you, I plan on only taking a *warm* shower this morning."

"The relief," I mumble, the toothbrush still in my mouth.

"You don't mind, do you?" Noah asks, walking over to the shower, his hand resting on the faucet, ready to turn it on.

"That's fine. You can let it warm up," I say, trying to talk with a mouthful of toothpaste. I decide it's better to just stop talking and focus on brushing my teeth.

Noah pushes back the curtain, turning on the water.

"Thanks," he responds.

I keep my eyes on my reflection in the mirror, making sure my towel stays tightly wrapped around me as I rinse out my mouth. I'm giving it a good swish, so that all the toothpaste is gone when I catch Noah's reflection moving. I glance over to him and practically choke on the water when I see him stripping off his shirt. He has his back to me, and my eyes grow into saucers as I watch his muscles flex. He pulls the shirt up and over his head, revealing a tapered waist that grows wider until it gets to his thick shoulders. He turns back to me, meeting my gaze.

"Can I have some of your toothpaste?" His face is blank as he picks up his toothbrush, awaiting my answer.

I squint at him, wondering if this is some sort of trick he's playing. Standing shirtless in the bathroom, like the past forty-eight hours never happened. Some secret *Noah way* of torturing me.

It probably is.

I nod, handing him the toothpaste tube anyway.

He spreads the paste onto his toothbrush, leans past me to run it under the water, and pops it into his mouth. I shake my head, focusing back on my reflection instead of him. He rinses out his mouth as I look over myself. I still need to brush my hair and put on lotion, but I can do both of those things in my room.

"All right, I'm going to go finish getting ready," I state, turning back to Noah as he's stripping off his shorts and underwear.

My mouth falls slightly ajar as I take in his naked back, butt, and legs. My eyes slip across every piece of his exposed skin before I realize I should look away. I want to gasp and yell at him, but I'm not sure my mouth would even work if I wanted it to right now. Noah doesn't glance over his shoulder to see if I'm watching him. He just drops his clothes on the floor, steps into the shower, and pulls the curtain shut.

"Okay," he calls out.

"Noah," I finally say, finding my voice, "I said you could turn on the water, not start showering."

"What? If I had waited for you to finish, we would've both been late. Besides, now, you can get ready at your own pace."

"I told you all I had left to do was to brush my teeth."

"And I managed to brush my own and get in the shower in the same amount of time," Noah says, drawing back the curtain just enough so I can see his face. And his stern *I'm right* look.

"Whatever," I mumble, grabbing my lotion. "I'll leave you to it."

I step out of the bathroom, making sure to close the door tightly behind me.

It crosses my mind that if anyone saw me now, it would look like Noah and I had showered together. Because he's already naked under the water, and I'm wrapped up in a towel, coming from the same bathroom.

The thought makes me uncomfortable.

Mostly because that's not what happened.

And despite Noah's innocent words, I'm not sure what to think. He acted so natural, so relaxed. But at the same time, he stripped naked in front of me.

I push the thought out of my mind as I walk into my bedroom and close my door. I put on lotion, get dressed in my uniform, brush through my hair, and run the blowdryer over it.

It only takes a few minutes for my hair to dry, and instead of thinking about Noah and his intentions, I decide I need to focus on myself.

I add a thick eyeliner and two coats of mascara, pairing it with a dark nude lipstick for something different. It makes my eyes and lips pop while still being appropriate for school. I spritz on some perfume, grab my backpack, and head downstairs.

Helen's sitting at the kitchen table, her legs propped up on a dining chair. She has a cup of steaming coffee held up to her lips and a book opened in front of her.

"Whatcha reading?" I ask, bounding into the kitchen.

I must take her by surprise because her hand starts to shake, and I half-expect her to spill her coffee all over herself.

"Oh dear," she fusses, looking flushed. She sits up immediately, setting her coffee cup on the table and pulling her book against her chest. "Nothing of importance."

"Aww, come on," I say, flitting past her to grab the French press and pouring myself a cup of coffee. "I'm always looking for a good book recommendation." I set my coffee on the table and sit down next to her.

She keeps the book tucked against her chest, her dark curls pulled back into a clip at the nape of her neck. Her cheeks are still rosy, like she's embarrassed, and she won't look me in the eyes.

"This isn't your sort of book," she says, shaking her head.

I snatch the book out of her hands, scan the cover, and immediately understand why she was trying to conceal it.

"*Taming the Duke,*" I read aloud with a grin. I glance up at Helen, who looks like she might pass out. "Tell me this is one of Gene's book club reads," I add, hoping my joke might break the ice.

"These books are usually best kept in the bedroom," she confides, looking over my shoulder to make sure no one is coming. "But I couldn't keep my eyes open any longer last night, and I had to know how it ended before heading off to work."

She nods her head once with her statement, like it couldn't be more factual.

"Well, if it's that captivating, maybe you'll let me borrow if you're done?"

"It's meant for the mature reader, dear," Helen says, taking the book back. "You know, us old, married women looking for a little adventure."

"You think it's too steamy for me?" I say with surprise.

"I suppose there isn't anything you don't already know about in it." She chuckles, taking a sip of her coffee. "Would your mother approve of you reading this sort of material?"

I wave my hand at her. "My mom's more the type to give me the book, so I'd be informed on the proper way to land a husband. So, if the character ends up with the duke, I don't think she'd have a problem with it."

Helen pinches her lips together, holding back a chuckle.

"Between us girls, she wins the duke over." Her warm eyes are glowing.

"With her wiles, right?" I grin, waiting for her answer as Noah joins us in the kitchen.

"Why don't you tuck this away in your room?" Helen says quietly, sneakily handing me the book under the table. "I'll have Noah start you some breakfast."

I take the book from her hand, making sure to keep the cover tucked against my chest as I run up to my room.

I glance back over the cover. It features a noble man with his hair pulled back into a ponytail and a woman in a long, silky gown.

It's got a classic historical romance feel to it. It's not something I would normally read, but from the way Helen was flushing at the table, I know it has to be good.

Or at the very least, it will be steamy.

I slide it under my pillow, knowing no one will find it there.

As I walk back downstairs, I can't help but wonder if Helen would have been concerned about the book's *mature content* if she had known what Harry and I were up to last night. If anything, Helen would be mortified. I'm not sure that letting Harry slip his hands into my underwear is exactly her idea of being young and having fun.

Though I am young.

And it *was* really fun.

The thought of seeing Harry today sends butterflies through my stomach as I get back to the kitchen.

"What's going on at school today?" Helen asks, looking between Noah and me.

Noah's standing in front of a blender, filling it with bananas, strawberries, and milk.

"Oh, is some of that for me?" I ask, moving beside him, completely forgetting about Helen's question.

"Do you want some?" he asks, raising his eyebrows.

"Definitely."

"Of course some is for you," Helen adds, a little late. "I told you I'd have Noah start your breakfast. Though I'm not sure a smoothie is a proper breakfast." She glances to the blender, her nose flaring.

"I'd rather think not," Gene says, joining us in the kitchen.

"Does that mean you'll prepare the toast?" Helen asks as Gene leans down, giving her a quick kiss.

I think it's the first time I've caught them kissing, and I instantly want to melt. I push out my lips in a pout, pinching Noah.

"Your parents are adorable," I coo quietly.

He leans toward me and lowers his voice. "My dad looks a little *too* happy this morning, don't you think?"

I glance between Helen and Gene, noticing how his hand stays on her shoulder, and instantly put two and two together. "Ohhh," I whisper, trying not to freak out. "Well, at least they get action."

"Fair," Noah says and then turns the blender on.

Gene looks at us with beady eyes, like the blender has

somehow offended him. When Noah's done, Gene puts in the toast as Noah pours the smoothie into two glasses and hands me one.

"Anywho, back to my question. Noah?" Helen asks.

"Nothing special, Mum. No tests, just the usual," he replies.

Helen turns her head in my direction, and I know she's going to ask me next.

"Same for me. Although, I've been meaning to ask, is it all right if I go to the Natural History Museum after school? Mohammad's taking his sisters and said I could tag along."

"Oh, that's a fine museum," Gene says from the counter.

"Of course that's all right," Helen says approvingly.

I glance over to Noah, watching as he takes his first sip of the smoothie. His cheeks are sucked in as he slurps, bringing definition to his cheekbones.

I feel like I should invite him, but at the same time, I feel like it's weird for me to invite him because I think it should almost just be a given that he goes.

"You'll come too?" I ask.

Noah glances up to me, his straw still in his mouth.

"Sure," he replies, dropping his eyes back down to his smoothie.

Smirking at me.
STATISTICS

WHEN NOAH AND I sit down in our seats in Stats, I stay silent. The entire morning has had a surreal feeling to it. Taking a long shower, Noah in the bathroom, seeing how close his parents are. Everything felt the same but slightly different. Slightly off.

Normally, we stop for coffee, but today, I had it at the house instead.

Normally, we're rushing to make our lunches, but Noah made ours in silence, not asking for my help.

The image of him in the bathroom this morning won't leave my mind. I glance over at him, taking in his brushed chestnut hair and creamy complexion. His white shirt is pressed, and his tie is set firmly at his neck. Everything about him looks orderly this morning.

I glance around, wondering what people think when they look at Noah.

Do they think about his hair?

Or his rounded lips and big smile?

Maybe they think about how smart he is.

Or about how well he plays football.

Which are all things that I would give anything to be thinking about right now. But all I can think about is seeing his naked body in the bathroom and the fact that I was wearing nothing but a towel.

It's not like he pushed me up against the door, eyeing the towel between us.

He never made a comment about how I looked or taunted me with his body.

He just got into the shower.

He just talked to me through the curtain like it was the most normal thing in the world.

But the thing is, it's *not* normal.

It's not normal for us to be such cordial friends.

Maybe his attitude this morning is our new normal. Maybe he realized when I was out on my date with Harry last night that things had to change.

I cross my arms, growing frustrated with myself.

With him and his relaxed demeanor.

A guy a seat over is vibrantly talking to him, and Noah lets out a deep, full-belly laugh. A girl a row over turns back at the noise, glancing at him. My jaw tightens as her gaze lingers.

"Noah," I interrupt, grabbing his attention.

He turns to me with a smile, tilting his head.

"Yeah?" he asks, his eyes on me.

I search his face, trying to figure out if this is all a facade. Maybe he's just pretending. Maybe if I wait long enough, he'll crack. He'll show his true feelings. But he just stays smiling, sitting there, looking at me.

My stomach twists.

"The shower, Noah," I say sternly, dropping my voice so no one overhears us.

"The shower, Mallory," he says back.

"Stop repeating me," I say, wanting to scream.

Because he looks amused.

And way too freaking calm.

His shoulders drop slightly as he glances away from me, his jaw twitching.

"What was going on this morning?"

"You're always the one going on and on about how long I take in the shower," he says, his eyes shifting back to me. "Well, this morning, you were the one taking forever, and instead of throwing a fit, I decided to work around you."

"Work around me?"

"I thought you'd be happy. You say you want things to be easy. For us to get along." He has his hands open in front of his chest like he's confused.

"So, getting along implies that it's now okay for me to see you naked?" I whisper.

"You didn't see *all* of me naked," Noah reminds me, his eyes on me.

"I saw half," I argue.

"The back half. Don't get too excited. It's not even my best side." He smirks.

"All right, you are being way, way, way too cocky and chipper for me this morning," I state, taking in his bright eyes.

"Mallory," Noah says, turning so he's facing me, "it's not like I joined you in your shower. It's not like you saw all of me naked."

"That's so beside the point," I fire back.

"What *is* your point?" he interrupts, arching a brow at me.

"My point is that you are playing dumb, and I know that you are. You wanted me to see you."

Noah pushes his hand through his hair and licks his lip. "I wanted to shower because I was sweaty."

"Yes, and you made a point of stripping off your clothes in front of me," I push the words out through my teeth, trying to keep my voice at a whisper. My gaze flicks to Mr. Johnson, who just walked into the classroom and is setting his bag down on his desk.

"What, did that bother you?" Noah asks, recapturing my attention.

"No, of course not. But it was inappropriate."

"Because you're dating my mate," he states, nodding his head.

"No." I look around us before I speak again. Everyone is in their own conversations, and Mr. Johnson hasn't formally started class yet. "Because you've admitted things to me before, and you can't just pretend that you didn't say those things or that I wouldn't notice."

I try to remain vague while still getting my point across.

"What did you notice exactly?" he asks with an annoying smile playing on his lips.

"Apart from your naked body?" I say sharply.

"Apart from that." He nods, his gaze honing in on me.

"I …" I start to speak, but I can't come up with anything.

"Interesting. Nothing comes to mind?" He leans back in his chair, looking amused.

I blush, feeling overwhelmed. Because the whole point was that he shouldn't have stripped in front of me because of our history. And now, all I can picture is Noah's naked body again, and then I scold myself for thinking about it because I shouldn't be.

And that is the point.

"Are you warm? You look flushed." Noah conceals a smile as he reaches for his backpack. "Here, have some water."

I look between him and the bottle, wondering if he's actually serious.

Because it's obvious that he's enjoying this.

And it pisses me off.

So, like the five-year-old that I apparently am, I swat it away. Only that causes it to fall out of his hand and onto the floor. It makes a loud noise, and I pray it didn't spill all over.

Luckily for us, it didn't.

But unluckily, the noise catches the entire classroom's attention, and now, everyone, including Mr. Johnson, is staring at me.

"All right there?" Mr. Johnson asks, sounding entertained.

"Sorry, Mr. Johnson," Noah says. "Mallory, for some reason, decided to attack my water bottle today."

I glare at Noah, my mouth falling open at his sarcastically drenched words.

He smirks back at me.

Mr. Johnson must pick up on it, too, because he replies, "How sad for the bottle. All right, class, let's go ahead and get started."

Our professor continues talking, but I don't hear a single

word he says because my whole mind, my whole body, is filled with liquid fire.

And I would give anything to just dump it all over Noah right now.

I want to watch as it pours over his perfect brown hair, dripping down to cover his sculpted eyebrows and annoying mouth. I would happily watch it fall down onto his shoulders, covering his stupid boy muscles.

I wouldn't want the liquid fire to hurt him, *obviously*, but it could stain his shirt and cover his face.

I crack my neck, trying to calm myself down. But I actually feel like I'm about to boil over.

There has to be steam rising from my ears.

Or my head.

I'm not sure where the steam is supposed to originate from exactly, but I know it has to be there. I sit as straight as a board in my seat, forcing myself to stay silent, to not explode all over this class, and to keep my eyes on the front of the room.

But then I hear the water bottle crinkle, and my eyes betray me.

I glance over, seeing Noah take a long, exaggerated drink of water.

And he's staring at me.

I look back to the front of the classroom, avoiding his eyes.

I will focus on Statistics.

I will focus on Statistics.

I don't notice when he finally puts the cap on the water, slowly leaning down between our desks to set it on the floor. I don't notice how, when he does that, he puts his hand on the edge of my desk to keep himself upright. And I definitely don't notice how he spends the entire rest of class smirking at me.

Do you fancy him?
LATIN

THE SECOND THE bell goes off, I'm out the door. Mostly because I did *not* focus on Statistics. I was focusing on the clock. And every single second that passed by was slower than the one before it.

"I thought you were going to murder me in class," Noah says, suddenly at my side.

"Can you not realize that I'm trying to get away from you?" I reply, quickening my pace.

"You're doing a bad job of it," Noah says when I get to my locker.

"Noah." I glare at him because he's officially giving me a headache. I forcefully pull my locker open, grabbing my Latin textbook out before slamming it shut.

"Will you relax? I was teasing," he says, taking the textbook from my hand.

"What, do you plan on stealing my homework next? Sending me off to Latin defenseless?"

"I'm holding your book to be nice. But thank you for thinking of me in such high regard."

"You were being mean," I say, stopping in the hallway.

Noah looks down at me with concern, his brows pinching in.

"I was just messing around. I was teasing you," he says softer.

"Well, it wasn't funny," I say sharply, walking off.

When I get to my classroom, Noah is still following behind me with my textbook. I take it from his hand, still upset.

"See you at lunch, I guess," he says, nodding to Mohammad, who joins us, before walking off.

"I'm going to murder Noah before this week is over, I swear it," I growl, moving into the classroom. Mohammad follows me to our desks. "He has this way of making you look like a complete and total idiot while being an ass. And he gets away with it. Why does he always get away with it?" I look to Mohammad, feeling so lost.

"Because he's smart?" he offers, shrugging at me.

"Well, there's my answer. He's too smart. He's officially outsmarted me," I grumble, shaking my head.

"Someone's salty today."

"Someone's beyond salty."

"Oh?" Mohammad tilts his head, intrigued.

"I'm the entire Himalayan rock at this point."

"Oh, you're one of those weird pink-salt people, aren't you?"

"Yes. It's healthier," I say with a sigh.

"Well, would you mind not being a salty rock for me right now?"

I look over at him, noticing that his textbook, notebook, and pen are already on his desk.

"Why?"

"Mallory, I think we should talk."

"You're so serious," I say, noticing his change in tone. And the fact that he called me Mallory.

Mohammad's forehead creases, and he seems distraught. "Well, this is sort of serious," he admits.

"Okay, go ahead." I turn in my seat to face him, not sure where he's going with this.

"Saturday, at Noah's match, when you were crying," he says quietly, leaning in closer to me.

"That feels like a lifetime ago," I say, thinking about Saturday.

"Stay focused," he instructs.

"Okay. Yes, I remember."

"You said that you and Noah got into a fight. And the night before, you were acting super strange."

I blink a few times in understanding. "Mmhmm."

Mohammad looks around us, his eyes scanning the classroom. "Did something happen between you two?"

"Get real," I push out, shaking my head at him.

Mohammad tilts his head, not replying.

I swallow under his gaze.

"Physically, Miss America," he says seriously.

"No," I gasp.

"You asked Harry if he told Noah about what you two did. And then you told me that Noah was upset. You said that you two got into a fight. I'm just connecting the dots," he says frantically.

"Mohammad," I say, trying to warn him.

Because he shouldn't be connecting dots. He shouldn't be asking so many questions. Nothing good will come of it. Noah and I aren't anything.

"We should talk about it," Mohammad says, nodding at me.

"It won't do any good. At the end of every crazy, long rant I go on, there's nothing new to say. Nothing has changed. Nothing has happened," I reply, my stomach dropping.

I don't want to talk to him—or to anyone—about Friday. It was hard enough, experiencing it, and I don't want to relive those emotions. I don't want to be forced to explain how I felt.

Especially after last night with Harry.

"He fancies you," Mohammad says, completely catching me off guard.

I close my eyes, not sure what to say. Because Mohammad

didn't ask me a question.

"Where is this coming from?" I ask, feeling hurt.

He ignores my question, fidgeting with his hands in his lap. "Do you fancy him?"

"It doesn't matter," I say, my voice rising.

Mohammad narrows his eyes at me, glancing around. "Spill."

I shake my head, not knowing where to start. "I told you about *his* moves last week, right?"

Mohammad nods, following along.

"And I told you about how we talked, and things were fine. That we are friends and had it all figured out," I continue.

"I thought you *had* figured it out?" he says, like I've finally confirmed his point.

"I thought we had. But Friday night, after a few drinks, he sort of admitted his feelings again. Which is what led to the fight the next day."

Mohammad stares at me, eyes wide, and I can see the wheels in his head turning.

"Seriously?"

"Seriously." I nod.

"Did you tell Harry?"

"Of course I didn't tell Harry."

"Good." Mohammad nods, still working through things in his mind.

"There's nothing to tell. Nothing happened."

"I mean, that's some pretty juicy news," Mohammad disagrees.

"Sure, it's juicy. But it doesn't change one single thing. I'm with Harry. I want to be with Harry. We went on a date last night, and we talked about a lot. I really want to be with him. Only him."

"Are you sure about that?"

"Yes," I fire back, pushing my hair off my shoulders.

"Okay, okay," Mohammad says, holding his hands up in defeat.

"I'm sorry. I just … I don't know, Mohammad. It's been difficult."

"What happened on Saturday?" He asks the question as our Latin professor closes the door, signaling that class is starting.

"After class," I whisper, so he knows that our talk isn't finished.

Not that I wish it weren't.

But I know he's not done with the questions yet.

And I owe him answers.

Mohammad nods, giving me a sympathetic smile before opening up his textbook.

A pure annoyance moment.
LUNCH

"I THOUGHT THAT class would never end," Mohammad says with irritation.

"Were you dying for the gossip?" I ask halfheartedly, trying to lessen the tension in the air.

Mohammad doesn't reply. He just puts his hand on my elbow, leading me in a different direction than the lunchroom.

We walk opposite the flow of students until he's pulling me into a stairwell.

"I'm not sure this is exactly private," I comment, glancing up at the spiraling stairs that lead to the upper floors.

"Well, it's the best we've got," he replies.

I nod, knowing he's right.

It's not like we can talk about this in the lunchroom in front of Harry and Noah.

"The thing is, I don't want to ever come between your friendships. That's why I've kept this to myself," I start off.

Because he needs to realize that he's probably better off, staying out of it.

I want to tell him everything. I value his opinion. But I also don't want to drag anyone else into my mess.

Or my former mess.

"I'm sorry I got mad at you the other week about that. It was wrong of me," he says.

"It was understandable. I'm going back home soon, and nothing is going to change that."

Mohammad shifts closer, his gaze connecting to mine. "What happened?"

I stare back at him, knowing that he's going to freak out when I say the words. "Noah asked me not to sleep with Harry," I barely whisper.

"No," he gasps, his mouth forming a large circle and his eyes widening in shock.

"Yep." I nod, agreeing.

"*No. Freaking. Way,*" Mohammad says slowly, his expression a mixture of surprised and excited.

I look around the stairwell, making sure we're still alone. Because his eyes are going wild. He's searching around, trying to put all the pieces together.

But then his eyes stop, and he looks straight at me.

"And then you came downstairs and started doing shots and sat on Harry's lap."

"Well, when you say it like that …"

"Miss America," Mohammad scolds.

"I know," I huff.

Because he doesn't have to tell me. I know it was bad decision after bad decision on my part.

"So, that's why he was so upset on Saturday?"

"Harry had mentioned that I was a little frisky, and … well, Noah thought we had had sex."

Mohammad sucks in a long, heavy breath before letting it back out.

"Noah, like, *really* likes you." Mohammad's clear eyes flick up to mine.

I shrug back at him.

"He's made it clear that we will never be anything other than friends," I state, repeating Noah's words.

"That's what he keeps saying to you," Mohammad says, not sounding convinced.

"I don't know what's going on in his head, and that's why everything became so complicated. Which is why all I care about are the facts right now," I tell him.

"What are your facts?"

"Noah—at least, some part of him—likes me. But I want to be with Harry."

"Why?" Mohammad asks.

"What?"

"Why do you want to be with Harry? It seems like you're fighting so hard to be with him. Over and over, you've said that you want to be with Harry. You don't have to convince me."

The door to the stairwell opens, and I take a step back from Mohammad. He watches a girl passing us by, heading up to the first floor. Her gaze flicks between us. Mohammad's eyes follow her up the stairs until I hear the door open and close again.

Mohammad raises his brows at me, and I know I haven't

gotten out of his questions.

"Harry and I have a lot in common. I didn't expect to meet him and like him so much. He makes me feel comfortable, no matter where we are. He's funny and kind. He's a little outrageous sometimes, but he never puts on a front when we're alone," I answer.

"And Noah?"

I shake my head, trying to find words for Noah.

"We have chemistry. I can't deny that. But there isn't any consistency in his feelings. And that's not what I want from a relationship. So, even if we have a connection, it won't go anywhere. I feel lucky to be with Harry. He has a beautiful heart, and I really saw that last night. He has a lot of ideas and plans that he's starting to share with me, and that means something."

"Now, you're just sounding sappy," Mohammad says, his nose flaring.

"I should be sappy. I'm in a relationship with someone amazing. I shouldn't take it for granted," I state, pacing.

"Well, the fact that you're leaving doesn't help," Mohammad interjects. "Girls always get way sappy and romantic when tragedy is bound to occur. And guys, well, they can't help but want what's off limits to them."

"Those are some fair points." I nod.

"So, Noah fancies you, but he will never do anything about it, and he will never tell Harry. That really does put you in a pickle."

"Yes! Finally! Thank you. It is a terrible spot to be in. Because I genuinely like Noah. I like being his friend. Sometimes, I just wish everything else could go away. It would be easier."

"I'm going to give you a scenario, and you have to answer truthfully, okay?" Mohammad says.

I take in his serious expression and firm eyes. "Okay."

"Let's say, you lived here, and Noah and Harry weren't mates. We all went to the same school, but it wasn't this weird situation. They both fancied you, but they didn't talk to one another. What would you do? Who would you pick?"

"That's an imaginary place and situation," I reply, shaking my head.

"Why can't you answer the question?"

"Because it has nothing to do with the world we live in now. My answer would be irrelevant. Plus, how could I make that judgment anyway? It's not like I've dated both of them properly or anything. I have no idea what it would be like, being with Noah. Do you get what I'm saying?"

Mohammad leans his back against the wall, crossing his arms over his chest. "That's the problem."

"What is?" I ask.

"It's not an even playing field. Yet, somehow, you still seem to put Noah on the same level as Harry, who, from the start, has had the advantage. First kiss, boyfriend, dates," Mohammad goes on.

"Don't go there."

"Maybe if you just say it, if you burst the bubble, it will be done and over with. There's tension between you two, and you've never explored it. We always build things up in our heads, you know …" he says.

I nod. "What we can't have always has appeal. The opposite attracts us. That's what I tried to tell Noah. It's just some subconscious game, you know?"

Mohammad shakes his head, pulling his lips to the side. "Noah doesn't play games."

"You're the one who told me he was taunting me. He hated—like, *hated*—me when I first got here. I was loud and annoying. Demanding. Those were his words. Harry isn't like that. I think we could have a future together."

"A future?" Mohammad asks.

"Beyond high school. Beyond London."

"*Beyond?*" Mohammad says, rolling his eyes. "Sounds like a fantasy."

"It doesn't have to be."

"Did your date really change that much?"

I think about his question for a minute before answering, "Yeah, it really did." I smile. "I'm falling in love with him."

I look at Mohammad, hoping that he can see it in my eyes. Written on my face. That I *am* happy with Harry. That even though the idea of giving myself to someone is scary, it's also exciting.

"Well, this is a disaster," he replies, throwing his arm around my shoulders. He pushes open the doors, leading us back out into the hallway. "But, luckily for you, I'll always be here to help manage the chaos."

I bump him with my elbow, not able to keep a smile off my face.

"You're a good friend," I say, wrapping my arm around his waist. "But don't worry; there's no disaster. There's just history and the past. My future is calm and disaster free."

Mohammad openly starts laughing at me, his arm shaking on my shoulders as we walk into the lunchroom.

I unwrap his arm from around me, looking toward our table for Harry.

I haven't seen him all morning, which isn't unusual. But when my eyes land on the table, I only find Noah in our regular spot.

"I'll see you in a minute," Mohammad says, walking off toward the lunch line.

"Hey," I say when I sit down across from Noah.

He's already started his lunch, his sandwich half gone.

He doesn't say anything. He just grabs my lunch sack out from his backpack and slides it across the table to me.

"Where were you guys?" he finally says, breaking the silence.

"Oh, you know, Latin." I wave my hand at him, but Noah doesn't look convinced.

"Have you seen Harry?" I ask, scanning the lunch line. Well, what little of the line is actually left. It looks like everyone's already been through it once, only trickling back up for seconds.

"He's not here today," Noah replies, biting into an apple.

"That's weird," I say, my stomach dropping. "Wait, how do you know?"

"He told me."

I think back to last night. How Harry said that he had to entertain that guy who was coming into town. For a second, I feel worried that something happened, but I know that I have nothing to worry about.

I pull out my phone, hiding it under the table as I turn it on.

"I'll text him just to check," I say, not touching my lunch.

"Sorry about that, mate," Mohammad says, joining us at the table. He's got two brownies and a bowl full of pasta on his tray.

"Latin?" Noah says, repeating my excuse.

"Yeah, had to have a chat with the professor. Apparently, you're not supposed to talk in class," Mohammad rambles.

"You got into trouble?" Noah asks, glancing up at me.

"No," I reply quickly, trying to go along with Mohammad's lie. "I was just … asking Mohammad for help, and it looked like we were talking. A misunderstanding."

"Hmm," Noah grunts.

I feel my phone vibrate in my lap and see two texts come

through. It looks like Harry sent them around nine this morning.

Harry: *Blowing off morning classes. Try not to get into trouble without me.*

Harry: *Couldn't stop thinking about you last night. x*

"Harry said he was blowing off classes today. Well, at least morning classes," I say to Noah and Mohammad.

"I wish I could just blow off Monday classes," Mohammad moans. "If only the school had my dad's cell instead of my mum's."

"Would that make a difference?" I ask, looking over at him.

"For sure." He takes a big bite of pasta and then says, "My dad wouldn't fuss over it. Mum, on the other hand, would hunt me down."

"She probably would." Noah laughs.

I glance back down to my phone, deciding to text Harry back.

Me: *Missing you at lunch.*

I send the message, figuring that he won't respond, but my phone buzzes right away.

Harry: *That's because eating food isn't as fun without me.*

Me: *And why's that?*

Harry: *Because you can never keep your hands off me. Especially not during dessert. x*

Me: *Did something come up?*

Harry: *Just a hangover. No biggie.*

Me: *So, no school today.*

Harry: *Definitely not. Dad won't mind though. Fulfilled my duty.*

Me: *That makes me nervous …*

Harry: *It shouldn't. Couldn't keep my mind off of you.*

Harry: *Ring me after school. I want to hear about your day. x*

Me: *I will.*

"Uh, will you get off that thing?" Mohammad groans. He purses his lips, looking like he wants to murder my phone.

"What's your problem?" I ask, dropping my phone back into my bag as I open my lunch.

I'm glad that I heard back from Harry. I'm not exactly thrilled that he isn't at school, but I trust him.

Mohammad dramatically puts his elbows on the table and his chin in his palm with a sad sigh.

"Well, that's pathetic," I mumble.

"Olivia said to stop messaging her," he replies.

"What were you messaging her about?" Noah asks.

"Obviously, he was messaging her because of Friday night's events," I insist.

"Actually, I was messaging her dick pics," Mohammad says with another dramatic huff.

"Nooo," I state, feeling like my eyes are about to pop out of their sockets. Noah, on the other hand, looks like he's about to burst out laughing. "Mohammad, you didn't."

"I thought she'd like them," Mohammad says with sad puppy-dog eyes.

My mouth falls open, but then Mohammad starts grinning.

"Will you relax? I'm teasing." He chuckles.

"Oh, thank God," I say.

"You looked like you were about to have a heart attack," Noah says with a laugh, his chestnut hair shaking.

"I was!" I give Mohammad a little shove, but he just laughs some more. "So, were you actually texting her?" I ask, trying to get back to the true story.

"If you must know, she texted me. Apparently, she had fun the other night." He grins widely.

"What?" Noah says, practically choking on his water.

"I know. I was surprised too. She said, *Thanks for a fun night*," he says the words in a girlie, sultry voice. And even scarier than what she said is how good of an impression he does of Olivia's voice.

I look to Noah.

"Wow …" Noah says, sounding baffled. And I can't blame him.

"What did you say back?" I ask, sitting on the edge of my seat.

"Basically, I told her she was a goddess and could hit me up anytime."

"Well, that was … sweet, I suppose."

Noah blinks a few times. "Then, what happened?"

"Then, she replied and said she's always down to party with us," Mohammad says.

"Interesting," I comment, trying to figure out the motive for that. But I can't really find one.

"And then I chose to remark about the party always being in my pants … and she said she'd block me if I didn't behave myself," Mohammad says airily.

"She used the word *behave*?" Noah asks, his eyes flaring.

"Mohammad, I can't believe you had the nerve to say that," I gasp.

"Olivia's a girl who loves attention," he says, turning to

me. "And, yep, that was her word. *Behave*," Mohammad says the word excitedly, his pearly whites on full display. "Dirty, right?"

"So, you plan on giving her attention then?" I roll my eyes.

"Hell yes, I do. She let me snog her. That's huge," Mohammad insists.

"He's not … wrong," Noah agrees.

"This is all just a little too strange for me," I comment, biting into my sandwich. Noah layered on vegetables today. Carrot, tomato, and cucumber with what tastes like some hummus. "Wow, this is good."

Noah's lips pull at the corner, his eyes coming up to mine. "I'm glad you like it."

Mohammad glances from me to my sandwich with disinterest. "You two are weird. Choosing veg sandwiches over pasta and brownies."

"If it makes you feel better, I splurged yesterday. I had brunch with Naomi and Olivia and then afternoon tea with Helen."

"And you're just now telling me about this!" Mohammad exclaims.

"What did you get to eat?" Noah asks, glancing up to me with interest.

"A smoothie bowl and carrot cake plus everything with your mom. Tons of sandwiches and mini desserts."

"Back to the point," Mohammad cuts in, pushing his tray away from him. "What did she say?"

"Who?" I ask, confused.

"Olivia, Mallory. Come on, focus," Mohammad says. His leg taps up and down impatiently.

"Shit …" I mumble, remembering brunch and how we actually *did* talk about Mohammad. "You *may* have come up in conversation."

"Yes!" Mohammad says, bringing his closed fist in front of his chest like he's won something. "Wait, good things, right?"

"I'm going to summarize because it was a long morning," I say, trying to think back to what was actually said. "Naomi said that she was annoyed that Olivia kissed you because she had brought up first that you were fit even though she is sort of dating George."

"Wait, really?" Mohammad says, sitting board straight.

I glance over to Noah, who's listening intently.

"Yeah. And then Naomi started asking her about you two. Olivia said that there's something sexier about you now, that you've grown up. She said you were a good kisser, it was fun, she doesn't see it being anything more but that she doesn't regret it." I bring my finger to my chin, thinking. "And that's it."

Mohammad's lips are pressed tightly together, making it hard to tell where his thoughts are.

"That's all good feedback," Noah says to Mohammad.

"Good? Good?" he says, his voice breaking. "It's more than good. It's fucking phenomenal news."

"Yay," I say, shimmying my hands in front of me, trying to celebrate with him.

"Where is Harry when I need him?" Mohammad groans and slaps his own forehead.

"Hey, I'm trying to celebrate with you," I reply.

"You're doing a terrible job of it," Mohammad says, shaking his head. "But it doesn't matter because nothing can discourage me now. It's on. It's *so* on." He gets a determined look in his eye that I'm not going to try and tame right now.

"I wish I could say that this whole conversation was awkward, but I guess, thinking about it, we've had a ton of weird moments, haven't we?" I laugh.

"Like what?" Mohammad asks.

"How about when I walked in on Harry and Mallory after Naomi's party?" Noah answers, capturing my attention. He doesn't look upset. If anything, he looks amused by the memory.

"Shit, and that was only your first week here," Mohammad adds approvingly.

"I'm sure it was *nothing* compared to seeing you and Olivia on Saturday morning," I kindly remind Mohammad. "Because that was mentally scarring."

"I remember how mad I was on your first day of school when I saw you at our lunch table. And then, again, when you were my partner in Art," Noah says with a reminiscent smile.

"I thought you hated me," I say, rolling my eyes. "Oh, what about seeing you and Naomi dance together at her party, Mohammad? Although I guess that wasn't awkward."

"I'll always remember you snogging me," Mohammad says with a pearly grin. "I was freaking out—like, *freaking out*—the whole time though."

"You make it sound like it was terrible!"

"It was! I love you, Miss America, but there are lines."

"Get over it. Aww, what about watching you sing karaoke? And Noah's terrible dance moves," I coo.

"I feel like this is not about awkward moments anymore," Mohammad interrupts.

"I think she's moved on to memories," Noah replies.

"And when we were snooping around before school." I laugh, remembering all four of us hunched down in the bushes.

"I'm not getting on the sentimental train," Mohammad says, shaking his head. "Besides, that had a purpose. It wasn't for fun."

"You're right. There's nothing remotely funny about the

fact that we were *investigating* our professor," Noah says, his eyes sparkling.

"Not our professor, *your* professor," Mohammad reminds as the bell goes off, signaling lunch is over.

I rush to finish my sandwich as everyone starts to get up from their tables. I spent so much time talking that I barely ate.

"Save it for later," Noah says as we get up.

He grabs my apple and bag of chips, and I hold out my bag for him to put them in.

"Good idea," I reply. It will be the perfect snack between classes.

"So, we're still on after school, yeah?" Mohammad asks, walking between Noah and me as we exit the lunchroom.

"Yeah." I smile, excited about meeting his little sisters.

"We'll have to go to the primary wing and get them. So, want to meet in the common room after the last bell?"

"Sounds good," Noah confirms.

"See ya!" Mohammad calls out as he walks off in the direction of his next class.

I walk next to Noah in silence, watching as everyone stops at their lockers, getting their notebooks for their next class. Luckily for us, we can go straight to Art since we don't have anything to turn in and our projects are in the classroom.

"You know, you missed a few moments," Noah says, turning toward me.

"Sentimental memories or awkward moments?"

"Your choice, I guess," he says, not adding anything more.

"Well, what did I miss?"

"Hmm," he draws out, a smile forming on his mouth. "What about when you thought I was going through your bag, looking for your knickers?"

"That was more a pure annoyance moment."

"Or what about when you ran into the doorframe in my room?" he continues.

"I was flushed," I defend, giving him a little shove.

He lets out a deep laugh, clearly enjoying memory lane. "Because you saw me naked."

"I was so hungover after Naomi's party. Remember the night before, eating food in bed with Harry?" I smile.

"I carried you into the kitchen." His eyes catch mine as we make our way up to the first floor.

"You did," I confirm, my mind drifting back to how Harry was on his knees, begging me to cook for them.

"What about when you had chocolate all over your mouth after our popcorn feast?"

"That's embarrassing, not awkward," I say as we get to our classroom.

"It was cute," Noah says, shaking his head and stopping in the doorway. His eyes slip from mine, down to my lips.

For a minute, I feel breathless under his gaze, but then he starts chuckling, his eye squinting up at the corner.

"You're remembering me with chocolate on my face, aren't you?" I ask, pushing past him into the classroom.

"Yep." He nods, following me to our seats.

A true poet.
ART

ALTHOUGH I ENJOYED memory lane with the boys during lunch, it only momentarily distracted me from the things that Mohammad had said before lunch. It bothers me all through the beginning of class while Mrs. Jones goes on and on about a class project.

I was practically yelling at Noah to start acting normal in Statistics. Which I know was wrong and makes no sense. Because he *was* acting normal.

Our new normal.

Our *friend* normal.

But all of my feelings came rushing back when I talked to Mohammad. The way that Noah had looked at me when he asked me not to sleep with Harry. How upset he had been the next day.

At least I knew *that* Noah. Now, it feels like he's putting on a show. Like he's pretending to be fine.

The only problem is, I don't think it's a show. I think he might actually be okay with things now.

And that bothers me.

It *really* bothers me.

"Why didn't you wake me up to run with you this morning?" It's the first sentence out of my mouth after Mrs. Jones tells us to continue working on our projects. She also said that she would hand back our last project before class is over.

"What?" Noah asks, obviously not following.

"You ran without me this morning," I repeat.

"I didn't want to wake you up," Noah says, confused.

"It's not like you've had a problem with waking me up before," I argue, trying to prove my point.

"You're upset that I went running without you?" he asks, his fingers coming up to loosen his tie.

"I'm trying to understand why you did. Actually, I know why you did," I correct because I need to get this off my chest. And I need to get straight to the point.

"Hold that thought." Noah stands up. I watch as he goes over to the corner of the room and gets our projects. "Talk and work," he says, setting them on the desk when he gets back.

I look over my canvas, feeling flustered.

"I need paint," I say.

"Grab me some paint too," Noah says, examining his peacock.

I glance down at it, noticing that only half of it is done. But it's coming along nicely.

I get our paints and brushes and am back at our table quickly.

"So, you were saying that I intentionally didn't ask you to run this morning," Noah says as he dips his brush into a deep blue and then carefully places it on one of the peacock's feathers.

"We haven't talked about how things are supposed to be now," I clarify.

"Yeah, I realize that," he replies, but his eyes stay glued to his canvas.

"Isn't it something we should talk about?" I ask, setting down my paintbrush. Because I can't paint and talk to him about this.

Noah brings his eyes up to mine and shakes his head. "I told you, I was drunk. And you don't need to worry about me slipping up again."

"So, that's it?" I ask, frustrated.

"I don't know what else there is to say, Mal. Do you?"

"I guess not," I reply with a sigh, picking my paintbrush back up. "I just think that we should at least think about what we said. What it means. Don't you?"

Noah smiles, glancing over to me.

"It's better not to go in circles. We're friends. Things are okay, all right?"

I try to give Noah a smile, but I just feel like everything is off.

This weekend was so full of girl time and dates and tea

and Harry that I barely got to see Noah. And since then, he's been strangely chill.

"But things aren't okay. You're acting different."

I focus my eyes on my canvas, trying to keep my hands busy. I mix black with a deep purple for my top layer of paint, wanting it to be dark enough to really contrast with the eggplant and gold below it when I sand it down.

"I'm trying to be respectful," Noah says, his grip tightening on his paintbrush.

"I'm all about respect, but you're starting to freak me out. You're so calm all of a sudden."

"You're upset with me because I'm calm?"

"I'm upset that you're *acting* calm. Key word: *acting*. You're not regular, normal Noah at the moment."

"Would you care to clarify what you think of as *regular, normal Noah*?" He lays his paintbrush down on the table.

"Actually, I would," I say, turning on my stool to face him. "Regular Noah is grumpy about this or brooding about that. He thinks about deep things like art and sex, and he loves to give advice," I say, trying to imitate his deep voice. Which ends up just sounding really silly.

I scrunch my nose as Noah lets out a heavy laugh.

"Is that what you think I sound like?" He grins, pulling his lip between his teeth.

"I'm trying to tell you that you aren't *cool as a cucumber* Noah. You're Noah—deep, thoughtful, passionate Noah. It's not in your nature to be so chill about everything that's happened."

"You always say I'm passionate," Noah says, his eyes focused on his canvas as a sad smile crosses his face.

"Look at me," I demand.

"What do you want, Mal?" he says, his voice catching. He runs his hand through his hair, his fingers tensing. "Look, I'm doing the best I can. I am desperately trying to treat you the way a friend is supposed to treat a friend, okay?"

His brown eyes plead with mine, his thick eyebrows dipping forward. He stays staring at me, but I watch his jaw twitch and his fingers move to his tie, struggling with it.

I swivel myself back around on my stool, so I'm facing the front of the classroom again and not him.

"I'm sorry," I whisper, feeling like a jerk for pushing him.

"You actually think I don't care," he states, shaking his head.

And he looks … hurt.

We sit through the rest of class in silence until Mrs. Jones comes to stand in front of our table.

"I have your projects," she says brightly.

I glance up at her, taking in her pleased expression and hopeful eyes. It's sort of weird, seeing her so happy. Maybe it means we did well.

"Great." I smile back at her. Because I can finally give my collage to Helen.

And from the looks of it, I likely got another A.

"Mallory, I loved your sunset. The piece you wrote was quite moving. Well done," she says, handing it back to me.

I glance down at my paragraph, seeing my high score.

"Thanks Mrs.—I mean, Professor Jones. I had fun doing it," I reply, but she's already moved toward Noah.

She's looking at him like he's her shining beacon of hope, and now, I know who the eyes were actually for.

"Noah, I have to say, I am very impressed. You are a true poet," she compliments, setting down his project and paper on our table.

"Thank you." Noah flushes shyly.

She pats him on the shoulder, lingering for a moment. But then she's off again, continuing to pass out the last of the collages.

"I'm assuming she liked it," I say, trying to break the silence between us as Noah peeks under his paragraph at his collage.

I glance over to his paper, seeing that it is actually a poem.

I turn my head, trying to read a line of it when Noah folds it, tucking it into his backpack. He puts his forearms over his project like he's trying to hide it as the bell goes off.

I place my project into a folder and am careful not to crease it when I put it in my backpack.

"Mallory," Noah says, finally looking at me.

"Yep?"

"This is for you," he says, holding out his project.

I take the paper from his hand and look across it. His collage is in the shape of a spiraling circle. It's a mixture of gray and black and blue.

"You did your project on confusion, right?"

His collage is amazing. Each piece flowing and fitting perfectly with the next.

"It's a storm."

"Oh?"

"It represents you," he says, looking between his project and me.

I catch his gaze. "Great …" I start, knowing that this can't be good.

"No, *it's you*," he clarifies, standing up.

"It's me?"

"Just … hold on to it," Noah says firmly.

"Should I be offended?" I ask, looking over his storm collage.

Because what does he mean, *it's me*? Confusion, a storm, dark colors. None of those things seem good.

"Are you offended?" he asks.

"I'm not sure what to think," I admit. "But, Noah, it's really cool. I mean, are you sure you want me to have it?"

Noah throws his backpack over his shoulder. "Of course I want you to have it. I wrote something to go with it. Something that explains things."

"So, can I have that?" I ask, looking back down at his project as we walk out of the classroom.

"No," he replies easily.

"No?" I question.

"Nope." He smiles at me and then takes off down the hallway.

"Wait, why?" I call out.

"What fun would that be?" he yells back with a smile.

But then he's gone.

I tuck the project into my backpack, making sure it stays safe as I make my way to Geography.

Lose their appeal.
GEOGRAPHY

I SIT DOWN in my regular seat in class, ready for the day to just be over. Well, at least for classes to be over. My brain feels burnt out from thinking. My mind continuously shifts from my date with Harry to my talk with Mohammad to Noah giving me his collage.

The collage that he said is about me.

I want to look over it again. Study it. Try to figure out what it means. But honestly, it would be a waste of time.

Because Noah already told me.

It's about me. About confusion. And it's a storm.

I don't blame him for thinking that about me. Because,

normally, I'm put together, straitlaced Mallory. But lately, I've been all over the place. And he's right in essentially saying that I've practically been a natural disaster.

I glance behind me, sad to see Harry's seat empty.

His absence makes me uncomfortable. I'm used to him always being at my shoulder, chatting away in my ear.

He has a way of bringing me out of my head and into the moment. But today, he's not here to pull me out of my thoughts.

So, I have to do it myself.

I get out my geography notebook, trying to keep my mind in check. I think back to what we learned in class last week. I tell my mind to shift to thoughts of positive and productive things, fighting my urge to dissect all of the conversations I've had over the last few days.

I smile to myself, thinking about meeting Mohammad's sisters after class. I can't wait to see what their personalities are like and how Mohammad interacts with them. It will be fun to explore the museum. I've heard a lot of great things about the Natural History Museum, and it wasn't one of the places I visited with my parents on our last trip to London.

The classroom quickly fills up, and I catch Olivia's eye as she walks through the door with Naomi. Olivia's hair frames her face in soft waves, and she is wearing an easy expression as she moves to her regular seat.

Naomi gives me a wave before glancing to the empty chair behind me.

"No Harry today?" she asks me from the front of the classroom.

"No," I reply, shaking my head.

"Well, that means you're sitting with us." She smiles, walking down my aisle.

She grabs my notebook off of my desk before nodding her

head at me to follow her. I glance toward Olivia, wondering if I should put up a fight and stay in my regular seat or if I should give in.

Olivia is watching Naomi, but she doesn't look upset. I grab my bag and decide to follow her. I take the open desk in front of her, turning around to face her and Olivia.

"So … you talked to Mohammad today?" Naomi asks.

I can tell she knows that I did, and she wants me to dish.

"Well, yeah." I smile. "I have Latin with him. Plus, lunch."

"I saw him at lunch." Naomi nods.

"What are you getting at?" Olivia chimes in, sounding confused.

"I just wondered what he made of Friday night," Naomi confesses.

"That horse is dead and beaten," Olivia says with annoyance.

"I think we all had a nice time Friday. And brunch was fun yesterday," I admit.

"It was." Naomi smiles.

"Why are you so interested in Mohammad anyway?" Olivia asks, flitting her eyes from me to Naomi.

"I don't know." She shrugs. "I guess I'm just bored, and this is the juiciest thing that's happened all weekend."

"What about your date?" I ask her.

"Of course, it was amazing. I don't know though. George is just so … predictable, I guess," she confides.

"Over him in a day?" Olivia smiles, pushing her hair off her shoulder.

"He says all the right things. He's sweet and charming. He's a dream come true," she goes on.

"But?" Olivia cuts in.

"But that makes it easy to fall for him. And I also think

he's the type who might hurt me once I do," she replies with a sound nod.

"You should give him a chance," I offer. "It sounds like you're just scared."

Naomi lets out a sigh, crossing her arms over her chest. "I suppose you two are right."

"As per usual." Olivia grins and lets out a soft laugh.

I feel more than a few pairs of eyes on us and glance around. At least three guys in our class are staring at Olivia.

And I can't blame them.

Between her full hair, hourglass shape, and soft, confident voice, she really is beautiful.

And her laugh is one to be matched.

"You know, maybe you should sit with us at lunch." The offer comes out of nowhere, and I'm as surprised to hear the words come out of my mouth as Naomi and Olivia seem to be.

"Really?" Olivia asks, her smile fading.

"We're sitting together now, and it's nice. Plus, it's to my benefit because it eliminates me as the go-between," I say.

"The go-between?" Olivia questions.

"At lunch, Mohammad wanted to know what you had said, and you want to know what Mohammad said. The boys are worried that we can't get along, or you're curious what was talked about. I don't know. That could all just be eliminated if we moved forward off of Friday and talked."

"Even when Olivia and Harry were dating, we only sat at the guys' table maybe once, twice a week," Naomi cuts in, looking to Olivia. She doesn't sound at all convinced by the prospect of joining us for lunch.

"Why?" I ask.

"Lunch is my time to de-stress. I also like to chat with our friends, and they sit at a different table. Anyway, boys tend to be disgusting at lunch. They play with their food and have silly conversations. It's better this way—to have some separation. It's the only thing that keeps them cute and interesting," Naomi says mischievously.

"So, you think if you sat with them at lunch, they'd lose their appeal?" I laugh.

"I don't know," Olivia cuts in. "I think there is something hot about watching a guy eat."

"I might be with Naomi on this one," I reply, thinking about lunch. "Harry eats so unhealthy, but at least he isn't messy. Mohammad can destroy his food in thirty seconds. And he always mixes his courses. One bite brownie, one bite pasta." I shake my head at the thought.

Naomi lets out a string of giggles and covers her mouth. "See, exactly what I'm talking about. Boys are strange creatures. But luckily for them, they're adorable."

"What about Noah?" Olivia asks, her eyes slipping from Naomi to me.

"He's actually not a bad eater. Except he's super picky. He's generally slow. I think, for him, lunch actually is his time to just eat," I reply.

"Well, I think eating lunch together would be … interesting," Olivia states, her eyes staying on me.

"I do too," I agree.

"Would we all actually feel comfortable with that?" Naomi asks, looking unsure.

"Of course," Olivia replies with a smile.

She sounds certain, but I'm not so sure.

"All right …" Naomi says, her voice rising. "Anyway, Mallory, what are your plans for this week?"

"It's your last week here, right?" Olivia asks softly.

"Yeah." I nod, feeling a little uneasy. "Uh, well, tonight, I'm going to the Natural History Museum with Mohammad and his sisters. And Noah."

"No Harry?" Olivia questions.

"Not today."

"That should be fun," Naomi cuts in. "My parents are insisting on a family dinner out tonight."

"That will be nice," Olivia offers, turning her attention to Naomi.

"I think it will be," she agrees.

"What about you?" I ask Olivia.

"Mum and I are shopping tonight and then going for Italian. There's this amazing place a few blocks away from Harrods with the best pasta."

"That sounds divine," Naomi chimes in.

"Isn't Harrods too busy for you?" I ask. "The last time I was there, it was absolutely insane. Crazy busy."

Olivia nods understandingly. "It is if you're going through the entire store. But generally, I go with a purpose. The busiest parts are the hallways connecting the different departments. I think if you go just into, say, the handbag department, it isn't bad."

"I'll have to give it another shot," I say.

"I would," Naomi agrees. "You can't beat the selection."

Naomi's rounded eyes shift to the front of the classroom. I follow her gaze, seeing that Mr. Pritchard is seated at his desk, looking through a stack of papers, like he's about to start class.

Naomi grabs my hand, examining it. "Your nails are holding up nicely," she says, her eyes moving over my extensions.

"When did you have them done?" Olivia asks.

"Last weekend."

"So, you'll want them filled this weekend," she replies, glancing down at her own. They're painted a classic red and even longer than mine.

"We should go get them done together," Naomi suggests. "I think I'm ready for something more fall-themed. Maybe a bright orange or soft gold?" she asks, holding up her nails to us.

Olivia shakes her head. "No orange. But a soft gold would be nice."

"Pink is usually my color," Naomi adds.

"Is red yours?" I ask Olivia.

"That or pink," Naomi answers for her.

"Like I always say ..." Olivia smiles, looking at Naomi.

Naomi rolls her eyes but grins back. "Your nails should always be one of two colors and your perfume always the same," Naomi says, finishing Olivia's statement.

"What color do you want?" Olivia asks me.

I look down at my nails, taking in the blue gray color. "I think, next time, I'll get black or a deep burgundy maybe."

"A rich wine color would definitely be beautiful for fall," Naomi agrees.

"I'll probably get my extensions off though," I say.

"Nooo." Naomi pouts.

"They're driving me crazy."

"But they look great," Olivia states, like that somehow makes up for their annoyance.

"Yeah, I just don't think they're for me," I say as Mr. Pritchard does his best to quiet our classroom. I turn back around in my seat, facing him.

"Quiet," he growls, standing up from his desk.

We all do as we were told, and the room silences.

"Now, we've got a busy week ahead of us and an exam coming up on Friday."

"Ugh," Naomi groans from behind me. It's loud enough for me to hear but quiet enough that Mr. Pritchard doesn't.

"We're going to finish our chapter today, and tomorrow, I will hand out your study guide. You'll be allowed to work on it with a partner for the entire class. Wednesday and Thursday, we will then spend reviewing," he clarifies.

More primal.
4PM

WHEN CLASS IS over, my hand aches from writing so much. Mr. Pritchard wasn't joking when he said we would have a busy week. He spoke even faster than usual with his back to us, scribbling across the whiteboard the entire time. His handwriting is almost illegible, and between that and his quick but quiet voice, I strained the entire class to get everything written down. I say good-bye to Olivia and Naomi and head to the common room.

I spot the boys easily, finding Noah with his back against a brick wall, his arms crossed over his chest. Mohammad is standing in front of him, and from the looks of it, he's telling an entertaining story. His arms are flying out around him, and he's wearing a huge grin on his face.

Noah buckles over with laughter as I approach them.

"Hey." I smile, looking between them.

"Hey," Noah replies, still smiling. He pushes off of the wall, grabbing his backpack off the floor.

Mohammad looks between us. "Well, are you two ready for the hounds of hell to be unleashed upon you?" he asks, raising his eyebrows.

"Mohammad! You're terrible!"

"Just wait," he says with a wink, nodding his head for us to follow along behind him. "You'll find out for yourself soon enough."

Mohammad leads us down a long hallway before pushing through a set of doors connecting our building to the primary school.

"It's kind of crazy that this is all the same school," I comment, taking in the new surroundings.

The hallway is brighter, and bulletin boards are hung outside of each classroom. The name of the teacher is pinned up with what looks like artwork or projects from the class.

A group of kids in uniforms pushes past us, walking through the hallway with their backpacks.

"Why do we never see them out front?" I ask Mohammad.

"It's the same school but technically separate wings and buildings. There are two entrances even. One for primary, one for secondary," Mohammad answers.

"So, they want to keep it separate," I state, nodding along.

"Thank God they do. Could you imagine us all being mixed up? It would be a nightmare," Mohammad replies.

"We're only allowed in the primary building after school's over," Noah says, continuing. "Drop-off and pick-up times. Otherwise, if you're caught here without reason, they'll send you straight to the office."

Noah and I follow behind Mohammad until we get to another common room. It's similar to ours, but there are little kids running around everywhere and tons of parents.

"Mo Mo!" a little girl exclaims, running straight up to Mohammad.

He squats down, and she launches into his arms.

"Hey," he says, picking her up and giving her a hug.

"Want to say hi to my new friend?" Mohammad whispers to the girl in his arms.

She excitedly nods her head.

"This is Mallory," Mohammad says, turning to me.

She squishes her head down close to Mohammad's chest with a grin on her face.

"Hi," she whispers.

"Why don't you tell her your name and how old you are?" Mohammad insists.

She holds out her small hand in front of her, holding up five fingers. "I'm Leela."

"Hi, Leela. It's nice to meet you. I'm Mallory."

She giggles before looking away.

Two other girls join us, the younger looking shy.

"And these are my sisters, Maya and Nina," Mohammad continues as Leela wiggles out of his arms. He sets her down, and she takes off running. "Maya is ten, and Nina is eight."

"Hi, I'm Mallory." I smile at them and give them a wave.

"Hi," Maya says, smiling back.

Nina peeks over her sister's shoulder, not sure of me yet.

"Don't be shy," Mohammad insists.

Maya looks the most like Mohammad, her skin a rich chestnut color, matching his. All four definitely look related. Maya has black hair that rests on her shoulders and a long, straight nose. Nina has longer hair that's parted on the side with thick waves falling well down her back. She has softer features, her rounded nose set centered below warm eyes.

I catch sight of Leela, who is now hiding behind Mohammad's leg. She has the lightest hair of all of them, almost a caramel brown that wisps around her face. But she shares Mohammad's sparkling eyes and wide grin.

I'm instantly taken with her.

"Noah and Mallory are going to come with us to the museum," Mohammad instructs, looking between Maya and Nina.

"Cool," Maya says nonchalantly, holding on to the backpack straps at her chest.

"All right." Mohammad nods, grabbing Leela's hand.

"No," she says, pulling away from him and pushing out her bottom lip. She stomps next to Mohammad, crossing her arms over her chest. "I walk on my own."

"No, you don't," Mohammad replies with a huff. He glances over to Noah and me. "Want to hold Noah's hand?" he offers.

Leela grins, hiding behind Mohammad's leg again, apparently over her fit.

Noah holds out his hand to her with a smile. She giggles and then runs over to him, delicately placing her hand into his. Then, she swings his hand in a dramatic swoop as they walk. It's the most adorable thing I've ever seen.

"Nina, give me your hand then," Mohammad says to his sister, who puts on a pout.

It's easy to tell that Maya is old enough to walk on her own, and I think she knows it. She watches her sisters with warmth, but also with a certain amount of pride that you have when you're allowed to do something others are not.

It's only a ten-minute walk to the museum, and Leela holds on to Noah's hand the entire time.

Nina must forget that she didn't want to hold Mohammad's hand because she happily walks next to him, glancing at the different faces that pass us by on the street. When we get into the museum, Mohammad lets go of her hand.

"Can we see the animals first?" Nina excitedly asks Mohammad.

I glance around, taking in the huge central room. It's two stories high with large fossils set into place, showcasing the structure of long-lost animals.

"This is insane," I say to Noah, who followed me over to one of the displays with Leela.

All three of us are staring wide-eyed at the remains of a dinosaur.

"So big," Leela whispers.

"It is, isn't it?" Noah replies.

"Do you mind if we see the animals first?" Mohammad asks, walking up behind us with Nina and Maya in tow.

"Yeah, that sounds great," I reply absentmindedly.

I feel like I've been pulled into a different world, walking into this building. It just has a magical quality about it.

"I want to see a giraffe," Leela exclaims, tugging at Noah's hand.

"All right." He chuckles, smiling down at her. "Let's go see if we can find one."

She nods enthusiastically before letting out a stream of giggles. Maya and Nina lead the way, Mohammad at their side. We move down a long hallway before entering into a large, open room.

"Look, the giraffe." Leela points, bouncing up and down.

I follow her finger to the large stuffed giraffe in the center of the room. There are numerous animals, different species of birds, and cats spread out. The girls are already off. I watch Maya walk slowly, her gaze intense on every animal she passes by.

"Don't touch that," Mohammad says to Nina, who has her hand outstretched toward an elephant.

"I won't break it," she replies, dipping her thick brows in.

"It doesn't matter. You can't touch," Mohammad replies, pushing her forward as we circle the main floor.

"What do you think?" Noah asks at my side. His eyes are on Leela, who is bouncing from one glass encasement to the next.

"It's a little creepy," I admit. "I guess, on one hand, it might be good for learning. But on the other, something just feels weird about it."

Noah nods, his eyes shifting to me. "Yeah. It's not my favorite room in the museum."

"What is your favorite room?" I ask as we walk up a wide staircase.

Leela is at Mohammad's side, and Nina and Maya are a few steps ahead.

"I'm not sure I have a favorite, but they do have a room called Images of Nature that's cool."

"Why do you like it?"

Noah stops in front of a glass encasement, his eyes scanning across a section of birds. "I guess I like the interpretation. Something about it shows the action in a way that this doesn't. It shows movement and life. And you can see how we've changed our approach and relationship to nature and to animals."

"So, you like it because you're an artist?" I grin, bumping into his shoulder.

Leela looks up at me through thick lashes and grabs on to my hand.

"Look, it's a bird," she coos, tapping on the glass.

"It is," I agree, smiling at her.

NINA AND MAYA lead us through the first and second levels before weaving their way through the museum. You'd think that, after a while, they'd get tired, but they never seem to.

Part of me thought when we got here that they'd get bored or put up a fight. But it's actually a really cool museum.

And each time we go into a new section, they're completely captivated by something.

"Leela!" Mohammad calls out as she goes running off.

Mohammad rolls his eyes as Noah follows her, standing at her side.

"He's surprisingly good with kids," I comment to Mohammad.

He waves off my observation. "That's because he doesn't have to deal with them all day, every day."

"Neither do you," I fire back. "But at least you get to be the oldest."

"Oldest." Mohammad dramatically rolls his eyes. "Please. Everyone says that older siblings get what they want. They're demanding and bossy. Well, think again. I get nothing that I want because I was followed by God's three gifts to my family. Shiny haired angels who will forever run our household."

"Come on," Noah cuts in, joining us. "You know that your family is just waiting for the day that you get your life together and head off to uni." Noah raises his eyebrows at Mohammad, teasing him.

"I'll make them proud, of course. Get myself a respectable degree, marry a woman my mother approves of, and then move into the house next door," Mohammad replies sarcastically.

"Sounds like your personal nightmare," I tease.

"Basically. But I'm the only boy. So, as long as I find a suitable woman and pick a career that will make me money, my family will respect me," Mohammad replies.

"Seriously?" I cut in, noticing his change in tone.

"Yeah. I mean, that's their dream for me."

"It's not a bad dream," Noah comments as we move to the next room.

"It is if it's not what he wants," I disagree.

"Who knows what I want? But right now, I don't want to even *think* about a wife or a career," Mohammad says with a shiver. "Come on. Let's get a snack at the café."

Mohammad waves Maya, Nina, and Leela over.

"Mum wants me to get some food in them while we're

out. They're wired from traveling and all this excitement," Mohammad says, motioning to the museum around us. "But you can be sure, the second we get home, they'll turn into cranky and tired demonesses."

"The wheels will fall off the wagon." I laugh. Because he's probably right.

"WHAT DO YOU want? Leela, do you want a warm toastie?" Mohammad asks when we get to the café.

It's fairly busy with a few people already in line.

Leela is peering into the glass display case, her eyes on a chocolate brownie, while Maya reads over the menu.

"Cocoa, cocoa, cocoa," Leela repeats in a high-pitched and very insistent voice.

Her display gets her a few smiles and a few glares from the people around us.

Noah lets out a chuckle.

"All right, all right, you can have hot cocoa," Mohammad gives in, waving her back over to him.

"Mo Mo, can I have a brownie?" Leela asks, batting her eyes when she gets beside him.

"You're having cocoa," he insists.

And I can tell he's trying not to use the word *no*.

I see her eyes light up as her forehead creases, and it looks like she's about to throw a fit. Mohammad must see it because he squats down next to her.

"All right, which do you want? Cocoa or a brownie?"

"Hmm, cocoa!" she declares.

"Right," Mohammad agrees, placing her hand into mine. "Why don't you and Mallory go find us a table? Nina, do you want to go with them?"

She nods, moving beside me.

"What do you want?" Noah asks me.

"Uh …" I stutter. Because I haven't even looked at the menu.

He waves me off. "I'll just order you something."

"Let's go," Leela insists, pulling at my arm.

I give in to her, Nina at my side. I look around the café, finding an open table with six seats.

"How about there?" I offer, pointing to a table in the corner.

Nina nods at me, and Leela pulls out of my grip, running up to the table. She hops into the middle chair, shifting in her seat.

"I sit by you," she says, looking at me with stern eyes.

"All right," I agree, sitting down in the far corner by the wall.

Nina quietly sits across from me.

"So, I heard your brother decorated the house for your arrival," I say, trying to make conversation.

Nina looks at me excitedly. "Yes. Mohammad put up flowers and streamers!"

"We ate cake!" Leela shouts.

"Aww, was it yummy?" I ask.

She nods sillily, bouncing her head back and forth. Maya joins us at the table, carrying a tray filled with sandwiches.

A few seconds later, Mohammad and Noah come over, both holding trays.

"All right, we've got five hot chocolates, one coffee, five toasties, six bags of crisps, and one apple tart," Mohammad calls out.

Nina and Maya both grab their sandwiches and crisps as Mohammad passes out the hot drinks.

"We got you coffee and the tart," Noah says to me, taking the seat next to Leela. "But if you want, I can trade you my sandwich."

"No, that sounds perfect."

Mohammad sits between Nina and Maya, breaking up the girls. Everyone eats, content.

Well, everyone, except Mohammad, who practically inhales his food. Maya looks over at him with disgust, watching him shove a handful of crisps in his mouth before swallowing it down with a gulp of hot chocolate.

"Noah, can you check Leela's hot chocolate?" Mohammad asks, finally coming up for air.

Noah nods, taking a small sip from her drink. "It's not too hot," he confirms.

"Do you want some of my cocoa?" she asks me after taking a big gulp.

"Aww, thank you. But I have coffee," I reply, leaning down toward her.

She brings her hand up to my cheek, staring at me. "You're beautiful," she says with a smile.

"Thank you." I grin at her. "You're beautiful also. And your sisters too," I comment, looking at Maya and Nina.

Nina is focused on her sandwich, but Mohammad is watching Leela and me while Noah and Maya talk.

"Do you like Mo Mo?" Leela asks with curiosity.

"Mohammad's my best friend," I confirm.

"No!" She shakes her head vigorously.

"Do *you* have a crush?" I ask, wondering if that's what she's getting at.

"No, no, no."

"She does; she does," Nina says, hearing us across the table.

"I like Harry," Leela says with a bright smile.

"You do?" I ask, looking at Mohammad.

His shoulders fall with her statement, and he rolls his eyes so far back that it's like he's staring at the heavens for help.

"Mmhmm." She nods. "He always gives me a lolly, and last time Mo Mo and Harry took us for cocoa, he gave me his brownie. No one else."

"He gave me some," Nina cuts in.

"No!" Leela shouts.

"Leela, enough," Mohammad says, stopping their argument.

"What about Noah?" I ask, trying to change the subject.

Leela whips her head over to Noah, who is in the middle of a conversation with Maya. He must sense our glances because he looks over at her with a smile.

"Noah's silly," Leela insists, watching Noah make faces.

"*He is?*" I ask.

He sticks out his tongue.

"See." She giggles, her eyes on him.

He pushes his finger into her belly, tickling her. I raise my eyebrows, taken aback by his playfulness.

"Maya, why don't you tell Mallory about your music?" Mohammad instructs.

"I play the violin," she says, looking at me across the table.

"That's awesome."

"Thanks. I practice at home every day."

"She's going to be off and in music school before I ever finish secondary school," Mohammad says warmly.

"What about me?" Nina pouts, crossing her arms.

"What do you like to do in school?" I ask, giving her all of my attention.

"Art," she says softly.

"Noah loves art too," I offer.

Nina flushes, her eyes staying glued down on her tray. Mohammad lets out a groan at her obvious blush.

We finish our food and cocoa, and then Mohammad leads us back through the museum to the front entrance.

"All right, we should be off," he says, ushering his sisters outside. I can tell he's over this outing. "Maya, hold Nina's hand, please."

Maya looks at Mohammad like he's crazy, but Mohammad insists again.

"Maya," he says firmly.

She takes Nina's hand, looking annoyed.

"All right, Leela, say bye," Mohammad says to his sister.

Leela throws her arms up next to Noah, and he picks her up.

"Bye," she whispers, hugging him.

"Bye bye," he replies, giving her belly a small tickle before setting her back down.

"It was nice to meet you," I say, smiling at the girls.

Leela waves at me before grabbing on to Mohammad. Nina waves shyly, and Maya gives me an actual smile.

"I'll see you at school," Mohammad says, nodding to me and Noah.

And a second later, they're off, going down the long sidewalk leading to the museum exit.

As I watch them, I can't help but grin.

"That was really fun." I smile, practically feeling high.

Mohammad's sisters each have a distinct, lovable personality. And there's just something about kids. They have a way of pulling at your heart.

"You're glowing." Noah laughs, looking me over.

"I can't help it. Everything about this afternoon was a breath of fresh air."

"What was your favorite part?" he asks as a shiver runs through me.

The cold October air has officially set in, and even though the weather's almost the exact same in New York City, I'm never quite ready for the transition. I take in a deep breath, accepting the cold as we walk in the direction of the Williams' house.

"It was all of it," I answer. "The museum, the coffee. We did something new and fun, but it felt really wholesome. We got to learn and hang out. And kids are ... I don't know. It sounds silly, but they're just so pure. They don't hide their emotions. They let you in, and you can see when they're happy and sad. I like that."

"Mohammad's sisters can be a lot sometimes. But this afternoon was fun," Noah admits.

"You know, you're surprisingly good with kids."

"It's not hard. Kids, they're just mirrors. And they want constant attention. If you can accept those two facts, I think it's not that bad," he replies.

"I'm sure it would be a lot to live with them full-time. But it was a special afternoon for me."

"I appreciate you inviting me," Noah says, glancing at me.

His words take me by surprise.

"You didn't need the invitation. You know you're always invited to stuff like this."

"Yeah, but you were right. Things got heated this weekend. Anyway, you didn't have to ask me to come. You could have gone by yourself with Mohammad and his sisters. But I appreciate it."

A smile pulls at my lips. "So, does that mean you had fun too?"

"Oh, definitely," Noah banters back.

"And what was your favorite part?" I say as we turn onto our street.

"Hmm, I thought the birds were pretty cool," he answers.

"Uh, no. They were creepy, just hanging there, dead and stuffed. That whole animal display section was just ... weird," I disagree.

"You asked what *my* favorite part was," he points out, raising his eyebrows at me.

"Fine, I guess you're allowed to have your opinion," I tease. "I like seeing what everyone was drawn to. I always find that part interesting."

"Yeah. It's hard, trying to keep up with the *hellhounds* though," Noah says, quoting Mohammad.

"They were fast. And intrigued by everything." I laugh.

"I can't imagine babysitting three girls who want to be independent."

"I don't know. It was pretty fun."

"You were taken with Leela," Noah says, eyeing me.

"She was adorable. And sweet." I pout, just thinking about her cute little face. "You and Maya talked a lot."

"She's bloody smart. And she's super dedicated to her music. Mohammad wasn't exaggerating when he said she'd probably be off to school for it before him. She's amazing."

"Wow. That's really cool," I reply as we get to the house. Number 32.

Noah unlocks the door, and I drop my bag and slip out of my shoes the second we get inside.

"All right there?" Gene says from the living room.

"Fine, thanks." I smile, pulling off my jacket.

Helen must have heard us come in because she pops her head out from the kitchen.

"How was the museum?" she asks with excitement.

"Fine," Noah replies as he hangs up his coat.

"Dinner's almost finished. Why don't you two run along and change?" Helen instructs.

"All right," Noah says, grabbing his backpack.

"I was thinking about having Gene light a fire after dinner," Helen adds. "There's a chill in the air. If you two want, you can do your homework down here tonight."

"You'll make hot cocoa?" Noah asks instinctively.

"If you'd like," Helen replies.

"Cheers, Mum," he says, walking through the living room to the kitchen. He places a kiss on his mother's cheek as I move toward the staircase.

"But you've already had hot chocolate to—" I start, but Noah's quickly at my side, covering my mouth with his hand, smiling innocently at his mom.

"We will go change," he says, pushing me up the stairs.

Gene looks at us, confused, but must not care too much because, a moment later, he's looking back down at his book.

"Hey," I argue, pulling Noah's hand off of me.

He continues to push me up the stairs, and it isn't until we're in the hallway that he lets me turn around to look at him.

"You were going to rat me out to my mum," he says, looking at me, appalled.

"I was just stating—"

"You were just stating that I shouldn't be allowed two hot chocolates in one day," Noah says, arching an eyebrow.

"I mean, it is a lot of sugar and chocolate."

"Are you trying to tell me that I'm getting fat?" He cocks his head to the side, looking exasperated.

I drop my chin and let out a groan. "I didn't mean that," I say as Noah pulls off his tie and starts unbuttoning his shirt. "I was just commenting on how you've already had one today. I wasn't *judging* you."

As I am speaking, Noah takes off his oxford shirt and the white T-shirt underneath it. He looks down at his naked stomach, his hair falling onto his forehead as he examines his flat core and chest.

"Hmm. I didn't think I was getting fat. But if you think so …" He looks up at me questioningly.

I roll my eyes, not about to play this game with him.

"I didn't say you were fat," I correct, crossing my arms over my chest.

"Well, you've hurt my feelings," he says, pushing out his bottom lip. It's like his eyes form into big puppy-dog saucers as he looks at me.

"I apologize." I know that he's teasing me and decide it's better to just let him have his fun and then be done with it.

"Apologize for what?" Noah asks, blinking a few times. His lips are curved upward, but they're pressed firmly closed as he keeps a straight face.

"For insinuating that another hot chocolate wouldn't be good for you."

"I know that you care about my health and my physique and just want the best for me," Noah says, finally cracking a smile. "So, I think I need to show you that two hot chocolates in one day won't break my diet," he says as he grabs my hands and places them on his bare chest.

I step back at the warmth, but Noah moves with me, keeping his hands on top of mine.

He guides my palms down over his chest. Across his hard stomach.

I can feel his muscles tense under my fingers.

I suck in a breath and try to convince myself that if I'm holding my breath, time isn't moving forward. And if time isn't moving forward, that means, this isn't actually happening. It's just some half-second getting lost in the reality of my life.

But it's not.

And I'm firmly aware of that fact when Noah pushes my hands down to his waistband and then drags them back up to his thick shoulders. He takes a step closer, moving my hands along his collarbone, to the edge of his rounded shoulders, and down over to the top of his back.

"What do you feel?" Noah asks matter-of-factly, taking another step closer to me.

I feel like I'm about to pass out.

I feel like my hands are about to burn off, leaving little stubs at the ends of my arms.

But I know that isn't the answer he's looking for.

"I feel muscles," I state.

And with my words, it's like the moment is gone.

"Exactly." Noah smiles, removing my hands from his skin.

He holds my wrists out in front of his chest before letting them go. And the moment he drops them, it feels like they practically fall to the floor. They're heavy, and I can barely register that those hands that were just all over him are mine.

"And muscle needs fat, protein, and carbs. The more muscle mass you have, the more fat and calories you burn, even when resting." He raises his eyebrows at me like he's won and then adds, "I'm going to change for dinner."

A second later, he's gone while I stay, standing still, frozen in the hallway.

Because what the fuck?

Like.

What.

The.

Actual.

Fuck?

My mouth drops open as I think about his blatantly pompous, self-affirming attitude. I cannot believe for one second that he actually just did that to me.

And he was enjoying himself!

I try to relax.

Maybe this is a good thing.

Maybe this means that Noah is through his whole *pouting about me being with Harry* phase, and he's moved on to just annoying me again.

Yes.

This could be good.

I try to convince myself that it's a good thing that he feels comfortable teasing me again.

And that's what's important.

I shake my head as I push into my room. Then, I shut the door firmly behind me and fall onto my bed. I don't bother to change. Instead, I grab my phone out of my bag, calling Harry's number.

I told him I'd call him after school, and it's been a good two hours since classes were over.

"Was beginning to think you'd forgotten about me," Harry answers, his voice seeping into me.

"Sorry," I reply quickly. "I went to the museum after school with Mohammad, Noah, and Mohammad's sisters."

"Ah, how was it?" Harry asks with interest.

"Mohammad said he messaged and asked you about coming. You said no?" I think back to what Mohammad said at the museum when I asked about Harry.

"Yeah, wasn't really in the mood for screaming kids and a packed museum."

"But I was there."

"You're upset I didn't come?"

"I just missed you today."

Geography was different without having him there, and after last night, I did really want to see him at school.

"I missed you too. And last night."

"How did last night go?"

"It was fine. He's less of a prick than I remember, but after a few drinks, it didn't matter anyway."

"Thus the hangover."

"Thus the hangover," he agrees.

"Did you take him to the club or …" I ask, giving him a chance to tell me.

"A curious little cat tonight," Harry teases. "We had drinks in his suite, which had a fully stocked bar."

"Oh?"

"Anyway, had a few scotches to take the edge off. It also lessened his incessant chattering, and he turned out to be an all right bloke. Ended up going out to the club. Sent him home with a girl."

"Wow," I exhale, my stomach tightening.

"I slept at my house," he clarifies. "Alone, in case you were wondering."

"I wasn't. And … the drugs?"

"He took a few hits of weed before we left, but that was it."

"Nice," I comment, silently thankful that it wasn't anything more than that.

"I told you though, I was expected to entertain him."

"And did you enjoy yourself?" I ask, feeling less freaked out about things now.

"I won't lie. It was fun. We got pretty toasted at the club, but all I could think about was you," he says, his voice dropping.

I roll onto my side, letting the phone lay on my ear.

"While some other girl was trying to dance with you."

"You know me, babe. I wouldn't do that. Anyway, we stumbled back to his hotel. I made sure he was off to his comfy bed with his woman and then took a cab home."

"Sounds like a romantic evening," I tease.

"Very." Harry chuckles sarcastically.

"I don't know," I insist. "It kind of was. I still can't believe our date. Pizza. A chocolate-covered strawberry bouquet. You spoiled me last night."

"I had every intention of spoiling you."

"So you could get lucky?"

"I could get lucky with you without any of that," Harry says easily.

"What makes you so sure?" I ask, smiling into the phone.

Because he's right. I'm always the one trying to move things along.

I *always* get caught in the moment, wrapped up in the way that he makes me feel.

"The way you look at me. It's easy to tell that you want me."

"Mmhmm," I agree. "Well, will I see you at school tomorrow?"

"You can count on it."

"Is that all I can count on?" I ask.

"Why don't you come over tomorrow after school and find out?" Harry offers.

"Will we study?" I grin into the phone.

"Absolutely not," Harry banters.

"Well, I would love that."

"It's a date."

"It's a date," I agree. "Wait, aren't Tuesday nights your, uh … squash match things?"

"Aww, look at you. You know my schedule," Harry says with enthusiasm.

"Come off it," I reply, feeling my cheeks flush.

"Nah. Every other week," Harry answers.

"Okay, cool."

"See you tomorrow then?"

"See you tomorrow," I agree.

"Promise to think about me tonight," Harry instructs, his

voice dropping.

"I don't know … there are so many things to think about," I tease.

"How about you think about the way I made you feel yesterday when my hands were between your thighs?"

Harry's words make my chest pound.

"Harry, I have to go down to dinner," I whisper, my whole body warming.

"Well, maybe you should ring me before bed then. I can tell you exactly what I want you to think about when you're good and alone."

"That's tempting," I stutter.

"How about I show you tomorrow instead?"

"Deal," I agree, immediately relaxing.

"Bye, babe," Harry replies before ending the call.

I let my phone slide out of my hand, dropping it onto the ground. I want to stay in bed forever.

Hide away in this room.

Because hearing Harry's voice makes me feel flushed and excited.

I missed him today.

But I know that I need to get down to dinner.

I quickly change into jeans and a sweater, worrying that I was probably on the phone for too long.

I head downstairs, taking my geography and art folders with me. Helen already has dinner on the table, but Noah isn't downstairs yet. After a few minutes, he joins us, and we sit down to eat.

ONCE WE FINISH dinner, Helen urges us into the living room. Gene lights the fire before getting comfortable in his chair. Helen makes hot cocoa in the kitchen, and Noah and I sit on the floor and spread our homework out on the coffee table.

"Here we are," Helen says, bringing in two cups of hot chocolate.

Noah gets up and goes into the kitchen, coming back out with the other two cups in hand. He gives one to his dad and the other to his mom.

"Well, this is lovely." Helen takes a sip of her cocoa, letting out a long, relaxed exhale.

"This *is* rather good," Gene agrees, pushing up his glasses as he takes a sip.

Noah and I work on our homework while Gene and Helen read. We sit quietly, not talking, but all together.

And it's nice.

The warm fire.

Being in a space where everyone is together.

It's a lot better than sitting up in my room, trying to study. Because everything becomes a distraction.

I consider giving Helen my art project, but I kind of want to do it when we are alone. Not in front of the whole family.

I also realize that if I open my art folder, I will see Noah's collage. I decide to wait and focus on my reading for Geography instead.

AFTER A GOOD hour, Noah slams his textbook shut.

"I think I'm done for the night," he states, causing Helen to look at the clock.

I glance up, seeing that Gene's already fallen asleep in his chair. Helen notices, too, a warm smile forming on her face.

"We ought to be off to bed as well," Helen agrees, waking Gene up.

They take our mugs into the kitchen and then say good night.

"Are you going to bed?" I ask Noah as we go upstairs.

"Nah. I'll probably play some games for a bit. What about

you?" he asks.

"I don't know. Maybe read for class."

Noah nods, giving me a smile before heading into his room.

When I'm back in my room, I walk over to the window and touch the glass. Cold air is seeping in, and there's a chill in the air.

I pull Noah's sweatpants and a thick sweatshirt out of the drawer and then change into them before grabbing my textbook and curling up in bed.

I can hear the sounds of Noah's game coming through the wall, and it's sort of like a lulling white noise. But at the same time, it's kind of distracting. I try to stay focused on my chapter but end up tossing it to the side.

I walk to Noah's room, pushing gently on his door. He's seated in his gaming chair, a video controller in his hand. I close the door behind me and study the screen. He's playing some game where he's a soldier running quickly through thick, tall grass. He glances over, seeing me, but keeps playing.

I fall onto his bed, watching as he runs toward the little red arrows marked on the screen, which I'm assuming are the opponents.

But then he pauses it and turns around to look at me. "You're in my bed."

"Yeah." I laugh. "Way to notice."

Noah clicks a few buttons, exiting the game before getting up and moving toward me. "You're in my bed *and* in my sweats."

"I just came to chill. Watch you game. I could hear you in the other room."

"You're distracting."

"What?" I ask as Noah slides next to me on the bed. His weight shifts the mattress, causing me to fall toward him.

"I thought you were reading."

"I'm kind of over reading for the day," I admit.

"You have to take breaks."

"Like you?" I ask, glancing over his shoulder to the home screen of his game that's flashing in the background.

"I did most of my homework," Noah replies.

I roll my eyes. "Of course you did."

"So cheeky this evening." Noah laughs, relaxing into his bed.

"Yeah, well … something about being sassy just gives me energy."

"You're always sassy."

"Mmhmm."

Noah rolls onto his side, his eyes wandering down my body. "You've claimed these for good then?"

"Should I take them off?" I ask, looking down at his sweats and instantly regretting my decision to wear them. No matter how many times I think things should just be normal between us, I don't know if they ever will be.

"Take them off …" Noah repeats my words, his eyelashes fluttering. "Hey, if you feel like lying in my bed in just your knickers, then why not?"

"Noah," I say, feeling my cheeks flush as he lets out a deep laugh. "I meant, do you want them back?"

"No, I don't. I like when you wear them," he admits.

"You do?"

Noah nods, his hands moving to the waistband and pulling on it, seeing how they gape around my hips. "They're too big."

"I know," I say with a laugh. "Did you expect them to fit me?"

"No." Noah shakes his head, still looking at his pants. He plays with the strings, his fingers running over the waistband.

"You still wear them though?"

"They're comfortable," I answer.

"They don't fit you properly," he disagrees.

"That's the point. All of my stuff fits perfectly against me. I like these because they are soft and loose."

"So, it has nothing to do with me then?" Noah says, his eyes connecting with mine.

"What would it have to do with you?"

Noah pushes out his bottom lip and shakes his head. "I guess nothing at all."

"No, come on. I want to hear it." I laugh, taking in his silly expression.

"Well, if you're going to nick my favorite sweats, I'd at least like to think you did it for sentimental reasons as opposed to *they're loose*."

"I know what you want me to say," I reply, leaning up onto my elbow.

"And what's that?" he asks, his eyes flicking up to mine.

"You want me to say that I wear them because they remind me of you," I state matter-of-factly.

"No," Noah replies, adamantly shaking his head.

"No?" I question, wanting him to explain.

"Nope. I would never put words into your mouth."

"Really?"

"Of course not. Too many times, we tell people what we want them to think or do. Feel even …"

"Then, it's not a question of what I want or think. What does it make you think?" I ask, grinning. I feel like I've won again in one of our verbal battles, and I know that he's going to have to answer me.

Noah looks shocked, but I see his lips pull at the corner. "I would say that seeing you in my sweats, well, it's normal, isn't it?"

"Normal?"

"Well, given the option, I prefer seeing you in them rather than myself." He chuckles.

"See, I told you, sentimental."

"Not sentimental," Noah disagrees. "More primal."

"Are we animals now?" I laugh.

"Do you want to be?" Noah almost growls, his mouth widening into a smile.

But then he dips his head down to my neck, shaking it back and forth like he's mauling me. I can't help the stream of giggles that escape my mouth at the sensation.

"That noise." I grin, swatting him away.

"Did you like that?" he asks, laughing now too.

"I think it's the funniest and weirdest noise I've ever heard you make," I say as I sit up, wiping at my wet neck.

As Noah smiles, his tongue slips down onto his lip. I watch it, following it as it moves across his lip and then retreats back into his mouth. Noah's whole face is glowing, his cheeks forced up with his smile. When I finally make it up to his eyes, I see him raise an eyebrow at me, and my breath catches in my throat with the motion.

But then Noah closes his lips, his cheeks slipping back into their regular spot on his face.

"No more slobbering on my neck," I state, lying back down on his pillow.

"I'll do my best," he replies with a dramatic eye roll.

"Don't sass me with an eye roll," I say sternly. But then I crack, giving him a smile. "Who would have thought you could have such a long conversation about sweats?" I say, my mind drifting back to the pants.

"Not me—that's for sure," Noah replies. He keeps his lips pulled flat, but I see the hint of sarcasm sparkling in his eyes.

"You're being a brat tonight," I huff.

"Mmhmm," Noah agrees, laying his head down next to mine on the pillow.

"What am I going to do with you, Noah Williams?" I breathe out, looking back at him.

Noah glances down, his fingers moving to the strings again, playing with it. But then he's looking back up at me, and it causes me to swallow hard. Because Noah's hair is in his eyes. And my fingers ache at my sides to brush it off his face. My eyes glide down to his Adam's apple, his neck pushing out toward me, his head tilting back.

"I think, whatever you want, Mallory James," he says, looking back at me seriously.

His rounded lips are closed in a straight line, but I see his lips twitch as he gives me a one-sided smile. I blink a few times, as he pushes out a long breath through his nose. I stare at Noah, feeling like I've been sucked into a dream.

Neither of us moves.

We just stay where we are with our heads on the pillow. Noah's eyes slip across my face, and I watch him study me.

I look back at him, letting my eyes explore his skin.

It's like his words are hanging in the air around us. They don't mean anything. Or maybe they mean everything.

But it doesn't really matter.

I keep myself there, in that spot, for as long as I can. Until Noah suddenly sits up, running his hands through his hair and glancing at the clock.

"I should get to bed," I offer, sitting up with him.

"Yeah," Noah agrees, nodding at me.

I give him a small smile as I stand up.

"Good night," I say, turning back to him when I get to his door.

"Good night, Mal."

TUESDAY, OCTOBER 8TH
Rip off her dress.
6:15AM

"WHAT IS THIS?" Noah's voice slips through my bedroom, waking me up.

"What's what?" I groan, rolling over onto my side. I pull my comforter up around my neck, trying to cocoon myself. I'm not ready for the day to start yet, and I'm absolutely *not* ready to get out of bed.

The bed gives next to me as Noah sits down.

"Whoa," Noah exhales.

His excited tone pulls me out of my sleepy morning daze, and I roll over to see what he's doing. When my eyes land on him, he's leaning his back against my headboard, flipping through *Taming the Duke.*

"It's just a book," I groan, rolling back over.

"It's porn," Noah disagrees. He flips from one page to another, the sound of rolling paper filling my ears.

"It's romance," I reply, wiping my eyes. I blink a few times, trying to get my eyes to cooperate with me this morning.

But they really don't want to.

They're cloudy and heavy. And all they want to do is stay closed and go back to sleep.

"It's definitely porn. Well written porn though," Noah

says observantly.

I let out a small huff, knowing that there's no going back to sleep now.

Because we all know boys and porn—or, well, this *supposed* porn. And he's assumably not going to give up on the conversation before exhausting it.

I roll back over in his direction, glancing up at him.

"Courtesy of your mom," I reply, sitting up.

"Eww," Noah says with a wince. "Was she reading this?"

"She finished it before giving it to me." I smile. "Us girls have to stick together, you know?"

Noah drops his chin, looking at me, unconvinced. I glance down, taking in his body clothed in a long-sleeved black top and jogging pants.

"Is this what girls want?" he continues, his eyes scanning across the page. "For a man to ... barrel into the bedroom and rip off her dress?"

"Basically." I nod.

Noah starts reading. *"For the usually reserved and guarded duke, all of his defenses were down. He wasn't hiding behind formalities or societal rules. He was more animal than dignified man, spreading her legs wide apart—"*

"Oh my God, can you stop reading?" I flush, trying to grab the book from his hands.

But Noah marks the page with his finger and extends it up over his head.

I try to climb on him to reach it, but I'm half asleep, and his shirt is that slippery material. I roll back over to my side of the bed, throwing my head down into my pillow and giving up.

"Why are you in my room?" I ask grumpily as Noah chuckles.

"I brought you coffee."

I instantly sit up, wondering how I could have missed the coffee. I look around Noah and notice a steaming mug sitting on the bedside table. It's next to my clock, and I squint my eyes, reading the time.

"It's six fifteen. Are you mad?" I let out a heavy breath, feeling like I might cry. Or pout-cry. I'm not sure which. I just know that I want to curl back up into a ball and sleep for another forty-five minutes.

"I'm taking you on a long run this morning. So, I thought you'd need the extra energy."

"I'm sleepy," I disagree, burrowing myself in the bed.

"Well, that's too bad."

"Noah," I whine.

"Nope." He shakes his head firmly. "This is your punishment."

"For what?" I squeak.

"For getting salty with me yesterday about not asking you to run. So, there's absolutely no way you're getting out of this."

"I should have never brought it up," I huff.

"Nope," Noah agrees.

"Fine," I sigh, sitting up in bed.

Noah hands me the coffee cup and then says, "Let's check out this book." He shifts on my bed, crossing his legs at his ankles, getting comfortable.

"I thought you wanted to run?"

"You need your coffee first," he replies.

"I bookmarked my page. You might as well pick up there then," I say, leaning my head back against my bed frame.

"So, this is what you do in bed at night."

"Not typically." I laugh, the warm coffee relaxing me. "But I have to give it to your mom. This book has a way of sucking you in."

"Which part are you at?"

"They just met for the first time. The beginning. He likes her—clearly." I smile, thinking about the chapter I read last night.

Noah opens it up to my tabbed page and starts reading. "*Mr. Taylor paces the length of the hallway, taking it in long, brisk strides. He wraps his fingers together, his knuckles tensing. Harriet doesn't know what to do. Is she to intervene? He hasn't noticed her hiding in the corner, watching his face contort as thoughts consume his mind,*" Noah says before letting out a laugh. "Sounds like he's upset about something."

"He's upset by his feelings," I clarify. "He doesn't know what to do. He's taken with her but mad at himself for falling in love."

"Oh my," Noah says, his eyes flashing.

"Keep going," I insist.

"*But a moment later—and too soon—Harriet is caught. Mr. Taylor spots her, and she knows the exact moment when she is no longer hidden in the shadows. Mr. Taylor's strides halt, and his back, before arched, extends itself, pulling him taller and taller. It's as though a delicate hand rose up the back of his spine, elongating him. And not a moment later, his entire frame turns, focusing in on the shadow.*"

"She's been caught," I say, waggling my eyebrows.

"What does that mean?" Noah asks, glancing over to me.

"It means that they're alone in a dark hallway. And they have feelings for each other."

"Ah," Noah says. "*And Harriet knows when Mr. Taylor has found her eyes. She's tried all night to keep her gaze concealed, hiding behind her lashes. Though, even now, hiding in the shadows, she knows there is something between them. Mr. Taylor extends his long legs, slinking toward her in the shadows. He walks like a night cat, cautious and calculating. But once his*" *hands find her hips, that caution is gone. He pushes Harriet against the doorframe, unlacing her bodice until her breasts are bursting out toward him,*" Noah says, his voice rising higher and higher with each word. "This is very sexy," he says, clearing his throat.

"Shall I open a window for you? Are you getting flushed?" I tease, fanning him with my hand.

"If anyone's getting flushed, it's you," he replies.

"I don't know. This seems more up your alley."

"What, historical romance?" Noah asks with a chuckle, his nose scrunching up.

"No. They just talk differently in these books. Everything is vague and has a hidden meaning."

"I'm not sure if *he was about to ravish her* has a hidden meaning," Noah replies, amused.

"I mean the way they talk, silly," I clarify, taking a sip of my coffee.

"The formality?"

"Mmhmm. I'm always saying you're old and wise."

"Like a fine wine," Noah says, his eyebrows rising as his cheek pulls up on one side. "Was I born in the wrong era?"

"Nah. That wouldn't be fun." I take another sip of my coffee before handing it to Noah, motioning for him to set it back down on the bedside table.

"Because you wouldn't know me?" he asks.

"Obviously." I smile, laying my head back against the bed frame. I'm not really ready to get up yet, but the coffee has at least woken me up enough to keep me from falling back asleep. "It's sort of romantic though. The book."

"What, their sex?" Noah asks.

And I can't blame him for thinking that because it is the part we left off on.

"No, just their love. I mean, he's falling in love with her."

"It sounds like he's falling in love with her boobs," Noah disagrees.

"I thought you said body, mind, soul. It doesn't matter because there's no distinction," I fire back.

"We both know that attraction can just be surface level."

"Well, I guess we'll just have to wait to read and see. Then, we can find out if it goes beyond the surface."

"From the sounds of it, they're going to take a lot of time enjoying the surface," Noah says. "*Plunge, consume ...*" He goes on, flipping a few pages ahead.

I let out a squeal, covering my eyes.

"It's kind of erotic, isn't it?" Noah says.

"No, it *definitely* is."

"When you read this stuff, are you just, what, supposed to get off from it or—"

"Noah," I say, my face flushing.

"What? We can't talk about that?" he asks.

"The point is that you're falling into an imaginary world," I clarify. Because I *do not* want to be talking about *getting off* with Noah.

"Is *this* world so bad?" Noah asks seriously.

"It's just a story. It's about how one couple fell in love. It's about what passion and romance mean. It's supposed to take you somewhere else for a while, I guess."

"So, that means that you don't get turned on by it?" Noah asks, looking over at me.

"That's personal. And it's kind of weird to think about, seeing as *your mom* gave me the book."

"Stop reminding me," Noah says, flaring his nostrils.

I roll my eyes in response.

"But you didn't answer my question."

"Why do you want to know if I do?"

"Because it seems like something you'd get turned on by.

But that's just my opinion," Noah says, getting up off the bed.

"Wait, which part?" I ask curiously.

Noah sets the book on the side table as he answers, "Sweeping her off her feet. Throwing her against a wall. I can see you fancying both."

"Romance and ravage?" I ask, throwing off my covers and getting out of bed.

"Mmhmm," Noah answers as I walk toward my dresser.

I pull open a drawer, getting out my workout pants and a sweatshirt.

"Maybe I'm one of those girls who just wants to be treated like a princess," I argue even though that's completely not true.

"Maybe you're a princess in the respect that you have nice hair and smell good," Noah offers, leaning his back against the door.

"But not in the bedroom?" I ask with a surprised laugh.

Noah shakes his head. "Nah. You want to be romanced *out* of the bedroom."

"And what about *in* the bedroom?" I ask, moving to my desk to grab a hair tie.

"In the bedroom, you need … someone else in control," Noah finally replies.

"But I love to be in control," I disagree, collecting my hair into a tight ponytail.

"That's the problem. There are times in life when you have to be able to … let go."

Noah smirks at me, and I can't help but give him a little shove.

"Come on. Follow and talk," I say, moving him out of my doorway. I walk across the hall to the bathroom and pick up my toothbrush. "Enough about me. What do you think about the duke?"

I throw toothpaste onto my brush and start brushing my teeth as I listen. Noah leans against the doorframe, crossing his arms over his chest.

"I think he's obsessed with her—or sex—and he can't think straight."

"And you're not? What sixteen-year-old boy can come to that conclusion? Besides, he likes her."

"Of course I'm not. They're desperate for one another. That's lust, not love." Noah shakes his head.

"But by the end of the book, they'll be in love. So, does it really matter?"

"Well, hopefully, they will be, or it'd be a rather shit book, wouldn't it?"

I hold up my finger, rinsing out my mouth. "I don't think you can write off their love just because it's sudden and passionate. Not everything has to be slow and thought out, you know? Don't you ever just want to … I don't know … grab someone and kiss them? Or scream? Or run? I know you feel that passion. Expressing it isn't a bad thing."

"If you weren't so slow in the morning, I'd already be on my run," Noah states, cocking his head to the side. He taps on the doorframe with his knuckles. "I'll meet you downstairs."

I close the door behind him and quickly change. When I get downstairs, Noah's standing at the front door with his shoes on, ready to go.

OUR RUN IS shorter than normal, and we have to take a different route to end up back at the house in time to get ready for school.

Noah said it was because I spent too long drinking my coffee.

But I said it was because he spent too long reading my erotic book.

And that shut him up pretty quickly.

When we get back to the house, I'm wide awake. I shower and change for school, deciding to wrap a thick sweater around my shoulders because of the chill. I add a dark navy eye shadow to my lids, which matches my uniform, and a swipe of mascara.

Something about the color puts a smile on my face. It makes me feel like fall has officially arrived.

I decide to switch up my bag, using an oversized purse to put my notebooks into. I take out my and Noah's art projects, making sure to be careful. I tuck them into my desk drawer to keep them safe.

I throw the gold chains of the purse over my shoulder and then head downstairs.

I find Noah in the kitchen with his Chemistry book open. He's scribbling across a sheet, writing out illegible answers.

"Last minute attempt to finish your homework?" I ask, glancing over his shoulder.

"I couldn't be bothered with it last night," Noah admits.

"Do you understand the material, or are you just filling it out, so it's complete?" I ask, curious.

"Nah, it's not that hard," he says, looking over the sheet. "Want to grab some juice today? I already made our lunches."

I follow Noah's gaze to the counter, seeing our filled lunch sacks.

"Sounds perfect," I answer.

"Cool."

Noah shoves his homework into his folder, rises from the table, and then puts his folder and our lunches into his backpack, zipping it closed.

"Where are your parents?" I ask, taking in the empty kitchen and living room.

"Already off to work," Noah answers. "They slipped out

while you were still in the shower."

"Aww," I draw out, my lips pulling to the side.

"Aww what?" Noah asks, walking toward the front door.

"I don't know." I shrug as we both put on our shoes. "I feel sort of silly for even thinking it."

"No, tell me," Noah insists, looking up at me as he ties his shoes.

"I guess I just like having them around in the mornings. It's nice."

"Sometimes, it's nice to have the house to ourselves though," Noah comments, pulling on his coat.

"Yeah, sometimes. But not in the morning. Or right before bed. There's something comforting about having someone downstairs when you wake up and someone still up, reading, when you go to sleep. You know?"

"Yeah, I guess," Noah replies as he opens the front door.

I zip up my coat as we step outside.

"Don't get me wrong; I love alone time. But I do really like your house and the company," I say as we walk.

"Maybe we should trade places for a bit. You can stay with my mum and dad, and I'll visit your family in New York."

"Do you think it would be weird for you? I mean, the whole exchange thing?"

"For sure. I'm don't know how you've managed it, honestly."

"What do you mean?"

"It had to have been hard to come here. The idea of making new friends, staying at a new house. It's impressive. I'd never do it."

"But your sister's the type who would?" I ask.

"Mia definitely is. She's like that though. She's always moving from one spot to the next. I can see her living in a ton of different places. She has a way of fitting in naturally wherever she is."

"How do you think it will be when she comes back?" I ask, looking over to Noah. "Speaking of seeing our families, are you excited to see her?"

"I've missed her. But I like your company too," Noah replies, glancing over to me.

I smile at him.

It's weird to think about what it will be like when I go home. It's only days away at this point.

Noah squints his eyes as he thinks. "Every time we've spoken, she goes on and on about loving Greece, so I can see her coming back a convert. She'll likely want to dress like she did there or prepare the traditional foods for my parents. She's just one of those people who's constantly seeking out variety."

"That could be fun though. You'll get to eat a bunch of Greek food and hear all of her stories. And maybe she'll bring you back something. A seashell. Or maybe a piece of art." I smile.

"I don't need any gifts." Noah grins. "But, yeah, she would be the type to bring me back something."

"Maybe I need to think about getting my family a gift."

"I think you being home is the best gift you're going to give them."

"I've only been gone two and a half weeks," I point out.

"That's so strange." Noah shakes his head, disbelief flashing across his face.

"What is?"

"It feels like you've been here a lot longer than that," Noah offers.

"It actually does." I laugh as we stop at a red walk light. "Do you want to go grab the juice, so I can get us some coffee?"

"*Us?*" Noah smiles, his eyebrows rising.

"Fine, *me*," I restate, pursing my lips.

"Yeah, that's fine," Noah agrees. "But can you grab a few granola bars? You ate through my locker stash."

"You had a locker stash?" I tease with a grin.

And it's easy to imagine organized stacks of granola bars tucked perfectly into the back of Noah's locker. Always at the ready.

"Yes, and you destroyed it," Noah states.

I roll my eyes. "Fine, I'll get you some granola bars and meet you at school."

Noah nods before walking off. I head to the coffee shop, grabbing an assortment of granola bars for Noah and a bag of crisps for Harry, and then order a cappuccino to go. The man working behind the counter cracks a smile when he sees my pile, and I feel the need to clarify that they're not all for me. He nods like he understands, but I'm not convinced he actually believes me.

I throw the food into my purse, grab the coffee, and head to school.

When I get into the common room, I don't see Noah anywhere. I sit down to wait on one of the couches, seeing that we still have about ten minutes before classes start. I watch the front entrance, hoping to see Harry walk in.

Or Noah.

Or at this point, even Mohammad.

But when the warning bell goes off, signaling we only have five minutes until class, I decide to give up on my effort and head to Statistics.

Think about going home.
STATISTICS

RIGHT AS THE bell rings, Noah strides into class. He doesn't look flushed or like he rushed.

He doesn't even look tense. If anything, he looks pleased with himself. Like he secretly knows that he couldn't have timed his entrance any better.

He smiles to Mr. Johnson as he walks past his desk, and I swear, I hear at least three girls collectively sigh at his grin.

"That was a bit close," he comments, sliding into his seat.

"Where were you?" I ask, taking a sip of my coffee. "I waited in the common room."

"Apparently, not long enough," Noah replies, setting a brown paper bag onto his desk.

"I didn't want to be late." I watch as he pulls out two juices and a paper container.

"There was a line. And they had these blueberry muffins that I had to wait for."

Noah hands me the container. I open it, immediately getting hit with the scent of warm sugar and blueberries.

It smells like heaven.

And it will be amazing with my coffee.

"Ahhh," I squeal, looking between the muffin and juice, trying to figure out what to eat or drink first. I reach my arms out for Noah, wanting to hug him.

"What are you doing?" He chuckles, looking at my extended hands.

I can't quite reach him because there's a bar on the side of my desk, barricading me in.

"I'm trying to hug you." I laugh, wiggling my fingers at

him.

Noah leans away from me, his eyes squinting with his grin.

"You're so strange," he says, shaking his head.

"Give me your hand," I insist.

Noah gives in, placing his hand in mine. I give it a quick, hard squeeze before dropping it and turning my attention back to my muffin.

"There's no eating in class, Miss James," Mr. Johnson says, eyeing my muffin.

My mouth quivers, instinctively pushing out a pout.

Because he didn't even give me a chance to sneak a taste.

He could have at least let me steal a bite before telling me to put it away.

I look up at him with puppy eyes.

"But it's warm," I whisper to myself, closing the top of the box.

"All right, let's settle down, please," Mr. Johnson says coolly, standing up behind his desk.

I glance over to Noah, still sad about my muffin. He gives me an encouraging smile, but it doesn't really help.

I look back to Mr. Johnson, who you'd swear was standing in front of a camera instead of a classroom. He has this subtle grin plastered on his face and just oozes a quiet confidence.

Usually, it's something I appreciate about him.

But not today.

Not after he denied me my warm muffin.

"Well, unfortunately for your weekly plans, I've scheduled a rather abrupt exam for Friday," Mr. Johnson says, instantly losing him more credit.

The entire class groans, but Mr. Johnson holds up his hand, stopping us.

"This examination is going to be multiple choice and very different from your last one. I've also chosen to give you an exam on Friday because it is all we will be focusing on this week. As long as you do your homework, you should be able to get through it without trouble."

"What relief," I say under my breath.

Noah's still looking ahead, but he lets out a small chuckle, which means he heard me.

I practically fall asleep, listening to Mr. Johnson drone on and on through class. He shows us how to figure out the population mean, its standard deviation, and its variance.

I hear the words coming out of his mouth, but I don't really register them.

My eyes shift between Mr. Johnson and the brown box on the floor containing my muffin. It's probably growing cold and lonely in there, and being forced to sit here and not eat it is torture. I glance over to Noah, watching him take notes.

Maybe having my eyes on him will keep me from thinking about how hungry I am. Or about the fact that I was just denied my breakfast.

But it doesn't.

And my hunger starts to annoy me.

Really, everyone starts to annoy me.

Because they're all sitting and taking notes like good students while I, on the other hand, am plotting out ways to wipe the smile off of Mr. Johnson's face.

But just when I think I might implode, he passes out our homework and says we can use the last ten minutes of class to start on it.

I turn to Noah, letting out a growl before burying my head into my arms on my desk.

"Someone sounds hungry," Noah comments.

I peek up at him to see he's looking over the homework.

"Someone is," I agree, pulling myself up off my desk.

"Have you talked to your parents in a bit?"

"No. I need to though."

"I'm sure they're getting excited for you to be home," he says, glancing up at me.

"I don't even want to think about going home." I shake my head, trying to erase the thought. I pick up my pencil and look over the questions.

"I don't like it either. But you should phone your parents," Noah insists. "Ignoring them isn't going to change things."

"I'm not ignoring them. I just … I don't know what to say."

"Why don't you test it out on me?" Noah offers, tilting his head with interest.

I roll my eyes, but Noah gives me a stern look, so I come up with something.

"Hey, Mom, Dad. I can't wait to see you too. I mean, *of course* I'm happy to come home," I talk, pretending to hold a phone up to my ear. "What, what are you saying? I don't sound happy? Well, actually, *no*. I'm not happy about it at all. I'm likely going to be miserable, and it will be the two of you who will have to put up with me."

I smile at Noah. "What do you think? Think they'll like my call?"

"Well, if they can appreciate your sarcasm, I'm sure they'll love it," he says, smiling back. "All right, homework. Question one. Do you have the answer?"

I look from Noah down to the paper in front of me.

"Uhhh …" I pause, trying to come up with at least somewhere to start.

"You weren't paying attention at all, were you?" Noah sighs disapprovingly.

"I was annoyed with Mr. Johnson," I whisper, glancing up at our professor.

"So, in retaliation, you decided to ignore his lesson and ensure your failure of the homework. Sounds logical," Noah mutters.

"See, that's where you come in. You're my statistical fairy godmother. And as such, I know you'll help me."

Ha!

Take that, Noah Williams.

"Godmother?" Noah says, his mouth dropping open. "That seems a little off."

"Nope. I think it's pretty accurate," I reply.

Noah's face flashes with concern at the comparison. "I still feel weird about it," he disagrees.

"What? Why? Uh, never mind. Just forget it," I insist, laying my palms flat on the desk.

"Well, first off, I'm not a fairy. And secondly, I pay attention. It's not magic," Noah replies, looking back down at his homework.

"Let's hope someone else decides to take pity and sprinkle a little fairy dust on me. Or at least, on my homework. Because, otherwise, I'm screwed."

Magical or something.
LATIN

THE SECOND THE bell goes off, I'm flying out of the classroom.

We only got through the first two questions out of the ten on our homework, which likely means that I'm going to be spending at least another hour on the assignment tonight.

But right now, I don't have to think about that.

All I have to think about now is how I'm going to finish this juice and muffin before Latin. I crack open the juice, handing Noah the muffin box.

"I thought I was going to starve to death in there," I say, taking a greedy gulp of juice. "His whole *no eating in class* rule made him lose major points with me today. Especially because he hadn't even started class yet."

"Well, technically, we aren't supposed to eat in class," Noah says, opening up the muffin box as we get to my locker.

I take another big gulp, getting half the juice down.

"I *technically* don't care. Besides, professors should let you eat. If anything, they should encourage it. It doesn't make any sense to me. If I'm hungry, I'm not going to be focused on class," I say melodramatically, opening my locker.

"If you don't stop talking and start eating, you're going to sit through Latin with the same lovely attitude." Noah smiles, handing me the box.

"You make a fair point," I agree, taking a bite of the blueberry muffin. And everything about this muffin is perfect. It's soft and sugary, but it has enough flour to not be too sweet or fall apart. My eyes grow as I take another bite.

"Good?" Noah asks, looking between my mouth and the muffin.

"So good." I extend the muffin out to him, holding the box under it to collect all the crumbs.

Noah tilts his head, and instead of taking the muffin from my hand, he leans in and takes a bite. I watch him nod as he chews, evidently agreeing with me.

"Yum," he replies, wiping at his mouth.

I nod at him before putting my Latin textbook into my purse. It's then that I notice Noah's granola bars.

"Oh, your granolas," I say, taking out two handfuls. I leave the bag of crisps in my bag, glancing around the hallway.

I still haven't seen Harry this morning.

"What?" Noah asks, looking around with me as he takes the granola bars from my hand and puts them into his backpack.

"Uh, nothing," I comment, bringing the juice back to my lips before shoving another bite of muffin into my mouth.

"All right, see ya," Noah says, giving my shoulder a pat before heading off.

I double check that my locker is closed before going to class, taking another bite of muffin as I get to the door.

"Oh my God, that's rude." Mohammad's voice floats over my shoulder.

I turn around and am instantly greeted with his grin.

"Want some?" I offer.

"Yes," Mohammad states, stealing a bite. He chews quickly, licking his lips. "Wow."

"I know," I agree, looking down at the remains of the magical blueberry muffin.

"Where did it come from?" he asks, eyeing what's left.

I hand him a big, fat crumb. "The juice shop."

"Anytime you want to go for juice, I'm down. Just give me a ring, and I'll be there," Mohammad says brightly.

"Does that mean you'll drink juice with me?" I ask optimistically.

"Probably not." Mohammad chuckles. "But I'd be open to trying any other food they've got. Muffins, cakes. I'll take one for the team and give you my fair assessment of their products."

"How generous of you." I laugh, taking another gulp of juice and finishing off the bottle. I look around the hallway. "Have you seen Harry this morning?"

"Not yet," Mohammad replies, stealing another bite of muffin.

Hmm.

"I had fun last night, by the way," I say, turning my attention back to him.

"Really?" he asks, his eyes widening. He gives his head a sideways shake, like his body is trying to reject my statement.

"Really," I insist.

"Well, it was nice of you and Noah to tag along. It was good to have some help and the company."

"I know you secretly love spending time with them." Because I saw him smiling at his sisters more than a few times yesterday when we were at the museum.

"I do. But that doesn't mean I can manage them. I swear, you get one happy, and the other is about to burst into tears. *Women*."

"Well, I'll give you that. It probably is a lot to manage."

Mohammad nods, dropping his hand into his pocket. "Do you think you can manage it for another night?"

"What do you mean?" I ask as I pick up the last piece of muffin and hand it to him.

"The girls had fun. Especially Leela. I swear, everything to her is magical or something. Anyway, they told my parents they fancied you, and … well, I had mentioned you coming around anyway. They brought it up. Invited you for dinner." His statement is more of a question, but I know that he worded it like that in case I wanted an out.

But I don't.

"*Awww*." I pull Mohammad into a big hug, squeezing him. "Of course I'll come. When?"

When I pull back, Mohammad's cheeks are tinted pink, but he has a smile on his face.

"Does tomorrow work?" he asks, grabbing the empty box from my hand and motioning for me to follow him into the classroom. He drops the box in the recycling bin before moving to our seats.

"Tomorrow's great. Can I bring anything?"

As Mohammad's about to answer, our professor stands up, closing the door shut right as the bell goes off. I scrunch up my nose, realizing that this is the end of our conversation.

"I CAN'T BELIEVE that we're expected to present in class tomorrow," Mohammad groans when class is over.

"It *is* kind of short notice," I agree as we exit the classroom.

"Short notice? More like *no* notice! We had today to prepare, and that's it," Mohammad goes on.

"Why are you so worked up? You're amazing at public speaking. If anyone can wing it and actually do good, it's you," I argue.

"That's beside the point. Why aren't you *more* upset? You're the one who's bad at public speaking."

"Ouch," I declare as we get to my locker. Number 75.

"All right, sorry. But you were the one who was so freaked out about presenting in Statistics."

I shrug in response. Because he's right. I was freaked out.

"I guess I'm over it now. At least for today. Besides, we're going to be standing up there together. It's way less scary with another person."

"It's not even about that," Mohammad continues. "It's about the principle. You're supposed to give students adequate time to prepare."

"What's really going on?" I laugh.

"I want you to be on my side." Mohammad pouts. But he can't keep a grin from forming on his lips. His face fights it, his brows quivering until the smile wins out, spreading all across his face.

"I'm always on your side." I smile and put my Latin textbook away.

JILLIAN DODD

When I slam my locker, something diverts Mohammad's attention. His smile is gone, and I follow his eyes down the hallway until my own land on Harry. My cheeks ache to pull up into a smile when I see him, but then my eyes shift to see that he's leaning in, talking intently to Olivia.

"What do you think that's about?" Mohammad asks.

"I don't know," I reply, watching them.

Harry looks frustrated.

Or maybe concerned?

It's hard to tell, but he looks serious. And Olivia's expression matches his.

His head is dipped down, and Olivia is looking up at him with worry. They're talking quickly, and Harry shakes his head. His knuckles tense at his sides.

I glance back over to Mohammad, seeing that he's still watching them with the same amount of confusion and interest that I am.

"Something's up for sure," Mohammad comments as I look back at them.

Olivia has her hand on Harry's forearm now, keeping it there as they talk.

"I'm sure it's nothing," I insist, dropping my gaze.

Because whatever is going on between them, Harry can tell me about it himself.

I don't want to stand here in the hallway, spying and jumping to conclusions.

"I'll guess we'll see at lunch," Mohammad replies, giving my arm a quick squeeze.

"Yeah." I give him my best smile, but Mohammad holds my gaze for a few seconds too long, and I know he doesn't buy it. He's searching my eyes, trying to figure out how I really feel.

Finally, he just says, "Have fun in Art."

A beautiful person.
ART

"WHAT'S WRONG?" NOAH asks the second I sit down next to him. He's already in his seat, propped up perkily on his stool.

"Nothing, just kind of a weird moment in the hallway," I reply.

"A weird moment?" Noah peers over at me, his forehead creasing.

I decide to just tell him. "Olivia and Harry were talking."

He'll find out anyway at lunch because I'm sure Mohammad will bring it up. He can't help but be in on the gossip, and I know he'll have no issue asking Harry what they were talking about, point-blank.

"Oh. Are you upset about that, or ..." Noah stutters, sounding confused.

"No, of course not. It's not the fact that they were talking; it's how they were talking," I insist, pulling my lips to the side.

"And how were they talking?" Noah tilts his head, his eyes on me.

"Harry seemed worried. It didn't look like a pleasant conversation," I reply, my stomach doing a flip. "I don't know. I'm sure it was nothing. It just ... didn't feel right."

Noah nods, his chestnut hair bouncing.

It looks even softer than usual today. It's light and fluffy, having that airy feel about it. It's so different from mine, which is straight and flat. I try to focus on his hair instead of the flips occurring in my stomach.

"I'm sure he'll explain," Noah offers.

"He doesn't owe me an explanation," I say, trying to balance the truth with how I feel. "It's not that I don't trust him."

"All I meant is that if he's upset, he'll let us know. Like I said, heart on the sleeve. It's kind of impossible to not know how he's doing." Noah smiles, his eyes creasing at the corners.

My face instantly matches his, and I smile with him.

"You always make things so simple." I laugh.

"And you have a way of making things overly complicated. Maybe we both just need to find a happy middle?"

I vigorously shake my head, pinching my lips together to keep from grinning. "No, I disagree. I like your way much better. Everything's simple, easy, relaxed. You have no worries, and stuff gets resolved in its appropriate time." I'm half teasing him but also half serious. Because I can always learn from Noah and his approach.

"It sounds like you're mocking me," he says, his voice dropping lower as he leans toward me.

His eyes are glued to mine, his cheek pulling on one side.

"Maybe just a little."

I hold my fingers out in front of me, pinching them together so they're almost touching. Noah looks down at them, lightly grabbing my wrist.

"I still can't believe you're able to get work done with these," he says, examining my fingernails.

I make my hand into the shape of a claw, curling my fingers in. "Are you scared?"

"Petrified." Noah chuckles. His fingers slip against mine as he examines my hand.

"I could actually do some damage with these things." I laugh.

"You still haven't given me a proper back scratch yet."

"Do you want one?" I tilt my head, searching Noah's eyes.

"Would anyone turn down a back scratch?" he replies, sounding appalled.

"The question isn't if *anyone* would; it's if *you* would," I say, raising my eyebrow at him.

"I'd prefer your regular nails than these on my skin," he says, running his finger over my extensions.

"So, the answer is no then?"

Noah brings his gaze back up to mine. "The answer is, I'll always take a back rub."

"I thought so. Besides, I would be careful. I wouldn't cut you or anything."

"I trust you." Noah nods, his eyes slipping down to my lips.

I swallow under his gaze, trying to get my stomach under control. I clear my throat, causing Noah to disconnect his eyes from mine as he drops my hand and turns toward the front of the classroom. He picks up his pen, and I watch as he clicks the top of it up and down, over and over. His muscular forearm flexes each time he does it, and I can't help but notice a few things.

Like when the pen clicks down, his forearm flexes.

When the pen retracts, his forearm loosens.

Noah glances at me, his head turning to the side. He looks between me and his pen, his lips parting. My gaze flicks to his plump lips. He always seems to have the perfect thing to say to relax me. Then, at the same time, he has this ability to make me fully distracted.

I'm not sure if looking at him is okay or if it's wrong, but it's more of an admiration. Because I can't just pick one piece of Noah that makes him Noah. Every piece is a part of him. His forearms. His lips. His floppy brown hair and brilliant mind. The way he's able to make everything seem so simple. The way that he holds my gaze.

It's like, when I'm with Noah, we're in this different world. I can't help but fixate on the small things with him.

The sound of his voice. The way my heart always feels lighter. And it's not in a sexual way. It's in a *he's a beautiful person* way.

Noah's eyes are all over my face, his golden brown eyes changing. They somehow always manage to darken and widen when I look at them.

It's a constant that's reassuring.

I can always count on his eyes' reaction to mine. And there's an immense comfort in that.

I can also see longing in his eyes.

I know that it's there.

But it's not the only thing that's there, which is why I think I always come back to him. He's my friend.

I break our gaze when Mrs. Jones starts talking. She instructs us to continue working on our projects for the day, so I get up and collect my canvas. Everyone else shuffles around the classroom, getting paint and picking up their projects from the holding racks.

When I sit back down at my desk, I look over my project. I still have to add my final coat of paint. After that, I can start sanding it down.

CLASS SEEMS TO fly by. Before either Noah or I realize it, the bell is going off, and we're putting our projects away.

"I love Tuesdays." I grin.

"Shortened classes are nice," he agrees, walking next to me out of class.

We head to the stairwell, going back down to the main floor and out into the hallway.

"Nice? More like amazing. Plus, I really enjoy Yoga. It's relaxing and good to get out of my head for a bit."

"Well, while you're in Yoga, finding your inner peace, I'll be at football practice, getting kicked in the shins," Noah banters, glancing over at me.

"Please. I know you love it."

Noah smiles. "Yeah, I actually do."

Another lecture.
LUNCH

WHEN WE GET to the lunchroom, Noah and I head straight to our usual table. Mohammad joins us a few minutes later with his lunch tray in hand. I look around, not spotting Harry anywhere. Noah gets out our packed lunches. I open mine to find leftover pasta and vegetables that Noah combined to make a cold pasta salad.

"Mallory, what do you want to do while you're still in London?" Mohammad asks me.

I glance up to him, trying to read his expression. "What do you mean?"

He sets down his fork, looking between Noah and me. "You've been here a couple weeks now, and it feels like you've just hung out with us."

"Ouch," I reply, my eyes shifting back to my pasta salad.

"That's not what I meant," he corrects. "I meant, if you had a free day, what would you want to do? Where would you want to go?"

I think about his question.

What would I want to do?

"I'm not sure. I like all of the things I've done, honestly. Hanging out with the Williams, with you guys. I've gotten to experience *life* in London as opposed to just running from one tourist attraction to the next."

My eyes flick to Noah, who nods in understanding.

"But this is your trip. Your time," Mohammad goes on.

"It's not just a trip," I disagree. But Mohammad gives me his *don't argue with me* look, and I know I need to come up with a better answer. "I've been doing things I like. I went shopping and out to brunch with Naomi. I had afternoon tea with Helen. I run through the park with Noah. We've partied together at Harry's, and I've already been out to a club here. I love all of those things. Getting takeaway sushi, trying new restaurants."

But Mohammad is not appeased. "What I'm trying to say is, if we go out, what would you want to do?"

"Hmm, probably shop." I grin, looking between Mohammad and Noah.

"Of course." Noah chuckles.

"So, you want to go shopping?" Mohammad asks with interest.

"Why not? And from the sounds of it, you two are offering to go with me," I say, looking directly at Noah.

Noah drops his fork, already shaking his head.

"I don't know about that," he starts, but Mohammad interrupts him.

"Of course we'd go. So, where are we going?"

I look at Mohammad, confused, trying to figure out what he's doing. *Does he really want to go shopping? Or is he just trying to do something nice for me?* I'm not sure what he's looking for.

"I think what Mohammad is trying to say is that we want to do something with you that *you* enjoy," Noah finally clarifies.

I look to Mohammad, feeling butterflies form in my stomach. I instantly want to hug him and kiss him and just generally squeeze him. My lips push out into a pout, but Mohammad holds up a finger, stopping me.

"I recognize that look. Don't get all sentimental on me. But Noah's right. You went to the museum with me and my sisters. You showed up for Harry. You're at all of Noah's matches," Mohammad lists off.

"Well, there is actually a place that caught my eye," I comment, remembering a shop that Noah and I passed once.

"Great," Mohammad encourages.

"It's this bookshop. It's right next to an Indian restaurant, and I remember stopping because of the amazing smell, but then I noticed these beautiful antique maps hanging in the window. It was a tiny shop, but it looked really interesting."

"As long as it isn't one of those shops where you can't touch anything, I'm down," Mohammad agrees.

"What?" I laugh.

Mohammad rolls his eyes. "Mum always makes me go shopping with her. Usually, I like it. After all"—he places his hand on his chest—"I myself have great style. Plus, I give great style advice. But then we end up in these home decor and kitchenware shops, and she's always smacking my hand, telling me not to touch any of the plates because she thinks I'll break them."

"That's why you just shouldn't go," Noah cuts in, getting straight to his point.

"No one likes to be treated like a little kid," I add, sympathizing.

"And yet, it continues to happen to me," Mohammad moans. "Regardless, let's check out the bookshop. Maybe even grab some food after."

"Yeah?" I ask, looking at Mohammad. I glance over to Noah, wondering if he's going to go along with this too.

Noah connects his eyes to mine, nodding in agreement.

"Yeah," Mohammad answers, taking another bite of his chicken. "Let's go on Thursday."

"Okay …" I start, feeling excited when a hand comes down on my shoulder. I watch Noah glance up, his expression not giving anything away.

"What's Thursday?" Harry asks as he takes a seat next to me on the bench.

He doesn't have a lunch tray, just a can of soda that's already cracked open. His forehead is creased, and his expression is heavier than usual.

"We're going to a bookshop and then for food," Noah answers, looking between me and Harry.

"Sounds … fun?" Harry replies, taking a sip of his soda.

"Something different," Mohammad cuts in.

"They were asking me what I wanted to do this week." I shrug, feeling my stomach flip.

"I'm sure we'll have a cracking time, as always," Harry replies quickly, placing his hand on my leg.

I grab on to his fingers, trying to figure out what is going on with him.

"No food today?" I whisper as Noah and Mohammad start chatting about Noah's upcoming match.

"Not hungry," Harry replies.

I let go of his hand, feeling my own start to shake. Because everything about his demeanor is off. He's usually flirty and warm. But right now, it's like everything I say slides right off of him.

"You sure?"

"Can't stomach it, to be honest," he says, finally glancing over at me. His blue eyes can't hide his feelings. It's like they're hollow. "Food looks like shit today."

"Hey. It's not that bad," Mohammad cuts in, overhearing him. He scoops up another forkful, bringing it to his mouth.

"Well, just in case," I say, grabbing my bag. I hand him the crisps that I bought this morning and give him an encouraging smile.

Harry finally smiles back at me, his eyes softening. "Always thinking of everything," he replies, wrapping his arm around my shoulders.

Even though he's being warm with me, something is definitely wrong.

"I saw you chatting with Olivia earlier. Anything going on there?" Mohammad asks with almost disinterest.

And I realize he did cut straight to the point. Harry doesn't flinch at his question, but Noah looks at him in interest.

I stay frozen, keeping my eyes down on my salad.

"Ah, you know, just this or that. She's always harping on me about something or other," Harry responds.

"What do you mean?" I ask, confused.

Because he completely avoided Mohammad's question.

"She's just being Olivia," Harry says, glancing over at me. "Trying to stick her nose in where it doesn't belong."

"I don't get it. Did something happen?" Noah chimes in.

I can feel Harry sit up straighter at my side, and he clears his throat.

"You could say that," Harry says, pushing out a forced laugh.

Harry looks uncomfortable. Like he can't decide if he wants to be sad or angry.

"Just more shit with the family. That's all."

"Well, if you want to talk about it …" Noah says, tilting his head.

I watch as his eyes soften with the mention of Harry's family, and I try to relax too.

After all, he and Olivia have history.

And she knows about what's been going on with his family. It isn't surprising that she might want to talk to him about it.

"I'd rather play billiards and have a heavily poured double," Harry replies, popping open the bag of crisps.

"That bad, huh?" Mohammad asks.

"I thought you wanted to ..." I start but stop myself. Because I thought we were supposed to hang out tonight, just the two of us. But it sounds like that isn't going to happen now.

Harry brings his hand into my hair, sliding his palm down over it once.

"Let's just all chill. Fuck off our coursework. Play some billiards and have a few drinks." Harry doesn't ask it as a question, but I can tell he's waiting for my answer.

"Yeah. Why not?" I agree. Because if he wants to just relax, all of us together, I'm fine with that.

"Mum probably won't let me leave the house since they just got home," Mohammad says, his lips pulling into a straight line.

Harry's jaw twitches slightly even though he nods in understanding before looking over at Noah.

"All right," Noah quickly agrees.

"Are you sure you're—" I start to say.

"Moving back to this bookshop visit," Noah says, interrupting me and changing the subject. "You should ask Mallory what she's been reading lately. More specifically, what she was reading this morning."

Noah's gaze shifts from Harry's to mine, and a smile plays on his face. I narrow my eyes at him, trying to figure out why he's just going along with this.

"New reading material?" Harry asks, his shoulder bumping into mine.

"Books are boring. I prefer the movies," Mohammad chimes in. "Or just people watching. You can learn just as much from eavesdropping as from a book."

"You're more of a *take action* person though," I say to Mohammad. "Not everyone's so bold."

"What can I say?" He grins. "I'm constantly on the hunt for new experiences."

I roll my eyes, looking over to Noah.

"Back to the book," Noah instructs.

"Well, what were you reading?" Harry asks, trying to follow along.

"Let me guess. Action," Mohammad says. "Spies, romance, travel."

"You could call it action …" Noah chuckles.

I glare at him because, now, he's just ruthlessly dragging this out.

And I know he's going to make it a big reveal.

"Spill," Mohammad insists, shaking his head like he can't take Noah's vague answers anymore.

"Smut," Noah says excitedly.

His eyes are sparkling, and it's annoying. I want to stifle out the sparkles one stomp at a time.

"I was *not* reading smut," I say with an eye roll.

"No?" Harry asks with interest.

"No," I repeat. "Noah was."

"Wait. What smut?" Mohammad asks, looking between us, confused.

"I found this book in Mal's room called *Taming the Duke*." Noah directs his statement at Mohammad, wiggling his eyebrows at him.

Mohammad must finally connect the dots because he looks over at me wildly.

"Is it hot?" he asks excitedly.

"Why don't you ask Noah's mother? She's the one who gave it to me!" I reply, crossing my arms over my chest.

"Helen!" Harry's voice breaks as his eyes go wide. "I think you've scarred me. Not our precious Helen," he insists, but I can hear the sarcasm in his voice.

"Enough about my mum," Noah cuts in, looking freaked out.

"Get back to the book," Mohammad instructs.

"It was … detailed," Noah replies, apparently nowhere near done with the subject.

"How did it compare to porn?" Mohammad asks me seriously.

"It doesn't compare to porn because it isn't porn," I defend. "It's a sweepingly beautiful romance."

"That means, it's positively dirty." Harry grins, looking at me, amused.

"Agreed. Girls say anything hot is romantic just so they don't have to admit it's hot," Mohammad says.

I scowl at Mohammad before turning my attention back to the perpetrator of this conversation.

Noah.

"Why did you bring this up? You're always the one who's saying that sex isn't dirty," I argue.

"It's not," Noah replies, taking my side.

"So, why are you leading them to believe that I was reading porn?" I grumble.

"You were." Noah shrugs, like he can't see where I'm coming from at all.

Because, now, I've moved beyond annoyed to embarrassed.

"Those were some pretty specific words. And scenes," he continues, putting the final nail in my coffin.

I cover my face with my hands, mortified.

"What is it about?" Harry asks as he brings my hands down away from my face, lacing our fingers together.

I look at Harry, feeling flushed, wishing that they would just drop it.

"What I can make of it so far is that it's about this duke who's quite posh but rather rigid. He's summering at a family friend's estate, and he meets their eldest daughter. She doesn't want to marry and is a firecracker, which is upsetting to him. Apparently, they have banter and eventually can't control themselves anymore," Noah informs, catching even me off guard.

"And hidden behind the polished duke exterior lies a sex maniac." Mohammad grins.

"Exactly!" Noah agrees.

"No. No. No," I cut in. "It's about love. And how that love is expressed …"

"Physically," Noah adds, raking his tooth across his bottom lip.

"Which we all know is just code for *shag-ging*," Mohammad sings out with a naughty smirk.

Harry lets out a deep laugh as Noah covers his mouth, trying to conceal a chuckle. I glare at him before addressing Mohammad.

"The key is love," I disagree.

"Yeah, yeah. I hear you. It's about love." Mohammad rolls his eyes. "Anyway, once you're done with it, let me read it. I'm always open to learning new tricks."

"Promise me you won't get your tips and tricks from porn," I say.

"What's wrong with porn?" Mohammad asks, offended.

"It's not good for men," Noah agrees.

"What?" Harry says, looking appalled.

"Well," Noah states, "it's easily addictive. Plus, it makes pleasure only about the ending. It's surface-level material that highlights only the physical. And sex is about a lot more than that. It's a process and definitely about the connection."

"But I'm not looking for a connection. I'm looking to get off," Mohammad insists.

"Fine. But if you do watch it, know that it's so far off from what sex is supposed to be. Sex is intimate and special. It shouldn't be taboo, but sex in porn isn't realistic or typical either. Women don't look or sound one way. And men shouldn't be expected to be these pleasure machines. It's just all wrong, if you want my opinion."

"Wait, does that mean you've watched porn?" Harry asks, eyeing me.

Mohammad and Noah both turn their attention to me, glancing at me with the same amount of curiosity.

"I'm not answering that."

"Hmm," Mohammad huffs. "So, you're saying I can't watch porn *or* shag a girl *just* for her body?"

"Nope," I reply.

"What bollocks," Mohammad mumbles.

"You're better off exploring your body and what you like and dislike on your own. Or with a partner you respect," Noah agrees.

"It's interesting that the two most vocal people regarding sex haven't *actually* had sex," Mohammad says. "Once you have it, you'll understand. Porn is necessary."

"What? Why?" I ask.

"For educational purposes. Trust me. You have to at least watch it once to know where all the bits are and what they look like."

"The bits?" I repeat, my eyes going wide.

"Maybe that's the whole point," Noah says. "You should be in a relationship with someone who you feel comfortable talking about those things with. You can learn together. Or at the least, we should be able to talk to our mates about it."

"Well, next time I want to have a wank, I'll make sure to ring you," Harry says with a grin, sticking out his tongue at Noah.

"I'd prefer not." Noah chuckles.

"I thought that's what you were getting at. You just want to be let in on the intimacies of my ... body," Harry teases.

"Come off it, you two. This is serious," Mohammad interjects, turning to me. "Mallory, promise to bring me the book when you're done with it."

"Yeah, I'll be sure to check if it's all right with Helen, too, since she lent it to me," I reply, rolling my eyes.

"I swear, I'll have it done and back to you in a day," Mohammad says seriously.

"Thought you didn't read?" Noah chimes in.

"Could you actually read it in one night?" I ask.

"Obviously," Mohammad says, like reading a book in one night is the easiest thing in the world. "If it's the right material, I'll read it as quickly as I have to. You have no idea what I have to go through when researching. Anytime I'm Googling anything slightly risqué, I have to be quick. You can never trust being alone in my house. There's always someone walking about, coming into my room, unannounced. My dad, my mum, my aunt. I'm not even allowed the sacred personal space of my own room. Constantly, my privacy is violated."

"That's why he has to wank off in the shower." Harry chuckles, looking at me.

"Well, that's your problem. You're a developing boy," I comment, putting two and two together.

"Can you not talk about me like I just hit puberty?" Mohammad says, his nose scrunching up.

"Sorry," I clarify, shaking my head. "I just meant, you need privacy to, you know ..."

"Wank off?" Noah chuckles.

"No, to *explore myself*," Mohammad mocks, looking at me as the bell goes off.

"Oh my Lord. I am officially done with you three and this conversation," I say, getting up from the table.

Harry stands up with me, moving toward the trash bins to throw away his can and bag of crisps. Noah and Mohammad are slow to get up, both still wearing devilish grins. And I can't help but grin with them.

I look back over toward Harry, watching him linger by the trash bin. His smile is gone, and he rubs his forehead, looking upset again.

"Hey." I smile.

He blinks a few times, looking at the ground before bringing his eyes back up to mine.

"Hey," he forces out, pushing a smile onto his face.

"Let's walk to class?" I grab his wrist, aching to touch him.

"Yeah," Harry agrees, lacing his fingers through mine.

His hand feels stiff, but he keeps our fingers together as we walk. I stay silent, not sure what to say. One second, he looks angry and upset, but then the next, he's joking around.

I can't read him today.

We leave the lunchroom and are halfway to Geography when Harry stops walking.

"Actually, no," are the only words he says as he turns to face me.

"No?" I repeat. "Harry, what is going on?"

He diverts his eyes, shaking his head. "Nothing."

"Harry." I hold his arm with one hand, my other coming up onto his cheek.

He brings his blue eyes back to mine, staring at me.

"Let's skip," he says, holding my gaze.

"What?"

"Let's go. Let's just go," Harry says, his voice pleading with me.

"I can't just leave," I say, glancing around the hallway. "It's the middle of the school day, and there are teachers and students everywhere. Even if we wanted to, we'd get caught. We can't just walk out without being noticed."

Harry shakes his head, putting his hand on top of mine. "Go to the loo and wait until everyone's in class. We can sneak out by the changing rooms."

"If we get caught, they'll call Helen," I insist.

"I don't care," Harry exhales, taking a step away from me. He runs his hands down over his face, his palms dragging from his eyes down to his jaw. "I'll text her. I'll tell her that I needed you," he insists, pulling his phone out of his pocket.

He doesn't give me a chance to answer before he starts typing on his phone.

"Harry, wait. I thought I was coming over after school. I thought it was supposed to be just you and me?"

Harry shakes his head, pushing his phone back into his pocket.

"I can't be here," he says, his voice catching.

"Why?" I ask, bringing my hands back onto his forearms. I rub my palms down his arms, trying to comfort him.

"I … why can't we just go?"

"Because you're not telling me anything. You have to let me in."

"I don't need another lecture."

"I'm not trying to lecture you," I say, my stomach twisting.

"If I needed a shrink, I'd go to the one my family has on retainer," Harry mutters, his jaw tightening.

"Excuse me?" I stare at him, not believing he just said that to me.

"You're my girlfriend, for fuck's sake. And my mate. Isn't it just enough for me to tell you that I can't be here?" Harry says, his voice catching again.

"I'm worried. I just … I want you to tell me what's wrong."

It's not even about leaving school at this point.

It's that he owes me an explanation.

"I don't need you to worry about me. I need you to be there for me." Harry takes a step away from me, looking like he might burst into tears. But a second later, his face changes.

Actually, it sets.

It becomes so firm and hardened that it's hard to believe the same eyes are looking at me.

"So, are you coming or not?"

"I …" I stutter, trying to figure out what to do.

Because he's right.

I'm his girlfriend and his friend. I should leave with him, no questions asked.

"You know what? Forget I asked. Go to class. Enjoy your time with Professor Pritchard," Harry says, holding his hands out in front of him. And it's like he's both giving up on me and feeling disappointed in me with one look.

He scans me over once before turning away from me.

"Harry," I call out, but he doesn't turn back.

He just moves past a group of students, and all I can see is the back of his shaking head. And then he turns and walks out the door.

I glance around, seeing eyes on me. But they don't stay for long because the bell goes off, and everyone rushes to class.

I stand motionless for a moment.

I wanted to follow him.

I know that I should have.

And suddenly, I want to cry. Because I know that he

thinks I abandoned him.

In his moment of need, I didn't show up.

I just stood there, silent, falling all over my internal monologue.

My mouth feels watery, and I open it, trying to come up with something to say. Maybe to myself. Maybe to the space where he was standing. But nothing comes out. I turn around and go to my locker, get my geography textbook out, and slam the locker shut. The noise echoes in the hallway, but I don't care.

I need to be angry.

Because if I'm not angry, I'm going to be hurt.

And I have to make it through Geography.

It's personal.
GEOGRAPHY

I DO MY best to slink into class silently, but I gain the entire room's attention when the door slams shut behind me.

"Shit," I mutter to myself.

"Miss James, kind of you to join us," Mr. Pritchard says dryly.

"Sorry." I wince, my lips pulling into a flat line.

But he must not have already started class yet because students continue talking, and Naomi waves me over toward her and Olivia as Mr. Pritchard writes out words on the whiteboard.

"Hey." Naomi smiles as I spy an empty spot in front of her. It's the only seat open in her row, and I'm not sure if it's a coincidence or if she saved it for me.

Olivia watches me the entire time, her eyes not giving

anything away.

"Hey," I reply, falling into the chair with a huff.

"No Harry?" Olivia questions, her gaze flicking to our usual seats on the other side of the classroom.

"He's not a fan of Geography," I say, not telling her anything more.

"Pity," Olivia says.

"But he was here earlier," Naomi comments, looking between Olivia and me.

"He was," I answer.

Olivia moves her gaze back to Naomi, her tone softening. "It's not that surprising he wanted to leave after everything with … well, it's personal after all," she says, glancing at me now, "and I'm sure he's already told you. So, best not to repeat it."

It actually crosses my mind that she sounds sincere, but then she gives me a tight smile, and I'm not sure that the sincerity is actually there.

"Well, hopefully, he's all right," Naomi says sympathetically. "Personal drama can be such a drag."

"It can be," I agree.

"But in more exciting news, I have a date with George tonight." She's beaming, and a huge grin is plastered on her face.

"This is your second date, right?" I ask, smiling back.

Just because my romantic life is a complicated mess doesn't mean that hers is. And I need to be happy for her right now.

"Third actually," she corrects, practically glowing.

"What are you two doing?" I make my voice go higher, trying to match her enthusiasm.

"He's taking me for dinner. There's this new pizza place that's supposed to be delicious."

"So, tell us," Olivia cuts in, cocking one eyebrow at Naomi, "does our dear George have any chance of getting lucky on this third date?"

Naomi mouths, *Olivia*, silently scolding her.

But I know it's all for show because she looks like a lightbulb now and is wearing a megawatt smile that could match Mohammad's.

"I don't know. I fancy him," she says.

"So, you'll make him wait," Olivia says, rolling her eyes.

"Probably." Naomi nods her head as Mr. Pritchard clears his throat, quieting the class.

We get paired up into groups and start to prepare for our upcoming test. I get put with a random guy I've never met before. He introduces himself quickly before focusing on the task at hand.

And although I don't want to be doing this right now, his determination is a good distraction.

I give in and focus.

I listen intently as he talks, because his soft tone combined with his fast pace is hard to keep up with.

But we manage to get through the study guide by the time the bell goes off. He gives me a curt head nod, like our formal business is done, before putting on his backpack and leaving.

My last week.
YOGA

I WALK WITH Olivia and Naomi to the changing room, my body moving on autopilot. I can't shake the way that Harry looked at me or Olivia's knowing comment.

It all just feels wrong.

But I try to keep myself calm and answer any questions that Naomi asks along the way.

She doesn't seem to notice my discomfort because from the moment class was over, she has been going on and on about what to wear on her date. I listen as Olivia gives her advice and don't disagree with her.

Which is annoying.

Because I wish she would just slip up. Say something rude or cold.

Something, anything that would warrant me getting angry with her.

But she doesn't.

So, I stay silent.

I excuse myself to the bathroom after I change—that way, I don't have to walk with Olivia to Yoga. And when I get up to the room, I already have the excuse that my usual mat is a few spots over from her, so we don't have to talk.

After our instructor, Amy, takes us through our warm up and into the flow, I feel like I want to cry.

But I know that I have to hold it in.

My stomach feels like it's going to come up through me and out of my mouth as I move into downward dog.

I want to keep my eyes shut, but I know that I can't.

Because the only thing flashing in my mind is Harry's upset face.

When class is finally over, I rush out of the room and back to the changing room. I keep my head down and stay focused, wanting to be out of school.

I'm mad at myself, frustrated with Harry, and feeling uneasy about Olivia. I only catch her eye once in the changing room, but that's all it takes.

Because I can see it written all over her face.

She's looking at me like she did the first week I was here.

When I was encroaching on her property.

And for a minute, the thought flashes through my mind that she's only being nice now, that she's only keeping her cool, because she knows something that I don't.

And because she knows that this is my last week at Kensington.

Which is something I've been trying to forget.

A storm.
4PM

"YOU READY TO go?" I say, rushing up to Noah.

He's waiting for me outside the changing room, his backpack and duffel on the ground next to him. I barely flick my gaze at him before heading for the exit.

"Whoa, what's the rush?" Noah asks, pushing off the wall and catching up to me.

"Just done with school for the day."

I charge through the doors, letting the cold air hit my face. I suck in a gasp, grateful to be free of those narrowing brick walls.

"You sure that's it?" Noah asks, glancing over to me.

"Yep," I reply flatly. I'm not sure why I'm being so short with him. I know it's wrong of me.

But you can add it to my list of fuckups today.

Because it feels like the list just keeps growing and growing.

"Mal," Noah says, grabbing my arm.

I try to continue forward, but he pulls me back, so I'm standing in front of him.

"Yeah?" I ask, itching to move.

"You're going to be like that, huh?" he asks, tilting his head at me.

"I'm not being anything. I'm just tired. And I'm trying to get home," I reply, wishing he would just let me go.

"You're tired?" Noah repeats, looking me over. "Well, you'd better wake up. Or take a nap. It sounds like we're going to have a long night ahead of us with Harry."

I blow air out through my nose, wishing he hadn't just said that.

"That's probably not going to happen now," I reply, looking down the street. My legs ache to move, and I bounce one leg up and down, ready to go.

"But at lunch—"

"Yes, I know what he said at lunch," I say, trying not to get upset. "But after lunch, everything just … and I … he's not going to want me there."

"You can't say that," Noah disagrees, looking distressed by my words. "Harry is crazy about you."

"Yeah, well, I feel like the worst girlfriend in the world, and the icing on the cake is, soon enough, I won't even be here. So, I guess that takes care of that." I start walking toward the house.

I'm not sure why I'm even going there.

I guess I just need something safe.

Something familiar.

I'll barely get up to my room before I start crying.

That's usually how the course of my meltdowns go. And I can feel it coming.

"Instead of being angry, why don't you try a new approach?" Noah suggests, back at my side. "Why don't we find a way to defuse the bomb?"

"The bomb?" I repeat, looking over at him.

"I see it ticking," he replies, raising his eyebrows.

I roll my eyes at him even though he's right. "I don't do well when I'm overwhelmed."

"Well, what would make you feel better?"

"Hitting someone," I say, half-kidding.

"All right," Noah replies, stopping me again. "Have at me."

"What?" I look at Noah and realize he's serious.

He extends his hands out to his sides, exposing his chest to me.

I shake my head. "I'm not going to hit you."

"Why not? I'd rather take one punch now than a night full of your pent-up energy. That's your problem, you know."

"What is?"

"You get overwhelmed because, well, you're pretty power-ful. And when you concentrate your energy on being angry, it's almost too much for you to handle. That's why we need to get it out of you. What else helps when you feel this way?"

Noah's eyes are firm but soft, and I know he's just trying to help.

I let out a long breath, wondering if he's right. "Usually, stuff like running or screaming. I need help getting out of my head. I don't get overly angry or anything like that. I just feel this overwhelming feeling of—"

"You don't like to lose control," Noah finishes.

I shake my head. "No, I don't."

"Well, there are a lot of things going on around you right now that you can't control," Noah says, stepping closer to me.

"I guess," I agree, keeping my eyes on the ground.

"If you need to get out your energy, let's get it out. Why don't we fight it out? You and me?"

"What?" I laugh, taking in his silly expression.

"Come on, slugger," Noah says, egging me on. He takes a step back, raising his hands into the air like he's about to fight me. "Now, I don't want anyone to get hurt here. So, rules are, you can only pretend punch me."

"Noah," I moan, shaking my head.

He throws a pretend punch out in front of him before taking a step back and kicking his leg into the air.

"You look ridiculous."

"I only look ridiculous because I'm doing it alone."

"How about you stop with the ninja moves on the sidewalk, and I'll defuse the bomb all on my own?" I insist.

"Hmm," Noah replies, his eyes narrowing at me. "You promise?"

I roll my eyes and grab his arm. "Yes, I promise," I agree, trying to drag him toward the house.

"All right, all right." Noah chuckles, finally giving in.

I glance over at him, feeling … better.

When we get home, Noah puts his key into the lock and is about to open the door when I stop him.

"Thank you." I give him my most sincere smile.

"You don't need to thank me," he replies, shaking his head.

"I do," I counter, holding his eyes.

"Go ring him," Noah says.

"What?"

"Go ring Harry. You'll sort it out, all right?" Noah insists.

I nod at him, hoping that he's right as we walk inside.

"Hello, lovelies," Helen greets us at the door. She's putting lipstick on, watching her reflection in the mirror.

"Hey, Mum," Noah says, taking in his mom's outfit.

She has on a tailored black and gold wrap dress that accentuates her waist and shows off her chest.

"Wow," I say, noticing her figure. "You look beautiful."

"Oh, thank you," she says as she pops the cap back onto her lipstick. "Gene and I are having drinks and then dinner with close clients of mine tonight."

"That sounds nice," I reply, slipping off my shoes before hanging my coat up.

"It will be, if Gene ever gets himself down here," Helen says, eyeing the staircase. "Who would have thought a man could take so long to get himself ready?"

"Mum, he just wants to look smart for his woman," Noah says playfully, placing a kiss on his mom's cheek. "After all, he's got to look top-notch if he's going to be standing at your side tonight."

"Noah," Helen says, batting at his chest. Her cheeks tint a rosy pink, and I can't help but grin at their interaction. "You flatter your mother too much, dear. It's not good for my ego."

"I disagree," Noah replies, dropping his duffel and back-pack before falling onto the couch.

"Long day?" she asks her son, noticing his sigh of relief as he leans into the sofa.

"Long practice."

"Well, that's how these things usually are. If you want to be good, you're going to have to work for it."

"You're starting to sound like Coach," Noah says.

I stay standing by the front door, feeling stuck.

"All right, dear?" Helen asks, noticing.

"Yeah. I think I'm just going to head up and start study-ing if you don't mind."

"That's fine, sweetie," she says, rubbing her palms over my shoulders to comfort me.

Her touch is unexpected, but even more surprising is that I react by wrapping my arms around her.

"Oh," Helen says, but then just as quickly, she is hugging me back.

I close my eyes in her arms for a long minute.

She gives me a smile and then rubs her hand against my

back. "I'm afraid you and Noah will be on your own for dinner. Do you think you two can fend for yourselves?"

"Yeah, that's fine."

"Don't worry. I'll make sure we eat." Noah grins at his mom.

"I'm not at all concerned about you," Helen says pointedly. "Your appetite is growing by the day, and my bank account is shrinking along with it."

"Mum!" Noah laughs, looking amused.

"I'm teasing, my love. But make sure to get some proper food. I don't want to come home and find out you filled yourselves up on ice cream and crisps. I want something of substance in you both."

"I promise I'll make sure to feed Mallory a healthy dinner," Noah says.

"And for yourself."

Noah rolls his eyes but agrees, "And for myself."

"I'm serious, Noah," Helen warns. "Don't be cheeky. I'll be checking the freezer before I go."

"Warning understood." Noah nods easily.

"Oh, Gene," Helen calls out with a huff. "We need to be off, dearest, or we'll be late."

She looks to the stairs, waiting, but doesn't get a response.

"Men," she mutters, shaking her head before going upstairs.

"She's not joking," Noah comments when his mom is gone.

"What was that about?"

"She'll check the ice cream before she leaves. If we eat too much of it, we'll never hear the end of it."

"Really?" I laugh.

"My sister finally realized the key was to just leave the ice cream in the freezer and go out and buy a new bin. She would eat it outside the shop and then get rid of the evidence."

"Smart." I laugh, shaking my head. "Well, I'm going to change and study for a bit."

Noah sits up and then nods his head at me.

I grab my purse and go up to my room. The second I'm alone, I grab my phone and stare at Harry's name.

After a few moments, I finally work up the courage to click it.

I listen to it ring, but there's no answer.

Me: *I'm sorry about today.*

Harry: *Don't worry about it.*

I feel instant relief when he texts me back.

Me: *Do you want to come over?*

Me: *We can just hang out. Or study. Whatever.*

I don't know how else to say it. I try to be casual about it, but I also want him to know that I want to see him. That I'm sorry about how things went today. My phone buzzes, and I read his text.

Harry: *Not tonight.*

Me: *I was joking about the studying.*

Harry: *I'll see you tomorrow, Mallory.*

I hit Call, feeling frustrated with his response. He can't just blow me off. Shut me out.

"Yep," Harry answers.

"Harry, what's going on?" I ask, desperate to figure things out.

"Nothing," he breathes out defensively.

"Obviously, you're upset."

"Clearly."

"I'm sorry that I didn't leave with you today. Just, please, let me make it up to you."

"I just … I need some time," he says, his voice raspy.

"Time?" I question, feeling my heart come into my throat. "Harry, that's ridiculous. I'm really sorry I didn't leave with you. I just—"

"You weren't there for me," he states simply, but I can hear the hurt in his voice.

"What? Like Olivia? I saw you two this morning. Look, I'm sorry that I froze in the hallway. If I could, I'd go back and make my legs move, but I can't." I realize I'm more frustrated and hurt than I expected.

I thought I could be levelheaded about this, but my insides feel like they're flipped upside down.

"You don't know what you're talking about," Harry disagrees, sounding emotionless. "I'll … I'll see you at school tomorrow."

And then he hangs up. The call ends, and I'm stuck frozen, listening to the silence.

And I can't believe him. I can't believe that he would say that to me.

Or just blow me off.

I want to scream. Or cry. At the fact that I didn't leave today. At the fact that he won't tell me what's going on.

At the fact that he's shutting me out.

Again.

Instead of reacting, instead of sitting here upset, I decide to do something productive. I decide to do my homework.

I get out my statistics folder and textbook, opening up to the chapter we're on, and read through the part of the chapter that we went over in class today, trying to piece together everything.

Reading is a good distraction, and the explanations that the textbook gives about the formulas actually make sense.

I pull out my homework and scan question three.

I'm working through the formula quickly and am onto question four when Helen calls out, "We're off."

I get up off my bed, popping my head out of my door. "Bye. Have fun," I call out, seeing them at the base of the stairs.

A second later, I hear Noah say, "Bye."

And then they're gone.

I go back into my room and close the door. I move back to my statistics homework, trying to keep my energy focused on getting the assignment done. It isn't until question eight that I get stuck and pull out my art textbook. Mrs. Jones decided, on top of our project, to give us some homework, making us search through our textbook to identify different transformative techniques used in painting.

I can barely stay focused, my mind slipping back to my conversation with Harry. I feel anger boil in me, and I end up throwing my pen against the wall, having to grab a new one out of my bag. My textbook slides off my bed in the process, resulting in a loud thump.

"Uh, I hear some intense pencil throwing happening in here. Are you beating up your textbook as well?" Noah says, eyeing my textbook on the ground as he walks into my room.

I lean over, pick it up off the floor, and toss it on my bed. "Humanities is a joke. There are more productive things to be learning about than paint," I retort, plopping down onto the edge of my bed.

"You're having trouble," Noah notices, picking up my homework.

"Where does Mrs. Jones get off, assigning us this stupid homework anyway? In Stats, I can't figure out which formula to use, and then in Art, there's no formula, and you have to go with your gut. I don't get it. Why can't I just answer yes or no?"

"Mallory," Noah soothes, sitting down next to me.

"I'm sorry," I reply, standing up.

I can feel tears threatening, and I know that I won't be able to fend them off this time.

"I'll help you with your homework," he says.

I shake my head. "It has nothing to do with my homework."

"You talked to Harry then?"

Tears slip down my cheeks as I nod at him. "I don't understand. It's like he's flipped a switch."

Noah strides toward me, pulling me into a hug. I cry on his shoulder, feeling a sob escape my throat. Noah's hands wrap around me more firmly, and he starts to rub my back. I fold into him, trying to gain a little composure.

"Come here," he says, pulling me onto the bed.

He wraps me up in his arms, lying down with me. I burrow into his chest, feeling his wet shirt against my cheek.

"I'm sorry."

"You don't need to apologize. Do you want to tell me what happened?" Noah's voice is soft, and he continues to rub my back.

I stay tucked against him, my face hidden.

"He asked me to leave school with him," I explain, wiping at my eyes. "After lunch, he told me that he needed to leave. He couldn't be at school. He asked me to go with him, and I froze. I stood there, like an idiot. He'd just … surprised me. He looked so hurt, Noah. Like I had abandoned him or something. And then he left. I called him, and he said he needed time. But I don't even know what's wrong. I don't know what to do. I'm worried."

"I'm worried too," Noah agrees, his hands still drawing circles on my back. "And it's not fair that he's doing this to you. You don't deserve it."

I glance up at Noah, watching his forehead crease.

"I was the one who should have been there for him. I messed up."

"No, you didn't. Harry's going through a lot, but he's handling it like shit. Especially with you."

"You can't say that."

Because I know that Harry is handling it as well as he can. I just wish he would give me the chance to show him that I could be there for him. That he would tell me what's wrong.

"I shouldn't. But I can. You deserve better than that."

I look at Noah, completely caught off guard.

Because we're talking about Harry.

His best friend.

"You love Harry."

"And you do too," Noah replies, his lips pinching closed. "And it's clouding your judgment."

"My judgment?"

Noah pulls back but keeps his eyes on me. "You can love him and not be with him. I love Harry, but he shouldn't be in a relationship if he's going to treat someone like that."

"It's easy to judge. Relationships aren't perfect," I say, watching Noah's expression stay firm.

"Mallory, we're talking about Harry. You know I love him. I want the best for him," Noah says, his voice catching.

"I know you do," I insist.

"I don't like seeing you hurt."

When he pulls me back against his chest, I think, now, I'm the one hugging him. Comforting him. Because he holds on to me like he needs it. Like he's just as much upset about Harry as I am.

"ALL RIGHT, DONE." Noah grins, closing all three of the textbooks.

History, Art, and Statistics.

Noah insisted that we get up, move to the kitchen, and finish our homework. He promised it would only take ten minutes, but it is really an hour later before we're finally done.

I know that he just wanted to change the conversation. To focus on something other than Harry and our stewing pot of mixed emotions.

And I needed to get out of my room.

Out of bed with Noah.

And the homework was a good distraction. But it didn't do anything in the way of cheering me up.

I give Noah my best smile in response, trying to be grateful that we have the rest of the night free.

"What's it going to take to perk you up?" he asks, shifting in his chair.

"You want me to perk up, don't you?" I reply, knowing that I need to. If not for Noah, then at least for myself.

"You don't have to do anything. It's all right to be sad. But I don't like seeing you sad. Come on. Just indulge me here."

"Indulge you …" I think about what it would take to perk myself up. What I want. What sounds good.

I can't help it when food crosses my mind.

"It would take a massive, juicy, delicious avocado. I'm talking ripe and creamy perfection. There's nothing better than an avocado sliced on warm toast. A dash of salt and a coffee on the side. Mmm."

"I love that you go straight to food." Noah grins, letting out a heavy laugh.

"What was I supposed to go to?"

"Avocado toast is good," Noah continues. "But expensive."

"So expensive!" I agree. "It's, like, fifteen dollars just for my plate when I go out for brunch. To think, avocado, bread, and black coffee. Who knew three simple ingredients would become such a pricey fad?"

"It's ridiculous."

"Problem is, it's good. So good. Uh, warm, crusty bread and the fresh, chunky salt on top."

"I feel like you're getting wet for some avocado toast right now." Noah laughs.

"Noah," I shush, flaring my eyes at him, urging him to be quiet.

Because did he just say *wet*?

"What?" He laughs, sticking out his tongue. "It's okay. Certain foods make me horny too."

"Like what?" I ask, tilting my head at him.

"Like ... fresh orange juice."

"Why?" I laugh.

"It's delicious. And it wakes me up." Noah smiles.

"All right, what else?"

"Chocolate for sure," he continues, bringing his hand up to his chin.

"Chocolate is like that for everyone," I argue.

"Yes, but chocolate is best with fruit. Or, say, like a raspberry and chocolate baked oat square. Between the fresh raspberries, rich chocolate, and salty and earthy oats ..."

"You really do get turned on by it." I chuckle.

Because Noah looks like he's in food heaven. At least, he is in his mind.

"What else for you?" Noah asks, eyeing me.

"I don't think about food like that," I reply, shaking my head.

"Come on. I know you, and I know that you're picky

323

about your food. You always take a minute to absorb the flavors. I don't believe for one second that you haven't thought about food that just … gets you excited."

"You're going to laugh."

"Try me."

"That blueberry muffin today. That was pretty good." I smile, thinking about food that I absolutely love.

"It was good." Noah nods. "You have to give me something else."

"I don't know. I really love olive oil pasta. Something about the oil and hearty pasta, mixed with fresh herbs and vegetables. It's delicious."

"It's the oil."

"Probably." I chuckle. "I guess, all together, it's just so good. The roasted vegetables and salt," I say, licking my lips.

"Right, well, maybe we should be off for some pasta then." Noah grins, his eyes slipping down to my mouth.

"*Very funny*," I say, shaking my head at him.

"What? You made it sound so good that, now, I'm craving it too."

I have no idea what Noah is even saying because all I can hear is the word *craving* echoing in my ear. Noah's eyes are innocent enough, but his mouth is pulled up on one side, and he's staring at me expectantly.

"What about sushi?" I offer.

Because sushi is a safe choice. It's little wrapped up pieces of healthy deliciousness that isn't remotely sensual.

There won't be candlelight. Or delicious olive oil. There won't be rich sauces or creamy desserts.

"Fine … but let's try a new place. It will be fun."

I nod, my chest deflating as I relax.

"Itching to get out of the house?" I ask.

"I'm hungry. Practice was intense. And this way, I can

order as much as I want."

"Whereas, with takeout, you have to pre-select," I say, finishing his thought.

"Yep. Plus, it will be good for you to get out. Get dressed up. A change of scenery."

"You're making me sound pathetic."

"Well, I did come in your room to find you crying over your art homework," Noah points out.

"I started crying after you came in," I correct.

Noah tilts his head, giving me his *you can't talk your way out of this* eyes.

"Fine, I'll change."

SO, IT TURNS out that I was totally wrong about sushi not being sexy.

Because when we walk into the restaurant that Noah picked out, it has dim lighting and a modern interior. Everything is crisp and orderly.

The tables are all identical, illuminated by low lighting and strategically placed candles.

"This is fancy," I comment, surprised Noah would take me to a place like this.

And he even dressed for it.

He has on a thick brown sweater and dark jeans. It's plain and simple, but it's a stark contrast to his usual sweats and uniform.

"The menu looked good," he replies before we get to the hostess.

She grabs two menus and leads us to a table in the center of the room. When we get seated, I glance around, taking in the elegant lines and orderly staff.

"It's beautiful," I say, noticing the unusual glass staircase rising up from behind the modern bar. Because it is practically transparent, it gives the illusion that patrons walking up to it are floating in the air.

"It's a cool restaurant," Noah agrees.

"You were right. I needed to get out," I admit, settling into my chair.

Something about being here makes me remember that I'm not some high school sob story.

I'm not the center of the world, and my problems are fairly minimal in the scheme of things.

Harry and I will work it out.

I shouldn't spend the entire night being upset.

"You're pretty easy to read," Noah says, looking at me over the menu.

"You think so?" I ask with a laugh even though I know that he's right.

"It's kind of funny actually. It's always easy to see exactly how you're feeling."

The glow in the room lights up his face, and I try not to stare. I break my eyes from him, looking down to the table.

"So, where do you think your parents went?" I ask, changing the subject.

"Probably some posh spot," Noah replies. "Mum loves that sort of stuff when they go out."

"But you don't?" I ask, noticing his indifference.

He shrugs. "I don't like all of the extra stuff. I can appreciate delicious food. A calm atmosphere. But I don't like when people fuss over getting dressed up or going somewhere expensive just because it's what's done. I hate that people feel the need to impress people they don't even know."

I nod, getting his point. "So, how are you supposed to rectify those feelings with beauty? I know you appreciate art," I point out.

"Let's take you, for example," he replies, leaning back in

his chair.

"Uh oh …" I tease.

Because this can't be good.

"You dress smart, and you like nice things. But I think you like them because they suit you. You pick out pieces that will last. You don't—at least, in my impression—wear certain things or go certain places to impress anyone. You clearly don't buy into the hype of things, which I like."

"Yet you chose this place?" I point out, looking around us.

Because it's filled with beautiful people. Beautiful food. The mood is set. Every detail was thought of. It's beautiful, but it also comes off as the type of place you either fit into or you don't.

"Mallory," Noah says, leaning into his elbows on the table. "Have you *seen* the menu? Look around. The food looks phenomenal," Noah goes on, his voice light and airy.

"So, it comes down to the food?" I laugh, raising my eyebrows in question.

"I guess we'll have to find out."

Noah and I place our order, and our food quickly arrives, one plate after another.

I start off with miso soup, taking a gulp of the comforting liquid.

"You said before that you wanted to sell real estate, right?" Noah asks in between bites.

"Yeah."

"Have you ever thought about commercial spaces?"

"I don't know. Not really," I admit. "I guess it depends on how my career goes. I always imagine myself selling residential spaces."

Noah nods, glancing around the restaurant. "I could see you selling places like this. You've got a good eye. And good taste."

"It's definitely something to think about."

"You could work with individual clients. Help them find locations that would suit their needs. But it would go beyond a vision just for a home. You might have to find a place and help them visualize how it could become a store or restaurant. Even office space," Noah suggests.

"Look at you over here, planning my future," I tease.

"Just offering some inspiration."

"What made you think of it?" I ask, picking up an avocado roll that Noah insisted we include in our assortment of food for *obvious reasons.*

"After our conversation about food, I realized you have good taste. And you have an eye for beauty. I think you can see what people want. Plus, it might serve as more of a challenge for you."

"Do you think I want a challenge?" I ask, picking up a rainbow roll and popping it into my mouth.

"Well, you like to feel accomplished," Noah says, his lips pulling at the corner. "Which is why, after getting your homework done, you always manage to look like you've overcome the devil himself."

"Well, if Statistics isn't the devil, I'm not sure what is."

But my mind shifts back to commercial real estate as I watch Noah finish off his plate.

He's not a slow eater; he just never seems to stop.

"I'm starting to think that you're just pushing for me to sell restaurant spaces, so you can visit for free food."

"That *would* be one of the benefits," he says with a laugh.

"Do you think you'll keep growing?" I ask, remembering what Helen said. That Noah's been eating more and more, especially with the added workouts and running suggested by his coach.

"Maybe. Guys tend to grow well into their early twenties."

"So, you've got more filling out to do," I reply, looking Noah over.

His shirt is already pulling across his chest and arms. I think if he gets any bigger, he'll have to start buying new clothes.

"What, now you think I look too thin?" he asks, glancing down at himself.

"No." I smile, shaking my head.

I think Noah's just about the opposite of scrawny. He's long but lean. And you can unquestionably see the outline of his sculpted frame.

"Do you remember the day you first got here?" Noah asks, tilting his head at me.

"I mean, yeah, of course I do. What do you remember?" I ask curiously.

"I remember that I was surprised to find you in my room," he answers, watching as a waiter clears the plates from our table.

"Really?" I ask, a grin forming on my face. "I think you were more angry than surprised."

"I remember the way you narrowed your eyes at me. How you were just lying across my bed."

"You were so mad at me." I laugh, thinking about my suitcases. "I think you actually hated me from the minute you saw me."

"I didn't hate you."

"No?" I ask, not believing him.

"No. I thought you were rude."

My mouth drops open at his statement.

"And stubborn," he adds.

"Oh, even better," I say, rolling my eyes.

"I liked you."

"What?" I ask, looking at Noah.

"And I was mad at myself for liking you."

"Really?"

Noah nods.

"I don't open up to … really anyone. But you can. You can talk so casually or closely with almost anyone. Always speaking your mind and going on."

"You make me sound so charming," I reply, not sure about his compliment.

"I was amazed. I felt so comfortable with you. I found you in my room, and when I pushed you, you never cracked. And you were so relaxed."

"You were testing me?" I ask, keeping my eyes on Noah.

"Not intentionally. Um, what was your first impression … of me?" Noah asks hesitantly.

I lean back in my chair and think about my options. But I decide to go with the truth.

"My first thought was, *Holy shit, he's hot.*"

"What?" Noah laughs, his eyes creasing at the corners.

"Until you opened your mouth." I grin.

Noah's eyes are sparkling at me, and I know that he can tell I'm joking.

"Then, what was your first impression of me?" I ask.

Noah's eyes shift to the corner like he's reliving the experience. "I was quite sour about your cases."

"Obviously," I reply, letting him continue.

"I thought you were beautiful. And you were so stubborn. God, you're stubborn."

"I am not."

"You are," he corrects, leaning in toward the table. "And I knew right away that you were going to be trouble."

"Trouble?"

Noah nods at me. His lips start to rise at the corner, but

he keeps it in check.

"Trouble," he repeats. "You were too pretty and too stubborn. You were bossy but relaxed. I wanted to hate you, but I couldn't. And I knew that conflict would be troublesome."

"You thought all of that the first day you met me?" I ask, feeling a little light-headed at his words.

"You were this huge storm that just came rolling into my life," Noah replies, nodding his head. "And that was before your first day of classes, when I found out you already knew Harry."

"A storm," I repeat, my mind fixating on his word choice.

Because Noah's collage was of a storm.

He said it was about me.

And when he said it, I thought it was a terrible thing. I thought he meant that I just came in and destroyed everything.

"The perfect storm," he adds, taking me out of my thoughts. "And I had no idea how to handle it. You. Any of it."

I can't help the question that comes out of my mouth. "Do you now?"

I'm not sure why I asked it, but I did.

"I think I finally realized you can't contain a storm," he replies, looking at me. "You just have to let it run its course. If it consumes you in the process, well, it will be a beautiful ending, won't it?"

"You make it sound like I'm going to destroy you."

"I guess that's up to you." Noah chuckles, not taking me seriously.

"Do you think I'm going to hurt you?" I ask, feeling like this conversation is getting way more serious than I ever expected.

"Don't worry about hurting me."

"Noah, is it … is it okay that we're here together?"

"Why wouldn't it be?" he asks, tilting his head at me again.

"We're usually out with Mohammad and Harry," I comment, realizing what this looks like.

And what it's starting to feel like.

"We usually are," he agrees. "But not tonight."

I hear a tinge of sadness in his voice, and I think it's because the same thoughts crossing his mind are also crossing mine.

We're supposed to be with Harry tonight.

It's not supposed to just be Noah and me.

This time, it's just the effect of a messed up situation that I put myself into.

That I put *us* into.

And I'm sitting here, watching Noah look at me from across the table like he can't decide if he should be happy or sad to be out with me.

Because he knows how I feel.

He knows that I care about him.

But I care about Harry too.

And tonight, it was supposed to be Harry.

I wanted it to be.

But he's not the boy who is sitting across from me.

WEDNESDAY, OCTOBER 9TH
I can't be here.
6:45AM

WHEN MY ALARM goes off on my phone, I turn it off, and all I can see on my home screen are texts.

What the heck?

There must be at least ten of them, which all came through around one and two in the morning.

There's a missed call from Naomi.

Text after text from her.

Naomi: *Oh my God, I hate George. I will forever hate him.*

Naomi: *Olivia was out tonight and saw him. Apparently, Harry and George were plastered. George was chatting up some other girl.*

Naomi: *I don't understand.*

Naomi: *Why would he do that? We just went out together.*

Naomi: *Olivia's saying that he's a total player.*

Naomi: *That he ... snogged her.*

Naomi: *Not Olivia. Some other girl.*

Naomi: *And Harry and George got into a fight. I thought you should know.*

Naomi: *I'm sorry. I just don't know who else to talk to right now.*

My stomach immediately lurches, and my whole body starts to shake.

Harry was out with George last night?
They were drunk?
George kissed someone else?
And what about Harry? Was he with Olivia?

I TEXT NAOMI back with shaky hands, trying to think about her and how she must be feeling instead of myself.

Me: *Hey, I'm so sorry. I just got your messages this morning. Do you want to meet before school? What can I do?*

I'm not sure what to say. Mostly because I feel like I'm going to puke. Part of me wishes the texts had woken me up. Maybe then, I could have gotten more information out of Naomi as opposed to these small bits and pieces of the story.

I want to call Harry immediately.

To demand that he explain himself.

But I know that I won't call him.

Mostly because I messed up yesterday.

Harry was right.

I wasn't there for him.

And I don't know the whole story yet.

All I know is what Naomi told me, which is just that Olivia, Harry, and George were together. And that Harry and George fought.

I get out of bed and go into the bathroom to shower.

I take my phone with me, keeping it on the counter in case Naomi replies. When I'm halfway through shakily shampooing my hair, I hear a ding come from my phone. I decide to finish showering, the impending message motivation enough to quicken my pace. I wrap a fluffy towel around my chest, brush my teeth, and then comb through my hair, parting it straight down the middle.

I look over myself in the mirror, trying to keep my eyes from wandering down to the reflection of my phone.

Another text chimes out, and I'm slightly terrified to read it.

I'm sure it's just from Naomi and her response to if she wants to meet or not. But there's also a chance it's from Harry. Or even Olivia. Or maybe it will be from Naomi, telling me news that I don't want to hear.

I know I'm being ridiculous, so I grab the phone and read the message.

Naomi: *Meet me in the common room? 7:30?*

Naomi: *I'm gutted ... I wish I could talk to Olivia about it, but she warned me. And she was right.*

Me: *It's his loss. You're amazing. I'll be there at 7:30.*

I click Send on the text, grateful that she didn't bring up Harry. I go back into my room and change into my uniform. My stomach feels all over the place. My hands are lightly shaking as I run the blow dryer over my hair until it hangs flatly at my shoulders.

I add a touch of mascara and some lip balm before grabbing my bag for school. I look in it, realizing my textbooks are still in the kitchen.

I pull open my door, finding Noah in the hallway.

He's still in his pajamas, his hair a sleepy mess.

"You're ready?" he says, surprised, eyeing my uniform.

"Yeah. I need to get to school," I reply, trying to shift past

him.

"Whoa." Noah puts his hand on my arm, stopping me. "What's going on?"

I'm not sure what to say. So, I just pull up Naomi's texts and hand him my phone. His eyes scan across the screen as he scrolls through her messages. When he looks back up at me, his face is covered with concern.

"Give me five minutes, and I'll be down," he says, keeping his brown eyes on me.

I shake my head. "Naomi probably just needs some girl time," I insist.

"And what do you need?"

"I need some air. I'll meet you out front. I'll make us some toast to go, okay?"

Noah nods at me before going into the bathroom. After he closes the door, I head down to the kitchen.

I find Helen at the table, a cup of coffee in her hand. She's dressed for work, her keys and purse on the table.

"Morning." I give her a smile before popping some bread into the toaster.

"You're off early this morning," she says, watching as I rush around the kitchen.

I grab two napkins and fill up a mug with coffee to take with me.

"Yeah, Naomi wants to meet before school," I explain, putting the lid on my coffee. "She's pretty upset. The guy she's been dating ... apparently, she isn't the *only* one he's dating."

"Oh, poor dear," Helen says understandingly. "Well, try to have a good day."

"Thanks," I reply as the toaster goes off. I put both pieces of bread into the napkins and grab two bananas to go. "Oh, I almost forgot. Mohammad invited me over for dinner tonight.

Is it all right if I go?"

"I don't see why not," Helen replies warmly. "I'll be out for work today, but you'll be home after school?"

"Yeah," I reply as I walk to the entryway. I slip on my shoes, checking the time on my phone.

"Mallory, your coursework," Helen says from the kitchen.

"Right." I shake my head. I start to walk toward her but then look down at my shoes, not sure if I should have them on in the house or not.

"It's fine," Helen says, waving me in. "Are you sure you're all right?"

"Just a little frazzled this morning."

I head back into the kitchen and grab my and Noah's homework off the table before throwing it into my bag. I realize I forgot my coffee, too, and grab it off the counter.

I give Helen an apologetic smile and then head back to the front door.

"Noah, dear, I'm off," Helen says from the kitchen.

"All right, Mum. Love you," Noah calls back to her as I throw on my coat.

"Have a great day," Helen says before heading into the garage the same time that I step out the front door.

I suck in a gulp of the cool air, letting it clear my head.

I'm about to sit down on the front stoop when a car pulls up to the sidewalk, and I instantly recognize it.

It's Harry.

I instinctively get up as the door opens, and Harry gets out of the car. His head is down, but it's easy to tell that he isn't quite ready for morning. His shirt isn't fully tucked in, and his tie isn't tight at his neck. His blond hair, which is usually combed perfectly, is a mess.

When he closes the door, his eyes finally meet mine. And when they do, I can't keep from staring at him. My insides lurch as I take in his black eye. It's bluish yellow, and the only thing that I can think of is the similar bruise that Harry got from his dad.

"Can we talk?" Harry says, more matter-of-factly than anything else.

I shake my head, my voice catching in my throat. I walk down the steps, wanting to move past him.

I can't be here.

I can't do this right now.

"No," I stutter, shaking my head.

"Please, we need to talk," Harry insists, pressing his lips together.

My breath catches in my chest with the motion. Because I feel like I already know what he's going to say.

And that he's going to break my heart.

If I let him talk, if I let him try to talk his way out of whatever he's done, I'm not going to make it to school. I won't be able to get through the day.

"Later, all right," I offer, walking past him.

"Mallory," he says, chasing after me.

"What?" I shout. I'm angry with myself for stopping. But I can't help it. I look back at him, my eyes scanning across his darkened eye to the frown set on his face. "Harry, are you okay?"

"You're asking me if *I'm* okay?" he repeats. His brows dip in as he glances away from me.

"Yes, I am."

"I'm fine," Harry says, his gaze meeting mine. "I … I messed up yesterday."

And there it is.

That's all he has to say.

Because I know exactly—*exactly*—what that means.

I nod at him, trying to stay levelheaded.

"Look, I have to go talk to Naomi. I'm supposed to meet her before school."

"Mallory, this is more important," he says, taking a step toward me.

"She was dating George," I snap, trying to make him understand. "And apparently, last night, she found out that he was kissing someone else. *She's upset.* And I need to be there for her."

I stare at Harry, feeling everything in me roll.

"Seriously?" Harry replies with disbelief. "You're going to go console her over the guy who punched me in the face?"

"What happened?"

Because he's not about to lecture me without explaining himself.

"It wasn't anything—" Harry starts.

But I cut him off, "What do you mean, it wasn't anything? You do have a black eye, don't you? And since when do you go out and party with George? What the fuck are we even doing, Harry? Naomi told me you were with Olivia."

"I wasn't *with* her," Harry says, shaking his head. "She just showed up at the same place. I needed everyone off my back for one night."

"No. You just wanted *me* off your back."

"Mallory," Harry says, his blue eyes softening.

"Just stop." I take a minute, picking my words. "You told me that you wanted me to be there for you. You said that you would let me in. And I know that you were trying to yesterday, but you didn't really even give me a chance. You wouldn't tell me what was wrong or give me two seconds to make a decision before shutting me out. What happened to the guy who was on our date? The one who said it was him and me?"

"I needed you yesterday," he says.

339

"I know that. But, Harry, I can't always be right there for you. Fuck, I can't be everywhere. If we can't do this now, how are we supposed to do this when I leave?" I ask, becoming more upset. And then the realization hits me. "I wasn't there for you … but Olivia was."

"I didn't say that," Harry says, his eyes growing serious.

"You're not denying it either."

"Do you want me to lie? Yes, I saw her last night."

"Make me understand. Tell me what's going on. I saw you two talking in the hallway. I gave you a chance at lunch to explain things, and you said nothing."

"I didn't have an explanation at the time. You're my … girlfriend. I thought you were just supposed to be there for me. You're supposed to be on my side."

"I'm standing right here, talking to you," I insist. "Maybe you should figure out an explanation. Because I'm trying really hard not to jump to conclusions right now. I know you're going through a terrible time. I know you are. But it's not an excuse."

"Why are you yelling at me?" Harry replies, shaking his head. "I came here to apologize for being a prick yesterday."

"Why am I yelling? I'm yelling because I woke up to fifteen texts telling me that my boyfriend was drunk last night, got into a fight, and was out with his ex-girlfriend," I say, running my hands down my face. "And every time you open up to me, I open up to you too. And yet, after each time you do, you freeze up. You stop yourself. You can't do it."

"I can," Harry pleads.

"No, you can't. And in your process of self-discovery, you're just dragging me along."

"You have no clue what's going on in my life," he says, his voice cracking.

He looks distraught.

"And whose fault is that? Let me clear some things up. I'm done. You want me off your back? I'm off. I'm over it. Feel free to do what you want, when you want. And with *whomever* you want. Just don't expect it to be with me," I say, pushing past him.

"What?" Harry asks, catching my hand. I should pull out of his grip, but I don't. "Mallory, I'm sorry." He keeps his hand wrapped around mine.

"You're *always* sorry," I say, feeling my hand start to shake in his.

"Fuck. Stop jumping to conclusions and just listen to me for a second."

"Harry," I insist, "you woke up and dragged yourself here for a reason. You're apologizing for yesterday. I can put two and two together."

Harry drops my hand. "You won't believe me. You've already shut me out."

"Can you blame me?" I ask, working hard to keep my voice steady and calm. "I need to go."

"No. Mallory, I didn't cheat on you."

"It doesn't matter," I reply, feeling upset over so many things.

"I'm not going to just let you declare it's over and walk away," he says.

"Yes, you are."

"No." Harry reaches for my hand again.

"Just stop!" I yell, feeling tears sting my cheeks. I step away from him, trying to make him understand. "You're breaking my heart, okay? More and more with each and every word. I don't want it to be this way, but it has to be. I can't keep giving you more. You're hurting me."

Harry stares at me, a tear slipping from his eye.

"You need to go," Noah says as he steps outside, closing

the front door behind him.

"Noah …" I barely get his name out of my mouth. I don't have the energy to say anything else.

Noah shakes his head at me, looking more upset than I've ever seen him. He's staring at Harry, his usually golden brown eyes practically black.

Harry wipes his eyes, looking between me and Noah, and then nods.

He sucks in his cheeks and swallows hard, glancing around like he's trying to figure out what to do.

"I'll go," he finally says. He turns around and then heads down the street.

I stay, standing frozen in my spot, until I can't see him anymore.

I want to collapse.

To fall to the ground.

But I dig my nails into my palms, knowing that I can't do that. Noah's looking over my shoulder, watching Harry like he might blow up at any moment.

But his face changes as he looks me over. He dips his head down, searching my eyes.

"I'm sorry," he apologizes, like I'm the one he told to leave.

"Please don't say anything."

"Mal," Noah says, bringing his hands onto my shoulders.

I look up at him, forcing my eyes to stop fogging over with tears. "I don't want to cry right now. And if you keep talking, I'm going to cry."

Noah keeps his eyes on mine, his forehead creased. His lips are pulled into a frown. He looks between me and the door but finally nods.

My nails continue digging into my palms at my sides as we walk. I feel a mixture of emotions.

But mostly, I feel hurt.

Noah constantly looks over at me. His eyes soft and concerned. I try to keep my focus on school. On getting to Naomi.

Because I know that she must be feeling terrible right now.

I squeeze my fists tighter, but then Noah's hand comes down onto my arm, holding up my hand. He opens up my fist as we walk, taking in the red nail marks on my palm.

I try to pull away from him, but he doesn't let me.

"Squeeze mine instead," he says, lacing his hand through mine.

As we walk to school, whenever I feel like my emotions are about to spill over, I squeeze tightly. Noah doesn't say anything, just like I asked.

But every once in a while, he squeezes back.

WE WALK IN silence until we're in the courtyard of Kensington. There are a few students milling about, but for the most part, it's quiet and empty.

I glance to the tree.

The central spot where Harry and I sat and kissed the morning we came here to investigate before school.

Someone is sitting in that same spot, seated with one leg crossed atop the other.

But it's not Harry.

It's Mohammad.

I let go of Noah's hand, practically running to him. I throw myself into his arms and wrap my hands around his neck.

"Nice to see you too." He chuckles, hugging me back.

"You're here," I say, the words tumbling out of my mouth. "I mean, why are you here?"

Mohammad pulls away from my hug, nodding to Noah.

"I *do* go to school here. In case you forgot." He grins. "But if you're referring to why I'm here so early, ask Noah. He messaged me."

I turn, looking at Noah as he approaches us. "You texted him?"

"I thought you could use the friendly face," Noah replies, his eyes shifting between Mohammad and me. He glances around the courtyard, his eyes scanning the students passing us by.

And I know that he's looking for Harry.

"Care to fill me in?" Mohammad says, pulling my attention away from Noah.

"I think I just broke up with Harry … I mean, the words that came out of my mouth gave off that impression. I didn't mean it. Of course I didn't. But … I don't know. Something in me snapped, and I sort of just declared that we were done."

"What?" Mohammad shrieks, his eyes popping out.

"And now, you see why I messaged you," Noah says to Mohammad as he runs his hand through his hair in frustration.

"What happened?" Mohammad asks, looking frantically between Noah and me.

"Harry and George went out last night, and Olivia was there. This morning, Harry tried to explain things to me, but I barely let him speak. I was so frustrated. I was kind of a jerk."

I know that I handled the situation badly.

"It's okay to be upset," Noah says to me.

"Did something happen between Harry and Olivia?" Mohammad asks, vocalizing what I have been worrying about all along.

"No. At least, I'm pretty sure. Harry said nothing happened." I realize it's already seven thirty-five. I wave my hand through the air and say, "I'll let Noah fill you in. He saw the texts from Naomi. I really need to go in and meet her."

"Wait, what does Naomi have to do with this?" Mohammad asks, looking even more confused.

"Just come inside in, like, ten minutes. I'm sure Naomi could use the cheering up. But let me talk to her first," I say to both of them before walking into school.

WHEN I GET inside, I easily spot Naomi sitting on one of the couches.

She has on her uniform, but she doesn't look anything like herself. Her hair is pulled up into a scrunchie, and her usually rosy face is a tinge too pale.

"Hey," I say.

Naomi brings her eyes up to mine, her brows dipping when she connects our gaze. She's holding on to her backpack in her lap like it's a pillow, and she automatically pushes out a pout as I sit down.

"Hey," she replies softly, her shoulders drooping.

I can't think of anything else to do but pull her into a hug. I wrap my arms around her, trying to make her feel better.

"Thanks," she says into my hair, hugging me back.

Naomi pulls away, and I move her backpack off her lap. I turn, pulling one of my legs up onto the couch so I can look directly at her. I rest my arm along the back of the couch, bringing my hand up to her hair, running down it once.

She doesn't say anything; she just looks at her hands in her lap.

I stroke her hair, giving her a minute.

"I feel like absolute shit," she finally says, her lips quivering.

"What happened?" I ask, trying to make sense of everything. "Didn't you have your date last night?"

"Yes!" she replies, her voice rising. "And it was perfect. We talked about our families, and he told me how much he fancied me. But I guess it was all just for show."

"This might be a bad question," I say hesitantly, trying to be gentle. "But had you two talked about being exclusive? I mean, is it something you can get past, or are you done with him?"

"He hadn't asked me to be his girlfriend," she clarifies. "But last night, he invited me to his mate's party this upcoming weekend. He was pretty clear that we could stay the night and have time to *ourselves*."

"Wow," I reply, shaking my head.

"What a wanker," Naomi growls, looking more upset now than sad. "He was just trying to get into my knickers this weekend, I'm sure."

"What can I do?"

Naomi pinches her lips, her eyes drifting up to the corner of the room. "Can you fix my makeup? I didn't have it in me to put any on this morning."

"I don't have any with me," I reply, my lips pulling into a flat line.

"I carry a touch-up bag."

She reaches for her backpack, pulls out a cute little bag, and hands it to me. Inside, I find eye shadow, mascara, blush, and lip gloss. There are also mini concealers and sample-sized perfume bottles, among other things.

"You're prepared," I reply, admiring her stash. "I think you've got more in your travel kit than I have in total."

"We really need to get you a proper full set of makeup." She laughs, shaking her head at me.

"You're probably right," I agree with a smile.

I apply gold eye shadow to her lids before coating her lashes with mascara. I glance at her cheeks, adding a little highlighter to her cheekbones and down the center of her nose.

"This feels nice," she says, letting out a sigh.

"It's fun to have your makeup done," I agree, dabbing gloss on her lips.

I add a little spritz of perfume to her neck and then look her over. Her hair looks cute up, but I pull down a few tendrils, allowing them to frame her face.

"You look beautiful." I hand her back her makeup bag. "You did before, too, but I hope it helps you feel better."

"Thanks." Naomi smiles and looks herself over in her compact mirror. "I just still can't believe it."

"At least you know now. It's better to know now than to fall madly in love with him and then realize he doesn't want the same things as you," I tell her, hoping she can see the bigger picture.

"That's what Olivia said," Naomi says with a sigh, putting her makeup back into her backpack.

"Where is Olivia anyway?" I ask, daring to bring her up.

"I'm sure she'll be here soon," Naomi replies mindlessly. "I just feel ridiculous. Oh, and you should know that Olivia wasn't out *with* Harry. I'm sorry if I made it sound like that. I'm sure I had you flipping."

"Harry came by to talk to me this morning actually."

"What did he say?"

"Nothing of use. I argued with him and basically left."

"Well, I know Olivia. Even if she wanted to get back with Harry, she wouldn't have done anything with him while you're his girlfriend. Not necessarily out of respect for you, but because she's prideful."

I nod, not sure what to say. Or if I believe her.

"Unlike George," Naomi goes on. "Who apparently will get with any girl he can find."

"You're better off," I insist.

"Better off with me," Mohammad says, dropping down next to Naomi on the couch.

"Hi." I smile at him, grateful for the interference.

Mohammad gives me a nod before turning his attention—and his grin—back to Naomi. I glance over to Noah as Mohammad slides his arm around Naomi's shoulders.

"Don't be cheeky," Naomi warns.

"I have to be," Mohammad replies seriously. "Look at you. You're absolutely stunning. It's George's loss."

Naomi gives me a sympathetic smile before looking back to Mohammad. "Well, thank you. I'll take the compliment."

I glance across the seating area to Noah. He sat on the couch opposite ours, and he's leaning back into the cushions with his arms crossed over his chest.

"You girls need to cheer up," Mohammad insists, looking between Naomi and me. "You're sitting next to some of the finest and fittest lads Kensington has to offer, yet you have nothing to say."

I look back over at Noah as he cracks a smile.

"Just because I'm not dating George anymore doesn't mean I'm ready for a new boy to fancy me," Naomi replies.

"Whoa, whoa, whoa. I'm not looking for a woman to fancy," Mohammad cuts in, eager to set the record straight.

"You're not?" Naomi asks, raising an eyebrow at him.

Her words catch me off guard, and I look to Noah, who is watching them intently.

Mohammad bites his lip before glancing over at me. He looks lovestruck with confusion and slightly impressed. Or maybe it's worry on his face. It's hard to tell because, a second later, he's staring at Naomi like she's the most interesting thing he's seen all day.

And seemingly, George has been wholly forgotten because Naomi is looking back at Mohammad with, well, flirty eyes.

"But maybe I should be ..." Mohammad banters with her.

Naomi replies with a coy smile.

I scrunch up my nose, sort of horrified that my visions of them getting together seem to be coming true. And slightly because it's like watching two animals dance around one another right before they mate.

And I definitely feel like I shouldn't be here, listening and watching.

Naomi looks up at Mohammad coolly, taking in his arm still wrapped around her shoulders. "I'd believe you more if you hadn't snogged by best friend the last time we were all together," she says, raising her chin at Mohammad. And raising a fair point.

"If I remember, you weren't exactly at that party alone," Mohammad replies quickly, his eyes still on her.

"Ugh, don't bring him up. I can't be bothered to hear his name again," Naomi says, shaking her head.

"Let's not talk about *him* then," Mohammad replies, fully taking over the conversation. "Let's talk about what *you* are doing Friday night."

"What?" I stutter, my eyes going wide.

"What do you have in mind?" Naomi asks.

But I can tell she's still listening because she looks over at me, her cheeks flushed.

Mohammad dips his lips toward her ear, saying something to her with a smile that I can't hear.

Naomi's mouth falls wide open as she listens. She lets out a giggle but then stops herself, pushing him away with her palm.

"It's a nice offer, but you'll have to do better," she says as Olivia joins us.

"What, partying without me?" Olivia sits down on the opposite couch.

I notice Noah glances over to her, his jaw setting.

"Piss off," Mohammad mumbles, looking upset at the sight of her.

"Excuse me?" Olivia says, her face paling.

"Either explain yourself or piss off. Because a lot of people were hurt last night," Mohammad replies.

I've never seen him so serious. Or upset. And he's definitely not budging.

"You're joking," Olivia says flatly. "I didn't do *anything*. It's not my fault Naomi fell for a fuckboy. And it's not my fault that Harry and George went on a bender and got in a fight."

"No, but your lovely rendition of the evening got around before anyone had a chance to explain themselves," Mohammad interrupts.

Olivia looks at me, her face flushing.

"Nothing happened between Harry and me," she states, her tone harsh. "Besides, even if something did, I don't owe anyone an explanation."

"Actually, you do." Noah is the one to speak up this time.

I look at him, surprised he even said anything.

"If you want to be friends with us, then we do need an explanation," Mohammad agrees.

"For fuck's sake. I ran into George and Harry on accident. And after we'd spoken yesterday, I was worried. I stayed with them to make sure he was okay. They were pissed but in good spirits. George, obviously, found someone of interest. I left Harry at the bar to use the loo, and when I came back, they were in a fight," Olivia says, talking a mile a minute. "Harry was upset, caught a cab, and left. That was it."

Noah's watching me the entire time Olivia speaks. It makes me self-conscious, and I try hard not to let a single emotion flash across my face.

I don't want to have a reaction.

I need to just listen in silence.

"All right then," Mohammad says with a nod.

"All right then," Olivia grumpily replies, getting up from the couch. She looks at Mohammad's arm around Naomi, and I can see her eyes trying not to roll back. But she does a good job, keeping them in place, and says to Mohammad, "So, do you want to walk to class?"

I remember from the first week that Mohammad said he had first period with Olivia, so her suggestion makes sense. But I also think she doesn't want to walk away from us alone.

"Yeah," Naomi says. She stands up from the couch, pulling me with her. "Thanks for showing up," she whispers, giving me a hug.

Naomi looks to Mohammad with a smile. His eyebrows rise as she nods at him, and he gets up to follow them.

"Later," he says to me, quickly catching up to Olivia and Naomi, leaving Noah and me in the common room.

"Should we head to class too?" Noah asks, but he stays on the couch.

I look at the clock as the first bell goes off, our warning that classes are starting soon.

I want to say no, that we should just sit here and stare blankly at one another. I could use the time to zone out of everything.

But if we do that, we'll be late.

"Yep, let's go."

It was hard to miss.
STATISTICS

"That was weird," Noah finally says, breaking the silence between us.

"So weird," I agree, turning toward him.

"Mohammad was … blushing," he replies, his creamy forehead creasing.

"Right! You saw that too?"

Noah scrunches up his nose and lets out a heavy chuckle. "It was hard to miss."

"I mean, I know I said I wanted them together, but that was a little fast," I say, thinking about the strange morning.

"I wouldn't get ahead of yourself. You did ask Mohammad to cheer her up," Noah says, bringing his hand under his chin.

"Yeah, cheer her up. Not flirt with her."

"He wasn't exactly flirting alone," Noah says, shaking his head once like he can't believe it.

"All right, class," Mr. Johnson says. "I'd like for you to go ahead and turn in your homework from last night."

"Oh shit," Noah mutters as I grab my bag.

I take in his worried expression and know what he's thinking.

"I've got your homework. I threw everything from the kitchen table into my bag this morning," I say, pulling out his stack of folders.

Noah lets out a sigh of relief.

"Thanks." He looks flustered as he takes his folder from my hand, gets his homework out, takes mine from my hand, and walks it up to Mr. Johnson's desk.

"So, how did we all get on with the homework?" Mr. Johnson asks as students move back to their seats.

I glance around, seeing frown after frown. And from the looks of it, Mr. Johnson's cool factor is quickly wearing off. Because his usually chipper class is looking at him like they want to murder him.

"I'm sensing it didn't go well," Mr. Johnson infers, running his hand across his jaw. As no one replies, he searches the classroom, his lips pulling into a flat line. "I'd like to hear your thoughts."

"It was hard," one girl says.

"It was hard," Mr. Johnson repeats, tilting his head. "Anyone else?"

"It took me over an hour," someone else says as the class riles up.

And I'm internally cheering for them. But I don't say anything. Mostly because I don't want to be one of those students who goes all power crazy when they're finally asked for their opinion.

"I remember this one kid in my class in New York," I whisper to Noah. "This guy was always silent. Finally, one day, the professor called on him and asked what he thought, and he just started spilling out every critique he had on his mind. It was negative after negative after negative."

"That's the problem with holding things in. They just fester," Noah whispers back as someone else tells Mr. Johnson that they couldn't even finish the homework.

"I know. It was surprising actually. But after that, he started talking more. It was like he got it all off his chest. And he wasn't wrong. His critiques were fair, and our professor even pointed that out," I reply, thinking about school in New York.

"So, your professor agreed with the student?"

"Yeah. And I think it made him like her more though. Because, sometimes, professors can get that sort of high-and-mighty vibe. I know that's not fair to say because education is important and their job is basically impossible. But still, I think it made everyone feel like they could speak up if they had a problem."

"You're not afraid to ask questions, are you?"

"Nope. Are you?"

Noah shakes his head. "No. But most of the time, the questions I think about asking, I never actually ask."

"Why?"

Noah glances up at Mr. Johnson. He's sitting at the edge of his desk, flipping through our homework assignments, evidently checking how much everyone got done.

"I guess I just get consumed in my thoughts. There are pieces of information that stick out to me, and I get fixated. I would rather work on one theory or problem for an entire lesson. Knowing how they created the formula, tricks for it, different ways of coming to the same answer. That's not really how they teach though."

"No, it's not. I think that might be my nightmare of a course. I want to know just enough to solve the problem." I let out a little chuckle.

"Problem is, there are so many different ways of learning. Everyone's different, but we have a system built for one type of student."

"That kind of sucks," I comment, realizing he's right. "Do you ever think you'd do better at the courses you didn't like if they were taught differently?"

"I'm sure I would. But doesn't matter too much. Whatever I want to know, I can always look up on my own."

Mr. Johnson interrupts our conversation by setting down our stack of homework on his desk and then says, "Let me defend myself firstly by saying, I am your professor, and as such, I'm entitled to assign you homework. And secondly, though it was difficult, you shouldn't need to prepare for your exam Friday because of it. So, you're welcome."

He gives us a heavy head nod, like his statement somehow addressed every complaint, and then instructs us to quiet down and open up our textbooks.

Try living it.
LATIN

"I'VE BEEN DYING to talk to you," Mohammad says as he slides into his desk.

Statistics dragged on, but at least Mr. Johnson didn't assign us any homework.

"History was terrible. There was way too much information coming at me from all sources. I was like a computer that was short-circuiting because of too much input."

"What?" I say, trying to follow along.

"I have History with Olivia and half, if not three-quarters, of our year's other chatterboxes."

"And ..." I state, still trying to understand.

"I got *all* of the details," Mohammad replies, leaning in toward me.

"I thought Noah told you everything?"

"Noah's useless," he replies, brushing off my answer. "He gave me a stream of facts that didn't imply or suggest anything."

"Well, let's hear it then," I say, mentally preparing myself for the gossip to come.

"Let's start off with whatever the fuck happened between

you and Noah in Art yesterday."

"Yesterday?" I ask, confused about what he's talking about. "What does that have to do with—"

"Well, from what I heard, you and Noah had a staring competition," Mohammad insists, like I should understand what he's saying. "One of the girls said—and I quote—'You could cut the tension between them with a knife.' Apparently, you two stared at one another for a solid minute, minimum."

"Oh God," I moan, dropping my forehead onto my desk.

Because this cannot be happening to me.

"That's not even the half of it. Half of the girls thought it was romantic. The other half think you're even more of a slag than before because not only do you have Harry, but now, you've also put some sort of spell on Noah. Their words, not mine."

"That's kind," I say, shaking my head.

"That's Kensington."

"What does it matter at this point?" I reply, not sure what else to say.

"I just thought you should know. So, what were you doing, staring at Noah anyway? I thought you said that was handled. And I saw you two this morning," Mohammad whispers, leaning closer to me, talking through closed lips.

"What do you mean?"

"You were holding hands," Mohammad says, his eyes widening with each word.

"Forgive me, but it was a rough morning. He was trying to support me."

"Luckily for you, I'm the only one who saw," Mohammad says, eyeing me sternly.

"And Harry?" I ask hesitantly. "I'm not sure what exactly Noah told you, but just because I was upset ... I still care."

"Harry's at school," he replies, softening his gaze. "He

came in at the last minute. I saw him before class."

"That's good."

"Mallory, are you all right?"

"Yeah … honestly, I don't know. I have this terrible feeling in my stomach about everything."

"You're knotted up." Mohammad nods understandingly.

"Yep."

"Well, news of his black eye will spread like wildfire, and then he's all you're going to hear about. So, mentally prepare."

"I hate this. We shouldn't be gossiping. We should be talking to Harry. *I* should be," I clarify.

"From what Noah said, he deserves a cold shoulder for a day."

The bell goes off, and Mohammad lets out a heavy groan. "Presentations today."

"I know," I reply with a frown.

"We're going to bomb it, aren't we?"

"Stop," I say, slapping at Mohammad's arm. "You need to be optimistic. We will do fine."

"Well, if we don't, why don't you be the one to explain it to my mum tonight? Then, finally, someone will understand the soul-crushing disappointment I apparently inflict on her each and every time I come home with shit marks."

"You're being dramatic," I say pointedly.

"What can I say? It's been a dramatic day. It's affected me," Mohammad says, his dark brows dipping in.

He gets a pout on his lips, and I can't help but grin at his cute face.

"Aww, is someone worn down from all the gossip? Well, try living it …"

"Yeah. That's a big *no, thank you* on that one."

"You'd just rather help me navigate it, right?" I tease.

"I did say I would be your guide, didn't I?"

"Along with my counselor, Latin tutor, advice giver, and best friend."

"How about we just say I'm *many things* to you?" Mohammad grins. "But most importantly, your best friend."

"And my source of gossip." I grin back at him.

"Obviously."

Like a sweet flower.
LUNCH

OUR PRESENTATION WENT better than we'd expected. Evidently, Mohammad had been overly dramatic about not doing good because he drove us through it. I'm not sure where it came from, but he did amazing.

And at the moment, he knows it.

He totally knows it.

"Did you see me? I was on fire. I was practically a Latin god!" Mohammad declares to the entire hallway on our way to lunch.

"You actually were," I agree, giving him full credit.

"I sounded like some ancient, sexy emperor up there. Like I was about to conquer a corner of the world and take its treasures as my own."

"And what did I sound like?" I ask, peering up at him.

"Well, you sort of sounded like you were reading lines," Mohammad says.

"How. Kind," I say each word in sync with a push, shoving him away from me in the hallway.

"It's not my fault you got stage fright, baby. I carried us all the way."

"You really did," I admit, shaking my head and just deciding to let him have his moment.

Mohammad's got a grin plastered on his face. I can tell he's thinking about our presentation, and each time he tries to wipe the smile off his face, it comes right back.

"Someone should have really recorded that. I'm telling you, maybe I should go out for theater. I could be the next James Bond."

"All right, buddy, I think you're getting a little ahead of yourself," I say, trying to rein him in. "Besides, I thought you were going to be a matchmaker. Or a detective."

"Well, seeing as your love life is a disaster and I couldn't find anything on our joyful Mr. Johnson, I might have to find a new profession."

"Luckily, you've got time," I say as we make our way into the lunchroom.

My stomach instantly knots up when I see Noah sitting at our usual table, alone.

I wave him over, following Mohammad as we get in the lunch line.

"What are you doing?" Mohammad asks.

"I forgot our lunches today," I comment as Noah joins us. "Busy morning and all that."

Noah's lips pull at the corner, curving up into a sympathetic smile. It's more of a twitch than a smile, but I think it's the best I'm going to get.

"Ah, it's better for you anyway," Mohammad insists, extending his head forward to see what they're serving today.

Noah keeps his eyes on me. I want to say something to him, but I just don't know *what* to say.

It feels like there's too much to say.

"Oh my God, I just realized ..." Mohammad says, turning to me. "I *could* actually be the next James Bond."

"What?" Noah asks, breaking his eyes away from mine.

"You said it earlier. I'm suave. I'm brilliant with women," Mohammad goes on, giving a girl in line a quick wink to prove his point. "I'm sneaky, I'm a mediocre detective, I have a way of always extracting information, and I'm matchmaker enough to see who's secretly shagging. All I need to learn are some action moves, and I could *literally* be Mr. Bond."

"Where is this coming from?" Noah asks with a questioning smirk.

"Oh, just wait …" I whisper to him, knowing that it's just a matter of time before Mohammad goes off again.

"This is coming from a man who has not only conquered Latin, but who has also conquered the world! I could apply for MI6 tomorrow and be accepted just on my public speaking skills alone. That's a thing, right?" Mohammad asks, his eyes way too bright.

"I'm not sure they'd let you in …" I reply, trying to avert this idea.

"I'm clean as a whistle. What are they going to find? A few pics of me with a stiffy? Big deal. That's all the dirt I've got," Mohammad insists.

"Mohammad and I had a presentation in Latin today. It went … well," I say, connecting the dots for Noah.

"Well? *Well?* It was a blinding success!" Mohammad exclaims, apparently disappointed with my underwhelming assessment of our presentation.

"Well done," Noah says, giving Mohammad a whole-hearted smile.

"Thank you," Mohammad replies with an approving nod.

We move through the lunch line and take our trays back over to our table.

I glance around, looking for Harry. I can hear Mohammad's voice in the background, but I'm not really listening to him.

"Mallory?" Noah says, breaking into my thoughts.

"Yeah?" I look up at him, but he looks directly to Mohammad.

"I was asking if you're still down for having dinner at my house tonight," Mohammad says to me.

"Yeah, of course. Sorry," I apologize, feeling bad for ignoring him.

"Don't worry. Things will blow over," Mohammad says.

"I don't know," Noah states, stabbing at a piece of his pasta.

"What's got your knickers in a twist?" Mohammad asks Noah.

"Harry was being a wanker this morning," Noah says, shaking his head.

"Harry's always an ass, and we love him for it," Mohammad replies quickly.

"Well, he was especially one today," Noah counters.

"Simmer it down with the testosterone, please," I say, not wanting to get into this.

"Don't blame me," Mohammad says, holding up his hands in defense. "I'm not the grumpy grouch of the table."

"There are no grumpy grouches at the table," I scold, flaring my eyes at Mohammad. And even if there were, he shouldn't be bringing attention to it. "I don't want you guys taking sides. And there aren't sides anyway."

"We're not taking sides," Noah replies, setting down his fork. "We're irritated."

"No, *you're* irritated," Mohammad corrects.

"You would have been, too, if you had heard Harry this morning," Noah says with frustration.

Mohammad looks over at me accusingly. "Things didn't go as smoothly as you made it seem this morning, did they?"

I bite my lip, not sure what to say.

"It wasn't good," I admit.

Noah nods in agreement, finally picking his fork back up.

I look around, my gaze finally stopping when it lands on Harry. He's sitting at a table with a different group of guys, but he isn't speaking.

Mohammad and Noah follow my eyes.

"He's sitting alone," I mutter, knowing that this isn't right.

"He's at a table full of guys," Noah retorts.

"It's what guys do. We fuck up. We sulk. Or fight it out. Then, we make up. It will be fine," Mohammad insists.

"But just because we're having trouble doesn't mean you both should have an issue with him," I say, trying to get them to understand. "You're his best friends. You're supposed to be there for him."

"If I talk to him right now, I'll lose it," Noah says.

"When he's ready to talk, he'll talk," Mohammad adds. "For now, just let him roll around with it."

I nod, knowing I have to respect their decisions.

Their process.

It's okay for me to be upset.

And it's okay for Harry to sit somewhere else.

At least for today.

"You kind of saved the day with Naomi this morning," I tell Mohammad, wanting to lighten up the mood.

"Who would have thought she'd be so cheeky?" he says with a grin.

"Who would have thought you'd notice?" I reply.

"She smelled fucking good too. It was distracting," Mohammad admits, shoveling in a spoonful of pasta.

Noah lets out a deep chuckle, his mood instantly shifting.

"What?" Mohammad asks, looking up at him.

"Well, you typically only notice someone's smell when

you fancy them," Noah replies.

His eyes stay on Mohammad, but all I can think about is Noah asking me about my perfume last week.

"That's not true," Mohammad disagrees, waving off Noah's assessment. "I notice everyone's perfume. I like the different scents. Just because I know what you smell like doesn't mean I fancy you."

"But there's a difference between knowing what someone smells like and being attracted to the scent, right? What did she smell like?" I ask.

Mohammad puts his finger on his chin, thinking. "She smelled like … peaches."

"Peaches?" I repeat.

"Yes. Juicy, sweet, delicious peaches," Mohammad confirms, sticking out his tongue.

"Oh. My. God. Ewww," I say, trying to erase his satisfied look from my mind.

"You wanted to know," he replies with a laugh.

"Wait. What do I smell like?"

Mohammad leans toward me, taking a sniff. "You smell kind of like a sweet flower."

"What?" I laugh.

"There's something floral to your perfume. But also something sweet."

"Yet you didn't compare my smell to food," I point out.

"I'm not sure I'm interested in eating flowers," Mohammad replies, looking at me like I've lost it.

"You know, there are edible flowers," Noah teases, finally chiming in.

"Wait, what do I smell like to you?" Mohammad asks.

I lean into him, bringing my nose in toward his neck. "You sort of have a mulled wine scent. It's warm and comforting. There are some soft spice notes but a fresh tanginess too. Maybe orange? I don't know if it's your cologne or just you."

"Either way, I'll take it. Mulled wine is bomb."

"Noah next?" I ask, looking to Mohammad.

"I don't need an analysis," Noah replies, shaking his head.

"It doesn't matter anyway. He doesn't wear cologne," Mohammad replies.

"He still has a smell," I insist.

"Yeah, his natural one. What good's that going to do?" Mohammad asks.

"That's my point. We should be able to smell him even better. His true pheromones," I say, nodding my head at Noah. "Go on. Smell him."

Mohammad doesn't look convinced, but finally, he leans toward Noah. "This feels weird."

"Analyze," I remind.

"All right, I smell … laundry detergent. Maybe a hint of shampoo?"

"Good work, mate," Noah replies sarcastically. "You've proven that I'm clean."

"What do you smell?" Mohammad asks me.

I wave Noah toward me, leaning in and meeting him halfway across the lunch table. His scent is strong and overpowering, but I can't figure out how to describe it.

"I do get that fresh laundry scent, but it's mixed with … I don't know … salt maybe? It's like that first hit of air you get when you arrive at the beach. But then there's also this super thick musk. Like he just ran a lap and doesn't stink, but you can smell it."

I pull away from Noah, sitting back down onto the bench.

"So, musky, salty laundry." Mohammad laughs, mocking Noah. "See, that's the description I'm trying to *avoid* by wearing cologne."

Noah lets out a deep laugh, smiling at Mohammad as the bell goes off.

Because you're hurting?
ART

"SO, DO YOU agree with Mohammad?" Noah asks as we sit down in class.

"Agree with Mohammad about what?" I ask, dropping my bag down to the ground.

"Do I smell like musky, salty laundry?" Noah's eyes are sparkling, and his mouth is pulled back into an easy smile.

"He's just being dramatic. But, yeah, kind of." I laugh. "I mean, you smell like you."

"I smell like me?"

"Mmhmm," I agree. "I also heard what you said about liking someone's smell ..."

"You caught that?" Noah says, running his hand through his chestnut hair. "I need to start picking my words more carefully."

"Maybe you shouldn't," I disagree. Because it's times like that, when Noah slips up, that I feel like I finally get a little insight into what he actually thinks.

Or feels.

"You seemed good at lunch. Distant, but good," he says, changing the subject.

"Did I really have a choice?" I ask, glancing over at him.

"Of course you had a choice," he replies, his chin resting on his palm now.

"I was just ... trying to keep distracted."

"Because you're hurting?"

"Because I'm dreading Geography," I say, giving him the honest answer.

"Don't go," Noah says, his eyes landing on me.

"What?"

"I don't know. We could leave," Noah offers, pulling his lips to the side.

I shake my head. "I can't do that. I'd be running away. Just like I was this morning."

"I thought you were just over the lot of it this morning. I didn't think you were running away."

"I was done with the conversation. Maybe with everything. I don't know. I need to talk to Harry."

Noah nods, staying silent for a moment.

"What were you running away from?" he asks.

"Getting hurt. I didn't let Harry explain because, honestly, I couldn't deal with it in that moment. But also because I can think what I want right now. I can just avoid it. And if I ignore it, if I'm just *done*, well, then I can run away from all of it. And avoid putting myself in a position to continue getting hurt."

"There's a difference between running away and ending something because it's what's best for you."

"Yeah, well … I guess I'll just have to go to Geography and see how things are."

"But you have a chance to be done. I don't understand—" Noah starts, looking confused.

"I'm going to, uh, go grab our projects." I cut him off, getting up from the table.

Noah doesn't say anything. And I really don't want him to.

Because I know what he's thinking. That I have a chance now, here, to be done with Harry.

But I really don't want to be. And that's what's freaking me out the most about going to Geography and facing Harry. The fact that maybe he took what I said literally and *is* actually done.

My insides churn.
GEOGRAPHY

I SPENT THE rest of Art silently working on my project. Noah didn't say anything, and I kept my focus on sanding down my painting, letting the bottom paint layers come through.

"I'll meet you after class?" Noah asks when we get to my locker.

"Yeah, sounds good. I'll meet you out front."

"Yeah." Noah nods, glancing around the hallway before looking back at me. He puts his hand on my arm. "Everything will be fine, okay?"

I give him a smile.

"It will be fine, I promise," I say the words, feeling like they're more for him than myself.

Because Noah has concern written all over his face. He nods his head some more before dropping my arm.

"Noah," I say, trying to pull him out of it, "I'm okay."

"I know," he replies, shaking his head. "I'm just frustrated."

"Are you okay?"

"I'll be fine," he says, loosening his tie. "I'll see you after school."

And then he's gone.

But the truth is, we aren't *fine*. And we're both worried.

I don't waste any time in getting to Geography, mostly

because I know if I do, I'll chicken out and hide in the restroom through class.

Which doesn't exactly sound pleasant.

I sit down in my regular seat, my heart pounding in my chest as students filter in. Olivia and Naomi come in together, glancing at me before taking their seats. As I move my gaze back to the door, my eyes instantly connect with Harry's. I take in his bruised eye and the sad look on his face.

It makes my insides churn.

When Harry sits down behind me, I can smell smoke, but with everything going on, I can't blame him for needing a cigarette.

I can feel Olivia's gaze on Harry and me and catch her looking at us out of the corner of my eye. But today, she isn't looking at Harry with longing.

She's looking at him with worry.

Harry doesn't say anything, and I can't take the silence, so I turn to face him.

"I'm sorry I yelled at you this morning."

"You don't need to apologize," Harry replies, his voice gravelly. He shakes his head, keeping his eyes on his desk.

"I do. Despite everything, it was unkind of me."

"I need to explain things to you," he says, lowering his voice. He looks up at me through his blond lashes, sending butterflies through my stomach.

"You don't."

"I do. Just not here," Harry says, looking around the room.

"Because of Olivia?" I ask, my mind instantly going to her.

"Because it's too public," Harry replies.

I stare at him, trying to figure out what *public* means when Mr. Pritchard starts talking. He puts us into groups to review for our exam, and I spend the rest of the class trying to think about Geography and not about Harry.

Or about what he wants to say.

What kind of favor?
4PM

HARRY'S AT MY side as we walk out of class, and when we exit the door, I run straight into Noah.

"I thought we were meeting out front?" I ask him, trying to steady myself with his arm.

"I had to walk past your class to get out front," Noah mutters, not really looking at me because his eyes are on Harry.

Harry looks back at him, but neither one says anything. I look between them, wondering who is going to speak up first.

I push past them, deciding to just walk home by myself.

I can hear them following behind me, but I don't turn around. I'm not interested in watching as they have a staredown or whatever it was that they were doing. If guys get mad, mope, and then make up, then fine. I'll leave them to it.

"Mallory, you said we could talk," Harry says, rushing up next to me.

"Let's talk," I tell him, glancing behind me to see Noah following along.

As I walk out of the school's entrance, I can't help but wish that this could all just be over.

Harry looks over to me and then back at Noah. He grabs my hand and then stops walking, pulling me to a stop with him.

"Noah, could you please just give us a minute?" Harry

says to Noah.

Noah's eyebrows dip in, and his mouth opens like he's going to respond. But he just looks at me.

"Mate, come on," Harry pleads. "You told me I needed to explain. I'm trying to."

"You what?" I ask, my voice rising.

"Mallory?" Noah asks. And it looks like he's trying to gauge if I'm okay with this or not.

"I'll meet you at the house," I reply with a nod.

Noah looks from me to Harry, holding his gaze. His expression hardens before he turns and walks out of the courtyard.

"Fuck, he's on alert today," Harry exhales, dropping my hand.

"He's worried about me."

"I know."

"You know?"

"I'm sorry. I should have explained things to you already," Harry says, his blue eyes scanning my face.

"I asked you yesterday, and you didn't want to say. So, what's the difference now?"

"My mum called Olivia," Harry states.

"She what?" I stutter, trying to wrap my head around what he just said.

"I know. I was just as surprised when Olivia told me yesterday." He looks down at my hand and hesitates for a moment before taking it into his. Then, he leads me over to a bench, and we sit down. "Apparently, I hadn't told my mum yet that Olivia and I … weren't together. She thought we were, which was why she reached out."

"Oh …"

"It was an honest mistake," Harry says, rubbing his thumb across my hand. "We broke up before everything with my dad, and, well, it never came up. Anyway, she called her to ask a favor."

"What kind of favor?"

"She wanted Olivia to help push me in the right direction. You know, being a girlfriend and all that, Mum thought she'd have some pull over me or something." Harry swallows, shaking his head. I watch his leg bounce, the motion making me nervous about what he's going to say. "My parents told me this week that they're coming home."

"What do you mean?"

"I mean, they are coming home … together." Harry's blue eyes connect with mine. He holds my gaze, letting what he just said settle in. "My mum called me yesterday before lunch. She said that she and my father had talked. Things with the divorce were getting too messy, and she said it would affect the company if they didn't rein it in."

"That's not good…" I say, seeing where this is going.

"No. But it's the only thing my parents seem to agree upon."

"Harry, what's happening?"

Harry takes a deep breath and then continues, "Mum informed me that she and Dad would return to London. And that we would, for the foreseeable future, be spending time together as a family. That we need to look united."

"She's not leaving him?" I gasp.

"She is," Harry corrects. "But the board isn't thrilled about the divorce. There's no room for emotion in business. And with news of the divorce getting out, my family's stability will be called into question. And if, God forbid, anyone realized my mum was leaving because of my dad's heavy hand, well, it wouldn't be good for the company."

"So, you're what? Expected to pretend to be a family?"

"The divorce will be temporarily put on hold while my

parents do damage control. We will appear as a happy family. Eventually, my mother and father will separate—agreeably— and it will all be done with."

I suck in a gulp of air, realizing what this means for Harry.

I ask the only question that I'm scared to ask. The only one I want to know the answer to. "Will you all be living together?"

Harry sucks in his cheeks but then gives me a forced smile. "Yes."

"No," I state, shaking my head.

"I threw a bit of a fit to Mum about that one," Harry admits.

"And what did she say?"

"She said that it was time I grew up. That, despite my father being a shit husband and dad, he's always been good at business. And if saving the company means keeping our family reputation intact, she's going to ask that I put myself in that position."

"She can't ask that of you. You cannot stay there," I disagree.

"You don't understand. She's doing it *for* me. She's worried we will lose everything," Harry stutters, licking his lip.

"Do you feel that way?"

"I don't know. She called me, and then my dad called me. He said that it was time I step up in the company. He said if I want a role in the future, I have to prove it now. When they arrive home, it will be the start of a beautiful show. I'm to attend meetings and parties. And I'm going to learn the business when I'm not in school. The clock's run out, and my time is up."

"They can't ask that of you. How are you supposed to know what you want? This is all just … wrong, Harry."

"It's not a question of want. It's a question of responsibility."

"To who? Your family?"

"I have nothing, except my name and what that name has built," Harry replies, sounding distraught.

"That isn't true."

"No one believes I can do it," Harry says, his eyes back on me.

"So, you want to prove them wrong? You're going to put yourself through this to prove your worth?"

"Maybe. Maybe this is the only way to show them that I'm not a useless piece of shit. I don't want it. But it's my reality."

"I thought *I* was your reality?" I stare at Harry, unable to stop the words that came out of my mouth. They slipped out of my lips, leaving room for all of my emotions to come flooding back in.

How amazing those words felt when he said them to me.

How kissing him makes me feel like I can do anything.

How hurt I was yesterday when he walked out and again this morning.

A tear escapes, but Harry is quick to wipe it away.

"There's nothing for me to say about the past few days, except for I'm sorry. I swear, I'm usually more fun than this. I guess, when you arrived here, so did my family problems. They've run parallel courses that I can't explain. You don't deserve it. I reacted out of frustration yesterday. I was shocked when Olivia talked to me. And then I heard from both my parents. I was too scared to say anything at lunch, and then I just … snapped. I needed to get out of there, and I wasn't going to wait for you. For anyone …"

"But you love Noah and Mohammad. You trust them. Why didn't you go to them, if not me?"

"I needed time to process it. To figure out what I wanted to do or say. Let's just say, if you're going to put on a show, you have to decide exactly what that show is. And unfortunately, Mohammad and Noah can always see right through my charades. I wasn't ready for that. So, I went out."

"Yeah," I reply, not sure what else to say.

"I messed up. Please, just don't give up on me. Don't lose faith in us," Harry says, grabbing my hands again.

I shake my head, feeling a pit form in my stomach. "Why shouldn't I? Despite everything, I don't know if this is the best time for you to be in a relationship. You have a lot going on, and I don't want you to feel like you're disappointing me. We can just be friends."

"No," Harry says, clearly upset. "I *really* don't want that."

"You don't want it because you think you're going to lose me. But I promise, you won't."

"Mallory," he says, wrapping his arms around my waist and pulling me against his chest.

It's the first time we've hugged in days, and I almost forgot how much I love being here.

In this spot.

Pressed up against him.

Harry leans his forehead against mine and looks down at me. "I wish I could say this with better timing and under better circumstances, but I've heard life doesn't really care about any of those things."

"Harry?" I ask, looking up at him, wondering what he means.

"I love you," he whispers.

"You're just saying that."

"I'm saying it because it's how I feel. I didn't expect to care for you so much. I didn't want to fall for a girl who lives a country away. You're so different from me, but we're so similar. I love you, Mallory James. I don't know what's going to happen with my family. I don't know what I'll be expected to do. I don't even know if I want this responsibility. Maybe it will be good for me. It could give me direction, straighten me up. Or maybe it will break me. I can't tell you what I don't know. But I know that you're the best thing that's happened in my life in a very long time. And yesterday, I knew right away that I'd fucked up. I reacted immaturely and was mad at myself. And instead of fixing it, I went out. That's on me. I know it is."

"You love me ..." I repeat, trying to absorb it all.

"I love you," Harry says again as his hands hug my waist tighter.

"But, Harry, this is a pattern. Over and over, you make these shitty decisions. And they affect us. They affect me."

"I'm not perfect. Being with me, it won't be perfect."

"Then, what will it be?"

"It will be ... us. When I'm with you, I feel like I'm the person I've always wanted to be. And I think you're extraordinary. I'm sorry if I haven't made that very clear," Harry says, breaking his forehead apart from mine.

"I just ... I don't know where we stand right now." The words hurt, coming out of my mouth, but I know if I don't say them, I'm just going to continue to get hurt.

"You need time?"

"I think *you* need time. And we don't really have any," I say, shaking my head.

"We have tons of time. I told you, New York isn't a problem. It won't change how I feel."

"We need to be realistic. Things will change; they're bound to. And is it really smart for you to depend more on someone who won't be here day to day?"

"I don't need day to day," Harry disagrees.

"You're a sixteen-year-old boy. You're telling me you're going to be fine with waiting months to see me?"

"Already thinking ahead?" Harry grins, his blue eyes connecting to mine.

And damn those eyes.

Because they have a way of cracking me wide open and seeping right into my heart.

"Look, I didn't tell the boys because I was embarrassed. And as embarrassing as it is to admit that, I have to. Because I acted like an idiot and hurt you in the process. I won't make that mistake again. I'm going to be the kind of boyfriend you deserve."

"That's a lot of pressure," I argue. "I think we should take some time to think through this first."

"I'm not in a rush. We aren't either."

"Aren't we?"

"Silly girl," Harry says, running his finger down across my cheek. "We've got our whole lives ahead of us."

"All I seem to be able to see of it are three more days. I leave on Saturday," I say, trying to get the point across.

"I really don't want to spend them with you angry with me," Harry says, his lips dropping down into a frown. "But if that's what you want, if you need time, I understand. Take whatever time you need, okay? You're not in a rush. I'm not going anywhere."

My hands start to shake at my sides.

I'm not going anywhere.

Harry's words settle into me, and I instinctively reach out to grasp him. I push into him, letting my head rest against his firm chest.

"It's all right," Harry says, wrapping me up in his arms. "I'm not going anywhere."

And I believe him.

I don't know what's going to happen. Or if I trust that we will make it as a couple. Maybe we won't.

But I know that at least he wants to.

He wants to try.

He's not willing to sacrifice me. He never has been. And time and time again, he's shown me that.

He keeps showing me that.

No matter what we're put through, we always come out of it together.

We're learning together.

I grasp on to him tighter, realizing for the first time that I don't want to lose him either.

Maybe it's selfish. Or maybe it's just love.

But I know that I'm not willing to walk away from Harry.

Not yet.

Not that simple.
4:30PM

"IS EVERYTHING ALL right?" Helen asks the moment I'm through the front door. She wears a look of concern on her face, her gaze staying on me.

"Yeah. Why?" I ask, worried by her expression.

"Noah came home in a huff," she says, waving me over to the couch. "Muttered something about you and Harry talking after school. About you being in a fight."

I sit down next to Helen, trying to organize my thoughts.

"Today was just a long day. Harry's had my head all over the place," I admit.

Helen nods, her eyes slipping over me. "Tell me in one sentence, what's the problem?"

"The problem is … Harry is amazing. And then he's not. One second, he's an open book, and then the next, it's like he's not only closed, but he's also somehow sprouted feet and walked off."

"Because he's a book?" Helen asks, trying to follow along.

I nod at her.

"I'm sure that's confusing."

"It is."

"Noah seemed quite upset by it all. It's a rare occasion for him and Harry to be at odds."

"Noah *was* pretty upset by it all. I don't think he liked how hurt I was." My cheeks tint pink at the thought of this morning. "I'm not sure how much Noah told you, but yesterday, Harry found out some news from his parents. It wasn't good. And he acted out. He left school, blew me off, got into it with some guy we know. Olivia ended up getting mixed into the picture, and I reacted. He tried to talk to me this morning to explain things, but I was hurt and just kind of ignored him. I thought he wasn't being fair to me, but I didn't realize what was going on. And after school, when he explained everything, I felt horrible."

"I know he is going through quite a tough time. It's admirable that you've been at his side through it all. But excuses are still excuses when it comes to bad behavior," Helen replies solemnly.

"You're right. And I told him that. I want to be there for him, but sometimes, he just makes it hard."

"I think Harry might be a little more insecure than you realize," Helen comments, looking to me. "And because of that, he's going to make it hard for you. He's going to put up walls that you'll have to break through. Noah and Harry's friendship, well, it has always been strong because of their differences. They care about each other deeply, and they don't have to try to be there for one another. They just are."

"I don't understand," I say, trying to figure out what she wants me to take away from that.

"Do you want my advice?" she asks, sitting up straighter on the couch.

"Yes."

"Do you *truly* want my advice?" she repeats, looking at me with concern.

And even though this doesn't sound good, I nod anyway.

"You need to learn to stop reacting immediately. You need to learn to trust Harry as your partner, if that's what you want him to be. I'm not saying to be naive. I'm speaking about having faith in the person you are with. Giving them the benefit of the doubt—always. You're not supposed to be their savior or their mother. You aren't their therapist or their guide. You're their best friend. You're their biggest advocate."

"You think I don't trust Harry?"

"What I'm saying is that you *want* to be there for Harry. You *want* to support him. Why do you think you aren't? You keep saying that you want to. Do you not believe you are?"

I look at her, feeling shocked. Because, somehow, Helen has managed to silence me.

"Maybe I don't," I admit, realizing she's right. "I do continue to say that. Sometimes, I feel like I have to put in so much effort into getting through to him. I keep trying and trying, and I always feel like I'm failing."

Helen takes my hands into hers, patting them.

But then she stops and looks at me seriously.

"Could it be because, though you might care for Harry, it might not be the right relationship for you? Or maybe not the right time?"

"I don't know. I want it to be. We have a connection that goes beyond friends. I know he wants to be with me, and I feel the same. I want to be with him. Maybe I'm just not convinced that it will actually work. With his family drama, Noah, and me leaving, it just seems like obstacle after obstacle."

"Well, sometimes, obstacles are meant to be overcome. And sometimes, they are meant to be warning signs. Life is about balance and realizing these things for ourselves."

"I appreciate the advice." I give Helen a smile and a nod of my head. "I feel like I have so many voices in my ear all the time that it can be hard to know what I want."

"You'll know when you know. May I ask, did you leave anyone in New York? You're a beautiful girl, sharp—"

"Like a boyfriend?" I interrupt, shaking my head. "No. I dated, but I never met someone who made me feel … fully myself."

"Do you find yourself feeling fully yourself here?" Helen questions.

I pull my lips to the side before giving her a heavy nod.

"You and Noah have grown close," she continues, her eyes shifting as she thinks. "It's easy to see how much he cares for you. He was quite upset."

"Noah's … imperfectly perfect." I smile, thinking about how much I'm going to miss him and his mood swings. "He's become my best friend. Don't get me wrong; he still drives me crazy sometimes, but I think we've mostly got this friends thing figured out."

Helen lets out an amused chuckle.

"What do you make of my son?" she asks, adjusting on the couch. "Woman to woman."

I think about Noah, trying to figure out how to describe how I feel about him.

"He's thoughtful. He has a way of making you feel comfortable and confident. He's a great listener. Very wise."

"I hope to raise the kind of boy who will make a good husband," Helen replies, like she's mentally thinking through the traits.

"He's a husband in the making for sure," I continue, trying to compliment her son even though, inside, I'm kind of freaking out.

Helen nods enthusiastically, like she wants me to go on.

"Not to be weird, but Noah is obviously nice looking. He's smart and easy to talk to. But he's also kind of noncommittal. I mean, his feelings change as much as his moods. And we're only sixteen—"

"Seventeen soon," Helen counters, surprising me. "And I wasn't suggesting you two think about marriage."

I flush at her response, realizing I completely misread her question.

"Uh, how did you know about my birthday?" Because I haven't told anyone yet that my birthday is next week.

"Your exchange paperwork, dear," Helen replies, her brown eyes on mine. "Anyway, I'm sure you'll have plans Friday night with your friends, but I would like to have a family dinner tomorrow night. I realize Saturday will be quite chaotic with your departure, so it's really our last chance to spend the evening together."

"I would love that." I smile.

Helen pats me firmly on the leg. I can tell she's happy with my answer but done with our conversation.

"I'd better head upstairs and change," I say, getting up from the couch.

"Have fun at dinner and make sure to let me know when you're on your way back."

"I will."

WHEN I GET up to my room, I quickly strip off my uniform

shirt and open up my wardrobe. I thumb through it, trying to find something that's both cute and formal. Meeting the parents—well, anyone's parents—is a balancing act of being friendly, listening intently, being relatable, but also not forcing anything.

It's a headache, in a nutshell.

But I can't wait to meet Mohammad's parents. And to get to see his sisters again. I pull out a pretty gray sweater that is trimmed with silver stitching. It would go perfectly with booties and a dark pair of jeans.

I pull open a drawer, grab a pair of jeans, and then throw them onto the bed.

I'm taking off my skirt when my door flies open.

I jump at the sudden motion, covering my bra with my hands.

"So, you and …" Noah starts, but the second his eyes take in my shocked state, his sentence stops.

"Turn around!" I insist, trying to cover myself as much as I can.

Noah looks me over, his eyes slipping down across my bare stomach to my tights.

"What, you've decided to just ignore my requests altogether?" I huff, dropping my arms.

Because it's no use.

"You're in tights," Noah replies, his eyes coming back up to mine. "And it's not like I haven't seen you in less—"

"All right," I say, cutting him off. Because I don't really feel like going down memory lane right now.

I walk over to the bed, throwing the sweater on over my head. I glance at my jeans, knowing that they're next. But that's going to require taking off my tights. And stripping like that in front of Noah is more than I can handle.

I tilt my head at him, spinning my finger out in front of

me for him to turn around.

He rolls his eyes before turning his back to me.

I quickly take the tights off and pull on my jeans.

"So, you and Harry made up," Noah states.

"You can turn back around," I instruct, falling back onto my bed.

I glance over at Noah, watching as he turns around. But his feet never move. They stay glued in his spot by the door.

"Yeah, we did."

"Lovely," Noah comments, shaking his head.

"Noah, come on." I push off my bed, moving toward him.

"I don't want to talk about it," he says, not wanting to meet my eyes.

"We need to," I say gently.

Noah looks up at me, his jaw setting. "No matter how many times Harry fucks up, you allow it."

"That's not fair. He's going through a lot."

"He always has an excuse," Noah replies, moving past me. He walks the length of my room before turning and doing it again.

"He's your best friend," I state.

Because he should be defending him.

"Just because he's my mate doesn't mean he's not a shit boyfriend to you."

"He wants to try," I say, thinking about our conversation outside of school. "And I do too."

"Mallory, listen to yourself. I overheard you and my mum," Noah says, stopping.

"Excuse me?"

Noah steps back in front of me, his shoulders dropping. "She said it kindly. He's trying. You're trying. You want to be there for him. Has it ever occurred to you it shouldn't be that hard?"

I can see that Noah believes what he's saying. In his mind, he's right.

I can see he's trying to help.

"Look, I hear you. But I'm not naive enough to believe that relationships won't have their challenges."

"Challenges? More like fucking mountain after mountain," Noah mutters, shaking his head again.

"Harry is special. And I'm not going to abandon him right now." This isn't really any of Noah's business.

"Is that what this is about?" he asks, looking at me, perplexed. He takes my hand, pulling me down to sit on the edge of the bed with him. "You think he won't be able to handle it if you ended things with him?"

I stare at Noah, feeling both caught and upset with his statement.

"It's not that simple. I …" I stutter, trying to explain it.

"You love him."

"I care about him," I correct, looking up at Noah.

"You can care about him and not be with him. You can even love him and not stay with him." Noah's words are gentle, and his face is soft. I know he wants me to agree with him.

"I know that. And you might not like to hear this, but I'll tell you anyway. I care about Harry. And when things are good with us, they're really good. I'm just trying to hold on to that."

"And what about *us*? Do you think this is fair to Harry? You don't have feelings for *only* him, do you?" Noah says, stroking my hand.

I can feel an ache in my throat as his hand grasps mine.

Noah looks at me like I could break his heart with one word.

And I really don't want to do that.

But I don't want to lie to him either.

"I don't know what I want … I don't know what I'm even allowed to have. Or what the point is anyway. I'll be gone in a few days. And like you keep reminding me, I'll be leaving you both. Two best friends. I owe it to you both to at least keep that intact." I drop Noah's hand, trying to get him to see that I'm doing exactly what he's been asking of me all along.

I don't see a choice.

I see Harry. A boy who cares for me. A boy who is trying.

And then I see Noah. A boy who, over and over, has told me he's not an option.

"If you break up with Harry, it won't affect our friendship," Noah says.

"It's not the breakup I'm worried about," I reply, getting up off the bed and needing some distance.

Noah gets up with me, looking more frustrated by the second. He's practically glaring at me.

"Well, while you figure your bullshit out, just please, leave me out of it. Either break up with him or suck it up. I'm not going to keep being there for you when he hurts you. I will not continue to do it," Noah says coldly before storming out of the room.

I close my eyes as he leaves.

I don't blame him for being mad.

He's right.

I keep going back to him. I keep letting him get in the way of Harry and me. I keep putting myself in a position to be vulnerable.

And it has to stop.

And the only way it will stop is if I set boundaries. If I tell the truth.

And the truth is, right now, I want Harry.

And Harry, he wants me too.

And that's more than I can say for Noah.

I've definitely noticed.
7PM

I RING THE doorbell, my stomach fluttering as the chime goes off.

"I thought you'd never get here," Mohammad says, opening the door and pulling me into the house.

"Someone's flustered," I notice.

"Well, if I had known how much of a fuss Mum would make over having a guest to the house, I'd never have invited you." Mohammad grins, pulling me into a hug.

"*Ouch,*" I reply but still hug him back.

"Well, it's the truth. I've not only cooked for you now, but I've also cleaned my room and hoovered the living room carpet. I've put more work in for you tonight than I put in to try and get a shag."

"Maybe if you put as much effort into getting to know a girl, you'd be able to shag whenever you wanted because you'd have a girlfriend."

"You're starting to sound like my mum. Have you been conspiring with her?" Mohammad banters.

"Does she want you to have a girlfriend?" I ask with interest.

"One she approves of. Always." Mohammad dramatically rolls his eyes before putting his hand on my back and leading me into his home.

"And none of them have caught your eye?" I ask as I take

in the modern interior of his entryway and formal living room.

"Fuck no. Most of them aren't even interested. It's just a courtesy to take the meeting because it was arranged by our parents."

"Yikes," I reply as we stop in his living room.

"Yeah. Imagine having to try to woo a woman who already has a secret boyfriend."

"I feel like that might work out for you though. Don't you want a woman who won't grow attached?" I tease.

"I want to have fun," Mohammad corrects. "Not end up in some dramatic soap."

"All right, I give. How would the soap go?" I ask, curious of the story he's probably already concocted.

Mohammad sits down into a low-slung gray chair. I sit down in a matching chair opposite him on the other side of the sleek marble coffee table. I look around, taking in the amazing architecture of the room, momentarily distracted by Mohammad's house.

"Well, likely, I'd get into someone's knickers. Because it's me, obviously. She might have a boyfriend already—hidden from her own family, of course. But then she is about to be found out, so she says that she's actually with me and not some guy her family doesn't approve of. Then, she begs me to pretend we're a couple to keep our parents off her trail, so I agree, the gentleman that I am. And because I want back in her knickers, thus, somehow, I end up trapped in a relationship with a girl my parents approve of, with a girl who will actually let me shag her."

"Sounds frightening," I agree, pretending to be mortified.

"It is. And that is why I don't date. But Mum's excited to have you nonetheless."

"What, did she ask if I was a love interest?" I laugh, thinking about me and Mohammad together.

"Oh, trust me, she knows you're not. I think she was disappointed though. I guess the prospect of any girl is better than none."

"Aww. If only she knew how coveted you were by the girls at Kensington," I say with encouragement.

"Exactly. And then once she found out you were American, I think she was relieved," he says, shooting me a wink.

"Hey!" I start, but before I can scold him, a little girl runs into the living room, jumping straight into my arms.

"Leela!" I give her a quick kiss on the cheek.

She lets out a loud giggle before wiggling out of my arms and running out of the room.

"Come on," Mohammad says, pulling me up out of the chair. "I'd better introduce you before they die from anticipation."

We follow the stream of giggles, moving down a set of modern glass stairs that opens up into a large dining room and kitchen. The entire room is oversized and bright. One whole wall is covered in moss that can be seen from every corner. My eyes scan across the room, taking in a table situated under a beautiful multitiered chandelier that looks to be as much of a work of art as it is utilitarian in lighting the space. I also see two large marble-clad islands that form the main section of the kitchen.

Leela is seated on a barstool next to a man, who is watching a woman standing in front of the stovetop across from them.

The woman looks up, a wide smile on her face.

"Mallory," she says warmly, throwing a tea towel onto the counter before meeting Mohammad and me halfway. "It's lovely to meet you. I'm Meera."

I smile back at her. "It's nice to meet you."

And I'm instantly struck by her. Mohammad's mom is beautiful. Which shouldn't come as a surprise because both Mohammad and his sisters are gorgeous, but I don't know. I guess I was expecting this overbearing mother. But she's practically glowing. Her warm brown skin is set against shiny black hair, which is pulled back into a very chic, sleek ponytail.

She gives me a kiss on each cheek in greeting. Leela's watching us, perched from the barstool, as the man who I'm assuming is Mohammad's father walks toward us.

"Hi there." He smiles at me. I immediately recognize his charming smile, Mohammad's matching his. "I'm Samar."

"Hi." I smile back, feeling a little flushed while taking his hand. "I'm Mallory."

"Welcome to our home. Can I offer you something to drink?" he asks.

"I'm fine, thanks," I reply, still smiling at Mohammad's dad.

He's wearing trousers and a button down that hugs his body. He has thick eyebrows that frame his face and the kind of five o'clock shadow that only comes with age. I break my eyes away from him, trying to pull my shit together.

Because Mohammad's dad is, like … hot.

And I've definitely noticed.

He's warm and inviting, and admitting that feels weird, but I'm sort of feeling like a schoolgirl blinded by a cute teacher.

"Right, well, I'm going to give Mallory a tour now that introductions are over," Mohammad interrupts.

I nod at him like an idiot, willing to go along with anything right now because I can't think about anything other than the fact that his dad has warm hazel eyes.

"Dinner will be ready in ten minutes. Be back downstairs

then," Meera says.

"Oh, don't fuss over him," Samar says gently, following behind her. He slides back onto a barstool, plopping Leela onto his knee.

Mohammad pulls me up the stairs, leading me past the main floor and then up to the first level.

"Mohammad!" I say the second we're out of earshot.

"What?" he replies, leading me down a long hallway.

The walls are papered in a metallic blue gray with oversized framed photos hanging perfectly spaced out along the wall.

I just stare at him, trying to make him understand.

"You never told me your parents were so young. Or beautiful. Or kind," I insist.

Because they aren't at all what I was expecting. Granted, I don't actually know them yet. But they are a good ten years younger than my parents and living in this modern, amazing home.

"I told you, Mum might as well be an officer of the queen; she's so strict. And Dad, don't even get me started," Mohammad says, stopping in front of a door.

"He was nice," I reply, not making any sense of this.

"Sure, he's nice. But where is he when Mum's about to roast me alive? He just sits there, admiring her ferocity toward me. He's a soppy old man," Mohammad disagrees.

"He's not even old," I fire back as Mohammad pushes into a room. I glance around, feeling completely confused for, like, the millionth time tonight. "This is your room!" I shriek.

"Mmhmm," Mohammad says, finally smiling at me.

Because he knows it.

He knows his room is awesome.

There's a king-sized bed centered on the wall. It's got one of those low frames, which makes it look sleek and dramatic.

A large flat screen is mounted on the wall opposite it with what looks like an entire gaming setup spread out below. He's got a desk in the corner that's lit on both sides with matching floor lamps.

"Mohammad, your house is insane. Why don't we hang out here, like, all the time?"

"Did you forget about the two watchdogs downstairs?" he asks, letting me explore his room.

"I'm not sure I buy that your family is traditional," I reply, taking in Mohammad's stack of homework piled on the floor next to his desk.

He sits down in a swivel chair, moving himself in a full circle. "That's what makes my parents truly sneaky. It's all an illusion. Though the house might seem forward and they're stylish, as expected, internally, at their cores, they're all about tradition."

"That's probably kind of hard to deal with," I say, thinking about how he's talked about his parents before.

He's said that his mom is strict and that his dad is soft. That they always fuss over him and that his sisters are little demons who just happen to look like angels. And I'm starting to wonder if maybe he is more sarcastic than I first thought.

"It's kind of funny. Out of everyone's houses, yours is the most like mine in New York. Its structure is beautiful in and of itself. The wide windows, perfectly spaced furniture, meticulously displayed art."

"It's different from Harry's and Noah's; that's for sure," Mohammad agrees.

"What do your parents do anyway?" I ask, taking in thick, rich curtains that are pulled open to display a wall full of windows overlooking a private courtyard.

"They're restauranteurs."

"Really?" I ask with interest.

"Yep. Dad's always had a thing for restaurants. Mum loves concept and design. She sort of has a sixth sense for that stuff, if you know what I mean."

I fall onto Mohammad's bed, feeling like I'm sinking into a cloud.

"Do you think they'd adopt me?" I ask, watching as he continues to swirl in his chair.

"If you want to become a doctor and take our name, they probably would," Mohammad agrees. "Or a lawyer."

"Hmm. Well, I'm thinking it's a no-go on that then," I reply, rolling off his bed. There's a door on the far wall of the room, and I decide to check it out.

"Closet," Mohammad says, seeing me approach it.

"Ooh la la," I reply, pushing in to see what it's like.

Because if his room is any indication, it has to be spectacular.

And it is.

Not only are his clothes well organized in dark wood cabinets with glass fronts, but it's also wide enough for a love seat to sit in its center. I notice Mohammad's uniform tossed onto it.

I take in a stretch of the wall, counting at least five designer belts hanging up in a row. My hands slip across shirt after shirt. There are rows of polos and button downs. And then there's the entire section of name-brand sweaters covered in designer logos.

"This is amazing," I say in awe.

Mohammad has moved into the closet with me and is looking over his clothes. "It's a pretty good collection."

"That's an understatement," I say, looking Mohammad over.

I always knew he dressed well, but tonight, he has that casual look that can only be elevated through designer pieces.

He's in a black Balenciaga hoodie and a pair of crisp blue jeans.

"Did I tell you I went shopping the other day? I got this gorgeous metallic dress." I sigh, thinking about it.

"Really?" Mohammad asks with interest.

"It's beautiful. I have no idea what I'll wear it for, but I know I'll wear it for something."

"Women," Mohammad says, ushering me out of his closet.

"Women what?"

"You're always buying shit that somehow symbolizes your future. It's mad."

"I'd like to say, *manifesting* my future. Besides, when I find something that I love and that just fits me, I feel fully myself."

"Thus you somehow become the woman that you've always wanted to be?" Mohammad asks seriously.

"Exactly," I reply, happy that he understands.

"Ha. I call that smart marketing."

"Says the guy with three Gucci belts," I point out.

"Black, navy, and brown. Those are necessary basics."

"I was going to say that you're starting to sound like Noah, but I think that statement just proved you're not." I laugh.

"I'm a little insulted you'd say such a thing," Mohammad replies, falling onto his bed. "I love Noah, but I definitely have better taste in clothes than him."

"Your fashion sense is just one of your many winning qualities," I agree, sitting down onto the bed too. "Today was such a cluster."

"What do you mean?"

"Well, Noah isn't speaking to me. And Harry told me he loved me," I reply, mentally going through the list.

"Fuck me, Miss America. I can't even handle this right now."

"You and me both."

Mohammad's eyes shift upward before coming down to meet my gaze. "What do you say we ignore it then?"

I smile at Mohammad and nod. "I think that's a great idea."

I bounce off the bed and finish exploring Mohammad's room. I check out his bedside table, finding a lamp and a single framed family photo. I pick it up, counting his family of six.

"You really are a Cullen-status family," I note, taking in their warm skin, rich hair, and matching wide, white-toothed smiles.

"What does that mean?" Mohammad asks, confused, looking to the photo.

"It's from *Twilight*," I explain. "The Cullens are a family of vampires. They're immortal and perfect. They sparkle in the light."

"Are you trying to say my family looks like vampires?" Mohammad asks, not following.

"No, they just … the Cullens live in a modern house like this. They're kind and alluring. What I'm trying to say is, your whole family is beautiful. And—cover your ears—your parents are hot."

"Oh God," Mohammad says, trying to shield himself from my words with his hands.

"I'm serious." I laugh, setting down the photo.

"Well, is it any surprise?" Mohammad replies, taking a different approach. "I mean, look at me." He's standing with his arms outstretched, practically beaming.

"Look at your family," I disagree. "It's crazy. Obviously, you're handsome. And your sisters are adorable. But, good

God, normally, the kids outshine the parents."

"Are you saying that my dad's fitter than me?" Mohammad asks seriously, his eyes going wide.

I break his gaze, moving away from the photo. "*Uhhh* …"

"Gross, Miss America." Mohammad's body does a little shiver.

"At least you know, one day, you'll likely look like him."

"I'll make sure to relay the message," Mohammad says with a dramatic eye roll.

"I'll murder you before you get the chance," I threaten, knowing that if anyone would actually do it, it would be Mohammad.

"Yeah, yeah." Mohammad waves me off.

"Speaking of your family, should we head down for dinner?" I ask, knowing that our ten minutes have to be up.

"Only if you promise not to hit on my dad," Mohammad replies, looking at me seriously.

"I promise."

UNFORTUNATELY, I THINK I break that promise the moment we step back into the kitchen.

"Mallory, Leela was just telling me about your time at the museum. She's quite taken with you." Samar gives me a warm smile, and instead of replying with words, I let out a nervous giggle.

"Isn't she pwetty?" Leela says, running up to my leg.

"Very beautiful," Samar answers, causing a flush to rise on my cheeks.

Mohammad looks at me like his eyes are about to pop out. But a second later, he's covering his hands over his face.

And I know he's disappointed in me.

I'm disappointed in me.

Well, more freaked out. Mostly because I don't know

where these giggles are coming from.

Because I, normal Mallory, am not a giggler.

But apparently, today, I am.

"Thank you," I reply, trying to keep my focus on Leela and not Mohammad's dad.

"A little over ten minutes, Mohammad," I hear Meera comment as she sets the table.

"I wasn't wearing a watch, Mum," Mohammad fires back.

"Mohammad, please do not use that tone with your mother," Samar cuts in easily. "I'd like to have a nice meal this evening."

"All right, we're ready," Meera says, setting the last of the plates onto the table.

"This looks amazing," I say, taking in the delicious spread.

"Don't let the presentation fool you," Meera says as we sit. "We picked up most of it from one of our restaurants."

"Regardless, it smells fantastic."

Leela plops down into the chair next to me as Mohammad takes a seat on my other side. Samar and Meera sit across from us.

"Wait, Mohammad, I thought you said you cooked?"

"If you call warming bread in the oven cooking," Meera says warmly. "Please, help yourself."

I look at Mohammad, wondering if he has anything to say to that accusation.

"Fine, maybe I didn't exactly cook. But I still had to turn on the oven," he replies before grabbing a bowl full of vegetables in front of him.

I smile at him as I reach for the salad.

"No Maya and Nina tonight?" I ask, noticing their absence from the table.

"Maya has extended violin practice on Wednesdays, and Nina has a playdate," Meera says. "Which leaves us with just

Leela and Mohammad tonight."

"Your daughters are adorable. I had a really fun time with them at the museum yesterday." I set down the salad bowl and then pick up a tray of sliced sweet potatoes, adding some to my plate.

"Thank you," Meera says proudly, glancing to Leela. "My children all have unique talents."

"And they're sweet and cute." I give Leela a big smile, and she grins back at me.

"We named our children quite intentionally," Samar adds, watching our interaction. "Leela, fittingly, means *to play*."

"That is fitting," I agree, thinking about her bubbly and outgoing personality.

"And Mohammad is *to praise*," Samar continues.

"Not much to praise here," Mohammad mutters next to me.

Meera lets out a huff of breath.

"You will find your path," Samar says to Mohammad.

"That is what university is for," Meera agrees. "You will choose your path, study hard, and get a good job."

"That's been a hot topic at school lately," I comment, thinking about all of the career ideas we've come up with for Mohammad.

"Oh? Anything to share, Mohammad?" Meera asks enthusiastically.

"Nothing our family would deem worthy as a career," he replies, stabbing a piece of chicken.

"Hush," his father instructs. "Share these ideas with us, if you would, Mallory."

I glance over to Mohammad and give him an encouraging smile. "Well, there's an ever-growing list when it comes to Mohammad's talents, but we've talked about a detective. A matchmaker. Even a counselor."

"My, my, our son and his ever-developing talents," Samar replies with a warm smile.

"What I hear is rubbish," Meera disagrees. "You need to find a career that will support you. Something reliable and dependable."

"Told you," Mohammad huffs, looking over at me. "Mum's always wanted a smarter eldest son than the one she got. I'm just a disappointment."

"You know that isn't true," Samar interjects, looking hurt.

"Maybe if you got your head out of the clouds and out of other people's business, Mr. Detective, you'd be able to devote more of your energy to your studies," his mother suggests.

"Mum," Mohammad groans, setting down his fork.

"Well, if it's any consolation, Mohammad has been a huge help in Latin," I say, trying to lighten the subject. Because I can see Mohammad's growing frustrated, and I don't want to cause issues between him and his parents.

"Has he?" Meera asks, sounding optimistic.

"He has. He was the most welcoming person to me when I arrived to Kensington actually," I go on.

"That's our Mohammad." Meera beams, apparently having forgotten that she was in the middle of drilling him over future career choices.

"Mohammad tells us you're staying with the Williams. How are you finding it?" Samar asks.

"They're an amazing family. They've been nothing but welcoming."

"They're good people," Samar agrees with a wide smile.

"And what have you made of your exchange so far? We understand you are from America," Meera asks, making conversation.

"Yes. New York City. And I'm not sure how to put into

words my time here. It's hard to even think that I'm on an exchange," I admit.

"Feels more permanent?" Samar asks, understanding me.

I nod. "I really didn't want to come here. I fought my parents on it. Begged them to let me stay in New York. And then I got here and just sort of fell in love with London. With the people at school."

"When is your exchange over?" Meera asks.

"Friday's my last day at school," I answer unavoidably. "I leave Saturday."

"These are good experiences to have when you're young," Samar says. "Traveling is very valuable."

"Does that mean you'll let me visit Mallory in New York?" Mohammad asks, taking me by surprise.

I smile over at him, happy that he would even consider flying across the ocean to visit me.

"Maybe we should consider *an exchange* for you," Samar comments, looking to Mohammad.

"No!" Leela exclaims. "Mo Mo can't go."

She crosses her arms over her chest, pushing her lip out.

Mohammad reaches over me, stroking her hair. "Don't worry. It would only be for three weeks. And it would be for educational purposes." He grins at her, sounding way too enthusiastic. And I think Meera can hear it in his voice.

"Upon second thought, I fear you might be too excited at the prospect of being out from under our thumb."

"He could always spend one of his holidays visiting family. In India or America," Samar says, giving in to Mohammad's hopeful face.

"We do have family who live in America," his mother says. "Samar's brother moved there and raised his children in California. Mohammad's cousin is doing her PhD. at Caltech, if you can believe it."

"How about I skip the exchange, wave toward California from the airplane, and go stay with Mallory in New York for a semester abroad instead? I could even look at universities while I'm there. Find my path," Mohammad insists, trying to convince them.

And unexpectedly, both Samar and Meera burst out laughing.

Mohammad rolls his eyes, sitting back in his seat, not as tickled about his idea as they seem to be.

"It was an admirable attempt, Mohammad. But I'm going to say the answer to that is no," Samar replies, glancing over to Meera like he is both in awe and can't handle Mohammad's apparent hilarity.

AFTER DINNER'S OVER, Meera and Samar bring Mohammad and me each a cup of tea and a tray of desserts before taking Leela up to bed.

"It was very nice to meet you," they say in unison.

"Thanks for having me over for dinner," I reply sincerely.

When they're gone, Mohammad drops his forehead onto the dinner table like he's exhausted.

"Should I add your name to the list of meltdowns that have occurred today?" I ask lightly, taking a sip of the tea. And it's actually not half bad.

"This isn't a meltdown. This is my attempt to forget the sound of your giggle that is now, so kindly, set on repeat in my mind."

"Sorry," I reply, taking a bite of dessert.

"Yeah, not sorry enough," Mohammad says, sitting back up and stealing the dessert straight out of my hand.

WHEN HE WALKS me to the front door, I pull him into a big hug.

"Thank you for tonight. It was fun, coming over. Meeting your family. Getting out of the house."

"I'm glad you came. And despite the career conversation, I had a good time. My family likes you."

"I like them too," I reply. "Now, give me a kiss."

"I don't think you need another boy on your lips," Mohammad points out.

"On the cheek, jerk," I say with an eye roll.

Mohammad nods and then kisses me on the cheek.

"See you at school," he says as I give him a wave goodbye.

We don't have secrets.
9PM

WHEN I GET back to the Williams' house, I find Gene and Helen in the living room. Helen has the television turned on, and Gene is in his usual chair, a book open in his hand.

"Hey." I smile, plopping onto the couch opposite Helen.

She fumbles for the remote, turning down the volume.

"How was dinner?" Gene asks with interest, marking a page with his finger.

"It was really nice. I didn't realize Mohammad's parents were restauranteurs. And Mohammad's house was so cool. Very modern."

"They're very well known in the city," Gene says with a smile.

"How do you think we end up on all those fabulous dinners out?" Helen points out.

"You're close with Mohammad's parents?" I ask, not realizing that they hung out.

"We try to get together every month—at least to talk about the children. But we always manage to entertain ourselves. It's become a sort of monthly tradition," she says.

"The boys have been friends for years," Gene adds, "but Helen and Meera get on well. And we have nice chats about work and food. They're good about keeping us up-to-date on popular culture."

"That's fun though." I smile.

Because I could see them all hanging out and having a great time. Gene knows a lot about wine, and Helen's an amazing cook. They both have important jobs and are very smart in what they do. And Mohammad's parents seem no different. They're driven and hardworking.

"It's always a nice time," Helen replies, but her eyes drift back to the television, which features a house renovation show. "Noah's upstairs in his room, dear. But you're welcome to join us down here. I'm watching a new home show, and Gene, of course, has his nose in a book."

"What's Noah up to?" I ask curiously.

"Likely on that game of his," Gene grunts from his chair.

Helen raises one eyebrow at him, and I have to give her credit for it. She manages the perfect arch of her brow.

"I think I'll just head up and read," I reply, getting up off the couch.

"Ah, your book." Helen gives me a knowing smile, nodding at me in approval.

I shoot her a wink and then head upstairs.

When I get into my room, I change into my pajamas and then pull out her book. But before I start, I decide I should probably call my parents.

My mom immediately answers the phone, an excited voice coming from the other end of the line. "Mallory," she says brightly.

"Hey, Mom."

"It's so good to hear from you," she continues. "And perfect timing. I've just booked your car for Saturday. Your driver will arrive at the Williams' house at eleven in the morning and then take you to the airport."

"What?" I gasp, feeling completely blindsided. "No, Mom. Helen is going to want to take me."

"Dear, please," my mom says, brushing it off. "There's a lot going on, but it's your father's special treat. He asked me *especially* to book it for you. He even mentioned that it was some sort of joke between you two."

"What's going on?" I ask, noticing my mom's high-pitched voice.

She sounds almost frantic, which is usually a good indication that she's very busy.

"There's just so much to do!"

"To do? For what?" I ask, confused.

"For your arrival home, of course," she says smoothly.

"Okay … well, as long as someone gets me from the airport, I'm not sure what else you have to do."

"There's always things going on, Mallory dear; you know that," my mother replies. "Oh, and speaking of your father, he's just walked in."

"All right, love you."

"Love you," my mom replies.

"Hey, sweetie." My dad's distinct voice comes through the phone, and it's like he's sitting next to me.

"Dad, why does Mom sound so frantic?"

"Well, hello to you too," my dad says, not missing a beat.

"Hi," I say, knowing that I shouldn't jump him with questions.

"In regard to your mother, she's just had a busy week."

"I guess life doesn't stop, even when I'm gone."

"She's looking forward to seeing you, you know," my dad says.

"Well, hopefully, someone is, or I might as well just stay here."

"You know that we miss you."

"I know, but, Dad, I'm not really ready to come home."

"Mallory, all good things must come to an end," my father replies, sounding very matter-of-fact.

"You don't understand. I can't leave. My body won't let me," I say, trying not to pout.

Because I can already picture it now.

Standing in the doorway on Saturday. A car pulled up to the curb.

I know that I won't be able to move.

"Sweetie, what's going on?"

"I can't come home yet. He needs me," I say desperately.

"Who needs you?" my father asks.

Who?

Both.

Both of them.

"Harry," I stutter.

"You can stay in touch. Visit. Isn't that what you're always telling me? The benefits of technology," my dad encourages.

"This isn't a joke," I reply, growing upset.

"Everything will be fine, I promise."

But he doesn't understand.

No one does.

Because I'm the only one who was put into this situation.

"You can't promise that," I argue.

"Do you not miss New York?" my father questions. "It wasn't that long ago when you threw a fit about leaving the city."

404

"I realize that …"

"And?"

"And I threw a tantrum. I know I did. I was a spoiled brat. And maybe I'm being one now too. But I care about everyone here too much to go. I'm going to come back to New York, having left the life I'm supposed to live."

I'm not sure where that even came from, and the words surprise me as much as they seem to surprise my dad.

"What makes you so sure of that?"

"A gut feeling …" I say, not having any other reasonable reply.

"I thought you didn't believe in feelings," my dad says teasingly, practically quoting me.

Because I'm always telling him that logic over emotion is the way to go. That our feelings change, they turn on us. They encourage us to make rash decisions.

They aren't dependable.

But that's life.

And I guess what I mean to say is that life is messy and filled with contradictions. Because you live it, you learn, and then you realize that everything you learned doesn't mean anything.

"You make it almost impossible to argue with you," I groan.

"Trust me, all right, Mal? Everything will work out. Your mother and I miss you. And we're really looking forward to having you home."

"I love you," I reply, knowing that I'm not going to get anywhere with him.

"Love you too," my dad says, clicking to end our call.

I want to stay in my room and wallow. I want to bury myself under my covers and never come out.

But I don't.

If I only have a few days left, I'm going to use them to their fullest and spend them making more memories. Leaving will be impossible anyway, so what are a few more things to add to this list of reasons I'll miss this place?

I hop off my bed and go over to Noah's room.

"Hey." I smile, pushing open his door.

I expect to find him at his desk or playing his video game, but he isn't. He's sitting up in his bed, his back leaning against the headboard.

"Hey," he replies.

"What's wrong?" I ask, taking note of his sullen face.

"I don't want to talk about things," he says, not bothering to look at me.

"About what things?" I ask, closing his door behind me.

"Mal, you know how I feel. I don't know what else to say. I'm just overwhelmed."

"Overwhelmed by what?" I ask, confused.

"By how I'm feeling."

"And how are you feeling?"

"Overwhelmed," he states again.

"Noah," I say, walking toward his bed.

"It's fine. I just … would rather be alone," he says, diverting his eyes.

"No."

"No?" he repeats, looking up to me.

"No, you're not going to sit here, alone, in your room. I'm not letting that happen."

"I would *like* to be alone," Noah says again.

I cross my arms in front of my chest and sit down on the edge of his bed. "And I said no."

"I don't need this right now," he replies, holding my gaze.

"What don't you need?"

"You. Here."

"What did I do?" I ask, tilting my head.

Because Noah is in a bad mood. And I'm not really sure why. I've been gone for hours, and he's had tons of time to pull himself together.

"Nothing ... I ... fine. Stay."

"Tell me what's going on," I insist.

"I would rather not."

"You need a distraction then," I say, moving to the next best option.

"Probably," Noah agrees.

"Well, luckily for you, I have one." I grin at him.

"What?" he says, raising his eyebrows at me.

"Well, since you're in such a *good* mood and you have some tension to get out, why not kill two birds—I hate that expression—why not do two goods with one set of hands?" I say, trying to think over what I just said.

And I'm not actually sure what I said made sense.

"What?" Noah asks.

"I have tension in my neck. You're tense. Why don't you massage your frustrations out on me?" I chuckle.

"That sounded ... weird," Noah says hesitantly.

"I agree; it did. But I didn't mean it weird. Sit up," I say, scooting in between his legs. I sit cross-legged, letting my knees rest against his.

"Why do I feel like you're getting the better end of this deal?" Noah asks as I get settled.

"Because I am."

"You always get what you want, don't you?"

"Yep." I smile, turning back to look at him. "Come on. Chop chop."

Noah's hands come up onto my back, sliding from the bottom of my ribs up to my shoulders. His palms are warm, even through my shirt, and I try to relax.

His fingers press harder into my skin as he moves them up to my neck.

"Ahhh," I let out a soft moan when Noah hits a knot.

"You're so tight," Noah says observantly.

"I'm always tight. Like Mohammad says, I'm always wound up." I laugh.

"Did he actually say that to you?" Noah asks, letting out a laugh himself.

"Unfortunately."

Noah moves his hands across my shoulders, and I stay seated up, my back straight. It feels nice, and I tilt my head to the side when his hands glide over the sides of my neck.

"Why don't you tell me why you're overwhelmed?"

"So, this was just a ruse to get me to talk, huh?" Noah huffs, his fingers pressing more firmly into my shoulders.

I roll my eyes.

"Fine, let's not talk," I say, shifting.

Noah lightly runs his fingers across my back, and it sends goose bumps down my arms.

"Feel good?"

"Mmhmm," I reply, letting my eyes close.

His fingers slip further down my back until they're where my back meets my waist.

"That tickles," I whisper, trying to arch my back away from him.

My body is surprised by the feeling, stuck between wanting to pull away and wanting more of it.

"Relax. I'll stop," he says, his fingers moving back up my neck.

"Today was …" I start, trying to wrap my head around the day.

"Today's over," Noah states, cutting me off.

I nod my head, agreeing with him, "Today's over."

My back starts to ache from sitting up so straight, so I turn around and look at Noah.

"Do you mind?" I ask, looking to his chest.

He must get what I'm saying because, a second later, I'm leaning back against him.

"Better?" Noah asks, his hand still on my neck.

"Way more comfortable," I reply, letting my head rest against his shoulder.

It's probably not the easiest way for Noah to rub my neck. But I don't really care at this point because I'm so comfortable that I don't want to move.

"You know," I start but then stop myself.

"I know what?" he asks.

I turn my head, finding his face close to mine. He's glancing down at me, waiting for me to say something. I turn forward as his hands slip up onto my shoulders and then down onto my arms. His fingers scratch lightly against my skin, bringing back those goose bumps. I push myself harder back against his chest, trying to relax at the sensation.

"Too much?" Noah asks.

"No, it feels nice." I close my eyes, thinking about what I wanted to say. "Next week, it's my birthday."

"Your birthday is next week?" Noah's hands come to a stop. "We have to celebrate then," he finally says, moving his hands again.

"I don't know …"

"We do," he insists.

"Wouldn't it be kind of sad? Weird?"

"No, I think it's important. Birthdays are very special."

"I don't know. Not much can top a neck massage today and sushi last night."

Noah laughs, causing his body to vibrate against mine.

"You have low expectations for your birthday."

"No," I counter. "I just like simple things, you know?"

"I know. But we should celebrate anyway."

"Are you going to get me a gift then?" I tease.

"Hmm, I'll have to think about it."

"Noah." I laugh, shaking my head.

"What do you want?" he asks, sounding more serious.

"I can't tell you what I want. That would be too easy."

"You're going to make me guess?"

"I don't need a gift."

"Mallory, I know you. And despite your love for other people's sweats, takeout, and massages, you love nice things. There will always be things you want or need."

"I guess I did come here with a good amount of stuff," I reply, smiling at the memory of all of my suitcases and the look on Helen's face when she saw them.

"Seriously though, if you could have something, anything, what would you want?"

"Anything? That's a big question."

"Let's call it a birthday wish," Noah offers.

"Those are supposed to be a secret."

"We don't have secrets, I thought."

"I feel like you're guiding my answer here, Noah," I say.

Noah's hands run up and down my arms, and I close my eyes, trying to forget about his question.

Because I don't want anything right now.

"No answer?" he whispers in my ear.

"I have everything I want right here," I say with a content sigh, not wanting to think about wanting other things or needing other things right now.

Noah's hands keep moving until I feel them all the way down on my hands. He's sitting up a bit, and I can feel his stomach tighten under my back as he leans up.

"Mal," Noah whispers, his voice in my ear.

But then my words register in my head, and my eyes instantly fly open.

Because what in the hell did I just say?

Noah's hands are on mine, and his chin is tucked down by my neck. I can feel every part of his chest and stomach against my back.

"I, uh …" I stutter, feeling stuck again.

I glance toward Noah, his lips grazing my cheek.

I shouldn't be sitting here with him. I should pull away.

I got too comfortable. I let my guard down.

I can feel Noah's chest rising and falling quicker against my back.

"I'm sorry," I say, suddenly sitting up.

I swallow, feeling my heart thumping in my chest.

"For what?" Noah barely whispers.

"For falling into this. For putting us in these situations. I thought I could just be … I don't know what I thought."

"You thought you could lock your emotions into a box," Noah replies.

I whip my head around, looking at him.

"I got too comfortable. That's all," I state, willing myself to be firm.

"I'm sure you're just tired then," Noah replies, giving me an out. "You should probably head to bed."

"Yeah, I should," I agree, getting up.

I look Noah over, wondering if I've made things worse or better by coming here.

By lying in bed with him.

By walking into his house.

His life.

"Good night, Noah." I give him a smile that's meant to be my version of sorry, but I think, in reality, I just frown at him.

"Good night," he replies.

I LIE IN bed, feeling confused. Because this is what I've been afraid of. I'm leaving in three days. And more and more, I find myself letting Noah push me further and further. I find myself pushing him. I find myself pushing us and our boundaries.

And maybe he's right.

He's going to have me begging for him before he gives in.

That's what it seems like.

And it's so, *so* wrong.

Because I do want to be with Harry. I can see a future with him. I can picture it perfectly. I can see exactly the kind of life we could live. The partnership we could have. We have so much in common.

I just don't know if we can overcome all of these obstacles.

His family.

My doubts.

Leaving.

Like Noah said, there's been mountain after mountain.

And with Noah, it's probably the simplest thing in the world. There wouldn't be a single struggle if he could ever admit that he wanted me.

But what is life without struggle?

What is love without struggle?

Are you supposed to be with the boy who fights for you? Who is willing to become a man for you?

Or are you supposed to be with the boy who says he cares about you? But to him, that caring means staying out of things. Out of the way. Because, in some ways, it means he's not willing to fight for you. He's willing to let you go, if that's what you want.

And that sort of makes it all worse.

THURSDAY, OCTOBER 10TH
Want this so much.
6:45AM

I'M WALKING TO the bathroom when I see Noah's door open. He steps into the hallway, still in his pajamas, but he has a towel over his shoulder. I look between him and the bathroom door, knowing we're both headed for the same place.

A smirk forms on his lips, and a second later, we're both running toward the bathroom door.

"Noah," I grumble, swatting at his back as he beats me there. I should have put in more effort, but it's too early to be running down hallways and trying to compete for time in the bathroom.

"You'll have to be quicker than that," Noah says, turning back to me. He looks a little too wide-eyed this morning as he sticks out his tongue.

I push against the door, keeping it open.

"You're not fair. I was here first," I whine, throwing a mini fit.

"I'll be quick. I promise," Noah says, shooting me a wink.

Then, he closes the bathroom door, and I hear the lock click.

Hmm.

I go back to my room and sit on the edge of my bed.

Waiting. And waiting.

And let me tell you …

He isn't quick.

Twenty minutes later, I can still hear the shower running, and it's starting to piss me off. Mostly because I could have been downstairs with a coffee right now. *But no.* Instead, I actually decided to *believe* what he said for once and ended up wasting precious time, sitting and waiting for him.

I let out a huff and get up off my bed. I go back to the bathroom door. I want to scream at him, but I know that approach won't work.

He'll just take pleasure in my misery.

I bang on the door, making sure I have his attention.

"Ha ha," I say over the noise of the shower. "Joke's over, okay? You've won the battle of the bathroom. I give up."

Gene walks past me in the hallway, eyeing me. But instead of helping me out by telling Noah to get out of the shower, he slinks past me and goes downstairs.

He looks back at me like I've lost it.

And I probably have.

And apparently, he's going to be no help.

Once Gene is gone, I continue knocking, knowing that Noah can hear me because the water's turned off.

A second later, the door flies open, and Noah pulls me into the bathroom.

"So, I won the battle?" Noah asks, entertained, as he closes the door.

His eyes are all over me, and I try to keep my focus on his face. On his wet hair.

And not on the fact that the only thing he has on is a towel wrapped around his waist. One that is sitting dangerously low on his hips.

Ignore him.

At least, ignore his body.

"You've made your point. Can I please have the bathroom now?" I say, keeping my eyes locked on his.

"You can't technically *have* the bathroom," Noah smarts off, coming closer to me.

I try to disregard his encroaching presence. But the smell of his shampoo hits me like a wall, and he's the definition of temptation right now.

Like candy.

And candy is bad for you.

I know how to avoid candy.

I can resist candy.

So, I need to resist Noah.

"What are you doing?" I ask, watching as he shifts toward me until there's actually no physical space between us.

He presses his hips into me, pushing me back against the sink. "What does it look like?"

I follow his eyes, watching as he looks at his exposed stomach, down to where our bodies are touching.

"Noah, I'm serious," I force out, trying to ignore the way I'm feeling.

Mostly because Noah is, like, basically naked. And he's not even teasing me anymore. There's no amount of teasing in what he's doing.

He's just … doing.

"I'm serious too," he replies, his eyes drifting back up to mine.

I watch as he looks across my face, biting the inside of his cheek as he does. I can see his cheek dip in as he scoots himself closer toward me until I can feel his stomach pressing against mine.

"You flirt with me. You tell me that you … like me," I say hesitantly, trying to make sense of what's happening.

"I know," he says as he slides his hands down over my

hair.

I close my eyes at the sensation.

"You push yourself as close as you can to me," I say, thinking about how much of his body is plastered against mine right now. "But you never *do* anything."

I open my eyes, looking up at him. Noah's jaw tightens, but he keeps his hands gently moving through my hair.

He doesn't say anything, but I want him to. I press my hips toward him, trying to get him to understand.

His eyes get big and his hands fall onto my shoulders. His fingers press into my collarbone, following them from my neck out over the edge of my shoulders.

"You talk and talk and talk. But you never do anything to show me that you're serious. It seems like a game," I reply, trying to stay focused on my thoughts and not on how his hands feel, running across my skin.

Noah stops his hands, but he keeps them on my shoulders.

"You want me to show you how I feel?" he asks, searching my eyes.

Everything about him is overwhelming right now. His dark hair and thick eyebrows. The way that he smells like *him* mixed with shampoo.

How I can practically feel all of him on my skin.

"I'm not saying that. I—I just … I feel like boundaries are being pushed here."

Noah lets his hands slide up the sides of my neck, back into my hair. I keep my eyes open as goose bumps form down my arms.

"So, what are you asking me?"

There are so many things I'm asking him. I'm asking him if he really wants me. I'm asking him why he would be willing to do this now.

"I'm asking you, do you have any intention of breaking those boundaries, or is this what it's going to be now—a constant struggle?"

"I'm making it hard for you?" Noah asks with surprise.

"Well, you're a little close," I reply, glancing down at his chest. At his abs. At his creamy skin that somehow always ends up being so much of a distraction to me.

"I didn't notice," Noah says quietly, his eyes back at my lips.

I bite on them under his gaze, feeling my heart speed up in my chest. Noah brings his hand up to my mouth, pulling my lips from under my teeth, and rubs the pad of his thumb across them.

"I did tell you, you know."

"Tell me what?"

"That I would have you begging for me before I gave in." His voice is heavier and thicker than I expected.

I pull away from him, upset by his words. "Is this a joke to you?" I ask. But I can't really go anywhere because Noah is pinned against me.

"Not at all." Noah shakes his head, bringing his hand from my lips to my waist. "But I have to know, is that what you're asking, Mal? For me to give in?"

His hands slip down over the top of my shirt, and I'm about to freak out. Because there are too many sensations.

My body is burning, and my chest aches.

My stomach is swirling, and my legs feel like they're shaking.

I don't know how I'm standing up, but I am. Everything in me is spazzing out. Because, yes, I want this.

But I also don't.

Some part of me isn't prepared for this moment yet. I bring my hands up onto his shoulders, trying to steady myself.

Trying to push him back. Trying to get some air.

When my hands land on his skin, Noah leans his chest closer to me.

I shake my head at him, feeling like I can't breathe. Everything is hot and steamy, and my head feels foggy.

Noah nods at me, not looking upset. He lets my hands stay on his thick shoulders as he leans back.

"Okay then," he says with a sigh. "Why don't you let me know when that's what you're asking?"

"I have a—"

"Boyfriend?" Noah finishes. "Yeah, I think that's debatable. Or am I wrong?"

I stare at him, not sure what I want to say.

"You're not wrong," I admit.

Because if I did, if things between Harry and me were fine, I wouldn't be in this position. I wouldn't have let Noah pull me into the bathroom. I wouldn't have let him press into me.

I wouldn't want this so much.

But things between Harry and me aren't fine.

Noah looks me over and then takes a step away. He moves his hand to his towel, tightening it against his waist.

"Shower's yours," he replies, giving me a once-over before opening the bathroom door and walking out into the hallway.

The second he's out of the bathroom, I slide onto the floor. Mostly because my legs aren't working.

My back rests against the door as I bring my hands up into my hair.

What is wrong with me?

I'm a bad person.

I'm beyond a bad person.

I'm terrible.

Harry. All Harry has done is apologize to me.

I should just accept it. I want to.

But I don't know if I can because of moments like this with Noah.

When I literally can't breathe.

When I can't think straight.

Part of me expected Noah to just move on. I didn't think he would become so blatant and obvious.

And I didn't expect to feel so conflicted.

I peel myself up off the floor and decide to get in the shower. Sitting around and overthinking it won't do me any good.

And Helen won't be happy if we're late to school.

Give me a choice.
STATISTICS

WHEN NOAH AND I sit down in our first class, my stomach still has butterflies in it.

I haven't been able to think straight all morning. And believe me, I've tried. I keep trying to push the thought of shirtless Noah out of my mind.

But apparently, my mind has other ideas because each time I glance at him, I don't see Noah like he is now in his uniform shirt. I see shirtless, barely-towel-covered Noah.

And now that I'm not confronted with his nearly naked body, my mind's had time to process what happened.

Which really just means I've—I mean, *my mind* has had time to reconstruct Noah's body in my head. It's like now that I can breathe again, the air to my brain has focused all of its attention on the sharp lines of Noah's muscles and exactly how and where they cut across his stomach.

Productive, I know.

Or how, when he was pressing against me, I could feel parts of Noah that I'd never felt before. And I felt them in places they shouldn't have been near.

Or how Noah actually does have an eight-pack. I would usually say six, but today, my eyes landed on two that were hidden really low on his belly.

"You want to stop at the bookstore after school still, yeah?" Noah asks, pulling me out of my thoughts.

About him. And his body.

"I do," I reply, looking over at him. I blink a few times, clearing my head.

"Get lost in there?" Noah chuckles as he notices my flushed cheeks.

Because fantasizing over Noah continues to hit me at weird times.

"A bit," I answer truthfully, taking in his light expression. "But I think that's pretty understandable after everything."

Noah looks to the front of the classroom, checking to see what Mr. Johnson is doing before saying, "You liked this morning."

"I don't know what you're talking about," I reply, not going there.

Noah turns to me, putting his elbows onto his knees. "You don't have to be with Harry," he whispers, making sure no one can overhear us.

"I want to be."

"You actually want to be with someone who isn't there for you?" he asks, his thick brows dipping in.

"Harry is special to me," I reply quietly.

"And what about you? You need to feel special too," Noah insists.

"Right, like this morning?" I shake my head. "That wasn't

special, Noah. That was hormones."

"I thought it wasn't anything?" he replies, a small smile forming on his lips.

"It wasn't."

"I know; you said. Answer me honestly, Mal. Does Harry actually put you at the center of his world?"

"The center of his world? Noah, he shouldn't. Hasn't it ever struck you that those types of relationships aren't healthy?"

Noah's forehead creases, and he leans away from me as someone walks past him to get to their seat.

I turn back toward the front of the classroom, thinking our conversation is over, but then Noah starts speaking again, "I'd rather be consumed than forgotten."

I turn and glare at him, my mouth slipping open. "Wow. You think that's what he thinks of me?" I ask, hurt.

Noah lets out a hard breath, his hands fidgeting with his tie. "No. But, Mallory, you said no to Harry before. Why?"

"Because I needed to get to know him."

"And have you?"

"Of course I have. He's had a hard time recently. But, Noah, he's there for me."

"And I'm not?" Noah says a little louder.

My eyes flare at him, and as I glance around us, I want to shake him. I don't understand why he can't see that he's doing this to us. That he's the one who has given Harry and me every chance to grow.

He's pushed us together.

And it's worked.

And Harry, despite his absence this week, *is* there for me.

Well, at least he says he wants to be.

"No, Noah, you aren't. You *tell* me you are. But you really aren't. Because you're either there with every fiber of your perfect fucking being or you are absent," I force out with a whisper. "You're either zero or one hundred."

Noah sucks in his cheeks, his nostrils flaring.

"So, there it is," he states.

"So, there it is."

"Well, if that's what you want—"

"You think it's what I want? I don't want to feel like this. I don't like feeling like I'm being pulled in different directions."

Noah scoots closer to my desk with frustration. "You cannot care about two people in the same way, Mallory. You cannot," he says, looking at me sternly.

"I didn't say the same way, Noah." I shake my head, knowing we can't talk about this here.

"Then, what are you saying?"

"I'm saying that if you didn't walk away from me every chance you got, things might be different. But you did. Over and over, you walked away from me. You made that choice. And now, I have to make mine."

"All right, everyone," Mr. Johnson says, interrupting Noah's imminent tantrum.

Because he looks like he's a volcano about to blow, and I'm secretly grateful for our professor's interruption.

"Let's go ahead and partner up. I want you to work your way through this quick review for the first half of class. Then, we'll go over the answers in preparation for our test tomorrow."

I silently scream at Mr. Johnson for letting us pair up in partners.

Why can't he just teach us?

Is it too much to ask for him to force us to sit in silence for an hour?

I take the review from the person in front of me, turning

around to hand it to the girl in the desk behind me. And then everyone gets up, moving into pairs throughout the room. I look at Mr. Johnson, waiting for him to assign pairs.

But he doesn't.

I let out a breath, knowing what that means. I glance around, trying to find someone besides Noah who isn't partnered up. I smile to a guy, and he smiles back.

Bingo.

But as I walk toward him, I can feel Noah at my shoulder, and the guy diverts his eyes and then turns toward someone else.

"I cannot believe you," Noah says at my side before moving to the far corner of the classroom.

He slides into a desk, hunching himself over in it. I sit down in the seat in front of him with annoyance.

"Well, I cannot believe you," I reply.

"So, you're going to leave this weekend and ..." Noah says, wanting me to finish the sentence.

"I'll leave this weekend with a broken heart," I reply.

"Because?"

"Because I'm leaving my two best friends. And ... my boyfriend," I say hesitantly. I'm not sure what else to call Harry. And calling him just a friend feels wrong since we haven't exactly figured things out.

"I hope you're happy with that decision," Noah replies, starting on the review.

"Noah, it's a decision you made for me."

"Me?" he says, looking up at me, confused.

"Yes, you."

I look down at our review, deciding to just start on the first problem. Because if not, Noah and I will just keep going in an unproductive circle.

"ARE YOU SAYING that I'm the only one who can change things?" Noah asks a few minutes later after I finally accepted the silence between us.

"I'm saying that, even after this morning, there's nothing to show for it. It meant nothing. It's a stupid game that's going to end with me gone."

"I'm not playing around with you," he says seriously, shaking his head.

"Sometimes, I think all you *are* doing is playing around with me," I reply, keeping my eyes on our review.

"Do you actually think that?" Noah asks, sounding hurt.

I look up and take in his pained expression.

"I don't know what to think. But, yeah, it *can* feel like that," I admit.

"Why?"

"Because you don't give me a choice. You push and push, trying to get me to crack. And then the second I'm about to, you stop. You say, *Never mind. I can't.*"

"I'm giving you one now," he says, his eyes meeting mine.

"You're what?" I ask, feeling my heart in my throat.

Because I'm pretty sure I know what that means.

"I'm giving you one. Now," Noah repeats, setting down his pencil. "You said before that I chose for you. I'm not messing around with you. I'm *trying* to make it less complicated. But my strategy is … failing miserably. So, it's your choice. You can do whatever you want. With *whomever* you want."

"You're not telling me what to do anymore?" I ask, feeling like every boundary just somehow disappeared between us.

"Not anymore," he says, looking down at his desk. "Things are so fucked right now anyway."

"Okay," I stutter, wondering what this means.

"I thought you'd be relieved," he says, squinting one eye

at me.

"Relieved?"

"Yes, relieved. Now, you can do what you want. I'm not telling you what to do. Or what *not* to do. Now, the pressure or conditions, whatever, they're gone. So … it's up to you."

"It's up to me," I repeat, trying to wrap my head around what he just said.

I glance to Noah, realizing that I leave in two days.

And that he basically just told me that he is no longer off limits.

I DON'T HAVE anything else to say after Noah's little *confession*. At least, that's what I'm calling it.

Because a confession is better than a transference of power.

And it's definitely better to think he told me a secret rather than he, in essence, handed me a key to *him*.

Maybe it is just a key to his bed.

Or maybe a key to his heart.

Or maybe it is a key to get myself out of the cycle we've been in. The one where I feel something, he feels something, and then it stops because of these other reasons, one of which is always him *removing* himself from the equation.

Luckily for me, I don't have to ask what *key* the confession was meant for because Mr. Johnson quickly breaks up our groups and then spends the second half of class going over our reviews.

BY THE TIME the bell goes off, I've all but lost myself in the boring, if not informative, review session.

"I thought class would never end," Noah says at my side.

"Did you want it to?" I ask, turning to face him in the hallway.

But then he glances over my shoulder, someone apparently catching his eye.

I turn around to see Harry looking at us.

I watch as Harry and Noah stare at one another, and I'm not sure what's going to happen. Yesterday, Noah was pissed. But when I look back, I see he isn't tense, and Harry cracks a smile before striding up to us. He gives me a grin before pulling Noah into a warm hug.

For a brief moment, I wonder if Noah will accept it. I haven't heard if they've talked or made up. I'm not sure they even need to.

Maybe guys just ignore one another and then hug it out the next day like they're fine.

And apparently, they do.

I watch Noah visibly relax in Harry's arms, hugging him back.

"All right, mate?" Harry asks him.

"Yeah," Noah replies, glancing down to me.

And just like that, their fight is over.

"Stats was dull," Noah continues. "Spent the morning reviewing for the exam tomorrow." Noah raises his eyebrows at Harry.

Dull?

Dull?

Did he actually just say class was dull?

I look at Noah, confused, but he just nods his head at me before looking back at Harry, who is wearing a sour expression, seemingly as a result of hearing we have an exam tomorrow.

"See you at lunch," Harry calls out with a dramatic wave as Noah walks off.

But then he turns to me, and all that lightness is gone.

I swallow, not sure what to say.

Or even what to do.

"So, yesterday," Harry says, not allowing for an awkward silence, "after school, we sort of left things open ended."

I chew on my lip as his eyes come to meet mine. And I can see the hesitation in them.

"We did."

"I realize I'm a mess and that I put you through absolute shit. You have every right to just slag me off, but, Mallory, I really don't want you to. I've never felt this way for someone before."

Harry's words take me by surprise. Normally, he isn't one to talk about his feelings so openly.

Or so publicly.

I look around, realizing that anyone walking past could easily hear him. I glance back to Harry, taking in his sullen blue eyes.

"Felt what?" I ask, wanting him to explain further.

Harry lowers his voice, dipping his head down toward me. "You know me. You see that I eat shit food. You've seen me hungover. You were at my house when I was at one of my lowest points. You know I don't give two fucks about school, that I love to party and hang out with the lads. You've been to my two favorite spots—The Arrington and Marco's."

"We've been through a lot," I agree, thinking about all the places we've been. The conversations we've had. The good times and the not so good ones. "I've seen a lot of different sides of you."

"I know you have." Harry smiles. "And yet, you still care for me. You know all of me. The good and the bad. Everyone who has loved me before, well, they've sort of left me. Besides the boys, I've never trusted anyone with my heart."

"You trusted Olivia," I state the obvious. I don't want to ask the question or hear his answer, but I have to. "You loved her, didn't you?"

"I don't know what else to say… it was mostly about sex with her," Harry says, his mouth forming a frown.

"I know it was more than that," I reply, shaking my head.

Because I can see the hurt in his eyes. I can hear the coldness in his voice. He doesn't look or talk about her like she was just some girl he was sleeping with.

And she doesn't talk about him that way either.

"Harry, she still cares about you. And trust me, I, of all people, wish that it weren't true. But you need to know that she hasn't abandoned you."

"It sounds like you're trying to convince me to get back together with her."

"I'm trying to tell you that she loves you. Or loved you—whatever," I reply.

"She's just territorial sometimes. And it really has nothing to do with you and me," Harry clarifies.

"It does," I disagree. "Because you keep telling me that I'm different. That you trust me with your heart. But you're only saying that because you've been hurt in the past. And you think that everyone's left you. But they haven't …"

"You think that I still want to be with Olivia?"

"I think that what she did hurts you more than you'll admit."

"Things *are* different with you, Mallory."

Harry looks upset, and my insides roll with his discomfort.

"I know they are," I agree, taking Harry's hand in mine.

"I don't want to be with her. I don't even want to be talking about her," he says, shaking his head.

"Then, let's forget about it, okay?" I say, looking up at him. Because deep down, I don't want to upset him. And I don't want to tell him what to do either. But I do want him to make his choices, his decisions, with rationality behind them even if they're emotional. "Walk me to Latin?"

Harry nods, wrapping his arm over my shoulders. He glances over to me, a flush coming onto his cheeks.

"Sorry, shit," he mutters, unwrapping himself from me, pushing his hand through his blond hair. "I don't even know if this is all right. Fuck, I don't mean to make you uncomfortable."

I smile at Harry, his flush calming my own uneasiness.

I grab his hand, wrapping his arm back around my shoulders.

"Harry, I said we needed time to think about things, not that you couldn't touch me."

"I just … I'm not sure how to handle this," he says, his eyes pulling away from mine.

He bites down on his lip, and suddenly, all I can see is the Harry I've always cared for. The boy who wants to be with me. His brows are pulled in, and his eye is still black and blue from his fight.

"There's nothing to handle," I say, grabbing his hand. "I just want you to take time and think about things with a clear head."

"I feel like we're broken up," he says.

And he looks like he's about to cry. It sends pain through my stomach, seeing him look like this. I shake my head, wanting him not to freak out. Because I see it in his eyes.

He is.

I grab his arm, dragging him around the corner. And then I press my palms into his cheeks, bringing him to my lips.

Harry kisses me desperately.

And I kiss him back with the same amount of force.

With the same need.

Harry pulls away, glancing around to make sure we're still alone.

"I needed that," he says, his eyes scanning my face.

"You put on a good show for Noah," I comment, finally seeing him look better.

"It wasn't a show. It's almost impossible to be sour when you're around him."

"But around me?" I laugh for what feels like the first time today, and it's a good feeling.

"Around you, it's just as easy. But things have been off."

"We need to go to class," I say, knowing if I don't move, we're going to be late. "You'll still think about what I said?"

"I will," Harry agrees, squeezing my hand before we turn the corner and I walk into Latin.

Last hurrah.
LATIN

"I THINK I just fucked up."

"Miss America, language," Mohammad says jokingly as he slides into his seat.

He smells extremely good today, and I can't help but notice. I take in his pressed shirt and combed hair.

"Why do you look so fancy?" I ask, momentarily distracted.

"Thanks for noticing." He wiggles his eyebrows at me.

"You never answered my question." I laugh, watching him fuss over his hair.

"It's a secret," he replies, sealing his lips with his fingers.

"You? Keep a secret? No way. You'll crack before lunch."

"Why don't you crack? What did you just fuck up?" Mohammad sasses back.

I roll my eyes and let out a groan. "I kissed Harry."

"A little action at school." He grins, sticking out his

tongue. "I can dig that."

"You missed the fucked up part," I say, raising an eyebrow at him.

"You got caught?"

"I kissed him on accident," I admit, trying to explain. "We haven't kissed since—shit, I don't even know. Sunday? I didn't see him Monday. Tuesday was obviously not good. And even yesterday, after school, we just hugged."

"So, you snogged. What's the big deal?"

"The big deal is that I told him to think about things. I said I needed time. I said he needed time. With one kiss, I basically threw all of my advice for him to *think and reflect* to the wind," I insist. "And then there's Noah, but that's a separate can of worms."

"I'm not following."

"Harry is a wreck. And I'm not sure he's in a place to have a girlfriend. He was finally hearing me, but then he looked so sad and cute, and I had to go and make him feel better," I reply.

"At least it was with your lips and not some pity shag," Mohammad says, trying to console me.

"At least it wasn't that," I agree, nodding. "Regardless, I saw his relief after our kiss. Which I wanted him to feel; don't get me wrong. But Noah, in Stats …"

"What about Noah and Stats?"

"It doesn't matter," I reply.

Because there's no way to word what he said—or didn't say—without it sounding terrible for either of us.

And it wasn't terrible. It's the most he's given me in days …

"Chill out. It was just a kiss. And whatever happened in Stats, I'm sure it's nothing new. So, can we please get back to other important matters at hand?" Mohammad insists.

"Like?" I ask, trying to figure out what in the world could be more important than all of this.

"Like the party I've organized for Friday night." Mohammad beams. "Well, am organizing. It will be a *last hurrah* at Harry's before you leave."

"Do you think it's a good idea?" I ask hesitantly.

"No, I don't think it's a good idea. I think it's a *brilliant* idea."

"Right," I agree, wanting to let him have his party. "But, Mohammad, things are so complicated."

"Mallory, you're leaving." Mohammad's words are plain and simple.

Cut and dry.

"Like, *leaving*," he emphasizes, his eyes widening.

"I realize that," I say, a lump forming in my throat.

"When exactly are you leaving?"

"Saturday, late morning," I mumble back.

"Well, I've talked with Naomi. She's actually pretty creative. Wants to do a themed evening."

"Wait, you're planning it with Naomi?" I ask with surprise.

Mohammad nods. "It's going to be bomb."

"You're really excited, aren't you?" I laugh. "Wait, is that what the secret is? You're going to put the moves on Naomi today in order to win her over at the party tomorrow?"

"Sealed lips," Mohammad replies, eyeing me.

"I'm going to miss you," I sigh as class starts. "Will you visit me in New York?"

"No," Mohammad replies quickly. "You'll visit me."

"What?" I say, my voice rising.

"Mmhmm. I know you'll miss London. And obviously, you won't be able to stay away from *Mohammad*."

"No one could stay away from you," I agree with a grin.

Making things difficult.
ART

MRS. JONES COMES into the classroom in a hurry, dropping her things onto her desk. "Excuse my absence," she says, eyeing the clock and looking flushed.

I glance over at Noah, finding her whole display a little funny.

His lips rise into a smile, too, as he watches her.

"We're putting your projects on hold—at least for part, if not all, of today," Mrs. Jones continues, handing out a stack of papers to each table. "I'd like for you to identify the style found on each page."

I narrow my eyes at the stack, not sure why we're stopping our projects for busy work. And Mrs. Jones never gives an answer.

"Well, this is annoying," I mutter, eyeing the papers. "These have nothing to do with textures."

"Maybe she's helping give us ideas in a roundabout way," Noah comments, noticing my irritation.

"She probably just forgot about it earlier this week and is now punishing us."

"Or maybe it's in preparation for next week," Noah counters.

I glance down at the first picture and see a marble sculpture displayed on the page. Something about it reminds me of Noah.

"I think we've found your doppelgänger." I take in the subject's tapered waist, rounded shoulders, and hard jawline.

Noah glances at it, his lip rising into a lopsided smile.

"I'm not sure about that," he admits, shaking his head.

"Don't be modest. I can tell you're flattered." I grin, teasing him. "Besides, the resemblance is uncanny. Come on," I say, pointing down at the sculpture. "He even has your plump lips and symmetrical eyebrows. It's just not fair."

"Are you trying to tell me you're jealous of my eyebrows?" Noah wrinkles his nose at me, his eyes sparkling.

"Maybe just a bit. Girls are said to be beautiful. But honestly, I think people have it backward. I think guys are actually more beautiful than girls."

"That's just because you're into guys," he says, his gaze connecting with mine.

"Maybe I'm not," I tease, causing him to grin again.

"Are you trying to tell me you're into girls, Mal?"

"Would you be surprised?" I ask.

Noah thinks about my question for a minute. "I mean, you *are* always surprising me."

Noah's face lights up, his brown eyes taunting me. I push him a bit, shaking my head.

"But I think you're drooling over that statue a little too much to be *only* into girls."

I roll my eyes at him. "I'm not drooling. I'm appreciating," I say, holding up the piece of paper. "Besides, isn't that the point of art? To be appreciated?"

"I think the point of art is to make you feel something," Noah corrects.

"Either way."

It only takes us about half of the class to get through the papers, figuring out what Mrs. Jones wants us to declare about that piece or the next. We write our analyses and names on the back of each sheet and turn in the stack before grabbing our projects.

"A whole ten minutes left," I comment when we sit back down.

"That's loads of time," Noah says as he starts to paint.

I roll my eyes at his optimism.

"I think it will take me the full ten minutes just to figure out what I want to do next," I say, eyeing my painting.

"I thought you needed to sand it down?"

"I do." I nod, trying to find the motivation to work. But instead, I put my chin into my palm, watching as Noah rolls his sleeves up to his elbows.

I lick my lips, noticing how his arm flexes as he paints. With each stroke, it's like he gets more and more lost in the colors. In the process. And with each stroke, I get more and more lost, watching him. I try to distract myself by doing some sanding.

But it's hard to work and stare.

I let out a breath, hoping that it will straighten my head out. But something about Noah today has my mind so ... distracted.

The way that he focuses in on painting.

How, with each passing day, his shirt seems to get tighter.

How his dark hair has grown longer. Helen keeps mentioning that he needs a haircut, but I can't fathom it. I don't want a single piece of his hair to leave his head.

I'm so distracted by watching him that I don't notice him look over at me. His brown eyes darken. The second that the bell goes off, his hand is at my elbow, and he's pulling me alongside him.

"Where are we going?" I ask, trying to catch my breath. My heart is pounding in my chest.

Noah doesn't answer me, and he looks so serious.

A few seconds later, he's dragging me into a room and closing the door behind us. It takes me a minute to realize that Noah just pulled me into an empty classroom.

And all I can think about is how he even knew where to

find an empty room.

And how did he know that it would be empty?

Maybe it's just because everyone is at lunch?

"Noah?" I say, bringing my eyes up to his as he backs me up against the door.

His eyes are narrowed at me, and it's hard to tell what he's thinking.

He looks serious.

Frustrated maybe?

"You were staring at me in class," he finally says.

"I …" I don't know what to say. Because I was.

I *was* staring at him.

Noah's forehead creases, his thick eyebrows dipping in. "You have to stop staring at me," he says, his gaze flicking back and forth between my eyes.

"I wasn't staring …"

"You were." Noah's words stop me. "And you're making things difficult."

"Difficult?"

He sucks in a heavy breath and tilts his head back, and then he looks down at me.

My stomach is freaking out.

Like, literally. *Freaking. Out.*

Because it's dark in the room.

And we're alone.

And Noah is so close to me.

And he's looking at me like I have absolutely no idea.

No idea of what he's capable of.

No idea of what he's feeling.

Which is exactly my problem.

I have no idea.

And every part of me wants to find out.

I want to know.

Regardless of right, wrong, good timing, bad timing, I have to know. I want to know.

"Your eyes are all over me, Mal … and it makes it hard to focus. Hard to concentrate. You have to stop."

"Stop?"

"Staring at me."

"Fuck," I gasp, finally realizing what this is.

Noah's asking me to stop. To stop staring at him. To stop making him feel uncomfortable.

He's asking me to stop practically drooling over him.

And I'm instantly embarrassed.

I should just tell him, *Of course.*

I will stop staring at you.

I'm sorry.

My bad.

But no … what do I say?

"I'm not staring at you." I deny his words, pushing him away from me.

But Noah doesn't budge. His chest stays right in front of me, and I glance down, taking in his white shirt and tie. My eyes move across his chest, slipping over to his arms on either side of me before finally coming up to his eyes.

He just smiles down at me, raising one eyebrow.

"You're not?" He looks amused, and it pisses me off.

"No, I'm not. Now, if you'll excuse me, we—*I* need to get to lunch."

I cross my arms over my chest, narrowing my eyes at him. Because he needs to know that I'm serious.

That this isn't funny.

"By all means," he says, taking a step back, holding his hands out in front of him.

I'm not sure if he's trying to usher me out the door or giving in. Or maybe he's shrugging me off.

It's hard to tell.

But all I know is that, now, I'm pissed.

"This isn't a joke," I growl at him.

"It's a little funny," he says, his darkened eyes brightening.

"What is?"

"You're so angry. Fucking stubborn too. And to make it worse, you're a terrible liar. I see right through you. You do know that, right?"

Noah's grinning at me. And all I can feel is fire rising within me. Something so strong and powerful.

And all it wants is to be unleashed on Noah.

Because he's mocking me.

He's joking.

He's *taking the piss.*

And I'm about to blow up on him.

But then Noah starts laughing—his deep belly laugh—and pulls me into a hug. I'm completely caught off guard, feeling frozen in his arms.

There are so many things I want to say to him.

He can't see through me.

I'm not a terrible liar.

I'm not fucking stubborn.

So many things flash through my mind. I just have to pick one of them.

"You," I grumble as Noah laces his hands around my waist.

His chest is still bouncing as he laughs. He continually bumps against me, and it's distracting.

I try to pull away, but he doesn't let me.

"Noah, you're not being nice."

He just shakes his head, his eyes practically crystal now. "Come on. We've got to get to lunch," he says, not answering me.

He pulls me out of the classroom and back into the hall-way.

We're going to be late for lunch.

And I'm already trying to figure out what to say to Harry. To Mohammad.

But I have no clue what to say.

Because I have no freaking idea what just even happened.

Or what it meant.

All will be revealed.
LUNCH

"THERE YOU ARE," Mohammad says when we get to the table.

He's sitting across from Harry, and Noah moves around the table, plopping down next to him. Which puts me next to Harry and directly across from Noah. I slide onto the seat, trying not to look mortified.

"All right?" Harry asks, putting his hand on my leg.

I nod, momentarily closing my eyes.

"I was just telling Harry about last night," Mohammad continues, looking to Noah with a wide grin.

"Oh?" I ask.

"You had dinner at Mohammad's," Harry replies, filling me in on what he's heard so far.

"Yeah, it was really nice." I give Mohammad a distracted smile.

"It was," Mohammad replies, narrowing his eyes at me. "Except for the bit where you were wet for my dad."

"She was wet for your dad?" Noah says, flabbergasted.

"I know. Gag me," Mohammad replies, looking repulsed.

439

"Well, your dad does dress smart," Harry adds, not sounding surprised.

"First off, ew! I am not into Mohammad's dad. And secondly, you shouldn't be gossiping about me when I'm right here."

"Well, you shouldn't have giggled like a lunatic in front of my father," Mohammad fires back.

"He's funny," I say, shrugging my shoulders.

"He's really not," Noah disagrees.

"So, you've got the hots for Mohammad's dad," Harry says with a grin. "I never thought I'd have to compete with an older man."

I roll my eyes and remove his hand from my leg.

"Their love affair runs deeper than expected, boys," Harry says, his eyes growing wide.

"Ha ha ha," I state, ending this conversation. "Anyway, we had a great time. It was fun seeing Mohammad's house."

"All I know is, I can't wait to *not* be sleeping there tomorrow night. Are you getting excited for the party?" Mohammad asks.

"What party?" Harry and Noah say in unison.

"Shit. I guess I've only talked about it with Naomi," Mohammad says, a frown forming on his mouth. He looks between Harry and Noah like he can't believe he hasn't told them yet. "Tomorrow night, we're throwing Mallory a going-away party."

"Won't that be sort of sad?" I cut in.

"We're going to be with you regardless," Harry disagrees. "So, might as well drink and mourn the impending loss together."

"I guess you're right," I say.

Because party or not, I'm going to spend my last night with Harry, Mohammad, and Noah.

"It will be fun," Noah agrees.

"A smashing time." Harry grins, getting wound up.

"Let's hope so. You don't mind hosting it, do you?" Mohammad asks Harry.

"Why not? Mum and Dad don't arrive till next week, so the house is ours."

I glance between Harry and Noah, feeling sick to my stomach at the thought of Harry's parents coming home. I'm not sure if he's told Noah the news yet, but Noah looks back at me with the same concern.

"Uh, so, Mohammad," I say, trying to push away the thoughts, "how did this whole planning thing with Naomi come up? You mentioned a theme?"

"A theme?" Noah asks.

"I'm not revealing anything," Mohammad says, shaking his head.

"How are we supposed to prepare for a themed party when you won't tell us the theme?" I ask.

"All will be revealed at lunch tomorrow," Mohammad replies, rolling his eyes. "Naomi and Olivia are going to sit with us. Naomi wants to explain everything."

"I don't think that's a good idea," Harry states, glancing nervously at me.

"It will be fine. I already talked to Olivia. There's no issue," Mohammad insists.

"You talked to Olivia?" I ask, wondering if that's the secret he wouldn't tell me about in Latin.

"I had to," Mohammad says. "After the tension yesterday, we had shit to get sorted. Besides, I'm not going to plan you a going-away party and then let some girl ruin it. I want it to be fun—for everyone."

"And will it be?" Noah asks, trying to follow along.

"Yep. I set ground rules and everything." Mohammad

smiles before moving back to his lunch.

"Right …" Harry says, sounding conflicted. But then he turns to me. "Mallory, it's your party. You can invite—or un-invite—anyone you want. As long as the four of us are there, I'm happy."

I smile at Harry, feeling my heartbeat pick up in my chest.

"I know," I agree. "And honestly, me too."

Mohammad rolls his eyes, but he doesn't say anything. I expect him to since he's the one who is planning the party, and I know he's going to want other people there. But out of respect, I think, he holds his tongue.

Noah doesn't say anything either. He just sits, staring at me as we finish lunch.

WHEN THE BELL goes off, we all get up.

"We're still going to that bookstore after school, right?" Mohammad asks.

"Yeah." I smile at him.

"I'm not sure we'll be able to do dinner though. Mum wants us to spend the evening at home," Noah reminds me.

"Right. We'll have to skip dinner and just do the bookstore," I say, my lips pulling into an apologetic line.

"Hmm. I feel like I'm getting the shit end of this deal," Mohammad says as we walk out of the lunchroom.

"I'd say you should join us, but I think Mum just wants family tonight. Last dinner and all that," Noah says.

"Last dinner," Harry repeats as we get to my locker.

Noah and Mohammad walk off toward their classes, but Harry stays at my side as I get out my textbook for class.

"Last dinner," I say back with a not-so-steady nod.

Pushed me away.
GEOGRAPHY

"Lunch was interesting," Harry comments as we walk into our classroom.

"Mohammad was feeling dramatic this afternoon," I say, sitting down at my desk.

"He was," Harry agrees, dropping into his seat behind me.

There's an emptiness in his words, and it makes my stomach ache.

It's like we're just talking to fill the space.

This silence between us.

"Look," Harry says, interrupting my thoughts, "I know Mohammad has big plans for tomorrow night, but I don't give two fucks about any of it. I just want to spend the night with you. Come over after school or come over early before the party. Anything …"

I search Harry's eyes, seeing the sincerity in them.

"I feel like we're going to be setting ourselves up for a disaster," I say. "Hugging, kissing, making up. Yeah, it will be great for a day, and then what?"

"Mallory, you're the girl I want. I don't care if I have to go to New York to see you," Harry replies, leaning in toward me as he speaks.

"Don't you understand how hard this already is for me?"

And I know what I'm doing. I can feel it in my stomach.

I'm distancing myself from him.

But I'm doing it, so neither of us continues to get hurt.

So, that way, when I leave, I've already shut this down. So there are no unanswered questions.

No what ifs.

"I can't imagine what it's like for you," he says, shaking his head. "But just because you're leaving doesn't mean you have to give up on us."

"I'm not giving up on us." I turn around to face him. "I'm trying to spare us pain, okay? I care about you, Harry, more than you know. And this isn't going to be fun—me leaving."

Harry's blue eyes frantically search mine. He dips his brows in, tilting his head. "You love me, don't you?"

"What?" I reply, completely caught off guard.

"You're afraid of getting hurt. You think I'm going to hurt you," Harry says with relief.

"I'm scared this *situation* is going to hurt both of us," I correct.

"You have it so wrong," he says, putting his hand on top of mine.

"Harry, I know you love me. I believe you when you say you do. But I think you love me because you think I love you. And the truth is … I probably do. But what about me? Do you know me inside and out? Do you like every single part of me? How can you say you want me and you love me when every time something comes up, you aren't there for me?"

"You think I don't know you?" he asks, pulling his hand away.

"I think we both love the idea of being with one another. We both love the idea of what we could have together. We're both living a fantasy."

"It's not a fantasy," Harry corrects.

"Isn't it?"

"It just feels like one to you because … every time I open up to you, a second later, I shut down again. I let you in, and then I pull away. I know I'm doing it."

"Yeah, and that's a problem," I insist.

"It is. But at least I realize it is. I'm a fucking twat. A bag of shit. I know I am. I just had to wrap my head around things. When my parents told me they were coming home, I lost it. I felt a weight inside my throat that I thought was going to sink through me. I could have sworn that I was going to suffocate or be ripped open from the weight. I … I don't know if you know what that feels like, but it's not good. And here I was, making promises to the best thing that's ever walked into my life, apart from the lads, and I just …"

Tears threaten to spill out of my eyes, but I push them back.

"I was stuck. I was sinking, and the first thought that flashed into my mind was *I am going to break her because my parents are going to break me.* Someone who is broken cannot love. Someone who is broken cannot touch something without breaking it."

I stare at Harry, feeling my insides roll at his words.

"So, you pushed me away?"

"Yes." Harry shakes his head before letting out a heavy breath, looking disappointed in himself. "Isn't it better to push someone away than take them down with you?"

"I don't have the answer, Harry."

"When I woke up Wednesday morning, I felt terrible. I'd let myself drown in despair the night before because it was easy. It was easy to react. To walk out, to drink, to do something. Any action that let me feel like I had some amount of control. But after that, I realized it wasn't the mature thing. It wasn't the right thing. I should have explained things. I should have shown you my weaknesses instead of trying to run from them. But I'm learning, Mallory. I swear to you, I am."

"I know you are. I see it every time we work through something."

Mr. Pritchard clears his throat before announcing that

we'll be reviewing for our test tomorrow. I want to hold Harry's eyes, but I can't. I turn around, facing the front of the room until Mr. Pritchard tells us to pair up.

"Did you and Noah make up?" I ask, turning back to Harry.

"We didn't make up. We talked."

"So, you told him and Mohammad about your family?" I ask quietly.

Because I never brought it up with either Noah or Mohammad, and things sort of just went back to normal between all of us.

"I called them both," Harry clarifies.

"Really?"

Harry nods, his forehead creasing. "Noah's protective of you. I can't blame him. But, yeah, I told him what was going on, and I think he understood."

"He always does," I reply, thinking about my conversations with Noah today. All of which have basically been about how I shouldn't be with Harry.

About how Harry isn't in a place to have a girlfriend.

How I *supposedly* deserve better.

It makes me wonder if Noah is saying something different to Harry. Or maybe he does understand what he's going through. Maybe he understands too well, and that's why he's telling me I don't have to be with Harry.

I let out a huff, reading over the review. "Should we get started?" I ask.

Harry nods before handing me his pen.

Give me a chance.
BEFORE YOGA

"That review was ridiculous," Naomi says as we walk toward the changing rooms.

Harry is at my side, and Olivia is at Naomi's.

"I hate reviews," Harry agrees, running his hand through his hair.

"You just hate studying." I laugh, smiling at him.

The rest of class flew by, and Harry and I actually managed to stay focused on reviewing. Mostly because I kept us on track, knowing that if I didn't, he'd probably fail our exam tomorrow.

"*I* definitely do." Naomi laughs, glancing over to Olivia.

"Nah, studying can have its benefits," Harry whispers into my ear.

His breath is warm on my cheek, and my mind flits back to *studying* at his house last week.

"It's not that bad," I whisper back.

Harry looks over to Naomi and Olivia before grabbing my hand.

"We'll catch up," he says to the girls before stopping me in the hallway.

"Hurry up," Naomi calls back. "We need to party plan before Yoga." She gives me a wide grin but continues walking with Olivia down the hallway.

"Not that bad?" Harry asks, looking down at me. "I feel slightly insulted."

But I can tell he's not. The sparkle is back in his eye, and he's towering over me with that cocky grin.

"Maybe you should be," I reply, my lips pulling up into a smile.

"Or maybe I should remind you how much you love studying with me," Harry says, placing a kiss on my cheek.

Harry checks around us for a professor. I follow his eyes, not finding any. A second later, his mouth is on mine, and he's gently biting my lip.

My stomach swings forward at the sensation, trying its best to get closer to him.

He pulls away quickly, putting enough space between us so we don't get into trouble.

"You're not being fair," I reply, distracted by his kiss.

"I'm not trying to be. I'm trying to show you that I care," he says seriously.

"Well, I believe you," I say with a sigh, leaning back against a locker.

"Will you tell me what's wrong?" Harry says, lacing his hand through mine. "You've gone on and on all day about me not truly loving you, about you leaving, about us getting hurt. But you haven't told me what's really bothering you."

"I feel like all the things you just said are reasons enough to be bothered," I reply, trying to brush off his question.

"Of course they are. But they aren't … it."

"It, huh?" I state, looking up at him.

"Just tell me," Harry says.

I think over his question. About how I've been feeling. All of the conflict.

"The truth is that I believe you love me. I guess I just don't believe that you're *in love* with me," I say hesitantly.

"I've put on too good of a show, huh?" he says, pinching his lips together in understanding.

"What do you mean?"

"Of course it would seem like that to you because I've only just told you I love you. I haven't gotten the chance to show you yet. Not properly," Harry says, his face softening.

"Show me?"

"I've told you with my words that I do. But my actions haven't exactly reflected it. I know that. And that's all I'm asking for. Give me a chance to show you—with time, with action—what you mean to me."

Harry's words ring in my ears.

Give me a chance to show you.

I want to say no. *No, we don't have time. No, you've had your chance. No, I don't care about you.*

No. No. No.

But instead, I nod yes to him.

Because I want to give him a chance.

I want to see what we can be.

I don't want to leave, shutting him out.

So, I nod.

I nod yes.

Eye to eye.
YOGA

I QUICKLY CHANGE into my workout clothes, walking into Yoga with determination.

"Can we talk?" I say, catching up to Olivia before class.

She looks at me, disinterested at first, but then she agrees with a nod. The girl she was talking to walks into the studio, but we stay outside the door.

"Look, I wanted to talk to you about Harry," I start before I chicken out.

"This can't be good," Olivia mutters, her nostrils flaring.

"No, it's not like that," I correct, wanting her to pay attention. "I'm leaving, okay? And you at least deserve to know what he thinks."

"Are you trying to set me back up with him or something?" Olivia says, confused.

I shake my head, not wanting to say the word *no* to her.

"When you told Harry to put on a face about his dad, you messed up."

"Thanks for the history lesson," she retorts.

"Just listen. Harry thought that you didn't care about him. He thought that you cared about what other people would think. He thinks that no one loves him, Olivia. And … and he told me yesterday that he loves me."

"Why are you telling me this?" Olivia asks, her face paling.

"I'm telling you because he's *so* wrong. Mohammad loves him. Noah loves him. The Williams love him. *I* love him." I let the words finally come out of my mouth. "And I know that you love him too."

"What does it matter? He's with you, and he thinks absolute shit of me," she replies, glancing away from me.

"Why did you say those things to him?" I ask, needing to understand.

"I was trying to help him, Mallory. His dad *hit him*. What should I have told him? To tell everyone? His family is *important*. If his dad found out that other people knew, he would be furious. And I couldn't protect him. The only way to protect him was to lie. To tell him to lie."

"But it meant you would lose him. It meant he thought you didn't care," I say, my brows dipping in.

"It meant that he was safe," she corrects. "As long as he stayed quiet and stayed out of trouble."

"You and I both know that's not Harry."

"I told him to lie, knowing that it would hurt him. But I wanted to hurt him. I wanted him to stand up and be strong.

LONDON PREP: BOOK 3

And he did. And I think he did it because he was angry with me. Maybe he was being prideful. I don't know," she goes on.

"You did what you thought was best …"

"Of course I did," she says. "I know I'm some joke to you. But at the time, I did what I thought was right."

"And what about Tuesday?"

Olivia shakes her head, her blonde hair falling over her shoulder.

"Tuesday was not my idea of a fun time. I went out with a different group. I was trying to distract myself. And then, of course, who do I run into …"

Her gaze flicks over to mine as her mouth hesitates.

"I'm sure you want to know what happened. What we talked about."

I shake my head. "It's none of my business."

Olivia stays quiet as a girl walks past us, moving into the room.

"You're a good person, Mallory." She says it like she's trying to convince herself. "My parents are sort of going through something similar to Harry's, and I didn't find out about his parents until his mum called me."

"Your parents are too?" I ask, dropping my shoulders.

"It's very private," she insists. "I don't know exactly what's going to happen. It's a family matter. But when his mum called me, I had to talk to him."

"I know. And I'm sure it crossed your mind that she called you, thinking you were still together," I reply. "At least, it crossed mine."

Olivia smiles warmly. "That's just lads for you. Never letting their families know anything."

"Thanks for that." I smile back at her.

Because she could have said yes, that it did mean something.

But she didn't.

"Tomorrow night, Mohammad's having a party for me. A farewell party. I know he talked to you about it, but I thought I should tell you as well. I'd like for you to come."

"Are you sure?" she hesitates. "Obviously, Mohammad chatted with me about rules. Anyway, I figured after all of his efforts to insist that I behave, you thought it was because I wouldn't or something."

"I think Mohammad was a little wounded to find out you were out with Harry the other night," I inform.

"I thought as much." Olivia says. "Though, from Naomi's reaction to me kissing Mohammad and their apparent joint party-hosting skills, I'm not sure he'll stay sour for long."

I grin at her, feeling so much better.

"I hope you're right," I admit as we walk into class. "I could see them together."

"Unfortunately, I can see it too." Olivia smiles, sitting down onto her mat.

I feel a little stuck, my mat being a few over from hers. But she doesn't look like she's done talking, and Amy hasn't started our practice yet.

"Can I ask you something?" Olivia says, her eyes coming up to mine.

I nod at her.

"What's your end game?"

I roll my neck, knowing that question was coming. "I don't have one. I care about Harry, and I know he's going to go through a hard time soon. With me leaving. With his parents."

"And you want to date him, what, internationally?" she asks, shaking her head at me like it's impossible.

Which it probably is.

"Maybe he'll forget about me. You know, one of those

452

out of sight, out of mind sort of things."

Olivia squints her eyes up at me like she's trying to understand.

"It's not what I want," I clarify. "But I do want the best for him. And that includes your friendship, I think …"

I don't know where any of this is coming from.

Maybe it's been a long time coming.

Or maybe, as I say the words, I'm actually realizing them.

But something about my impending departure has me being more vocal.

More truthful.

"I think that you need to explain to Harry why you said what you said. He deserves to know that you … love him. Even if what you told him to do was wrong, it came from a caring place."

Olivia's cheeks tint pink. "Why would you want me to tell him that?"

"Because he deserves to know that he can depend on people he loves too. That not everyone just abandons him. He's special to more than just the guys. And I think he's going to need all the support he can get. Don't you?"

"He will," she agrees.

And for the first time, it feels like Olivia and I are actually seeing eye to eye.

I was kidding.
4:10PM

"I THOUGHT YOU'D never come out of there," Mohammad moans as I walk out of the changing rooms. He's leaning with his back against the wall, his body slumped in on itself.

"Class ended, like, twenty minutes ago. I had to rinse off."

"Rinse off? I could have been showered and to the other side of London in the same amount of time," Mohammad groans.

"Just ignore him." Noah smiles. "He's hungry."

"He's starving," Harry teases, greeting me with a wink. "Did you ask Noah for one of his granolas? He's got a secret stash, you know."

Mohammad pushes off the wall, grabbing his backpack off the floor before dramatically throwing it over his shoulder. "Granola shmanola. I want some chips and a fizzy pop."

I wrap Mohammad in a hug, trying to give him moral support.

"Well, if you behave yourself on our outing, maybe we'll finish up with enough time to stop and get you a snack," I tease, rubbing his apparently *starving* belly.

"One complaint later, and you totally cave," Noah replies, his eyes slipping from Mohammad to me.

"What can I say? I'm a sucker for making people feel better."

"You give in too easily," Harry replies as we push out of school. "You could have at least gotten something out of it before you agreed to feed him."

"Oh, like what?" I ask, wanting to brainstorm.

"Like … the theme for the party," Harry suggests.

Noah lets out a dramatic sigh. "Naomi was already out here, drilling me about it."

"Wait, what?" I ask.

"She was picking his brain for ideas," Mohammad clarifies.

"How do you know? I was the only one out here, talking to her," Noah asks Mohammad.

"I suggested it," he states with that *no duh* voice.

"Why wasn't she picking my brain?" Harry says with a pout.

"Well, would you have had ideas for her?" I ask.

"I don't know. What did she want to know?" Harry asks Noah curiously.

"She was just asking me about the party. She had a list of questions." Noah shrugs.

"And?" I ask.

"No," Mohammad cuts in. "It's supposed to be a surprise."

"I hate surprises," I say with a pout.

"Do I at least get a hint?" Harry asks. "After all, I am technically the host."

Mohammad's brows dip in as he thinks about a hint. "Think … fish."

"Fish?" Harry repeats, dropping his chin.

"Oh, I know. *The Little Mermaid*! An Under the Sea theme." I grin, pleased with myself.

Mohammad makes the sound of a buzzer going off. "Wrong."

"Hmm," I huff.

"I know." Harry grins, turning to us as we walk out of school and toward the bookshop. "Fish and Chips."

"Nope." Mohammad smiles.

And I think with every guess we get wrong, he gets prouder of his secret planning skills.

"Well, this is some bullshit," Harry finally says.

"Any other guesses?" Mohammad asks.

"I'm not going to continue guessing because I hate being wrong. And I feel like I'm going to just be wrong over and over."

"Aw, no fun," Mohammad says, sticking out his tongue at me.

"Well, maybe you should reconsider your theme," I reply. "Because if it were Under the Sea and I had been right, you could have required costumes."

"Costumes are a hard no," Noah cuts in.

"Even if the costumes are revealing?" I ask pointedly. "I could have put on long mermaid hair and worn a little starfish bra."

Mohammad's eyes widen with approval.

"I think we should vote to change the theme," Harry declares.

"Shit, maybe you're right," Mohammad says, bringing his hand up to his chin. "I'll have to talk it over with Naomi."

"I was kidding," I insist, realizing they're taking this way too seriously.

But no one replies.

"They do realize I was kidding," I say to Noah, moving over to talk to him.

"You got yourself into this one. All your talk about starfish bras," Noah says, his eyes slipping down me. "I can't help you now."

I frown at him.

"Well, just know, if I'm forced to wear a mermaid tail tomorrow night, then you'll have to wear one too," I say, trying to get my point across.

Noah wrinkles his nose, not liking the idea.

"Fine, I'll talk them out of it," he says.

"Thank you." I smile as I point out the bookstore.

AFTER SPENDING WAY too long in the bookstore, we all exit, empty-handed.

I had every intention of buying a classic novel for my dad or a beautifully bound book for my mom, but instead of searching through the racks, most of our time was spent listening to Mohammad's theatrical renditions of the synopses. Harry then followed it up with his theory of how the books would end, and Noah would come to an answer on whether they were plausible or not.

So, overall, our time was well spent.

Noah walks onto the sidewalk with a grin. "We should head back."

"I probably need to get home too," Mohammad agrees. "But that was more fun than I'd expected—I'll give you that."

I smile at Mohammad before glancing over to Harry. Because I know he has an empty house to go home to.

"It was fun," I agree as I take ahold of Harry's hand.

Noah glances down at our interlaced hands before bringing his eyes up to Harry.

"Do you want to come round for dinner? I'm sure Mum wouldn't mind the company." Noah smiles, apparently changing his statement from earlier when he said dinner included only his family.

Which makes sense because Harry really is one of them.

And Noah knows it.

Harry's face flashes with surprise, but a second later, he's waving off Noah's invitation. "I'll let good old Helen and Gene have Mallory tonight. Besides, we'll have her all to ourselves tomorrow."

Harry looks down at me, and I can tell he's conflicted. He wants to come, but at the same time, I know he wants me to have this night with them.

I smile at him, squeezing his hand.

"If you were going to invite Harry right in front of me, you might have considered inviting me as well," Mohammad mutters, kicking at the sidewalk.

"Awww. You know you're always welcome," I say, giving him a big hug.

"Like I need another night with you," he replies.

"Already sick of me?" I tease.

"Whatever," Mohammad says, shaking me off.

As he does, Harry moves in front of me.

He dips his head down, giving me a quick kiss on the cheek, his mouth lingering at my ear. "I'll see you tomorrow, angel."

I close my eyes, letting his words sink in. But then he pulls back and moves on, pulling Noah into a hug and laying a sloppy, wet kiss onto his cheek.

Noah grins back at him.

Then, Harry wraps his arm around Mohammad's shoulders. "I think we're both this way," he declares, swinging Mohammad around on the sidewalk in the opposite direction that Noah and I are headed.

"Bye!" I call out with a laugh.

I watch as they walk. Mohammad's stumbling as Harry leans against him, seemingly already in the midst of a conversation. I can see him bring his hands out in front of him and hear Mohammad's laugh.

"Ready?" Noah asks, watching them with me.

"Ready."

Things will change.
6:30PM

THE HOUSE SMELLS amazing.

Like, *amazing*.

I'm immediately drawn into the kitchen, kicking off my shoes when we get into the house. I drop my backpack and move through the living room. There are platters spread out across the table and candles lit.

"You've outdone yourself," I comment, my eyes practically popping out as I take in all of the food.

"Oh, Mum," Noah says, his voice rising.

Helen's cheeks flush with pride as she moves beside us, admiring the table. "Well, I did promise you a home-cooked meal."

And did she deliver.

There are plates and plates filled with food. Bread, mashed potatoes, French beans …

"This looks delicious," Noah says, dropping his bag onto the kitchen floor before wrapping his arm over Helen's shoulders.

"It does," I agree before moving to the oven and peeking to see what the delicious smell is.

"A roast with vegetables," Helen says, lowering her head to look in with me.

"Wow," is all I can manage to say.

Because Helen did all of this *for me*.

"I've found the perfect pairing," Gene says, joining us in the kitchen. He's examining a bottle of wine in his hand, his eyes scanning across the label.

"Lovely," Helen replies, snatching the bottle from him.

He almost jumps back, surprised by her sudden motion.

"Oh, you've arrived," Gene says, looking over at us for the first time.

"Perfect timing, it seems," Noah replies, dropping down into his chair at the kitchen table.

"Impeccable timing really. It's as though you had a warning on when to be home," Gene comments, arching an eyebrow.

Noah pushes out his lips, shaking his head at his dad. "I like to think it just worked out that way," he disagrees.

I glance over to him, not sure if it actually *did* work out like that or if Helen texted him, saying when to be home.

"Will Harry not be joining us?" Helen asks, eyeing the extra plate she put on the table for him.

"He thought we should have a family night to ourselves," Noah says, his face falling.

"Poor dear. You'll be seeing him tomorrow though?" Helen asks, checking on the meat.

Noah nods at her as I take a seat at the table. I stare at Harry's plate, feeling so much guilt for not insisting that he join us.

Gene grabs the wine from the counter and sets it on the table before bringing over four wineglasses. He pours one for himself and Helen and then pours a glass, handing it to me. I take it cautiously, but he doesn't blink an eye before pouring Noah a glass, too, handing it to him across the table.

"Your mum mentioned something about Harry and his family," Gene says, raising his glass at us before taking a sip.

"Well, apparently, his parents are coming home together," Noah informs.

"That's ridiculous," Helen says, her eyes widening.

"Yeah, it is," Noah agrees.

"Did he explain why?" Gene asks.

Noah looks over to me, and I know he wants me to explain. I want to crawl under the table and hide, but I know they care about Harry just as much as me.

And that they have a right to know.

And to be concerned.

I rehash everything that Harry told me, noticing Noah's lack of surprise at my statements. Which means that Harry actually did tell him everything.

Noah nods as I finish my explanation.

"That's quite complicated," Gene says with a frown.

"It is," I agree.

"And completely mad," Helen interrupts. "I cannot believe, after everything, she'd do this to him."

"I don't know what we can do," Noah says, bringing his palms down onto the table.

Helen nods, but she doesn't look at all convinced. Gene must notice because he puts his hand on her shoulder.

"Give your mother and me a chance to talk about this," Gene says. "Then, we can have a chat with Harry and get his opinion on all of this."

I nod, agreeing with Gene. Someone has to say something. Because everything about Harry's family's plan is crazy. It's layer upon layer of wrong. And sometimes, I think that they've somehow convinced Harry that it isn't.

That it's normal.

"Yes, Gene and I will discuss it," Helen confirms. "But for now, let's be done with this conversation. It's time to eat."

Helen pulls the roast out of the oven, plating a portion for each of us before delivering it to the table.

I stare in amazement as Noah scoops pile after pile onto his plate. I take a small helping of everything, wanting to try it all.

"I'd like to make a toast," Gene says, grabbing his already-half-empty wineglass. "Mallory, it's been a delight having you here. We hope that you've had just as wonderful of a time as we've had."

Gene smiles at me, and I can't help but smile back at him.

I look to Helen and Noah, seeing them both smile too.

"Cheers," Noah agrees as we all clink our glasses together.

"Any other plans for tonight?" Gene asks as we eat our meal.

"We probably need to study," I admit, hating the words as they come out of my mouth.

"Nonsense. Have some more wine," Gene disagrees, topping off my glass.

I've barely drunk any of it, mostly because I wasn't sure if I was supposed to. But Noah's sipping his, and Helen is drinking hers, too, so I think it's just one of those celebration-exception rules that I'm not supposed to bring up.

Noah tilts his head before taking another sip.

"Study for what?" Helen asks with interest.

"I've got a History test, and we've got a Stats one too," Noah answers.

"And I have Geography," I add. "Nothing like sending me home after making me lose my mind over exams."

"I'm sure you're as prepared as you can be," Gene interjects. "Besides, they always say that last minute cramming isn't of much use. You either know the material or you do not."

"I'm not sure I agree with that," Helen replies, her face flashing with concern.

"Don't worry, Mum; we've been preparing for them all week," Noah says.

"The best thing you can do is have your wine, watch a show, and relax. Go up, review your notes, and get a good night's sleep," Gene instructs, taking a bite of the roast.

"Are you suggesting a movie, wine, and popcorn before an exam, Dad?" Noah grins.

"This once—and likely only this once—I am." His dad smiles back.

"Oh, Gene," Helen fusses. "I'd think you'd had one glass too many, giving out that kind of advice."

Gene waves her off, pushing his glasses up his nose. "I think it's a perfect idea. There's not much that can beat Noah's chocolate popcorn and a show."

"It's only because you're a chocolate addict." Noah laughs. "It's really not that special."

"I think anyone sane would take chocolate popcorn over studying," I reply. "Besides, it's not even fair. They're sending me off to New York after having exams in half my classes on my final day."

"Were you expecting a warmer farewell?" Gene asks, his eyes sparkling.

"I think that's probably the warmest good-bye Kensington can manage," I say, stabbing at my roast. "Though maybe I'll stop in and say good-bye to Headmaster Compton. And Ms. Adams. You know, make the rounds."

"I think they've seen you in their offices quite enough, dear," Helen replies, taking a sip of her own wine.

Impressed with her comeback, I raise my eyebrows, looking over to Noah.

"So, Mallory, are you happy to see your family? I'm sure they're growing excited for your arrival home," Gene says, pouring himself another glass of wine.

His questions tonight surprise me. I'm not sure if it's because I'm finally leaving or because of the wine, but he's especially talkative tonight.

I shrug. "I guess I am."

"Well, that was unconvincing," Helen says solemnly.

"What about you? I bet you can't wait to see Mia," I say brightly, wanting to change the subject.

"Mia actually rang us tonight. I think she's in the same boat as you, though she's slightly more optimistic about coming home."

"Really?" Noah asks with interest. "Last time we spoke, she made it sound like she wanted to stay in Greece forever."

"I think she misses her friends and the city," Gene says.

"Of course she does. She's been gone too long." Helen's forehead creases with her reply.

"Aww. You're excited to see her." I smile.

"Mia's kind of like you. She's got a big … presence," Noah states.

"Yes." Helen nods in agreement as her eyes get that sad puppy-dog look to them. "I'd find the house rather dreary if you were to leave and Mia wasn't to return straightaway. Girls always give a house life."

"Ouch, Mum." Noah looks at his mom, pretending to be offended.

"Your mother's being rather cruel to us tonight," Gene says with a grin, glancing over to his wife.

"You know I didn't mean it like that. I love you both to bits, but I swear, sometimes, I think you'll do my head in."

"Would things be better if we both were just gone from your life, Mum? All but vanished?" Noah says jokingly.

"Well, the house would be tidier," she says back, weighing the option. And apparently not playing his game.

Gene lets out a chuckle but then covers his mouth with his hand, stopping himself.

I look from Gene to Noah, smiling with them.

Because I love how they talk. How Noah is always able to be so serious but also so silly.

It's just one of those things that makes him, *him*.

Noah looks at me happily, a smile still playing on his lips. I hold his gaze, feeling butterflies form in my stomach.

But then I notice that Helen is watching him. No, more like she's observing him watch me. And it seems to make her unhappy.

It makes me uncomfortable, watching her admire Noah. Because I know she sees that he's happy. That he's happy, looking at me.

And that I'm going to leave.

And things will change.

I clear my throat, trying to divert everyone's eyes.

"That was an outstanding meal," Gene says, leaning back

in his chair.

"It was," Helen agrees with a firm nod of her head.

"Thank you so much for making all of this. It was so, so good."

"It was my pleasure," Helen says.

Noah gets up, helping her clear the table.

I try to help, too, but everyone insists that I sit down and drink my wine.

I take another sip, watching as they box up the leftovers and clean the dishes in the sink.

"I think I'm going to put on the popcorn," Noah says, glancing over at me.

"Uh," Gene says, reaching for his stomach, "I'm not sure how you'll get it down. I'm stuffed."

Noah just shrugs as Gene looks over to me for my input.

"There's always room for chocolate," I say, giving him the only answer I know.

Gene lets out a chuckle.

"Well, I'll leave the rest of the bottle with you two then. If you're going to have chocolate, you might as well pair it with some delightful wine."

I smile at Gene, knowing that leaving us the rest of the wine is a real sacrifice for him.

"Why don't you go look for a movie?" Noah says to me, turning on the burner to start the popcorn.

Completely offended.
9:30PM

"ALL RIGHT, LOVELIES, Gene and I are off to bed. But have an extra bite of popcorn for me," Helen says, placing her hand on my shoulder.

"Night, Mum," Noah calls out from the kitchen.

"I definitely will." I smile, standing up in front of the couch. "I know I'm not leaving until Saturday, and we'll have all morning together, but thank you. You've treated me like one of your own. I don't think I could have managed this without you." I keep my eyes on Helen, wanting her to know how sincere I am.

She's given me nothing but thoughtful and heartfelt advice.

And with everything that's happened—with Harry, at school, the fight, letting me have sleepovers, taking me for tea—she's been there for me.

"Oh, dear," she replies, her lips quivering. She hugs me, patting my back firmly. "You're a lovely girl, Mallory, and we will dearly miss you. You'll have to write and visit, of course."

I nod at her over and over. "I promise I will."

Gene watches our interaction, and when I pull away from Helen, he gives me a warm smile as he rubs Helen's back, soothing her. She looks stuck between wanting to cry and laugh, but she ends up just smiling at Gene and me.

"All right," Gene encourages, helping her turn toward the stairs.

I watch her go, sitting back down on the couch. Part of me wants to cry at the somewhat early good-bye, but I know I shouldn't.

"Well, what do you want to watch?" Noah asks, joining me on the couch.

I pull my legs up under me, sitting crisscross, and turn to face him. Noah hands me the popcorn bowl and sets the wine bottle on the coffee table.

"Hmm. Something funny maybe?"

Noah shakes his head, dipping his hand into the popcorn.

"What about an action movie?" he suggests.

"Maybe," I reply, narrowing my eyes. "What about a romance?"

Noah scrunches up his nose and shakes his head.

"How about … a kids movie?" I offer.

Noah's eyebrows rise with interest.

"Something light would be nice," he agrees, settling into the couch.

I flip through the channels, looking for a movie, finally landing on an animated one that's halfway over. "How about this?"

Noah nods, bringing another handful of popcorn to his mouth. He chews it before looking at me. "I'm surprised you didn't want to go upstairs and finish your book," Noah says, his lips pulling up into a smirk.

I roll my eyes. "I think the duke will have to wait until tomorrow. Maybe I'll try and sneak him into school."

"Could you imagine?" Noah says with a laugh, his eyes creasing at the corners.

"I think the professors would be more mortified than us." I laugh too, letting the scenario play out in my head. "Besides, we still have that ammunition about Mr. Pritchard and Miss Gunters."

"That's not ammunition. If they're happy, then who cares?" Noah replies.

"Who cares? Everyone would care," I argue. "That's juicy stuff."

"*Juicy gossip*," Noah corrects, shaking his head. "And private."

"I think Mohammad would disagree with you there. You know, he messaged me earlier. Wants us to bring bagels to the common room tomorrow morning."

"He's really doing up this whole last day thing, isn't he?"

"He is. I still can't believe I have two tests tomorrow."

Noah shrugs. "It's just a few tests."

"Just a few tests?" I gape. "Who would have ever thought you'd be so chill about the prospect of failing?"

"Well, I won't fail," he simply states.

"Not even History?" I ask, knowing his lack of enthusiasm for the course.

"You have a point."

"Well, luckily, I studied for Stats and Geography all week, so I should be okay," I say, taking a bite of popcorn. "It's kind of funny though, isn't it?"

"What?" Noah asks, tilting his head.

"Just that we're sitting down here, watching a movie and drinking wine from the bottle the night before we have exams. Who would have thought?"

"Crazy, huh?" Noah grins.

"Actually, yeah. I figured you would have demanded that we study or something."

"I'd rather spend time like this," Noah replies, taking another bite of popcorn.

I watch him lick the chocolate off his finger.

"How did your talk go with Harry today?" Noah asks, finally bringing it up.

I grab the bottle of wine, taking a large gulp. Noah watches my mouth, reaching his hand out to take the bottle when I'm done.

"It was complicated."

"It always is, isn't it?" Noah says tentatively.

I want to tell Noah what happened. That I kissed Harry. Explain *why* I kissed Harry.

But I'm scared to tell him.

I'm scared of how he'll react.

But if I've learned anything over the past few weeks, it's that it's better to speak up and be upfront than to lie.

"Harry was pretty upset. He thought he was losing me," I say, trying to find the courage.

"And?" Noah asks, his voice flat.

"And I kissed him."

"Ah," Noah says, taking another swig.

"I thought you preferred white?" I say, attempting to crack a joke. But it doesn't work.

"I'd prefer anything at this point."

"I don't want Harry to hurt."

"After I told you, after what I said in class, you just … kissed him?" Noah asks, setting down the bottle with disbelief.

"I know," I reply, grabbing the wine and taking another drink.

Noah shakes his head, falling back into the cushion. "Well, at least you knew you had a choice. There was no question," Noah says solemnly.

"No, I didn't. I … just—"

"It's okay. We don't have to talk about it."

I stay quiet, turning back to face the movie. Because he's right. I have nothing to say for myself.

I watch the screen, hoping to come up with something to say—anything.

But I don't.

"I wish things could be different." Noah's the one to break the silence, his words sounding more like a reflection than anything else.

"I do too," I reply, looking over at him.

I watch him.

He keeps his eyes on the television, but I know he sees me.

And I'm confused.

I'm confused because I want Noah.

And I want Harry too.

Harry's beyond what I thought I wanted out of a boy-friend. He's someone I could see a future with. With Noah, it sometimes feels like I can only see the moment. I get so caught up in things with him. In my feelings.

But I'm not sure that Noah and I could ever be more than friends. I think, physically, we could be. But emotionally?

It's so hard to tell.

To know.

But when it's just us, sitting here, it's difficult. Because I see Noah. I really see him and how beautiful he is.

How his creamy skin glows in the light of the TV. How his eyes are set below a row of dark lashes.

"You're staring at me again," he says, still not looking at me.

"Are you surprised?" I ask, not denying it anymore.

Noah's hair moves as he shakes his head. I turn back to the movie, but I can see out of the corner of my eye that his hand moves on the couch. It shifts next to my leg, and I can't help but take it into my own.

I play with his fingers, knowing that this is probably the most I'll ever get to feel them.

See them.

That this is my only chance to pretend that everything else isn't happening.

Noah lets me run my fingers across his hand. Lets my palm slip around his forearm. Lets my fingernails scrape against the inside of his wrist.

Noah closes his eyes, his lips parting as he lets me explore his skin.

I keep my eyes on his hand, only looking up to glance at the television. To make sure I remember that we're sitting in his living room.

That we're still in his house, in London.

I do it to remind myself that I'm here, with him.

It's not some fantasy in my head.

That it's real.

The movie finishes quicker than I want it to. I stand up as soon as the credits start rolling, like it's some alarm going off in my head.

Noah gets up from the couch, picking up the wine bottle and popcorn bowl and taking them into the kitchen.

I turn off the lights in the living room, standing awkwardly at the base of the stairs as Noah rinses out the bottle.

"I'm going to go brush my teeth," I call out, not sure what else to do.

I walk upstairs and go straight into the bathroom. I wash my face, letting the cold water clear my head.

I pick up my toothbrush, put paste on it, and shove it into my mouth. I brush my teeth and rinse out my mouth, looking over myself in the mirror. My heart starts to pound in my chest as I hear the stairs give.

Noah walks into the bathroom, looking slightly distraught. His face has hardened like his mind is made up, and he turns to me. He looks completely different from a minute ago, when we were lazily lying on the couch. When he was so nonchalant about doing the dishes.

"I can't let you leave without experiencing this."

"Experience what?" I ask, feeling my voice catch.

"This," Noah says, his fingers slipping across my collarbone.

My eyes flutter shut at the sensation. "You mean, experience me?"

"Yes."

"What do you want, Noah?" I ask, trying to figure out what he's really looking for.

"I want you." Noah's brown eyes are locked with mine as

his statement leaves his lips.

Those perfect lips.

"The last time you said those words to me, you told me they were a mistake."

"It's not a mistake that you're here. It's no coincidence. I want all of you. Your body, soul. Everything," he says.

"You want my body?"

"I want to experience everything with you," he replies.

"Noah," I say, trying to get his attention.

"Yeah?"

"That's a lot."

"I know you want that too," he replies. "Your body's so easy to read."

I blink a few times, trying to stop my chest from pounding so hard. Because right now isn't the time for emotions and feelings. It's the time to be rational.

And it sounds a lot like he's saying he wants to be with me.

Like, *be with me.*

Physically.

"Are you saying you want to have sex with me before I leave just because we have chemistry? Are you kidding me?" I ask, looking up at him, frustrated.

"That's not what I'm saying at all," he replies, his eyes widening. "We haven't even kissed, Mal."

"And whose fault is that?" I argue because he hasn't answered my question.

"Do you want that?" Noah asks, tilting his head to the side.

"I'm not answering that."

Noah shakes his head. "It doesn't matter anyway. Once we kiss, we won't be able to stop. I know we won't."

"How could you know that?" I ask, looking up at him.

"How could you *not* know that?"

"We stop ourselves all the time. Point proven by the fact that we haven't kissed," I say, trying to brush off his words.

"We haven't kissed because you're with my best friend. I care about him so much," he says. "That's the only thing that could be equally as powerful as this. And you know that."

"Please." I snort.

"Don't make me prove my point, Mal."

"Prove your point?" I ask.

Noah takes both of my hands into his, bringing my palms onto his chest. He tilts his head back, slipping my hands up his thick neck, over his jaw, and onto his cheeks. His eyes flutter, and I feel stuck to his skin.

"What does that make you feel?" Noah asks, opening his eyes back up.

"I'm touching you, Noah," I say, needing to state a fact. I can't tell him how it makes me feel. I can't say that it makes me feel like if my hands stay on his creamy skin for one second longer, I'm never going to take them away again.

"And what do you feel when you touch me?"

"I ..." I stutter, turning away from him.

Because Noah and I are like a bomb that's about to explode. Of course, touching him is intense. But if we give in—if I give in—we *will* explode. Us coming together will be the end of us. And we'll hurt ourselves and everyone around us in the process.

"It's overwhelming, isn't it?" Noah says, nodding his head like he understands that I can't say anything.

"I know that you think you want to experience ... me. And I'm not saying that we don't have a connection. But it won't be a good thing, Noah."

"How could it not be a good thing?"

"You keep talking about needing to experience me ..."

473

"Of course I do. You're everywhere, Mal."

"You're missing my point."

"What is your point?" he asks.

"My point is … I think that you think if we have sex, you can get me out of your system."

Noah's face flashes with pain. "You think I think that?"

"What else am I supposed to think?" I say, feeling a little hurt. "You go on and on about experiencing me. But you don't want to be with me. You will never be with me. So then, that means you could only want my body. If you don't want *me*, you don't want my heart. My soul. You're wrong, Noah."

Noah's mouth falls open, and he looks completely offended by my words. He runs his hand through his chestnut hair and then turns to me.

Suddenly, he picks me up off the ground and sets me down on the bathroom sink. His hands move to my cheeks and then into my hair. And his body is sandwiched between my legs.

"Noah," I gasp as he presses our foreheads together, looking up at me through dark, thick lashes.

His nose dances against mine, and I can feel his lips barely graze my skin. I connect my eyes to his, wondering if he's going to kiss me.

I open my mouth more, ready for him.

Because I can smell his musk all around me. His creamy skin is so close to mine. And I know that here, in this place, I could never say no to Noah. Whatever he wanted, I would give him. Because deep down, maybe I want it too. Or maybe it's because I'm curious about what it would be like. Maybe we will kiss, and it will be a letdown. Or I'll know it's right. Maybe it's been me all along who has wanted this. Not to be with Noah, but to get just a small taste of him, so that way, I could move forward, at least knowing what it was like.

"Mal," he whispers, his brown eyes pulling my gaze up from his lips.

I don't answer him, but I keep my eyes transfixed on him, so he knows that I'm listening.

So that he knows he has my attention.

"When I taste your lips for the first time, it's not going to be because I'm curious. I don't want to just *shag* to get you out of my system. When I have you, I'm going to demand nothing short of everything because our feelings, our bodies, will require it. So, when we are together, there will be no distinction between body and soul and heart and you and me."

"But I'm leaving. How can you have all of that, say all of that, when I'm leaving?"

Noah shakes his head. "I'm telling you this because you shouldn't think for one second that I want only your body."

"It doesn't change the fact that you want to experience that with me, and then I'll be gone."

"We're already experiencing it. Stop focusing so much on sex," he says, his hand coming to my jaw, his finger slipping against my lips.

"Noah—" I start to say something. But I can't say anything. Because I want this too. To just experience this feeling.

I focus in on Noah's finger, how it's rough against my lips. I take in the way he smells.

Then, I let my hands explore him.

My fingers wrap around his waist, feeling how it tapers in and widens as I move up to his back. His finger stays at my lips, my throat tingling at the sensation.

I listen more closely, hearing his heavy breath like it's my own.

I glance down and watch him lick his lips.

And I know that, finally, we're going to kiss.

Finally, I will be able to have another part of Noah Williams.

I tilt my chin up, and his nose brushes against mine. I close my eyes, waiting. But he doesn't do anything.

Instead, he drops his hand from my cheek.

And I feel a gap.

An absence.

I keep my eyes shut, wishing that something else had happened.

That he had kissed me.

That he had told me not to go.

That he had told me how he felt about me.

That he had told me he loved me.

But when I finally open my eyes, I already know that I won't find Noah in front of me.

Because he's gone.

FRIDAY, OCTOBER 11TH
You don't get it.
6:45AM

"WE'RE GOING TO have fun today," Noah says, climbing into my bed.

"We are?" I mumble, rubbing my eyes.

"Yep," Noah replies, shifting next to me. "We need to."

I open my eyes a sliver, enough to see his floppy brown hair on my pillow.

"It's my last day," I state, the reality sinking in.

"That's technically tomorrow," Noah says.

I close my eyes again, knowing that I can't avoid it anymore. "I need to pack."

"I think we should run."

"Run?" I ask, opening my eyes again. "No. No. No. We should just sleep in. Skip school. Let's blow it all off."

Noah tickles my stomach, causing a giggle to escape my mouth.

"We can't skip school," he replies, rolling me over onto my side.

"Why not?"

"Well, Mohammad would be very disappointed. He's got big plans for you tonight, evidently."

"Apparently," I repeat, flaring my eyes.

"And a little goose told me they might involve mermaid

tails and starfish bras. Can you imagine?" Noah grins.

"Did you just call me a goose?" I laugh, pushing him away from me.

"A little goose actually."

Noah's full-blown smiley this morning, and it's kind of contagious. I shake my head at him, trying to hide under the covers.

"This little goose wants to go back to sleep," I mumble.

"This little goose should come for a run," Noah argues, coming after me under the sheets. His fingers find their way to my stomach, and his palm rests on top of my shirt.

I glance over at him, making out the outline of his cheeks. His jaw. His lips.

"Tell me the plan, and then I'll go," I agree.

"The plan?"

"The plan for today. Walk me through it. How do we— or I—how do I get through it?"

I look over at Noah, hoping he'll know what to say.

What to do.

"We just do," he says simply.

I let out a groan, turning over onto my stomach, trying to hide. Noah starts rubbing my back, his nails dragging up from my tailbone to my shoulder blades and back down again. It feels amazing.

"You can't hide away under here."

"I can," I chime back. "And I have every intention to."

Noah's fingers stop on my back, and I shift, rolling over to face him. I want to pull the covers off from over our heads to get some air.

But the darkness, the privacy, it's kinda nice.

It makes everything feel like a dream. Because we haven't gotten up or started our day. Everything that happens between now and when we get out of bed doesn't count. It's just a dream.

A memory.

"Last night," I say, bringing it up, "you left."

Noah pulls his hand away from me, moving onto his side to face me. He tucks his head into his elbow, letting his arm prop it up.

"I think it's best that nothing happened," he says. "It would have just made it harder on everyone."

I close my eyes, disappointed. I didn't expect a different answer.

"Harder on you," I say.

Noah clears his throat, his eyes diverting from mine. "Well, I'm not thrilled it's already Friday."

"You almost kissed me."

"Yes," Noah says.

"You're not denying it?"

"What's the point?" he replies, licking his lips.

"Because I'm leaving. I thought you would kiss me because I was leaving," I clarify, trying to work through these feelings.

"I wanted to," he says, his eyes coming up to mine.

"But you didn't. Why?"

"Because I told you, I wouldn't have been able to stop. And if that were to happen, I don't want you with someone else."

"Everything's a mess."

"It's a disaster," Noah agrees. "And I don't want to hurt anyone."

I look over at him, seeing the concern in his eyes.

"No. You just don't want to hurt Harry."

"No, I don't," he agrees.

"But you're willing to hurt me?"

"No. I'm trying *not* to hurt you."

"You're messing with my head. You're so back and forth. *I want you; I don't. Start; stop. Do what you want to; no, don't,*" I grumble. "And maybe it's for the best. Things with Harry and me, well, I think they will be okay."

"Mallory," Noah says, shifting on his side.

"What?"

"You're wearing my sweats," he comments, his eyes shifting down to my legs.

"I am."

"You can talk to me about anything. And you look at me, like …"

"Like what?" I ask, bringing my eyes back up to his. "Like I care about you? I do, Noah. Of course I do."

"It's more than that." He starts playing with the strings of his sweats.

His sweats that are on me.

"What does it even matter? I'm leaving."

"Which is why it's best this way," he says with a sigh, dropping the strings.

"What is?"

"For everything just to end. You're not going to be able to be away from Harry, from me, Mohammad. You're not going to be able to handle how much you'll miss us. I know you. And if more happened between us, it would just make it worse."

I bring my hands down to my chest, almost cradling myself. "What are you saying?"

"I'm saying, your best chance is to just end things now and forget about us. Forget about me."

I stare at him, feeling a hard, painful pounding in my chest. "How could you say that?"

"Do you think I enjoy saying that? Do you think it doesn't hurt me too?" He brings his hand up onto his face and then covers his eyes with his palm, letting his elbow fall back onto the bed.

I roll onto my back, staring into the dark comforter. "I think if you cared about me at all, those words would never have left your lips."

Noah pulls down the covers, making me look at him. He runs his hand down over my hair and onto my shoulder. "I'm saying it because I care."

"You're not hearing me," I reply, swatting his hand away.

Noah's eyes flare, and he drops his hand. "What would you like me to say? Tell me."

I shake my head, feeling anger rising.

What do I want him to say?

What do I want him to say?

"I want you to say that nothing else matters, Noah. I want you to say that Harry, the distance, all of it, that none of it matters."

"Of course it matters."

"You don't get it."

"I get it. I get what you're asking me to say."

"But you can't, can you?" I reply.

"Mallory, no matter what I say, you're leaving tomorrow. And it would be selfish of me to speak up now. It would be selfish, and I won't do that to you."

"So, instead, you're telling me to forget you?" I ask harshly.

"I'm telling you … that I want to go for a run."

As I look at Noah, I know that tears are going to escape at any second. I bite my lip, trying to keep them in. Noah looks down at my lip, his forehead creasing. And then he's sitting up, pulling his shirt off over his head. I want to ask him what he's doing, but he throws it onto the floor and then lies back down, pulling me against his warm chest.

He holds on to my head, pressing my cheek into the spot just below his collarbone.

"Relax, okay? Let's go for a run. And then ... I'd like to make lunch. Something delicious, of course," he says with a lighter tone. "We'll pick up the bagels that Mohammad wants. And then we'll go to school."

I try to focus on what Noah wants to do. On what he's telling me. But a tear escapes at the thoughts floating through my mind.

"You won't do it, will you?" I press my palms into Noah's chest, angry with this situation.

Angry with myself.

"Kiss you?" he asks, pulling back. He looks down at me, his lips parting. "Is that what you want?"

"Yes."

Noah's eyes are all over me, but then he closes his mouth. "I can't do that to you."

"You'll let me leave, not knowing what it's like?" I push, letting my hands explore his chest. I know that I shouldn't. I know that he doesn't want me to. I know that with every finger that moves, I'm hurting Harry.

I'm jeopardizing their friendship.

I'm jeopardizing our relationship.

But my fingers don't seem to care. They're too distracted by the creamy skin in front of me. By the warmth and muscle and comfort.

"You don't think I've thought about that every day? I told you yesterday, I was letting you decide ... and you kissed him, Mallory. You fixed things between you and Harry."

"You're stupid sometimes." I shake my head, pressing my face harder into his chest.

"What?" Noah asks, his hands resting on my shoulders.

I pull away from him, so he can see my face.

So he can hear me clearly.

I move to sit cross-legged, wanting to explain this to him once and for all.

"You're so annoyingly oblivious. I did it because I'm scared. I'm scared that you keep telling me to forget you. I'm scared that, after tomorrow, I won't hear from any of you again. And at least with Harry, if we're okay, if I leave, knowing we're okay, I know I will hear from him. I will see him. But with you, I can already tell ... you'll be gone."

"You made up with Harry, so you wouldn't lose him?"

"I made up with Harry because I love you both. And I know that he loves me too. He doesn't want me to leave and forget him." The words practically burn, coming out of my mouth, but they come out anyway.

Noah closes his eyes, bringing his hands up to his temples. "So, because he told you he loved you, that's it then?"

"You had every chance to tell me or show me how you felt. But you didn't. This morning, I even went as far as to ask you. So yeah, I guess that's it."

I look up to Noah, not sure what to do. I guess neither of us has the answer. We both want this, but we're afraid of it for different reasons. Noah thinks he will hurt me. He's scared that he will hurt Harry. And I'm scared of wanting someone who wants me to just forget them.

"Come on. Let's go run," Noah says, pulling me up from the bed. "I think we both could use the fresh air."

WE DON'T SAY anything as we run. I just push myself further and further, wanting to stay one step ahead of his pace. Maybe it's so I can feel like I'm winning. So I can show Noah that I can keep up with him.

But really, it's because anytime I slow down, my mind starts to wander.

When I push myself, my mind can only focus on performing, one breath in and one breath out—instead of naked skin, and Noah, and my bed, and the fact that he wouldn't kiss me, and last night, and Harry, and how much I care about him, and how terrible I am for begging Noah to, in essence, break Harry's heart with one motion.

By the time we get back to the house, I'm out of breath, and I have completely run out of thoughts.

I put my hands on my knees, hunching over to take in a gulp of air. Noah drops onto the stoop, trying to catch his breath too. I can feel that my shirt is soaked through below my sweatshirt. My cheeks feel hot, and my mouth is dry.

Noah has sweat stains under his arms and around his neck. His cheeks and the tip of his nose are both rosy. Probably from a combination of our intense run and the cold air that's been beating against our faces.

"Feel good?" he asks, his chest still rapidly rising and falling.

"Felt great actually," I reply, finally standing up straight. "There's nothing like running to clear your head."

"Or clear sexual tension," he comments.

I glance over to him, not sure if he actually said that or if I made it up in my head. But the smile that forms on his mouth tells me that he *did* say it.

I sit down on the stoop with him, giving my legs a break.

"I think running can clear out just about anything," I admit.

And for some reason, I feel better. Maybe it was the run or the fact that Noah and I had finally said everything there was to say this morning, but I have no more questions. There aren't any more chances for what we are to change.

And despite that hurting, it's comforting to know that this is how it is.

"That or a cold shower," Noah replies. He gets up and then extends out his hand to me. I take it, letting him pull me up after him. "Why don't you shower first? I'll work on lunch."

"You should throw in some of those leftovers from last night. Dinner was so good," I say, thinking back to our meal.

"Have you ever had a mashed potato sandwich?" Noah asks as we walk into the house.

"I haven't. But something tells me I'm about to."

Noah grins at me before going into the kitchen. I run upstairs, shower, and change into my uniform. It's a bittersweet feeling, putting this uniform on for the very last time.

Even though I hated it when I got here, there's something very homey and comforting about it.

It's nice to just get dressed for school. To not have to worry about what outfit I want to wear. There's enough wiggle room to make it my own but not enough to get lost in the endless choices that go along with wearing whatever you want.

I decide to put on my red lipstick, figuring if I'm leaving, I might as well go out with a bang. I add a dark eyeliner and a couple coats of mascara, leaving my hair straight.

I throw on a sweater as I head back downstairs, knowing I'm going to need it.

I go to my bag, checking to make sure I have all of the textbooks from the house. I don't want some annoying email coming to me in a week, saying that Kensington is charging me a small fortune because I forgot to return one of their textbooks.

"I'm going to run up and have a shower. Lunches are on the table," Noah says as he moves upstairs.

"Sounds good," I reply.

I throw our lunches into his backpack and then grab my statistics notes. I decide to make myself a coffee and read over them until Noah is ready to go.

About ten minutes later, he's back downstairs, and I've managed to convince myself that I at least won't fail my statistics test.

"Ready?" Noah asks as I throw my notebook back into my bag.

"Yep." I nod.

When we get out front though, I stop. I turn around, taking in their house.

"Hang on," I say to Noah, who's already walking off down the sidewalk toward school.

"Did you forget something?" Noah asks, stopping.

"No. I just want to remember this."

I look over the Williams' house. The black lacquered door, the stoop, the white columns that match the houses next to it. And then the one thing that makes it unique.

Number 32.

I try to lock every detail into my mind, and when I finally feel like I have it, I turn back to Noah.

"All right," I say, catching up to him on the sidewalk.

"Bagels?" Noah asks, giving me a sympathetic smile.

"Bagels," I agree.

As we're walking to the bagel shop, I hear Noah's phone go off. He must have forgotten to silence the ringer because it dings three consecutive times in his pocket. We both look at one another before he pulls out his phone.

"Mohammad," he tells, scrolling through the texts. "He wants us to get six bagels. Even requested the kind he wants." Noah chuckles.

"That's not really surprising." I laugh.

"He also said don't worry about coffee. They'll have

some." Noah hands me his phone, so I can read the texts.

"He's really going all out today, isn't he?" I ask, scanning the messages.

"You know Mohammad. He likes to be busy. I think this is his way of saying he cares about you and that he'll miss you."

I smile. "I think Mohammad could be the only person to do that while also demanding his own custom bagel."

"That's pretty accurate." Noah grins.

When we get to the bagel shop, we place our order at the counter and then sit down at a table to wait.

Noah keeps his backpack on, but I slide mine off my shoulder, getting comfortable in my seat.

"I've been meaning to ask you, have you given my mum your project yet?" Noah says, making conversation.

"Not yet. I want to wait and give it to her tomorrow. Sort of as a parting gift."

"Sentimental," Noah comments, his eyes on me.

"I love nothing if not a good tragedy," I say easily.

"Dramatic as ever." Noah smiles.

"Always. I have to have some consistency in my life," I tease.

"She's going to love it. And I'm glad that you have my project to take with you."

"I still can't believe you compared me to a storm." I laugh, thinking about his gift to me.

Noah's smile widens, and it reaches all the way up to the corners of his eyes. "Well, everyone is allowed their own interpretation, aren't they?"

"They are. However, I'm not sure why you couldn't have chosen to compare me to something more beautiful. Like a landscape. Or maybe a flower. Something delicate."

"Delicate? I'm pretty sure that it shouldn't have come as a

surprise that I chose a storm. After all, I did compare you to a bulldozer," Noah points out.

"Always so charming." I laugh as the shop worker calls out his name.

We both get up, grabbing the two bags filled with bagels, and then head out the door.

Noah keeps his eyes in front of him, looking out like he's lost in his head.

"Whatcha thinking about?"

"Do you remember how I said I wrote something that would explain the collage?" he says, glancing over to me as we walk.

"I do."

"Well, I would like to give that to you tomorrow. As *your* parting gift."

"Noah," I say with hesitation.

"You can save it to read for when you're back home. Maybe it will help you … I don't know … make sense of things."

"Make sense of what?" I ask.

"Make sense of how I feel," Noah says as we turn the corner.

"Why don't you just tell me now?"

But I know that he won't. Because he couldn't—or wouldn't—tell me this morning.

And I don't see that changing.

I think this morning made me realize that we won't work as anything other than friends. There are too many questions, too much baggage. It hurts to know that, but at least I know it now.

At least I can be sure that there's never going to be anything more between us.

Because if there were going to be, he would have kissed

me this morning. He would have told me how he felt.

But he didn't.

I know he cares about me.

It's just … not enough.

"That wouldn't be any fun," Noah replies with a coy smile. "However, I was thinking about something."

"Thinking about what?" I ask as Kensington comes into sight. I take in the towering building, the beautifully cut grass, and the encased courtyard.

"Well, I think it's only fair that if you get my sweats, then I get something in return."

"You're giving me your sweats?" I ask, caught off guard.

"I assumed they would just disappear, to be honest."

"And that I would be the culprit?" I laugh, shaking my head. "What do you want?"

"That shirt you sleep in would be nice," he says as we step into the courtyard.

"You want my pajama top?" I tilt my head, confused by Noah's request. I dip my brows in as I glance over to him. "Why do you want that?"

"Well, it only seems fair if you take my sweats."

"But I want your sweats because they're comfortable. So, tell me, are you going to wear my top around?" I tease him, trying to make light of his request.

Noah cracks a smile, rolling his eyes at my comment.

He holds the door open for me, letting me step inside first. I immediately spot Mohammad, Naomi, Harry, and Olivia, all seated in the far corner of the common room.

"It smells like you," Noah whispers once we're both through the door.

I whip my head from our friends to Noah. Noah keeps his brown eyes on mine, but a moment later, he's nodding his head in the direction of the seating area, putting his hand on my back to urge me along to our corner.

"We've got coffee," Naomi sings out as we approach.

"Sounds like you've already had one," I reply, giving her a smile.

"She had an espresso at the shop and has now moved on to hot cocoa," Olivia interjects, standing up.

She places a kiss on each of my cheeks. I'm not sure if it's the fact that I'm leaving tomorrow or that our conversation yesterday went well, but she actually seems happy to see me.

Naomi gives me a hug and then hands me a coffee.

"I'm slightly buzzed on sugar at the moment," she admits, gesturing for me to sit down onto the sofa next to her. "But when I smelled the espresso at the café, where I met Moham- mad, I just couldn't resist."

"Well, I appreciate you stopping to get us coffees," I say to her and Mohammad, who's sitting on the couch opposite us.

I break my attention away from Naomi and turn to look at Harry, who's sitting next to me.

"Hey." I smile, grabbing his hand.

"You're quite popular this morning." He smiles, pulling me into a hug.

"So it would seem." I laugh, hugging him back. And it feels good to be in his arms.

I rest my head against his chest, keeping my arm laced around his waist. Harry wraps me up, tucking me against him.

"This is nice," he whispers into my ear.

I squeeze him once, letting him know that it is.

"All right, I'm ready for my bagel," Mohammad says, opening up the paper bags we brought from the shop.

I glance over to Olivia, who has a coffee cup in her hand. She brings it up to her lips, taking a sip. Noah has a cup in his hand, too, but my guess is that it's hot chocolate. He catches my eyes for a second but drops my gaze immediately and moves to help Mohammad with the bagels.

I sit up, turning toward Harry.

"How are you doing this morning?" he asks me seriously, rubbing his fingers across my hand.

"Pretty good." I shrug. "I kind of feel stuck between trying to pretend it's a normal day and trying to enjoy every single moment."

"I figured as much. Mallory, can I kiss you?"

"You can always kiss me," I reply, tilting my face upward.

He gives me a soft, slow kiss, keeping his palm pressed into my cheek. When I pull away, Mohammad is handing me a bagel from across the table. I smile to Harry before leaning forward, taking the bagel from Mohammad.

"All right, I'd like to make a toast," Mohammad says, raising his coffee cup.

Both Naomi and I sit up, grabbing our cups as we listen.

Olivia and Noah already have their cups in their hands and are both looking at Naomi. Harry leans forward, holding out his own cup.

"Miss America," Mohammad starts, his eyes getting watery, "it's been a true pleasure, being your guide at Kensington. You've caused a fair amount of drama, and it's been an unforgettable three weeks. We're all going to miss you."

I grin at Mohammad, mouthing, *Thank you.*

Naomi puts her hand on my knee, giving me a smile.

"Cheers," Olivia says, raising her cup.

"Beautifully said, Mohammad," Harry adds as we all lean in, clinking our coffee cups together.

"Thank you," Mohammad replies with a small bow. "But this is just the start. Tonight, we'll be able to toast properly with actual alcohol."

"Thank God for that," Olivia comments, rubbing at her temple.

"Stressed?" I ask, noticing the bags under her eyes.

I'm not sure how I missed them before, but I think I was so distracted by her warm greeting that I really didn't see how she was doing.

"Didn't sleep well last night," she replies vaguely. "I'm just excited to be out of the house tonight."

"I'm excited too." Naomi smiles. "Plus, I can't wait to reveal the theme at lunch."

"You should just tell us now," I insist, actually wanting to know.

I glance over to Mohammad, who looks thrilled. He's chewing his bagel, but he can't keep the smile off of his face. When my eyes slip over to Noah though, he's expressionless. He looks like an abandoned puppy that's been left in the corner.

He doesn't say a word.

Or smile.

His bagel sits on the table, untouched.

"I've got to go review for the stats test," Noah says when he finally looks up to us. And within a moment, he's up and walking toward class.

Mohammad looks surprised, but the second he realizes Noah's left his food, he turns his attention to the bagel, claiming it as his own.

"Noah's ... a bit of a wreck today," Harry says uneasily.

"He's probably just stressed about tests," I reply, trying to brush off Noah's mood.

But Harry keeps his eyes on me, and I know he doesn't believe that.

"Noah cares about me," I start, lowering my voice so only Harry can hear me. "And I think he's not happy about me leaving tomorrow."

"Of course he's not happy," Harry says, taking my hand into his. His blue eyes shift as he thinks. "But he didn't just look unhappy. He looked …"

"He looked like what?" I ask, trying to figure out where Harry's head is at.

"He looked like he'd just lost a family member or something. He looked pitiful," Harry replies, taking a bite of his bagel.

"He kind of did," Mohammad agrees, overhearing us.

"Don't worry; that's Noah for you," Naomi adds with a shrug. "I told you, he's moody."

"My leaving is tough for everyone. I know it's hard for you," I say to Harry. "And it's hard for Noah too."

"I guess so," Harry says.

But something in his eyes is unsettling.

WHEN THE BELL goes off, we all clean up our breakfasts. Naomi and Olivia sound excited to sit with us at lunch today, and it's been entertaining watching Naomi sneak glances at Mohammad. I'm not the only one who's noticed, and each time I catch Naomi, I look over to Olivia. She sees it, too, and looks stuck between admiring her friend and wanting to roll her eyes at her.

I just smile at them.

"We'll catch up," Harry says, standing up from the couch at my side.

Mohammad gives us a wave before walking off toward classes with Naomi and Olivia.

The second they're out of earshot, he continues, "I'm worried about Noah."

And I can see the concern on Harry's face.

"Don't worry; he'll be fine," I reply, trying to soothe him.

"He'll get over me."

"Get over you?" Harry asks, dropping his chin.

"Yeah. I'm sure it's going to be weird, not having me around at first. Especially because I live there. I'm with him day in, day out. But eventually, you'll all have to move on with your lives," I say, basically rephrasing Noah's words.

"I need to talk to him," Harry says, still sounding worried.

I nod at him because I don't have the heart to tell him that it won't make a difference.

There's nothing to say.

"I also have something for you," Harry adds, putting his hand in his pocket. Then he extends his hand out to me, opening up his palm.

"It's a key," I say, taking the shiny silver key into my hand.

"It's my key to the country house," Harry says, biting his lip. "It's more of my promise than the actual key that's the gift."

"Your promise?"

"I want you to hold on to the key. And I want you to book a flight back the next holiday you get. Unless of course, you want me to visit. Which I'd be happy to do. But sometime this fall, I want to meet you there. I told you at the party last weekend that we could go," he insists.

I search Harry's eyes, my heart speeding up in my chest.

"This is too much," I insist. Because I can't believe he's actually giving me this.

"I was serious when I said that I wanted to show you how I felt. Let's go up there and make some new memories. We can take the boys or go on our own. I know everything's been off this week, but I love you, Mallory. This key is meant to show you that I don't plan on going anywhere. At least, not without you."

I immediately wrap my arms around his neck and throw myself against his chest.

"You like it?" he whispers.

I pull back, taking in his expression. I can tell that he was nervous about giving me the key.

"You really are showing me that you're serious, Harry, aren't you?" I ask, feeling like this could be a new chapter for us.

Maybe me leaving will be the best thing for us. It will give Noah and me distance. It will let me think about the future.

About Harry.

"I am," he replies with a wide smile. "Though don't think I'm going soft or any shit like that. I definitely intend on trying to bed you while we're there."

I can't help but grin at Harry as he jokingly waggles his eyebrows.

"I don't doubt that you will," I reply, pulling him straight to my lips.

"Is that a yes?" Harry asks.

"Yes." I smile. "It's a definite yes."

A future with me.
STATISTICS

"YOU NEED TO stop being so pitiful," are the first words out of my mouth when I get to class.

Because Noah looks terrible.

His brows are scrunched in, and he's staring down at his desk like he's forever given up on sitting up straight.

He looks over at me with a glare.

"Just leave me alone," he mumbles, bringing his elbows

up onto his desk. He drops his head into his hands and proceeds to ignore me.

"So, you're not talking to me now?"

Noah doesn't say anything. He just sucks in his cheeks and keeps his head tucked down in his hands.

I look around, taking in the eyes on us.

Well, on Noah.

Because apparently, I'm not the only one who has never seen him look this off.

I lean over toward him and whisper, "Pull yourself together. You're the one who said we needed to have fun today, and people are staring at you. Harry already asked what was wrong."

"I'm fine," Noah says harshly. "I just don't want to talk."

I lean away from him, wondering if he's doing it already.

Writing me off.

If he's officially detaching himself.

"So, you're ending our friendship a day early then?" I say coldly. "I mean, why wait until tomorrow when you can just start today?"

"I'm not ending our friendship," Noah replies. "But not everything is about you. And if this is what I want, then you have to respect that."

"So, you've changed your mind since this morning?" I state, not at all surprised.

"No. What I didn't realize was that after what you said and asked of me this morning, you'd come to school and pretend like everything is fine with Harry."

"Everything *is* fine with Harry. He wants to be with me. And this morning, it became crystal clear that everything between you and me is a struggle. And I really don't want any part of it."

"Well then," Noah says, looking like he wants to skewer

me.

I glare back at him but have to stop when Mr. Johnson starts handing out our exam.

I stay focused on my test, not looking over at Noah.

He can pout all he wants, but it doesn't change the reality of the situation. I'm going to leave, and Noah will never talk to me again. After all his big words and our intense moments, he's going to forget about me.

But Harry won't. Harry wants a future with me, and I think if I give him time, like he asked, I will want that too.

WHEN THE BELL goes off, most of us have already finished our tests and have been sitting silently, waiting for class to be over.

Mr. Johnson, despite getting grilled about giving us homework, was actually right. There wasn't anything on the test that I wasn't prepared for.

It wasn't hard and didn't take too long. No one asked questions or raised their hands.

I smile to Mr. Johnson as I leave class. Because I'm secretly going to miss him and his optimism.

Noah walks next to me in silence, and I don't bother trying to get him to talk. He has his eyes on the floor and his head hanging down. So much so that he almost runs right into someone, and I have to grab his arm to keep him from knocking the poor girl over.

"Noah," I scold.

"Hey …" Harry says hesitantly, coming up to us.

"Hey," I reply with a sigh.

Noah doesn't say anything, and I don't see him changing that now.

I look between Noah and Harry.

Harry holds my eyes, and then he examines Noah in his

pathetic state, his forehead creasing. I squeeze my eyes shut to keep from screaming at Noah.

But I calm myself down, give Harry a quick kiss on the cheek, and then say, "I've got to get to Latin."

Harry nods at me before patting Noah on the back.

As I walk off, I see Harry leaning into Noah. It looks like they're talking, but it's hard to tell.

And either way, I don't really care.

Nothing I say will change Noah's mood.

Maybe something Harry says will.

But I really doubt it.

It was shitty.
LATIN

"WELL, NOAH IS a disaster," I say to Mohammad when I sit down in class.

"Is that really a surprise?" he asks, moving to sit down on my desk as we talk.

"Not really," I say as I pull out my textbook. "I just wish he would decide how he's feeling. It pisses me off when he's all over the place."

"Give him a little time. I'm sure he'll perk up tonight."

"Maybe after a few drinks. But even then, I'm not sure it will do any good."

"Maybe finding out the theme to this evening's event will cheer him up," Mohammad offers.

"It couldn't hurt," I say with a smile.

Mohammad swivels around on my desk, moving off of it to sit in his seat.

"You know, I really appreciate you planning everything."

I look over to Mohammad. "It was fun to eat together this morning, and I can't wait to hang out with everyone tonight."

"What can I say?" Mohammad grins. "I'm a party planning machine. Plus, it's something to look forward to as opposed to the obvious."

"I get what you mean," I say, agreeing. "You know, it's my birthday next week."

I'm not sure why I tell Mohammad this now, but it feels like the right time.

"Really?" he asks.

I nod at him.

"I hate that you won't be spending it with us," he huffs, scrunching up his nose.

"I don't like it either."

"We should celebrate it tonight then. It can be a going-away-slash-birthday bash."

"I'm not sure that sounds very cheerful." I laugh.

"Well, what was your plan for tonight? I mean, seriously, Miss America."

I try to think of a better answer than the one that I have, but I can't come up with anything.

"Honestly … I figured I would just get drunk and try to have some fun."

"Solid plan." Mohammad laughs.

I roll my eyes in response.

"I know how that sounds, but I'm going to cry either way, so I might as well be tipsy if I have to do it. Noah will be in a terrible mood. I have no clue what will happen with Harry. So, I figure the best plan is to wake up and be so focused on my hangover that I forget how sad I am about leaving. I'll pack my stuff tonight and just roll up to the airport, get on the plane, and take a long, pathetic nap."

"That's depressing," Mohammad says with an exaggerated

sigh. "Though you're probably right. Bagels didn't *exactly* go as planned."

"Nope," I drawl out, agreeing with him.

"Noah wasn't in his usual chipper mood. I think everyone could tell."

"That's putting it lightly. Statistics was a disaster too. We had our test today."

"You bombed it, huh?" he asks sympathetically.

"I actually think I did great. But Noah was being pitiful. It was annoying."

"You mean, it hurt," Mohammad corrects.

I take in his soft eyes and raised eyebrows.

"Yep," I admit. "It was shitty, shitty, and shitty."

"Well, at least that means the day can only go uphill from here."

"I guess that's true." I laugh, wanting to see the bright side.

"I forgot to tell you, we're eating inside today," Mohammad whispers as class starts.

"*What*? No football field?" I almost pout.

Mohammad rolls his eyes.

"It's okay to break the tradition for something direr," Mohammad replies.

"What could be direr than the four of us eating out on the soccer field?"

"This party. Obviously," Mohammad insists.

"Mohammad, things are going to change when I leave, you know."

Because I feel like he's attaching himself to this party. Maybe it's because it's an excuse to talk to Naomi. Or maybe it's a distraction. His way of saying good-bye. I don't know …

"Yeah, life will go back to being boring as shit."

"What?"

"I'm really going to miss you, Miss America."

I push my bottom lip out, feeling so many emotions. "Mohammad, you're going to make me cry."

"No tears," he says, shaking his finger at me.

He gives me a little push on the shoulder, but he keeps his hand on my shoulder for a second longer than necessary.

And I know that this is the most meaningful thing I'm going to get from him as far as a good-bye.

But it's more than enough.

Talk about the party.
LUNCH

LATIN FLIES BY. Before I know it, the bell goes off.

"Finally," Mohammad says, his head falling back with relief. "I'm so ready for this day to be over."

"It's not over quite yet," I say as I put my Latin textbook into my bag.

"Two classes down, only two to go. Plus, *lunch*," he says as we leave class.

"Mallory, we need to talk," Harry says, practically jogging up to Mohammad and me. He looks over to Mohammad and adds, "Alone."

I glance to Mohammad because, *What in the world?*

Harry looks frantic. Like he's bouncing to tell me something. Like he literally can't wait.

"Whatever," Mohammad mumbles, looking at Harry like he's slightly mad about not being included.

"We'll be right there," I call out, knowing that this is completely messing with his *theme reveal* lunch plans.

Mohammad waves us off, and I give Harry back my attention.

"What's up?" I ask.

"He fancies you," Harry states, looking directly at me.

"What?" I ask, trying to follow along.

"He fancies you," he repeats, his eyelashes fluttering as he speaks.

"Who, Mohammad?" I ask, shaking my head. "No, he just wants to talk about the party."

"Noah," Harry says, cutting me off.

"Don't be ridiculous," I stutter, wanting to crawl under a rock and hide.

"This isn't some joke. He likes you … in a big way," Harry says.

"In a big way?" I ask, not even sure what that means.

"A *big* way." Harry repeats the words and lets out a sharp, unexpected laugh. He chuckles, almost to himself. "I sound ridiculous."

"You do," I say, trying to calm him down and bring him back to earth.

"What I'm saying doesn't even make sense. Noah doesn't just like you. He doesn't just fancy you."

"What are you saying?"

"I'm saying, he doesn't *just* like you in a big way. He likes you in a fucking cosmic way," Harry says, chewing on his lip. His leg is bouncing as he stands, his eyes flitting all around me, like he's had one too many coffees and is trying to process the information.

I look down at the floor, realizing that Noah told him.

Maybe he slipped up.

Maybe he wanted to tell him. To come clean.

But clearly, Harry knows now.

"Oh …" I state, not sure what else to say.

"Oh?" Harry yells. "He fucking fancies you, Mallory, and

all you have to say is *oh?*"

"So what?" I yell back.

"*So what?* So, how do you feel about him?" Harry's eyes look like they're about to pop out of his skull.

"I'm standing here with you, Harry. I agreed to work on things. I said yes this morning."

I stare at him, trying to make him understand.

"Why?" Harry asks.

"Why? *Why?*" I laugh. "Because I care about you. Over and over, I've chosen you. And you've chosen me too."

"This isn't something light to him," Harry says, running his hand through his blond hair.

"Noah and I are close. We're best friends. I told you it was going to be hard for him."

"It's more than that," Harry says, shaking his head. "And I can't do this. I'm sorry, but I can't do that to him."

"What are you saying?" I stutter, feeling the blood rush out of my body.

"I'm saying that three words from Noah is all it takes," Harry replies blankly. Like he can't believe this is happening.

"Three words? Three words for you to what?" I ask, trying to think about what Noah said to him.

"To end things now."

To end things now?

End. Things. Now.

"To end things?" I breathe out, not believing what I just heard. "Am I some sort of joke to you?"

"No, but, Mallory ... I mean, it's Noah." He looks fully conflicted. "How am I supposed to be with you when my best friend—"

"You're not fucking serious."

Harry opens his mouth but doesn't say anything.

"So, that's it."

"I don't know how I can be with you." Harry brings his hand to cover his mouth. He looks just as shocked by the words leaving his mouth as I do.

"Cosmic?" I repeat, feeling like I'm in a different universe. "That's what he said to you?"

Harry nods once, and that's it.

That's all I need to know.

A second later, I'm gone.

I'm walking toward the lunchroom.

Actually, I'm running there.

"Mallory," Harry calls out from somewhere behind me.

Maybe he's close, or maybe he stayed where he was, standing in the hallway.

I don't know.

And I really don't care.

Because all I can think about is what Noah must have said.

Those three words. And I know exactly what they were.

End. Things. Now.

The same words he said to me this morning.

It makes my blood boil.

I rush into the lunchroom, barely missing a girl with a tray full of food.

My eyes instantly find our table. I see Mohammad, Olivia, and Naomi all sitting down.

And then my eyes land on Noah.

I rush up to him, practically dragging him by the shirt, up and out of his seat.

"Cosmic?" I yell, feeling everything boiling over.

The entire table goes silent, but then Mohammad is up and at my side.

"Mallory," he says, trying to stop me but I won't let him.

"No." I hold out my hand, wanting him to stay away

from me.

I'm not going to sit down. I'm not going to calm down.

I'm going to get it out of Noah—here and now.

"Explain it to me, Noah," I say, tears threatening. "Why did you ruin everything?"

"Mallory, don't do this," Noah finally speaks, glancing around us.

He sucks in his cheeks, his eyes moving over my shoulder. And I know he's looking at Harry.

I can see that his focus is honed in on him.

"Harry and I were good, and you had to ruin it. What exactly did it take to convince him to dump me before I left? Three words?" I say, my voice becoming desperate. "You had *every single opportunity* to tell me how you felt. You had *every single chance* to tell Harry. But you didn't. And now? What's changed? What did you say to him, Noah? Because whatever you said implied that Harry couldn't be with me. You knew he would end things the second those words left your lips. You had to have. What were the three words? Say them to me."

"Mal, I ..." Noah stutters, his face going white.

"Nothing to say?" I push, wanting to pick a fight with him.

"I did it for you. I ... I had to tell him. It was the only way for us to keep our friendship. I had to tell him before you left."

I stare at Noah, feeling my heart break.

"So, as a way to preserve your friendship and because you couldn't handle the fact that I'm leaving, you decided to instruct everyone I care about to cut ties with me now? How dare you!"

"I had to tell him," Noah says more insistently this time. *He had to tell him.*

He had to tell him he had feelings for me?

Feelings he would never act on. Feelings that would allow him to end my relationship with Harry. Feelings that are so fucking weak that he already told me we wouldn't be able to stay friends.

"Cosmic?" I say, looking at him with disbelief.

Because there is nothing cosmic or good about that. There is nothing profound about throwing someone away.

I turn around to Harry, feeling betrayed.

By both of them.

And if they want to preserve their friendship and throw me away, then fine. I might as well ensure that it happens. Maybe if I play a part in it, I can pretend like it was my decision.

I turn back to Noah, filled with rage.

Filled with a decision.

"Well, shall we see then?" I growl, pushing against his chest. "I mean, I no longer have a boyfriend. I doubt any of you will ever talk to me again. That's what you want, right?"

"Don't do this." Noah's voice is a whisper, and his face is practically stone.

"Why not? You'll get everything you want, and I will leave with nothing. This will ensure it, so you should be happy," I say.

And suddenly, I'm kissing him.

Noah stands frozen.

For a minute, it's like I'm kissing a wall. Everything about Noah's mouth is hard.

I hear gasps around us.

Good.

Because that's exactly what I wanted.

If I'm going down, I might as well take Noah with me.

But then everything, all the noise and chatter, goes silent.

And within an instant, Noah's hardness dissolves. He becomes soft against me, his head tilting to the side as his mouth moves. His lips part, taking my own in between them. I hear myself gasp, caught off guard by his reaction.

I thought he would push me away.

I thought he would yell at me.

I thought his actions would prove to Harry that I wasn't wrong.

That Noah doesn't *actually* care about me. He just said that to Harry so that they could move on from me together.

Get a fresh slate when I was gone.

I thought maybe the kiss might even prove that there was nothing there. That this was all just some twisted fantasy in his mind. Harry would be able to see that, and he wouldn't ruin something good between us because of some ridiculous longing.

I thought I could kiss Noah to prove my point.

That it would break the spell.

That I could show everyone, with one kiss, that there isn't anything between us.

That he was being selfish.

I thought I could show him, with one kiss, that he had single-handedly broken my heart.

And I was sealing my fate with it.

I never thought …

I never thought that he would kiss me back.

Especially because I was upset, which meant that I pressed my mouth against his with force.

In anger.

But Noah is always surprising me.

I feel a shudder run through his body, sending the vibration through my own. And then his mouth opens to mine. His hand wraps around the back of my neck, pulling me closer to him. His lips part—those perfect lips I've noticed for weeks—and all I can feel is warmth. His tongue. The softness of his mouth.

I could never have imagined this feeling. No amount of thinking could have ever created this sensation in me.

His mouth forms its way around mine, and then everything is gone.

Everything disappears.

Time stands still.

At least, it feels like it does.

But I know that it hasn't.

And I know that the entire school is watching this.

Harry is watching this.

I pull back, instantly covering my mouth with my hand. I can barely feel my lips. Noah still has his eyes closed. But then he blinks them open, first keeping his gaze on the ground. But eventually, he looks up to me, his chest heaving.

"Is that what you wanted?" he whispers, staring at me.

"What?"

"You asked me why I had to tell him. That's why," Noah says.

"Noah," I start.

But he looks like he's about to cry. His eyes flick over my shoulder to Harry. I set my jaw and turn around to face him.

Harry looks stricken. He's standing, openmouthed, staring at us.

When I turn back to Noah, his face has hardened, but he takes a step forward, closer to me.

"I don't know how to forgive you for taking that moment away from me," Noah whispers.

And then he's gone.

He's walking away.

Out of the lunchroom.

Out of my life.

I turn back to Harry, feeling everything fall apart.

"I hope that's what you wanted to see," I say, staring at him.

He looks more hurt than I've ever seen him.

Everyone is silent.

Everyone is staring at me.

Mohammad.

Olivia.

Naomi.

I look over them all at once, one more time, and then I walk out of the lunchroom.

I will empty my locker, and then I'll go.

I'll leave Kensington forever.

Because I'm done.

I'm done with this place.

With those boys.

Who will choose one another, time and time again, over me.

I'm done with everything.

I've ruined everything.

My body starts shaking.

From rage.

From heartbreak.

From anger.

Because my first and last kiss with Noah was in anger.

Because the last image I'll hold of Harry in my mind is of his torn expression, watching us.

Because Mohammad looked at me like I had slapped him.

But suddenly, a small hand is wrapping around my arm, and I recognize the grip instantly.

"What, Olivia?" I say, swirling around to face her.

"I heard you in there," she says as I pull away and continue walking toward my locker.

"Yeah? So did the entire school." I just want her to leave me alone.

She's won.

She can have Harry.

"You kept asking what the three words were. And I heard them," she says.

"What?" I ask, stopping in my tracks.

"I overheard Noah and Harry in the hallway. I heard what Noah said to Harry. And I saw it … the moment when Harry went silent," Olivia replies, tears forming in her eyes.

"What are you saying?" I ask, feeling my stomach in my throat.

"I'm saying, I know that Harry cares about you. He loves you. He was … well, he was crying as they were talking after first period. But so was Noah. And I heard them," Olivia replies, wiping at her eyes. Because she had to see Harry mourning me.

" 'I love her,' " she says, her eyes coming up to mine.

"What?"

"The three words," she says, swallowing. "The three words Noah said to Harry were, 'I love her.' "

ABOUT THE AUTHOR

Jillian Dodd is the *USA Today* best-selling author of more than thirty novels.

She writes fun romances with characters her readers fall in love with—from the boy next door in the *That Boy* trilogy to the daughter of a famous actress in *The Keatyn Chronicles* to a spy who might save the world in the *Spy Girl* series.

She adores writing big fat happily ever afters, wears a lot of pink, buys too many shoes, loves to travel, and is distracted by anything covered in glitter.